THE SANDS OF VALYTHIA

THE TOKEN BEARERS — BOOK FOUR

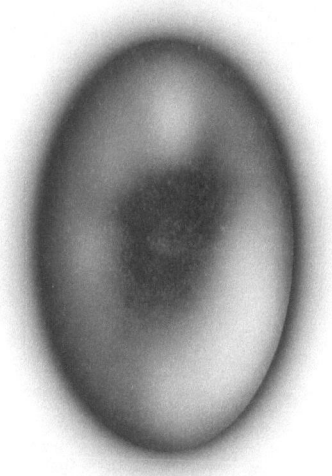

Books by Derin Attwood

The Token Bearers Series
Book One: The Caves of Kirym
Book Two: The Fortress of Faltryn
Book Three: The Trail to Churnyg
Book Four: The Sands of Valythia

THE SANDS OF
VALYTHIA

DERIN ATTWOOD

The Sands of Valythia

A Wordly Press Publication
Ashhurst, New Zealand
Phone 64 6 326 8066

First published by Wordly Press in 2016

Set in 12/18/24 Adobe Garamond Pro
This text uses English (UK) spelling.

ISBN 978-0-9941108-5-5

A catalogue record for this book is available from the National Library of New Zealand.

Wordly Press
www.wordlypress.com

Dedication

To Ron—always.

*And to Alistair who demands a new book every year,
the push is appreciated.*

Acknowledgements

Again special thanks go to Elayne Hand of Brightchick Photography, for the inspiration of the book cover, and Llyvonne Barber who adds the other details, including the divine artwork. She has always seen my vision, and then made it better. Thank you also for formatting the book interior and accepting pages of changes when I check the proofs.

My writing friends around the world who support me and help me solve problems when I have them, and celebrate with me when I don't. Those dear friends and writers close to home who pop in for tea, coffee, occasionally wine, and always lots of laughter. They allow me human contact in what is effectively, a very solitary occupation.

I'm especially grateful to my bestie, Della, for letting me talk my way around plot problems over coffee.

Last but not least, my family, particularly my son Garreth and my dearest, wonderfully supportive husband, Ron.

CHARACTERS ON THIS ADVENTURE

Name   *Relationship*

From The Green Valley

Amethyst	F	Found in the desert, adopted by Kirym
Arbreu	M	Aligned to Kirym, Teema and Bokum
Armos	M	Veld's second. Papa to Peet and Young Harby
Bokum	M	Joined to Zeprah, Papa to Sarel and Trayum
Findlow	M	Kirym's uncle, Lyndym's papa
Harby	M	Known as Old Harby. Armos' papa
Kirym	F	Veld's daughter, Aligned to Teema, Arbreu and Bokum
Loul	F	Headwoman, Kirym's mama
Lyndym	F	Findlow's daughter
Mekrar	F	Kirym's sister, Twin to Mekroe
Mekroe	M	Kirym's brother, Twin to Mekrar
Tarl	M	Kirym's eldest brother
Teema	M	Aligned to Kirym, Arbreu and Bokum
Veld	M	Headman, Kirym, Mekrar and Mekroe's papa
Walf	M	Hunter, Raffs family
Zelriff	F	Oldest woman in the family

Name		Relationship
From Faltryn's Tower		
Elm	M	Boatman
Crag	M	Hunter
Oak	M	Guard, Windrunner's great grandson
Starshine	F	Wind Runner's great granddaughter
Storm	M	Wind Runner's grandson
Willow	F	Healer (*deceased*)
Wind Runner	M	Headwoman
Arbryn's Family		
Arbryn	M	Known as Bryn
Dashlan	M	Eldest son
Enliah	F	Eldest daughter
Jeresaya	F	Married to Bryn
Larqeba	M	Youngest son
Qwinita	F	Youngest daughter
Rargo	M	Orphan
The Rock		
Ashistar	M	Guard
Baketer	M	Guard
Borboncha	M	Guard
Churnyg	M	Tree dwarf—Oak Family
Gynbere	M	Leader—Yew Family
Jetara	F	Shormel's maman—Oak Family

Name		Relationship
Mrilan	M	Old man
Rookham	M	Guard
Rosisha	F	Varitza's maman
Shurlyn	F	Old woman
Slaslow	M	Head guard
Thipin	M	One of triplets
Vellysh	M	One of triplets, sent to pick up Ibith
Zeffyn	M	One of triplets

From the Winterisle

Faltryn	M	Black
Iryndal	F	Blue
Ubree	M	Green
Othyn	F	Yellow
Egrym	M	Orange/Bronze
Arymda	F	Pink/Red
Borasyn	M	Purple

Prologue

A green dragon descended into the amphitheatre at speed, followed closely by a bronze. Just as it seemed they would crash into the ground, they levelled off. They flew so close to the ground, Teema, Kirym and the other three dragons, were buffeted by the wind they created.

Together the two dragons raced around the amphitheatre. The green slowly edged ahead until they were on the opposite sides of the field. They continued to circle, getting faster and faster, and then without warning they turned in towards the centre, now on a collision course.

At the last moment they twisted, met shoulder to shoulder and spun around each other, their colours beginning to blur. They drifted south until they were almost at the southern wall. While continuing to spin, they snorted a stream of fire into the pool of water near the south entrance. The water boiled and a cloud of steam rose and hung over the area, contained by the walls that surrounded the amphitheatre.

From the west, a yellow dragon streaked across the sky towards them. Without reducing speed, it turned its head and barrelled its shoulder into the two spinning dragons, knocking them head over tail in a tumble of wings, legs and a shower of scales.

The green and bronze lost control, disappeared over the eastern edge of the amphitheatre and hit the trees with a crash and a shower of leaves and small branches.

The yellow dragon circled sedately and landed softly near the western wall. Obviously female, she sashayed towards the group in the centre of the amphitheatre, her tail snaking two and fro across the grass, making the most of her entrance.

The green and bronze crawled over the eastern edge of the amphitheatre and raced towards her, skidding to a halt when the large blue dragon stepped between them.

1

Kirym Speaks

Three dragons stood in a semicircle in front of Iryndal. The two males, Ubree and Egrym glowered at the female, Othyn. She smiled smugly over their heads.

Each dragon was different, by face shape, horn number and placement of various lumpy or spiky eye ridges.

Egrym, the bronze had four horns, two sets of two. His thick eye ridges curved up at the outer edges. Close up, his scales were an amazing assortment of autumn colours ranging from pale apricot in the centre to deep bronze at the edge.

The green, Ubree, had two horns, much longer and thicker than Egrym's. They were wavy and one horn was twisted. He held his head high, and appeared to look down on everyone, even Iryndal who was bigger. It gave him an arrogant look. He stood tall, and kept his wings folded forward over his chest, the only one of the dragons to do this. He seemed to be the most wary of us, and kept his distance.

The yellow dragon's horns were long and thin, delicate. Webbed antennae-like growths fanned out from her cheeks, and her eye ridges were almost non-existent.

All three were smaller than Iryndal, *younger*, I thought, although they towered over Arymda and Borasyn.

Random pictures flashed through my head. A sped-up vision of recent events. I realised with amazement that Iryndal was showing the new arrivals what had happened.

"Oh wow, that's the weirdest thing, Kirym," murmured Teema.

"Interesting way to pass on information, don't you think?" I said.

He nodded. "Could make life easier if we had the art."

"Would it really?" I asked. He frowned.

Ubree and Egrym moved over to study Borasyn's pictures, but the yellow dragon, Othyn stayed with Iryndal. It looked as if they were still talking, but now I saw nothing of the conversation.

"You're right, that picture thing is a bit unnerving," said Teema. "I wonder what the yellow one is saying now."

"A private conversation, I imagine."

Teema and I walked over to join Sundas and Tarl, who stood on the far side of the northern pool, still open-mouthed at the dramatic arrival of the three new dragons.

"Of all of the things I've ever seen, this has to be the strangest," said Sundas. "With the talk of dragons, and even what we saw at Faltryn, I still didn't believe in them. Even now, I'm not sure I do. They aren't what I expected. It was like a dream. It only became real when the water turned to steam. It's a shame they destroyed the water though."

I shrugged. "It's a spring and it's already welling up again. It should be back to normal before morning. Tarl, can you and Sundas tell Mama, Papa and Wind Runner what's happening here. It's better that they know about the dragons before they meet them. Also warn them to beware of Gynbere's guards. A few of them travel fast, but they're scared. They may feel inclined to attack if they feel cornered. Papa may meet some of them before he gets here. He'll need to warn any advance scouts about them. I'd suggest hooding the fires too if you can, although perhaps it's too late for that now."

"Aye lass, wise advice," said Sundas.

They turned away, but Tarl spun back. "Kirym, I—I'm sorry I laughed at you when you talked about the dragons. I've always known you would lead the family when Mama and Papa can no longer do it. I was jealous, I have been for a long time. Stupid really! You clearly have skills I don't. I'll be proud to serve under you when the time comes."

I smiled. "You're the eldest and the leadership will go to you. I've no desire for it. The position I'll have is different to headman of The Green Valley. You'll do us proud when the time comes."

"But they can't just pass it on to me," he said. "Others will have a say in it."

"And you may be surprised at what they do say," I said gently.

He took a breath to argue, but shrugged. I could see he wasn't convinced, but at least he was thinking it over.

"Kirym," said Sundas. "You said you gained information from the dwarf whatshisname. What was it?"

"Borboncha," I said. "Oh he told us many things. Most importantly, he told us we'd been betrayed. Someone has passed on vital information to Gynbere and—."

"But that's not news," interrupted Teema. "We knew Rargo had done that."

"Not Rargo." I opened my pocket and pulled out a small masked figure made of marsh grass, an amethyst and three of the ornaments Salcan had made. "Borboncha dropped these, and I'm sure he did it on purpose."

Teema frowned. "But that's Amethyst's stone? I suppose Rargo could've stolen them, or maybe Enliah gave them to him."

"The last time I saw these," I held out the carvings and the amethyst, "was just before Gynbere approached us in his ibith. Rargo had long gone, and Enliah hasn't had a chance to hand them over since then. It's not the only thing Borboncha said though. Rookham knew Churnyg was alive. Rargo couldn't have known and that limits it to those who came with us from Faltryn, Bryn's family, Churnyg and Ashistar."

Teema frowned, trying to sort out the timeline. "Are you sure?"

I nodded. "When Gynbere charged into the clearing, he wanted Churnyg's body. So at that point he was convinced Churnyg was dead. Since then, he's discovered he isn't."

"So Ashistar is still loyal to Gynbere. Churnyg will be devastated. How will you tell him?"

"Oh, that's an assumption, Teema. There's no proof Ashistar has been disloyal. He hasn't been out of our sight since Gynbere left The Rock. He's had many chances to betray us while we were in The Rock, and yet he didn't. I can't see how or why he'd do it now."

"But no one else could've done it."

"Then we have a mystery, haven't we. I'll want firm proof before anyone is accused."

"I'm still gonna watch him," Teema mumbled.

"Well what's that?" Sundas pointed to the grass figure.

I studied it closely for the first time. It was a little bigger than my hand, made of long pieces of marsh grass, and looked like a doll with head, arms, a body and legs. The head was stuffed to give it a solid round, and a small half circle of shaved kellich skin was tied, mask like, around it. The half circle had two small holes in it that looked like eyes. I had no idea what it meant.

"Perhaps Borboncha didn't intend this to come to us."

"Is that what you really think?" Sundas asked.

"No. I'm sure he meant me to have it. So it means something," I shrugged. "Time will make it clear, I guess. Oh, one other thing. Gynbere knows about the amphitheatre. He may have assumed we knew about it. He knew we'd be here at about now. Either way he was looking for our leader. Why? Probably not for good reasons."

"Gynbere knows you're our leader, Kirym. Why didn't he tell his men?"

Sundas laughed and slapped Teema on the shoulder. "And let them know he's scared of a girl? Not a good look, lad."

"Perhaps not. Rargo will have heard us talk about Papa. But whatever Gynbere's reasoning, you need to go now. You'll not get far before dark. Hood your fire or keep a cold-camp overnight. Flames would be a beacon to Gynbere's guards."

"Aye, lass. We'll be wary. I think we'll travel through the night, if it's light enough. Moon dark was two nights ago, so I'm hoping we get a cloudless sky."

They hoisted their packs onto their shoulders and disappeared through the north-western entrance.

"Kirym. I need your assistance," called Iryndal. She was alone now. Othyn had joined Ubree and Egrym and was studying Borasyn's pictures.

"Othyn saw two children travelling by themselves somewhere to the west," said Iryndal. "They were quite unaccompanied. She felt they were frightened. It's been so long, I have little memory of humans, but I too feel this is not normal."

I clicked Teema's token. *Arbreu, is anyone missing? A child!*

No one has said anything. *I'll check.*

There was a long pause.

No. All of the children are accounted for. The only people not here are a few of the perimeter scouts. Veld is expecting most of them in before nightfall.

I nodded. *Tarl and Sundas are returning with news. I glanced at the lowering sun. If they can travel overnight, they should be there by morning.*

"Sooner, I think," murmured Iryndal. "Othyn," she called.

Othyn was beside Iryndal so fast, I didn't see her move.

"Children? Are you sure? From where?" asked Iryndal.

"Definitely children, but I no longer have the memories of place to identify them."

Iryndal shook her head and clicked her tongue in exasperation. "Then we will need to check on them. Take this male ..."

"His name's Teema," I interrupted.

Othyn glared at me, but Iryndal inclined her head and continued. "Take Teema and find them. Watch, but stay hidden. Do not approach until I get there unless they're in danger. In that case, do what is needed. Kirym, you will ride with me. Wear warm clothing, otherwise you'll freeze once the sun sets."

I packed the food I had collected into my shoulder pack, and swung my cloak around my shoulders.

Teema took the pack, but stared in horror at the two dragons waiting beside us.

"We have to ride one of them? They're huge."

"Othyn will take you to check out the children. Iryndal and I will join you presently."

Borasyn behaved for you, Kirym, but he'd have been happy to dump me in the middle of a lake. This one could do the same. Can't we go together?"

"Othyn is older than Borasyn," I said. "She's been instructed by Iryndal. You'll be quite safe. Climb onto her foot, then her knee."

"You'll come to no harm," said Othyn, as she raised her knee and Teema scrambled on to her shoulder. Moments later, they were in the air.

Iryndal was almost twice the size of Othyn. She had more spikes, layered from her forehead down her neck and along her back and tail. She flattened them for me to clamber onto her back. Her scales fitted into each other creating a smooth surface. However getting on was more difficult simply because of her size.

Her neck was thicker, but her neck ridges were prominent and easy to grip. Her scales were bigger and more flexible than Borasyn's, and they glowed in a way his didn't. The light blue edges shimmered as she moved.

She took off fast. I glanced behind, but Othyn and Teema had disappeared. Then Iryndal and I were high above the amphitheatre, with the land spread out below us.

Tarl and Sundas looked like ants from above, but quickly got bigger as Iryndal swooped down to land in front of them.

"I'll return you to your family," she said. "It's not safe for you to be out tonight."

They climbed up behind me.

"Less safe than this?" Tarl clung tightly to my waist despite Iryndal being still firmly on the ground.

"Yes. Iryndal is smoother to travel with than Borasyn, and much faster."

"You've done this before?"

My answer was lost in the swish of the air as we rose above the trees. With seemingly no effort, Iryndal raced across the treetops, swooping lower over open ground.

With the smoke from Papa's fires in sight, she landed. "This is close enough. You will be there well before sundown. Keep your people safe and close. Keep your knowledge of us to only those who need to know. Too much speculation can cause fear, and frightened people react badly."

Tarl looked pale as he slid off Iryndal's back. His knees buckled as he hit the ground, but he grabbed Sundas' belt, and remained on his feet.

They had scarcely stepped away from Iryndal and we were again in the air. Sundas' call of, "Thank you," drifted up to us, and then they were gone.

We travelled quickly now. Already the sun was tipping the horizon, and I wondered if we would find the children before night set in.

Iryndal's speed awed me. The flight line she took was not as direct as when she flew to Papa's camp. This time she circled east first, over a large bronze coloured area north of the amphitheatre.

I stared at it mesmerised, but then realised it was the setting sun, reflecting on a large body of shallow water.

Then Iryndal swung to the south and west to follow the path we had walked when traveling towards The Rock. Passing over Bryn's camp, I was shocked to see the blackened remains of his lodge. Its burning had implications I needed to discuss with him.

Soon after that a flash of yellow caught my eye. I had a vision of spring time daffodils, or the brightly coloured fruit of the dronger tree. Then we drifted in to land in a thicket of trees growing beside a small stream.

2

Kirym Speaks

Othyn had chosen her spot well. Two tiny figures in pale robes jogged into view slightly north of us. Our position meant we were not looking into the sun to see them.

"Oh my stars," I gasped. "Who are they? Where did they come from?"

Othyn sighed. "I was correct. Two children, and young ones at that."

"They're not known to you?" asked Iryndal.

I shook my head. "Iryndal, you knew the people of the land. Can you place the clothes?"

Iryndal frowned. "In all honesty, I can't remember. Kirym, I know the people of the caves and the trees, because you know them, and I've read your memories. Who else could they be?"

"Starshine talked of the cave people the desert people. We found Amethyst, but there were no sign of any others, but what chance is there, these two came from there?"

"None!" said Teema. "They couldn't get here, Kirym. We travelled that river from the fortress to the sea. There was no way across it. Wind Runner was certain no one could cross further north without a boat, and she was adamant the desert people had no boats. Anyway, even if they could get across, why would they allow their children to wander off like this? They must've escaped from the The Rock."

"Churnyg's people dress differently, Teema. These two are a different build, not as stocky. Also, they're coming from the west."

"Could they be from another world, Iryndal? Is it possible for the barriers to drop?" said Othyn.

Iryndal frowned. "They chose to close the gate to us, and to everyone, they said. That's why they set a gatekeeper."

"Could they have lost control?" asked Othyn.

"I need to think about that, but the gatekeeper had his own power over and above everyone. If the gate has been breached, the repercussions could be serious."

"What sort of repercussions?"

"Borasyn may know. He seems to have memories we don't. It would surprise me if the gatekeeper has lost his power." She sighed. "I haven't been given memories for many hundreds of seasons, but even so, there are changes in this land I don't understand." She shook her head. "Still anything is possible."

"It's getting late," I interjected. "What would you have me do about the children, Iryndal?"

"Talk to them. They're here for a reason. Wherever they're from, their families must be nearby, and those families need to be part of the gathering at the amphitheatre."

I stepped out of the trees and walked towards them. They were very alert, for moments after I appeared, they stopped and warily watched my approach. Their hoods, pulled well forward, meant I could not see their faces.

The lead figure fell to his knees, and his hood swung back. His face was lined with fatigue. He looked so similar to Amethyst I gasped.

"Can you help us? My people are in danger." The voice was deep, resonant, and matched the face, that of a man.

"What help do you need? I'll give you all I can."

"I'm Garanniis. This," he gestured to his companion, "is Morkeen."

Morkeen stepped back behind Garanniis, obviously wary of me.

"Morkeen, show manners," he barked.

She pushed her hood back and glowered at me. She looked even more like Amethyst than Garanniis did. If there had been any doubt in my mind they were from the desert, it was now gone. She had the same triangular face, creamy skin, similar almond shaped eyes and the thick long hair remarked on by Starshine. She was tiny, and seemed far too young to be travelling in this way.

I removed the stopper of my water flask and offered it to Garanniis.

As he lifted it to his lips, Morkeen whispered to him, trying to stay his hand.

"The offer of water is generous. Why would we not trust her? We must," he said gently, "else everyone will die."

He took a small sip, and handed the flask to Morkeen who did the same. She held the flask out for me to take.

""Drink please. There's plenty of water," I said. "I'm Kirym, and I'm so pleased to meet you."

She looked at me distrustfully and returned the flask to Garanniis who took another small sip.

Both of them were dusty and travel worn. Their feet were wrapped with strips of woven plant fibre, robes ripped, threadbare and stained at the edges. Morkeen's was torn at the knee where she had fallen; I could see grazes and a deep weeping cut through the hole.

I pulled a square of material from my pocket, a remnant of the petticoat I'd ripped strips off to bind Borasyn's foot. I pressed it to the flask to dampen it. Morkeen darted forward and righted the flask.

"Don't waste!" she snapped.

"There's plenty of water, Morkeen. I can refill the flask when it's empty. There's a stream quite close. Wash the dust from your faces."

She scowled again, but took the pad of material and having dampened it minimally, carefully wiped Garanniis' eyes.

He smiled in appreciation. "It's very generous of you to share your water."

"It'll be dark soon. My camp is just over in the trees." I pointed to the nearby copse. "Come and rest, and we can decide the best way to help you."

"I need warriors, builders and wise men. Are they close?" said Garanniis.

"Close enough, but first you need to rest and eat. There's is nothing we can do until morning." I smelled smoke, and knew Teema had set a fire. "Come, meet my companions and rest. How long have you been travelling?"

"The moon has darkened four times since we saw our people," said Morkeen.

"Resting one night will change little, and I need to understand exactly what you need. When did you last eat?'

Morkeen shrugged. "Recently."

"Three days ago," said Garanniis.

"Then you need food. My friend Teema has set a fire. A meal will soon be ready."

"We must keep going." Morkeen was near panic. "Garanniis, we need more than this child can offer."

I understood they were driven to complete their quest. "I have access to all of the things you may need," I said. "I've promised help and it is nearby, but I can't organise anything until I know exactly what we need to do."

Garanniis nodded.

Now I wondered how I could explain the two dragons, but decided I would wait and see how they handled it. I had no doubt they had heard everything we had said.

3

Kirym Speaks

Garanniis and Morkeen accepted Iryndal's and Othyn's presence with no comment at all. I made a mental note to ask Iryndal about that later.

Morkeen, plainly exhausted, fell asleep as soon as she sat down. Garanniis talked a little of the long journey they had made. Of the differences between the land he had come from, and the wonderful abundance of greenery around us.

I poured the remains of my flask into the skin-pot and set it over the fire to heat. Leaving our visitors in Teema's care, I cast about in the dying light for more food. I returned with a few root vegetables, and some late autumn fruit. It would augment the roots and mushrooms I'd collected earlier and the dried food we carried.

I returned to the fire to see Othyn hand Teema a fat gutted kellich to skin and joint.

"What food can we get for you, Othyn?" I asked.

"Dragons eat rarely, and when we need to, we collect our

own even from birth," said Iryndal.

Teema added the meat to the pot along with the scrubbed chopped vegetables.

I chose a few of my herbs to flavour the stew, and then sliced the fruit into a deep platter, added some chopped mint and a little honey.

"Can you find some fush grass, Teema? It'd make the night more comfortable for everyone. The ground is damp and I don't want anyone to lie directly on it."

He took Garanniis with him to gather it, and fill the flasks at the nearest stream.

Their noisy return woke Morkeen. Garanniis handed me a platter of berries.

I washed them and added them to the rest of the fruit.

"You use water carelessly," criticised Morkeen.

"We use it as needed, but there's plenty here. I realise it's less available in your land."

She scowled. "What would you know?"

"She's right, Morkeen," said Garanniis. "Teema showed me a stream. He said there are lots of them all over the land. It is so different to the river that edges our land. It was smaller, but I could reach it easily. I saw a fish. It was long and wriggly." He took a deep breath, and his face lit up. "I touched it."

Morkeen smiled at his enthusiasm. It transformed her face and suddenly she looked incredibly like Amethyst.

I felt a pang as I missed my wee girl.

Quickly, the scowl I was accustomed to seeing on Morkeen's face returned.

While waiting for the meal to cook, I cleaned Morkeen's wounds. The cut on her knee was not the worst of them, and my dress and petticoat were significantly shorter by the time I had ripped enough strips to use as bandages.

Teema dished up the meal. He and Garanniis ate heartily.

Every time I glanced over at Morkeen she was pushing the food about on her platter. However by the end of the meal, she had finished most of it.

She was horrified at the pile of fush grass we had cut. "Such a waste. Just because it grows doesn't mean you have to cut it down."

"It seeds well," I said gently, "and it thrives when thinned out. As it gets colder, the ground at night becomes damp. We wouldn't want you or Garanniis to get sick. We don't take it without care. This will travel with us and be used every night for the best part of a moon. Then I'll use the dried fibres for other things."

With the remains of the stew set aside for morning, Teema built the fire up and relaxed against a tree. "Tell us why you are here, and what we can do to help."

"Ahh," Garanniis sighed. "In retrospect I feel our journey is for nought. We've taken so long to get here, I suspect my people will have perished by now." He blinked away his tears.

"The sharing of your troubles may ease your heart a little, even if what you fear is true." I said.

"No!" Morkeen was on her feet, and backing away from the fire. "No, Garanniis. We will not tell them our stories and allow them to sit in judgement on us. We will keep our grief to ourselves. They have no right to know."

In the silence after her outburst, Teema sat with his mouth open. Garanniis went pale and suddenly seemed to be very distant.

"We can't help your people if we don't know their needs," I said.

"Dead people have no needs!" Morkeen spat.

"If you know for sure they're dead, then keep your knowledge deep in your heart. But if there is any chance even one of them has survived, you must let us try to help."

"If by chance they survived," she mimicked, "they'll have given up on us and returned to the desert to be killed by the monsters that have invaded our land. The moon will darken another four times before we could possibly return. Longer again for us to build a bridge over the river. Then we'll never find them because they'll believe us dead. If they see us, they won't trust their eyes. They'll hide thinking us ghosts sent to taunt them."

"Then the sooner we know where to go, the more likely it is they'll be rescued," I said.

"Morkeen," said Garanniis. "If we don't trust these people, why did we come here? We could've stayed near our families and called out to them daily until we had seen them all be torn to pieces and known there was no more hope. No more life for those we love. They begged us to get help, and this is the first we've been offered."

"We were searching for The Guardians, not these insignificant fools," she spat.

Garanniis shook his head. "I do fear Morkeen is right, though. When last we saw my people, they were surrounded by the largest group of fyrsha I've ever seen. My people had few defences, and while I told myself I was going for help, I wonder if my leaving was so I wouldn't see them ripped to pieces before my eyes. My land rejected me," he paused, "but I chose to walk away from my family."

"People are resilient. Sometimes when faced with the worst, they find a way to survive. I know we can get to where you saw them last and if we can do that, then there's a chance we can save them," I said.

"If and when you find them," snapped Morkeen, "and on the off chance they still sit beside the river, what do you intend to do? Wave to them? A fat lot of help you'd be. There's no way across the water. But even if there was now, they'd not be where we left them." She turned her back on us and sat staring stonily out into the darkness.

4

Garanniis

In the silence that followed, Garanniis picked up the flask and studied it. "Is water so readily available right across your land?"

Kirym smiled. "The stream Teema showed you is small. There are many similar that are much larger and equally accessible. There are lakes, great bodies of water, and smaller pools too. Garanniis, we want to help you, but we need to know what you need of us. What would you have asked from these guardians?"

"I hoped for what they originally gave us. A home." He sighed deeply, settled against a tree and closed his eyes. "Back near the dawn of our time, we existed as we could in the area between the arid sands in the west and the tribes of the eastern crags. We were harassed on all sides by wild people and wilder animals. There were a lot of border skirmishes. The Guardians descended on one battle and insisted the fighting stop.

The mountain tribes said they were only protecting what was their own. They said we prowled their borders and stole from them.

It was hard to define the border, but there were times we knew we had breached it. They also knowingly raided our land and took what they found. Naturally they failed to mention that, as they talked of our wrongdoings.

To an extent, they were right about us taking their game, but they had so much and we had so little.

As we explained our position to The Guardians, those from the mountain caves realised the hardship we lived under, and expressed regret for their actions.

The Guardians asked if it was now possible for us all to share the land, live peacefully together and learn about each other.

The leader who came from the nearest caves suggested we move into their caves with them, and we become one people together. Those from our family taken in battle were encouraged to return to us. A few did, but most declined. They'd become accustomed to the new comfortable lifestyle they led. They were happy to stay with their captors because they felt they had done well in the new community. Despite being taken in battle, they had not remained prisoners for long. They pointed this out to us, and assured us that we would have an equal footing in this new society. They encouraged us to join them.

We didn't trust them. We suspected that the price we would pay for their care was slavery, despite all their assurances.

We demanded they leave our land to us, as we would leave theirs to them. We wanted to be able to harvest all of our resources without threat.

Fortunately The Guardians understood our fears and our desire to remain as a people in our own land. They created the great river as a solid border between us.

We were taken deep into the centre of our land. At first we mourned the loss of the paltry riches the ribbon of greenery had offered us. We felt we were losing our freedom of choice. We quailed at the arid emptiness there, this seemed to be the bleakest of the bleak. We felt we were being punished for refusing the offers from the cave people.

But although the land was stark, it was also beautiful. We knew it would sustain us, although at a different level and life would now be harder for us.

However The Guardians had no intention of just dumping us in the dunes and leaving. Their leader chose a great flat basin surrounded by sand dunes to be our home. She walked to the centre of the land and fired a blazing arrow from a strange bow. It flew high into the air, landed and disappeared deep into the sand. A great fountain of water rose from the spot, and spilled over the land.

The Guardians built a reservoir to contain the water. Our homes ranged around it. A wall was erected to give us more protection from the desert. Trees and gardens were planted and suddenly we wanted for nothing. Although we were isolated we grew to love our home. We called it Valythia, which has many meanings. Land of Abundance, The Changing Land, and my favourite, The Peaceful Land."

Iryndal started, and stared at Garanniis. She took a deep breath, then shook her head, breathed out and closed her eyes again.

"We rarely saw other people after that," continued Garanniis. "Indeed it was many generations before anyone came near us. When they did, the visits were cordial, indeed they were a reason for much celebration. We encouraged our visitors to stay for a season or two knowing how difficult it was to travel through the desert and on many occasions they were happy to accept our hospitality.

To my knowledge, we never asked any of them where they

came from. The only people our history told us of, were The Guardians and the tribes, who we knew lived in caves in the wild crags. In truth our memories of the both were vague. We assumed our visitors came from the caves if only because they walked across the desert and were our closest neighbours. The accounts we had of The Guardians came down to us in stories, and many were contradictory. Some of our people even suggested they never existed, because the ancient stories also talked of a race of giants who rode great eagles and roamed the worlds they cared for. There was a suggestion that the stories had been mixed, twisted as they came down to us. Personally, I thought the stories all had truth. I assumed The Guardians rode the eagles, while the Cave People walked the land.

The last people to visit Valythia arrived in the heat of the summer which was unusual. The desert was not conducive to travel in the hottest season. We urged them to stay until winter, however they were adamant they would leave after just a few days.

We celebrated, dressing them in our finest robes. We dined through the afternoon and into the evening and offered such entertainment as befitted our guests.

In return they told us tales if the rest of the land, of the families and creatures that lived in it. These were wondrous tales, and we were suddenly eager to meet these people and creatures, or perhaps invite them to visit us.

Our visitors assured us that this could happen, and soon. They would bring a few of them to us initially. We could then join the families of the land in a great celebration. We would be honoured guests if we would be willing to venture to the green lands.

We were joyous at the thought of being included, of meeting others and setting up regular visits. We no longer saw strangers as a threat.

As the night died, we conducted our guests to our best lodgings. We bade them sleep so we could continue the entertainment when they awoke refreshed.

When they had failed to rise by midday, we entered their rooms to check on them. We could not waken them. Worried, we called our most esteemed physicians, but even they could not rouse them.

As the sun approached the horizon, a great black lizard such as we had never seen before crawled out of the western sands. It climbed up the outer dwellings, digging its huge claws in to them. Not designed for such treatment, they collapsed. The lizard pushed his way into the city, crushing every building in a frenzy of destruction. It dug through our gardens and destroyed them. The trees we had carefully nurtured over the seasons were uprooted and cast aside.

We cowered in the few remaining dwellings, but the lizard tore them apart. We gathered our families together and ran for our lives. Then armed with what weapons we could find, our men returned to save our sleeping visitors.

The lizard would not let us close. We planned an attack on the great beast, but he tore apart our reservoir and the resulting wave of water washed us out into the desert. Throughout the night we tried to re-enter the ruins of our home, but each time we were met with the glowing red eyes of the great beast.

By morning, Valythia had been turned into a heap of dust and the summer winds lifted it into the air, creating a dust storm such as we had not seen before. We struggled through the thick dust to our families, and shrank into the creases of the land. There was nothing we could do but wait until the winds disappeared.

When we woke, the air was again fresh and clean. Our beautiful city had disappeared. In its place was a wide plain surrounded by huge sand dunes.

There was no sign to show that our guests had died there, although nothing to show they had survived either. We hoped they had escaped and returned to their homes.

The water we needed to sustain our lives and crops had sunk back into the sands from where it came. The few plants we found, quickly withered and died. We dug down, trying to find the water, the sand oozed back into the hole as fast as we dug it out. As deep as we got, we found nothing, and when each morning came, the dunes had again grown and changed.

We knew there was water under the ground somewhere, but we really had no way of knowing which dune now covered it. The land was again as barren and featureless as when we were first taken there."

"Why were you not buried in the storm?" asked Teema.

Garanniis laughed. "One doesn't get buried in a storm. Sand will cover you, but what the wind blows onto you, is also blown away. At most a hands depth will build up over you."

"What did you do next?" Kirym asked.

"We thought initially to go to the caves to see if their people had returned safely, but our land had changed. It was as if the lines of the dunes had been altered. We had not travelled the land for many generations. We had lost the art of it, quickly got lost and wandered in circles for many seasons.

We wanted to live as we had lived, but we found it difficult to return to a peaceful, contented life. We again became nomads, strangers in our own land, always searching for a place, a time or a feeling of peace. It never returned.

As the seasons passed, my people became more and more incensed. They felt a deep resentment at the loss of their homes and security. They began to blame the visitors for what had happened."

"Why?" I asked.

"You know how it is when people sit around, angry at the harsh hand they've been dealt, and trying to find someone to blame for it all. Stories abounded, each more fanciful than the last, until no one seemed to know or want to know what had really happened.

Some of my people decided the lizard had come at the bidding of the strangers, that their visit was simply a ploy to infiltrate and destroy us. They saw it as a continuation of the border skirmishes that had happened hundreds of seasons earlier. Deep down, I'm sure they knew they were being unreasonable, but people are often irrational when grieving.

Time passed and eventually in our wandering through the sands, we happened upon the river that divided our land from that of the mountain people and we again discovered their caves.

They had prospered. They had built the ledges up, and now they lived in a great fortress in the cliff. We were awed by their defences. Their turrets and battlements towered over us.

Again we talked of approaching them, but the thought struck us that they had perhaps created the battlements to protect themselves from us. Perhaps this was proof their people had returned and felt Valythia and her people were a huge threat. My people now convinced themselves that the stories were true, and the battlements were to ensure we could not retaliate.

I wondered if they simply feared the great lizard. Whatever they feared, well, how could we be sure, and approaching them could be a disaster for us.

We were in torment now. Would approaching them again be seen as a declaration of war? Some thought it would. They worried that if we were seen, the antagonism of earlier times would begin again. The stories grew out of all proportion.

When a group of armed men appeared at their battlements, we fled in terror, fearful they had spotted us and were gathering their resources to attack us.

Although the strip of land along the edge of the river was the richest of the land we owned, our family leaders resolved not to use it if at all possible.

The decision was not one we could sustain. Valythia was a poor land, and there were times my people were hungry. Then we were forced to forage in the most abundant strip of land we owned. At those times, we were drawn again to look on our neighbours.

We were wary of the people and hid so they couldn't see us. But watching had a strange fascination.

Because of our needs, we ranged up and down the river collecting what food we could. Even though we thought it a great danger, we often spied on the magnificent fortress, and discussed the reasons for not approaching them. But still we feared the result of any overt approach.

Once as winter left the land, we were foraging along the river bank when we saw one of their boats sink far upstream from their fortress. After some time, the man who had been in it dragged himself up the bank onto our land.

He lay on the stones, blue with cold, and we worried for him. With evening approaching, he would have no chance to get dry or return to the fortress, so we gathered wood together, enough fuel to keep the flame high throughout the night. At dusk he was seen gathering food, and we made sure he found the store of wood beside the fire we had lit for him.

We were relieved. He was safe, but still we watched to

ensure he remained that way. In the dark of the night, we realised there was a problem and investigated. He had collected and eaten the tiny toxic mushrooms that grow on the roots of marsh grasses.

Through the night we nursed him. He was most distraught, screaming and thrashing about in agony. We restrained him, for his own safety as well as ours.

He appeared fearful of us, screamed and called us monsters, devils and wraiths. Just after dawn, he broke free of the ropes we'd used to protect him, overpowered our healers and ran off towards the fortress.

We followed, and eventually saw him rescued.

We watched to see what would happen. The people in the fortress saw us. They swarmed down from their battlements into their boats. Before too long, they were flooding up the paths onto our land.

We knew there was little point in trying to escape across the desert, assuming they planned to hunt us down and kill us. In the open dunes our prints would be obvious and we would be easily found, so we hid and watched.

However, they didn't go far from the river bank, but instead left baskets and platters of food, and returned to their fortress.

The food was welcome—it had been a particularly hard winter. The next day, they returned, replenished the food and built us a shelter, then left quickly so we could enjoy their gifts. They left clothes—quite different to ours—and we dressed warmly.

It was wonderful, but after a number of days, we saw our children begin to waste this excess of food. They became casual about the gifts offered and began to fight over different items.

We realised they expected this bounty to continue forever. It was not good, so we moved on. However the lesson we learned then was one of hope for a friendship in the future with our neighbours.

5

Garanniis

Time passed and we often returned to the land near the fortress. Generally we remained hidden, a lesson to our children, but occasionally we showed ourselves to our neighbours.

Those visits generally coincided with the end of the winter when our food stores had been exhausted. We argued about approaching the people and talking to them, wanting to ask if their travellers had returned home safely. The question always arose, if they hadn't would we be blamed? Each time our courage failed. We felt guilty at the failure and resolved that next time would be different.

We finally decided to make our approach towards the end of the next visit, but disaster hit before we had the chance.

Men from the fortress began to hunt on our land, and while initially they took only kellich and hairy becails, soon we were the prey.

They tracked our young women, and while the first who

were targeted managed to escape, eventually two were cornered and Foheem, a new-born whom they carried, was killed.

Before when these people had hunted, they had taken the kill home, but this time they walked away and returned to their fortress.

This was beyond our understanding. Our fears became overwhelming. In the dark of the night, we discussed what to do next.

Was this a token retribution for the death of their lost travellers, or the beginning of a bigger attack? Was it possible to talk to them, assure them we had cared for their people to the best of our ability? But then, if they'd held the grudge this long, would any explanation be acceptable?

We resolved to leave permanently, to return to the life we knew to be safe. Although it was a hard existence for our children, at least we didn't treat them as animals to be killed at a whim. We felt we could protect them better in our desert homeland.

I believed their people had died in Valythia, and now this seemed to confirm it. We understood the loss of family, and decided reluctantly we would leave Foheem with them. If they had someone to mourn, perhaps it would balance their other losses.

We collected rocks and Foheem's sisters spent the rest of the night building a bier for her, to show them our good intentions.

In the times we had visited, many people from the fortress had watched us, but one woman watched more often than the others. From the respect they showed her when she directed them, we understood her to be special, a leader perhaps. She was treated with reverence, and often gave directions to her people. She was always at the foremost when the gifts were delivered, and she had directed the shelter be built. Now she crossed the great river by herself, no mean feat because the currents were deceptively strong.

Instead of accepting our offering, she left Foheem's body on the bier and used some of the surplus stones we had gathered to build a small crypt-like tower over her.

This was foreign to us.

She appeared distraught and sat for a long time beside the bier. That mystified us even more. Why had she ordered the killing if she was so upset with the result? Although we had never seen evidence of other memorials built in this manner, we had to assume this was how they dealt with their dead.

Once the tower was finished, we left. Our grief for Foheem was great, and we resolved never to look on these people again.

I wished we had taken Foheem with us to care for her in the old ways and allow her to be with her ancestors, but a gift is a gift, and we could only take our memories.

Despite our decision to stay away, we occasionally did return to talk to Foheem and check her little tower.

The people from the fortress tended it often, planting and watering sweet smelling flowers around it, pulling the weeds that grew and replacing any stone that fell.

I began to feel that this was perhaps their way of leaving her with us while still caring for her, but my thoughts were not shared by many of my family. There were arguments between us now, and some left to live apart.

Things change of course. Seasons passed and now the people from the fortress travelled into our land.

This was something we didn't understand. They took nothing, didn't interfere with us at all, indeed I doubt they even saw us, but they built more small towers although none were as elaborate as that they built for Foheem.

Our elders initially wondered if this was their way of claiming our land or perhaps they were leaving their dead to watch us and report back.

I felt they were acknowledging the gift we had left them, but few agreed with me. I hadn't the age to convince them, and with so much anger against these people, I kept my thoughts to myself.

Eventually as the number increased, our elders decided they must be placed for their Gods, for although the cave people visited them again and again, they never attempted to reside near them.

We resolved to let them worship in peace, if that was what they were doing. They were not people we wanted to know. We thought if we didn't interfere with them, perhaps they would leave us alone. Some wondered if they were leaving us their dead as we had left Foheem for them, possibly an acknowledgement of our gift. I wondered it perhaps these were monuments to those long lost men.

With no agreement, we travelled deep into Valythia and avoided them. In doing so, our lives became harder. Time passed, and we entered a period when the rains came even less often than usual. Water became almost impossible to find. There was less food, and my people began to die from the hardship pressed upon them.

Recently I came of age and took up the robes as leader of my people. To fully undertake this position meant I had to journey into the dunes by myself, to contemplate the best way to guide my people and keep them safe. This trip took me away for a number of moons.

One night atop a large sand dune, I settled down to sleep and dreamed a new dream. In this dream gentle rains came, and the land blossomed. I watched as grass covered the dunes and great trees grew. Flowers bloomed, pools and rivers abounded. I was reminded of the area around the great city gifted to us by The Guardians near the dawn of our time.

In the morning I was reluctant to waken, knowing the

sands would no longer seem restful to my eyes.

The following night I again watched the land come to life. This time great flocks of birds sat in the trees, swam on the waters and darkened the sky as they flew across the sun and moon.

On the third night, many animals filled the land. The sun smiled on them and they prospered. The following night I saw my people join me and bask in all the land offered.

I was eager to fall asleep on the fifth night, but this time I saw the trees, flowers and grasses wither and die. The rivers evaporated and the pools dried up. The land died and with it the birds and animals. The sands of my dream were littered with desiccated sun-bleached bones of the dead.

When dawn came, I watched the sun rise on the arid land I had called home, and I knew I would no-longer accept living in a land that could not sustain us.

I wondered and worried about my family. Perhaps now it was time to approach the only people we knew and try to make our peace with them. If they required us to live in slavery, or give our lives in payment, then at least it would be quicker than slowly wasting away in Valythia's bleak arid sands and watching our children suffer.

That night I had no dream, and I knew it was time to return to my people. I set out as dawn broke, but my steps were heavy.

Although I knew the ways of the desert, I found by evening I had walked in a huge circle, and was standing once again on the spot I had spent the previous nights. The following day the same thing happened.

Fearing I could never leave this enchanted place, I sat where I had dreamed and idly sifted the sand as I wondered how to get back to my people.

Just under the surface of the sand, I discovered a strange stone. It was unlike anything I had seen before, blacker than the darkest night. The surface was smooth and it shone. It seemed to hold secrets deep inside it. When I picked it up, I wanted to keep holding it, but it was just a rock and I felt foolish.

I held it through the night. My sleep was dreamless. I woke feeling despondent, wondering if perhaps I was stuck here on this dune until my bones became as bleached and desiccated as those I had dreamed of.

I left, but by evening I again sat in the place of my dreams. In the back of my mind I wondered if there was perhaps another dream I needed before I could leave.

The stone lay on the sand where I had left it. I picked it up, slept holding it, and again no dream came to me. Despite the weight of the stone, when I left the dune the following day, I took it with me. I somehow hated the thought of leaving it alone in the sands, where it obviously didn't belong. Initially I had the fanciful thought that it came from Valythia, but I knew it couldn't have, it was the wrong colour.

This time, my journey took me to my people.

I resolved to not mention the stone to them, knowing it would cause arguments between those who now thought the whole city was a myth, and those who still blamed our last visitors for our loss.

In the moons I had taken to think of the future of my people, our situation had deteriorated. The land had always been populated with fyrsha. They hissed and spat if we approached them, but mostly left us in peace as we did them. After we left Valythia, a new variety appeared in our land. These were different, larger than any we had seen before, and much bolder. Now the numbers around us escalated. They even attacked the smaller variety we were used to.

They were swift, and didn't hesitate to attack us. Now when we travelled, our hunters had to be prepared to defend us at all times. Our children could no longer wander away by themselves to play in the sands as I had as a boy. When we stopped for the night, our safety depended on us crawling into the large patches of thorns that littered the bleak stony flats. Even the small flame our healers made, was of no use to us. Small fyrsha had fled at the slightest smell of smoke, but not these new beasts. We relied on the bravery of our young warriors, but more and more often we lost even them to the insatiable appetites of these vicious invaders.

Although I made no mention of approaching the people of the caves, I talked of leaving the land. Even this caused arguments. Some felt that dying there was better than facing the unknown or living on the charity of others.

Realising they would never agree to approach the cave people, I suggested we search for The Guardians. They had given us our dream home, Valythia, and I wondered if it was possible for them to rebuild it, or perhaps offer us other land, unwanted by others.

Not everyone was happy with this suggestion. Some thought The Guardians would blame us for the loss of Valythia, others that the city was a figment of our imagination and therefore The Guardians could not exist. Still, they followed me to the edges of our land, where eventually we again found the river and turned north. However the fyrsha still shadowed us, attacking at every opportunity.

One afternoon after yet another of our hunters failed to return, we chopped into an area of thick spiky plants, wanting a protective barrier around us overnight. There at the river's edge we discovered a fragile stone arch spanning the water.

By that time, the fyrsha had taken nineteen of my people and I knew if we didn't escape the land soon, I would have no one left to lead, or perhaps they would have no leader.

The flimsy arch was a tenuous link from our land to yours,

Kirym. I saw it as an immediate answer for our escape, although many felt it would be folly to use it.

I explained the only options open to them. If they didn't want to be hunted into non-existence, they would need to either cross over the arch and travel east in search of The Guardians, or follow the river north and approach the cave people to ask for protection.

They liked neither suggestion, and the arguments lasted throughout the evening and following day with no decision made. When they appeared to be about to reject both of my propositions, I suggested they offer their children to the fyrsha immediately, A kinder option, I thought.

I watched their shocked faces of. Never had I spoken to them so harshly, painted so brutal a picture.

Now they contemplated the days we'd need to travel to get to the fortress in the north. With the picture I had painted uppermost in their minds, they reluctantly agreed to try the arch. However no one would step on the flimsy bridge. And so with much trepidation, I made the decision to cross first.

I was safe, but the others hung back still fearful, and Morkeen bravely joined me.

Four fyrsha had prowled the edges of the thorny barrier, roaring with frustration, at their inability to reach us. It was also an invitation to others to join them. When a massive beast arrived and began to push into the thorny barrier, two young men, frightened by the growing threat of death around them, pushed their way to the head of the line.

I cautioned them to come singly and slowly so as not to stress the fragile span.

As they stood at the edge of the gorge, the fyrsha roared. My warnings were ignored. Despite continued cries from both sides of the gorge for restraint, the two remained together and sped up as they approached the centre of the span.

The stone crumbled. They were still running when they hit the water below.

Now no one else could join us, but my people urged me to journey on to find the guardians or someone to lead us to them."

Garanniis sighed deeply as he focused on the fire. "Morkeen is probably right though. It has been too long. To my shame I feel I raced away to get as far from the sight of death as possible."

Immersed in his grief, he would say no more.

He leaned against a tree and closed his eyes.

Kirym and Teema left him to rest.

6

Kirym Speaks

Garanniis' gentle snore was occasionally drowned out by the hiss and roar of the fire.

Morkeen had settled on the fush grass, although not without another objection at the waste that ended with, "but to not use it now you've cut it would be even worse." She placed a good thick layer for Garanniis to lie on and smiled her appreciation when Teema handed her his robe and cloak. She placed both over Garanniis.

Teema slept on the far side of Garanniis, almost hidden under layers of fush leaves.

When he was asleep, I covered him with my cloak, and rearranged the cloak and robe Morkeen had placed over Garanniis to cover her as well. I added another log to the fire, and walked to the edge of the thicket where Iryndal was watching the moon and stars.

The night air was crisp and cool enough for me to be aware of not having my cloak with me.

I gazed up at the sky. The stars appeared brighter than usual with the moon still below the horizon. "I love the sky here. There are so many stars that are different to those from my birth-land. I'm pleased though we still see the star we call the dragon-star. It was special to us back there, and it is here too." I paused. "Iryndal, Garanniis and Morkeen seemed not at all surprised or wary of you and Othyn when they arrived. Why?"

"Dragons have the ability to alter thinking in humans. Borasyn, Egrym and Arymda are not so good at it, they're not consistent in their abilities. It improves as we get older. The art is a protection for people who have never met us before. It would have been disastrous if Garanniis and Morkeen had run off in terror. When they realise we are here, they will accept that they've known for a long time, and won't really think about it." She pointed to the sky. "The owls are busy tonight."

I waited and watched. A short time later seven owls swooped across the rising moon.

It was strange having a dragon guarding the camp instead of Teema assisting me. When Iryndal suggested it, I worried she would tire, but she quickly reassured me.

"Dragons need little sleep," she explained. "We have the ability to rest and be vigilant at the same time."

She set my mind at ease also about her ability to hear and identify animals and even insects scurrying through the undergrowth. I suspected that she heard them well in advance of my hearing them, and indeed long before she mentioned them to me.

She paused. "Kirym, you can trust me to watch over you. Humans need sleep, if my memory is correct," she said.

"You're right we do, but I'm finding sleep elusive tonight," I said. "I've been trying to work out the best way to save the Valythians."

"You have a plan?"

"Yes. As soon as it's light, I'll go and talk to Mama and Papa, and let them know what is needed for the trip. I'll ask for some of Wind Runner's boatmen and their boats to travel north to where the gorge starts. There's a place to climb the cliff at the beginning of the gorge, so there'll be no need to go as far north as the fortress. It won't be an easy climb, but will take less time than going further. From there we can search for Garanniis' people. Hopefully they'll return with us and we can find them somewhere safe to settle."

"And how long would it take to get there?"

"We can travel much faster than Garanniis and Morkeen did, and we'll be able to help them to keep up, so we could be well into the desert in two or three moons if everything goes smoothly. Four, or more if there are delays which is a possibility. Winter's almost here and the stream from the stone circles may be in flood. The water will be icy, and although we will have the boats, we will be paddling against a strong flow. The gorge will probably be wider and deeper than when I last saw it and the water movement faster and stronger. Finding the Valythians may not be straight forward. I doubt they'll still be waiting where Garanniis left them. They'll have moved on, if only to find food."

"Have you forgotten about the gathering at the amphitheatre?" asked Iryndal. "It's planned for tomorrow."

"It'll have to go ahead without me. Garanniis has asked for help, and as I see it, that must take precedence. The longer we leave it, the less chance there is of finding any of his people, and we can't chance him losing any more of them. Mama and Papa can handle the gathering. They would anyway," I said.

Iryndal looked down at me, frowning. "Your presence is needed. Everyone must be there."

"But that must include the Valythians," I said. "We need

them too, or do you think they're dead? Because unless you're sure, we have to go and see. Every day we wait makes it more likely we will only find bones. We don't have a choice."

Iryndal clicked her tongue. "You say we, and you mean I. When you're a leader, you need to look at all of those available and use the most capable. Have you thought that someone else could do the job as well as you, Kirym? Or better?"

"Who?" I paused, but she didn't answer. "I've been in that desert, Iryndal. It's not an easy place to be. I wouldn't ask anyone to put their lives in danger. I of all people, have a little knowledge of the land."

Iryndal obviously had something in mind.

"Who would you suggest I ask?"

"Me!" she snapped. "Well me, and those I choose."

"But you do need to be at the amphitheatre. I may have to be absent, but I know you can't be. What happens when everyone else gets there without you?"

"Hmmm. You're right. We can't have the gathering until everyone is there, so let's arrange their arrival at a time that suits us."

"You can decide that?"

"In Faltryn's absence, I can influence the decision as to when we gather. All I know is that we have to gather, because you have arranged it."

She began to hum. It was a rich sound, so deep I could feel it vibrate through my feet.

Clouds boiled up from the east covering the stars and eventually the moon. They got thicker and lower and a wall of fog rolled towards us.

It was the most amazing thing I'd ever seen. I was reminded of the thick fog I had seen at the inlet when we saw the huge sea monster, and I wondered if Iryndal had been close by then, and used the fog to protect us. I laughed inwardly.

Perhaps it had simply been a heavy fog.

"You've built up the fire," said Iryndal brightly. "The night will be damper than anyone anticipated. By morning the fog will be so heavy, no one will be able to move from the comfort of their encampments. They'll stay where they are until the weather improves. We, however, will travel."

"Will you ask the other dragons for help?"

Iryndal laughed softly. "One doesn't ask when the answer may be no. I will simply tell them to join me." She sighed. "Othyn will want to assist because it is I who require it, and because it was she who discovered the desert children. Borasyn will almost certainly help because he found you and believes he has a proprietary interest. Arymda will do what Borasyn does. They are extremely close, and she feels protective of him. He is always sweet to her when he is the eldest, and she remembers that. Egrym and Ubree will refuse given half a chance, so it's best not to give them one."

"Why would they refuse?"

"Because they're male. Because they're my brothers. Because I am not the eldest and—well technically they should obey, but Faltryn's absence has caused problems in the past." She paused. "Garanniis talked of fyrsha, and he feared them. Do you know what they are?"

"I'm not sure, but Storm was stalked by a large black cat over there. I saw their paw prints and they're huge. I heard them roaring at night, but I didn't actually see them."

She nodded. "Hmmm. I have no memory of cats that size in the desert. Those I remember were small, very small. They kept the rats, snakes and lizards in check. I can't imagine there was a group I wasn't aware of, especially the size Garanniis described. Even the most prolific producers of offspring would take many hundreds of seasons to become as widely ranging as Garanniis implies. Somehow the normal way of things has altered."

"Iryndal, who were the guardians Garanniis talks of? Those who built the city for them."

"They were the first people we spoke to when we arrived in the land—those who had cared for all of the people of the land. They became the dragon riders."

I nodded. "Churnyg's people." I paused. "Would it help to have Churnyg or some of his people with you when you approach Garanniis' people?"

Iryndal looked at me quizzically. "I have all I need to make this journey. Churnyg has his own responsibilities to deal with."

I nodded. "What would you have me do while you travel to the desert?"

"I rather imagine I'll need you both you and Teema with me. I doubt I'd get Morkeen to cooperate or travel with us without you, no matter what I promise."

"Then we will need more equipment than we have here," I said. "Cloaks, food and water mainly, but rugs and boots would make life more comfortable for all of us. If we do find people, we will need stores for them also."

"I have a plan for that, too. Would you be prepared to get the equipment sorted now?"

I nodded.

7

Teema Speaks

Dreams are strange things, but was this a dream? Perhaps it was a nightmare, or maybe I was just deluded.

A fog had thickened, swirling around our small clearing, but appeared not within it. The dense fog was the only movement around me, for although the fire was bright, the flames seemed suspended, motionless, neither flickering nor burning. The embers didn't dull as time passed. The water heating in Kirym's leather-pot didn't appear to reduce in the heat.

A leaf seemed suspended above the fire. It didn't fall into the flames, but nor did it drift upwards in the heat. Smoke from the fire also hung motionless, while the fog roiled and swirled around the camp.

Was I asleep or awake? I was aware, but it was as if I was watching from elsewhere.

Morkeen and Garanniis nestled together on a thick layer of fush grass. More fush covered the robe and cloak I had lent them earlier.

I could hear nothing around me, even the night animals seemed to have taken the hint from the fog and stayed home. The only animal I could see was a small mouse. It stood motionless on a leaf in the clear area in front of the fire and stared at me, its eyes bright.

I reached out and touched it, pushing it aside. It skidded off the leaf, but no further and stood, still watching me. The leaf curled over him, sitting above his right eye giving him a rakish look similar to Larqeba at his most confident. Everything was heavily silent.

I struggled to keep my eyes open.

Something was important, so important I had to waken to check on it, however my brain was as sluggish as my eyes. Even breathing seemed to be a struggle.

Panicking I took a deep breath and forced myself to sit up.

The fog still pressed above and around the camp, thicker than ever although I couldn't feel the dampness I expected with it. The fire still glowed, the flames unchanged.

I started involuntarily as something loud snapped close by.

A limb on the fire burned through and fell onto the embers. Sparks scattered in the damp air.

The mouse jumped, spun around and disappeared into the undergrowth. The leaf hovered briefly, fell onto the embers, glowed red and disintegrated. The fog swirled in on me, thickening as the breeze moved through the trees. I was aware of moisture particles between the fire and me. The last time I had seen such dense fog was when we were taken out to sea by a huge monster from the ocean.

The damp tendrils of fog washed across my face. I shivered, and pulled my cloak closer. I glanced down fingering the warm material.

A slight movement caught my eye. Kirym walked into the clearing with an armful of logs. She placed two on the embers, poured in a little water from a flask into the leather pot.

She looked up and smiled, suddenly aware I was awake.

The log shifted on the fire and caught alight.

Something was different.

I shook my head trying to rid myself of the last vestiges of sleep. Then I realised.

My cloak and robe covered Morkeen and Garanniis. Kirym's cloak was draped over me.

However Kirym wore a cloak. A red one I hadn't seen before, and I knew it hadn't travelled with us from The Green Valley. It was Faltryn style.

"Where—where've you—where did that come from?"

She came and sat beside me, handing me a hot drink. "Shhh, don't waken the others. It's far too early. Iryndal took me to see Mama, Papa, Wind Runner and Findlow. They needed to know what we intended to do next."

"What are our intentions?"

"Rescue Garanniis' people, of course."

"Oh!" I looked around. "Is Veld here?"

She shook her head. "No. Mama saw no reason to send him with us. They have plenty to do where they are. She trusts we'll search well. We know the desert, they don't." Kirym quietly explained the plan she and Iryndal had come up with.

I nodded. "I hadn't thought of using the dragons to go there." I told her how I'd have handled it.

"That was fairly much my idea too. I never imagined the dragons would help us in this way."

"Oh! Well it'll be quicker, but a flight will still take time, Kirym. We'll need to take stores, boats to get the Valythians over the gorge, warm clothes for them to travel in. It'll take ..."

"Teema," she interrupted. "Papa has provided the equipment we need. It's coming with Othyn, Arymda and Borasyn. We'll leave in the morning."

"What about the fog? How will we see where to go?"

"We'll fly above it. As thick as it is, it lies low. It's there to keep everyone else quiet and in their camps until we return. No one can enter the amphitheatre until the dragons are ready for them, so there'll be no unwanted confrontations to worry about."

I stared at her as the importance of what she said sank in. "You mean they made the fog?"

She nodded. "Iryndal did it. It covers everywhere east of here, except for a small area around Churnyg's camp. They need to be able to hunt, and collect other food."

"Is Veld running short of supplies?" I asked.

"Goodness no. What put that thought into your head?"

"Well why not just take stores to Churnyg's people?"

"Because that wouldn't teach them to forage and hunt."

"But if you take them away from the camp, they could be in danger. Gynbere may have his scouts out, and they'll need to forage too."

"Storm, Bryn and Mekroe will teach Churnyg's people how to track and hunt. Starshine will take charge of the camp itself. The fog is particularly thick around Gynbere's camp. All of his scouts have returned. He has plenty of stores, and his people will be quite sleepy for the time we're away."

I snorted. "Bryn or Storm would do a better job for Churnyg's people."

"Starshine is born to the leadership, Teema. Anyway, she can ask for advice as she needs it. Little can go wrong. Iryndal has made sure everyone will be safe until we return. She's very efficient."

"Why didn't you talk to me before you left? I could've guarded the camp as usual. What if something had happened?"

She smiled. "You were asleep, and nothing could have gone wrong. We were in the field watching the owls when we made the decision. We moved fast because we had so much to do. Iryndal set up the protective circle and once the decision was made, I couldn't enter the thicket until it was raised. Nor could anyone or anything else."

"So that's why everything was weird. I wasn't sure if I was awake or dreaming. It'll be great if Iryndal takes over guarding from now on. We can all sleep every night."

Kirym laughed quietly. "It'd be tempting to allow her to do that. We mustn't though. We can't take the dragons for granted, and we need to keep our skills honed."

I told her about my dream.

"You were still alert, and that shows how much our training is a habit. We don't want to lose that art."

I sipped the warming fluid as she pushed aside the coals from the fire and pulled out a steaming leaf wrapped package.

"She cooked?"

"I did. I was on guard in the evening, and the early routine was the same as usual, Teema. Something is always prepared. It's not much. Just the rest of yesterday's fruit mixed with some nuts and ground grains. It needs to cool a bit before we can eat it. It's almost dawn. We'll leave as soon as everyone has woken and eaten."

"Kirym, at the inlet there was fog, and then that monster. But it was huge and black. Could other dragons be here without Iryndal knowing?"

"It was so big and I really didn't get a good look at it. I can't really put what I saw into perspective. We may never know what it was." She shrugged. "We shouldn't speculate. They haven't mentioned others, and I think they'd know. It could simply have been a sea creature with the ability to fly."

"Or a flying monster with a fondness for swimming and attacking small boats," I muttered.

The burning log collapsed. Garanniis grunted and sat up suddenly. He saw us, yawned and smiled. "I had such a strange night," he said. "Full of dreams."

He smoothed the cloak over Morkeen's shoulder, and accepted the drink Kirym handed him.

He smiled appreciatively. "Thank you. I slept well and we were so warm. Please don't go cold for us, we don't expect that."

"We didn't, and it'll be better tonight. We'll have more rugs," said Kirym. "And I'll have warmer clothing for you both quite soon." She quartered the steaming loaf and handed one platter to Garanniis, the next to me. "Eat. The next meal will be more substantial."

"Kirym!" I hissed, pulling her away from Garanniis. "This is all very well, but ..."

Before I could say anything else, Morkeen rolled over and stretched. She smiled sleepily at Garanniis. "Did you sleep well, Garan? Were you warm enough?" she asked, rubbing his back.

"Oh yes. Kirym and Teema are taking great care of us."

She sat up, pulling the cloak around her shoulders, and eyed the platter of food Kirym handed her with distrust. "You dish up such large meals. No wonder you all grow to be giants."

Wait until you meet Sundas, I thought.

Nevertheless, when Morkeen returned the platter to Kirym, she had eaten most of it.

As the black of night was replaced by dawn grey, Kirym rinsed the platters flicking the water onto the burning embers and packing them away with the other items not being used. She carried the pack away through the trees to await Iryndal's return.

Morkeen scowled at me, although it may have been that she happened to be looking in my direction as she did so. She seemed to wear a permanent grimace unless dealing with Garanniis. It was strange to see that look on a face so like Amethyst's.

"Waste! More waste. The fire was wasteful, and now when it is needed, she destroys it. Water for everything. Even washing,"

"What would you have Kirym wash with?" I asked.

"Sand. Works well, and it's reusable." Morkeen was shivering despite wearing Kirym's cloak.

I decided not to point out that we had no sand here, nor that different people had different customs. Instead I took a deep calming breath. "Would you like a hot drink?" I asked, handing the flask to her. "Kirym mixed juice from morlarl fruit in with it. It's warming in weather like this."

"Fire and hot food and hot drink? Pah, more waste!"

I tied the last of the fush grass together ready to be taken with us. I glanced up noting with satisfaction that Morkeen drank from the flask.

Garanniis returned from the direction of the stream with full flasks. "Such a rich land," he said excitedly, "but the weather. I've never known the clouds to come down like this."

"Just holds things up," grumbled Morkeen. "Bad weather keeps us here. So much for her promises of help."

Morkeen was beginning to annoy me intensely. She could scarcely blame Kirym for the weather. "It's unusual to have fog this early in the season, but it happens. It won't stop us though. Kirym still plans to begin the search for your people this morning."

As Kirym returned for the last of our possessions, the fire died. Suddenly I was looking at grey ash.

"Ah," said Kirym. "Iryndal must be close. Let's wait for her in the meadow." She picked up a pile of fush and disappeared between the trees.

I waited to hear Morkeen complain again. When she was silent, I glanced up to see her and Garanniis deep in conversation. Then she stood, grabbed a pack and a pile of fush and followed Kirym, leaving two loads. Garanniis picked up one, I took the other.

We stared into the thick mist. The slight breeze eddied around us creating all sorts of images. Sounds were distorted and more than once I jumped at something that was probably quite innocent.

Morkeen stood beside me, wearing Kirym's cloak. She shivered and Garanniis slipped my cloak over her shoulders as well.

"Here Garanniis, wear this." I wrapped the cloak I was wearing around his shoulders.

"No, Teema. If I am cold, you must be too. You've already done more for us than I've any right to expect."

"I'm used to it," I said. "Anyway, my robe is enough. I'll be loading the packs soon, and Kirym's arranged for more clothes to arrive with Iryndal."

He smiled his thanks.

Kirym squeezed my hand as I pulled her close and hugged her.

The mist swirled and suddenly darkened as Iryndal landed in front of us. Egrym and Arymda swooped past, identifiable only as pale colours in the fog. They circled and quietly landed beside Iryndal. Egrym carried a large pack similar to those we took when on extended hunting trips.

Arymda held a smaller pack which Kirym took and opened.

"Ah, warm clothing."

I recognised the boots she handed me. Memories of an embarrassing morning in the fortress city of Faltryn, when I realised I had been tricked into accepting gifts despite strict instructions from Kirym to refuse everything we were offered.

"How did you get these?" I asked.

"Iryndal told Wind Runner what we needed and she organised it. Faltryners have much warmer clothing than we do, and it'll be cooler in the desert now winter is almost here. There will be enough for everyone, including those we find in Valythia. We've food and water, and Mama sent extra remedies in case I need them."

8

Kirym Speaks

The dragons rose above the fog into bright sunshine. Ahead
the fog wall stopped abruptly, and glancing back, it looked
solid enough to jump on.

The four of us travelled with Iryndal. The scales around
her neck and shoulders rose and deflected the wind, ensuring
we were protected from the worst of the cold air. She wore
a webbing that harnessed us safely to her, even when she
swooped straight up or turned over.

At the beginning of the journey, Iryndal flew slowly to
allow Morkeen and Garanniis to get used to the new mode of
travel. Morkeen clutched my hand firmly, her eyes initially
closed tight with fear, but soon wide open with wonder.
Soon though, she relaxed, her eyes glazed over and she slept.
Glancing back, I saw that Garanniis was also asleep. Teema's
head rested on my shoulder. I knew Iryndal had removed the
stress of the new situation for them.

Early in the journey we skimmed over forests valleys, green

and brown clearings, and many small lakes and streams.

Salcan's hill was now covered with green, nature had done well in hiding the scar caused by the collapse of the cave. One of the trees, standing when we left, had recently fallen, the soil at its roots still raw and brown.

The canyon hill was to the south of our flight path but the ridge we had travelled along on our trip to Faltryn disappeared under us in a blur of greens and brown. No water flowed along the ridge now, and the bottom of river bed was tinged with the green of new grasses. Beyond there the land was alien to me, and Iryndal sped up so everything passed too quickly for me to calculate distances. Still I managed to get an idea of the land for future journeys.

A mountain topped with snow passed to our right, and even though it towered above us, the cold had a bite to it different from the air.

We flew very high, although Iryndal chose a lower pass when crossing the mountain. Even so, we were above clouds, and it was interesting to see the differences from above and below, with the sun shining through them.

Iryndal swooped down to land on a wide rocky plain just as the sun reached the meridian.

The other dragons were already there. A fire burned brightly. A meal had been prepared and was soon dished up. The stop was short, just long enough for us to eat. It was good to stretch and walk around, although I didn't feel at all cramped from the morning flight.

The dragons rose into the air together, but sped off one by one, Othyn first followed by Arymda, Borasyn, Ubree and then Egrym. I was able to watch their different flying styles, but noticed there were other visual differences. The dragon's underwing area was the same colour as the edging of their scales. Borasyn, Arymda and Egrym sported darker colours, the same as the token marks on their foreheads, while Ubree's was much lighter, and I suspected Iryndal's was also. Othyn was a golden yellow all over.

Ubree intrigued me most. For the first time I saw him close up and without his wings wrapped protectively around his body. His face had been familiar, and now seeing the long scar on his shoulder, I thought back to the day in Salcan's cave when Larqeba handed me a small carved figure of a dragon. I had assumed the line on the baked dragon's shoulder had been caused by a problem when Salcan had baked the statue, but now I saw it for what it was.

Again Teema, Garanniis and Morkeen snoozed through the journey, but I had much too think about. I was in awe at the speed we travelled. This was different to our early flights. Occasionally we travelled so high, the fine details of the land disappeared. Then I could see the shape of the coast, the hills and mountains.

Generally Iryndal didn't fly over the higher hills, but swooped around them, finding the lower saddles to cross.

It was cold, and I appreciated the warmer clothing Wind Runner had provided. Without them, we would have had an uncomfortable trip.

Iryndal had explained to me that on other flights, the dragons would go slower, and we would be able to see the land we crossed, and we would need to if we wanted to find the Valythians. If we travelled at that speed now, the trip would take more than six days longer, time we didn't have.

We landed beside the gorge during the afternoon. Although it was too late to begin a comprehensive search for Garanniis' people, there was time to search one or two close places for signs of life.

Look at the places you know. Become familiar with the unknown. Befriend those who need a gesture. Only two are needed to help Borasyn organise the camp.

Iryndal's message to me seemed to be contradictory, but

then I realised what she was suggesting.

"Garanniis, could you and Morkeen set up camp. Borasyn will help with wood and fire."

Garanniis smiled his agreement, and they both began to strip off the heavier clothing they'd worn.

"Teema, I'd like you to check the islands in the inlet. You could …"

"They fear water, Kirym," interrupted Garanniis. "They'd not go there."

"What would cause more distress, Garanniis? Water or fyrsha?" He frowned as I turned away. "It's a long shot, but we may as well eliminate the spot now. Egrym, will you take Teema?"

Teema dropped his pack. "What if we see them? I can't imagine they'll race out to meet me."

"At most there may be some indication they've been there. If there is, we'll follow up on it tomorrow."

Already he was on Egrym's back and with a downward sweep of his wings, Egrym was in the air and away.

I looked at the remaining dragons. Ubree stood watching the far bank through the trees, his wings again wrapped around his chest. Borasyn was drawing pictures in the soil, watched by Othyn and Arymda. "Othyn, could you fly north along the eastern bank of the river? Arymda could you do the same going south. Ubree, will you please take me along the far river bank. We may pick up some tracks."

Ubree sighed and shuffled around to offer his right knee to assist me to climb onto his back. He took off quickly.

Glancing back, I thought I saw Iryndal wink at me as we rose above the land. Then the camp was gone and we swooped up and along the river well above tree height. Out of sight of the camp, I leaned forward. "Ubree, I'd like to check the bridge Garanniis used. Do you think you could find it?"

He banked around a group of trees and soon we hovered

over the broken span. We could see how fragile it was even from this height.

A large clearing, partly walled by spikey plants, surrounded an area at the beginning of the western span.

"Oh my. I don't know how Garanniis and Morkeen had the courage to use that."

"Courage or desperation?" asked Ubree.

"Courage," I said emphatically. "No matter what else was going on, to even consider crossing was a feat."

"When the alternative is death, some decisions are easier made than others. Either way, this is not a structure to be used by anyone ever again. Let's make sure no one is tempted."

Without warning, he folded his wings and dropped abruptly onto the eastern span. The stone brought him to a sudden halt. I felt the strangest sensation as vibrations ran up his body. I was reminded of the smaller of the tremors I'd felt when the earthquake was beginning back in The Land Between the Gorges.

Ubree balanced on the bridge spar for a few moments. It broke with a resounding crack and splinters of rock flicked away. He spread his wings and soared up as the rock splashed into the water below. He dropped next onto the western portion of the span. Another crash and this time I watched the rocks hit the water.

Ubree followed them down running his feet in the water before again flying up to hover above the western bank. "Now nothing can get across. I suppose you want to land?"

"Yes, I'd like to see if they left any tracks. I may get an idea of how long they've been gone, and possibly the direction they went."

Still hovering well above the ground, Ubree twisted his head around to look at me. "I will allow this, but if I tell you to, you will get on my back immediately without question, without hesitation. If you're unwilling, then we'll simply return to the camp now. If you're slow in obeying me, your trip home will be less than comfortable because I will grab you. Is that clear?"

"Absolutely. I know you see and hear things long before I do. I will rely on you to keep me safe, as I will do my utmost to do the same for you."

He gave me the nearest thing to a smile I'd seen on him as he settled on the ground.

I slid off his back and searched the ground around the spiky enclosure. The plants left were still growing, their dead appearance normal for this type of plant. Around the clear area was indication there had been many more similar plants that had been uprooted and taken away. There were no foot prints.

"Did you expect to find any?"

"No," I said, "but it was worth looking. We know they were here, and it would've been nice to find some hint of where they went."

Ubree winced as he put his weight in his left front foot.

"How bad is it?"

He shrugged. "It isn't. Anyway I heal quickly. Some things are more important than a bit of pain."

"The wound on your shoulder didn't. The scar implies infection. How did it happen?"

He pretended not to hear my question.

"How long did you know Salcan?" I asked, changing the subject.

Ubree's eyes narrowed. "I knew he couldn't be trusted. He promised not to talk about me."

"He kept his promise. He didn't ever mention you. He had a small statue of a dragon. I put two and two together. I imagine you were the only dragon he met. I'll show it to you when we get back to my pack."

"Don't let anyone else see it." He looked quite pleased.

"Let's check north before light dies."

We flew as far as the beginning of the rift, stopping five times to check the ground. At our final stop, we found the first signs of people. An outcrop of blackened rock stood out starkly against the pale ground around it. A large fire had been set here, although enough time had passed for the ash to be blown away. On the edge of the scorched rock where soil had built up was a massive paw print. I was shocked at its size. The beast that made it would have been huge.

I pointed down the sheer cliff towards a grassy area beside the river. "That's where we camped on our journey south. Storm tried to convince me to turn back. He wanted us to join Wind Runner and the rest of the family instead of travelling through the gorge."

"Where were they?"

"East of here, tracing our path back to The Green Valley. They were initially aiming for the stone circles."

"You're lucky you weren't there when this beast came sniffing around," said Ubree, rubbing the scar.

"Does it still bother you?" I asked.

He grunted non-committedly.

"I have a salve that may help it. I used it on Borasyn's foot. It wasn't infected though and the wound disappeared quite quickly."

"Mine was a deep infection. It got into the bone."

"Does rebirth help?" I asked.

He nodded and looked resigned. "What is it about you that makes us want to tell you everything? Salcan talked of you, you know. He wanted to get you to help with my shoulder. I wouldn't let him. He said if I stopped talking to him, he was going to find you, whether I agreed or not. But it slowly got better. He did all right. What's he doing now? He talked of returning to his family, to you and his brother."

"He died, Ubree. Just over twenty days ago."

Ubree closed his eyes, and looked pained. Then he sighed. "I expected it. He wore death like a robe. I'm glad he got to see you though. He missed his family. Had some strange ideas, that one."

Ubree's head came up. "Now! We're leaving now."

I ran over and climbed onto his back. Moments later we were in the air. Ubree hovered above the land. The sun had long set, and the light was almost gone. The trees rustled in the wind, and nearby an owl hooted. In the distance, an animal roared.

The wind chased dark shadows across the ground. The small ripples in the land were vague in the growing gloom. One large dark shadow streaked over open land obvious only because it travelled in the opposite direction to the others.

"What was that?" I asked, although I was unsure if I had seen anything.

Ubree wheeled away, rising fast and headed towards the east bank of the gorge. "Something we'd best avoid."

It was dark when we arrived at the camp. We were guided in by the light of the fire, and assailed by wonderful smells of a waiting meal. Everyone else had arrived back before us.

As soon as I'd slipped off Ubree's back, Morkeen confronted me. "How did you know about those places? You can't see them from this side of the river."

"I was over there a few moons ago, and no, I saw no sign of your people."

"They wouldn't have let you," she grumbled, frowning. "How did you get back across the river? Why aren't we using—?"

"We didn't come across the river," I interrupted. "We followed the shore out to sea and returned along the coast that way. I'm not sure there is another way out, although maybe far to the north."

Morkeen turned away, her usual scowl softened by tears.

Garanniis and Teema dished up the meal as I removed the warm clothing I had worn for the day.

"Did you find anything?" asked Garanniis.

I told them about the fire remains, but didn't mention the paw print. "All of the charcoal from the fire had gone, so the chances are they took it with them. The ash has long since blown away."

"Well that's good news," said Teema, "because we found no signs at all. The dwelling isn't usable. The sea had washed away the soil around that big tree with the red berries. It fell and that left the dwelling vulnerable. That storm we were caught in must've blown it about a bit. One wall and the roof had collapsed. Animals have been through it, those things up in the trees, I think. Some of the baskets you left have been gnawed through, the contents eaten."

"Well I didn't think it would stay intact. Nature takes over very quickly. The islands?"

"Nothing big on them. Mostly rodents and birds," said Egrym.

"We never expected to find them in those places anyway," said Garanniis. "Where do we go tomorrow?"

"I've made a map," said Borasyn. "We can work from that." He indicated over to where he had been drawing earlier.

Teema picked up a torch and followed me over to look. "It's not bad either. I think he has the distances sorted."

"Hmmmph!" Ubree's breath was warm on my neck. He reached over my shoulder and stabbed a deep gouge into the hard soil west of gorge line. "There's a canyon here, but it's unlikely they'll have gone that far. It's too dangerous, but it's possible if all else fails. Rocks here in the north, I'll check them if we need to, but there are other more obvious places first. Massive thorn patch north west of here."

"I've seen them before," said Garanniis. "They're too thick and spiky to utilise. The home of the groaning ghosts."

Ubree snorted. "Just the wind."

"Whatever causes it, eliminate the area. My people won't go there. Searching will waste time."

Ubree frowned. "Tomorrow. Teema you and Egrym will check the northern side of the tall red rocks—the chimneys Kirym called them—right along to the end, and come back on the south side. Othyn you can take Morkeen and fly the gorge. That's in the gorge not above it, and the western side only. It's possible to climb down the cliff. Arymda, you do the same with the eastern side. Garanniis will help you. There are overhangs, and some of them are almost like caves. You'll need to watch carefully to find them all. I'll take Kirym with me."

"You can't tell us what to do. You're not the oldest," said Egrym.

"You can argue, but I've the most experience with the desert and what lives there. You're welcome to go elsewhere if you like, but you'll fly by yourself. When you don't return, I promise I'll look for your bones. Can't say I'll find them though."

"They would attack someone the size of Egrym?" gasped Teema.

"And they'd win," said Ubree.

"Fyrsha? Well, they might scratch him, but win?" said Garanniis.

"The ones you saw. What did they look like?" asked Ubree.

Garanniis grimaced. "Black, large crest on their heads and down their necks."

"Horns?"

"Yes, they have horns."

"What length?"

Garanniis held his hand up, fingers wide apart. "A bit longer than that."

"Juveniles! Think horns longer than mine, and the older the beast, the more cunning and vicious it is." He turned to the other dragons. "I've had a few run-ins with them. They're getting bolder, and they weren't particularly retiring when I first met them. None of you have any idea what to expect from them. But whatever you are thinking, it'll be worse. If you just fly away, they'll follow. They're fast, and they learn quickly. They can jump. High! So if you see one, go straight up and keep going until you're less than a spec in the sky. That's if you see it."

Garanniis was pale. "You think the big ones are hunting my people. Could anyone live through that?"

"They can!" Ubree sat beside the fire and blew on the flames. They roared into the night sky. His tail thumped angrily on the ground. "Tell me about the wind direction, Garanniis?"

"When it's hot, it comes from the north and west. The cold winds are more southerly. It has been more hot than cold over many seasons."

"Is that significant?" asked Teema.

I nodded. "The wind alters the direction of the sand dunes. It's easier to follow the line of the dunes, rather than cross them. If Garanniis' people travel towards the afternoon sun, the land would take them northwest."

"Unless they purposefully climb the dunes," interrupted Garanniis.

"If they do that, their tracks will be obvious from above. We'll see them easily," said Ubree. "We'll be flying much slower than we did on our trip here. It'll still take two or three days to check out the dunes. Where else would they go?"

"The rock plain," said Garanniis. "It's a huge area. The rocks are tall, and it's a warren of tunnels. Lots of places to hide."

Ubree shook his head. "The fyrsha would find them equally attractive. They can hide as easily as your people can. They're very good at ambush."

"There's the high blue basin. Tollick grass mainly. It's harsh and cold there. Icy winds, so it's unlikely they'd go there unless forced."

"What about the area where Valythia was?" asked Teema.

Garanniis shook his head. "We never found it. The legends say it was a barren wasteland before we arrived. It returned to that once the city was destroyed. The only reason we stayed was because of the protection offered by Valythia's walls and water."

"Will each of you dragons fly a different route?" asked Kirym.

Iryndal nodded. "Perhaps you can split up also. You see things differently, and four groups would make the search faster, although Morkeen and Garanniis may prefer to go together."

Morkeen scowled. "I don't need my hand held."

"Good girl." Garanniis smiled broadly.

"If you are to search tomorrow, you need to rest," said Iryndal.

Garanniis and Morkeen had laid out the fush grass and spread the rugs around. After we ate, they snuggled down together.

I tidied the area and placed food under the embers.

Teema dropped an armful of wood beside the fire. "You didn't tell Garanniis or Morkeen about Amethyst."

"No," I said, glancing around to see we weren't overheard. "I didn't want to complicate things. Garanniis told me his was not the only group. Amethyst could come from any of them.

I want us to focus on finding people. We'll sort Amethyst's family out later. Please don't mention it yet, Teema. You sleep now. I'll call you later."

Iryndal pushed more wood onto the fire. "You too should sleep, Kirym. I'll care for you all tonight. You'll need to be very alert tomorrow."

I was pleased for the suggestion, and pulled my rug over my shoulders.

Next thing I knew, Morkeen was shaking me awake. "Come on. The day's half gone. We'll never find anyone this way."

It was early and grey light was just beginning to touch the eastern horizon. Again a fire burned brightly, food and hot drinks awaiting us.

I drew my cloak close around me, it was cold here above the river.

"The dragons are over there looking at each other. They've had their heads together ever since I woke, and that was well before dawn," said Teema. "Haven't had a word from any of them."

"Ubree is telling them what to expect and what to look for." The words were out of my mouth before I realised Ubree's pictures weren't reaching anyone else. I grabbed a water flask and shook it. "Are they all full? What about food for the day?"

"Yes, I filled them and we won't need them all," said Teema, not realising what I'd said. "I've divided one of the loaves from the embers and wrapped part for each of us. We can eat well now and again when we return. Hopefully we'll have to prepare a lot of food for those we find."

I longed for Teema to be right.

9

Kirym Speaks

"A wasted day," scowled Morkeen. "They would have been too scared of the water to climb down to those caves. And searching the eastern bank was a total waste of time. How would they get there? You knew yesterday they'd gone north. That's where we should've been searching."

Morkeen and Garanniis had just returned from their search of the cliffs above the gorge as I dished the meal.

"Just past the fire remains we found yesterday, there was a great jumble of rocks. That would've been hard to travel through, so they may have turned back," I said. "The land beyond there is difficult.

"Why bother looking if they didn't go past the rocks."

"They might have managed to get through. Anyway I wanted to eliminate the fortress area and beyond. Each place we eliminate is one less to check tomorrow."

"We talked about this, Morkeen. We have to be methodical," said Garanniis gently. "The search areas suggested by Kirym and Ubree were the most obvious places for them to be."

She stamped away angrily to stare at Borasyn's map. Garanniis looked distressed.

"It's all right, Garanniis" I said quietly. "She's scared we won't find them, or that we'll find them too late."

Egrym and Teema flew in. "What was it like at the fortress, Kirym?" Teema asked before he had even dismounted.

"Cold and desolate. It was horrid there without the people. I hated it."

He shuddered. "Did you go in?"

I nodded. "Ubree landed on the battlements, so I could check the great hall and the rooms we stayed in when we arrived. Then he took me up to Wind Runner's window and I checked the rooms there. The dust hasn't been disturbed anywhere."

"What about the fires?"

"The smoke is closer to the northern wall than before, and just by the winter garden, it's burned through to the surface. There's a deep hole there. I could see the glow of the fire in it."

We sketched in the extent of our search on the map and made decisions about the following day.

Ubree wanted to check an area of caves where the stony desert met the sand. He gave out areas to the others. Iryndal and Borasyn would be at a central place to liaise the search, as these areas were closer together than our searches today.

Our meal, eaten as the sun set, was sober. Morkeen and Garanniis kept their thoughts to themselves, and both slept as soon as it was dark.

Teema sat up a bit later helping me prepare for the next day.

"It's a shame they hadn't gone to the red rocks," said Teema. There are a number of bigger caves on the northern side that could've been made safe, and I think they would have found adequate food there if they were careful."

"Fear and superstitions are strange things," I said. "Let's just hope they found somewhere safe."

The initial map drawn on the ground had been transferred to parchment. I now studied the details we had filled in. We had found many things, but no people, and other than the scorched rock, no sign of them.

"Why are you not asleep?" asked Iryndal. "You'll be too tired to be useful tomorrow. We did discuss this, Kirym. You can trust me to guard you well."

I pulled my cloak around my shoulders. "I do trust you, Iryndal. Sleep doesn't always come when invited."

I picked up a flask, warming my hands on it, but not drinking. "We're missing something. There's one thing we haven't seen at all."

"People?"

"Have you seen any fyrsha?"

Iryndal frowned. "I haven't. I didn't think about that." She closed her eyes. "No, and none of the others have seen them either. That could mean they've dispersed."

"If they were wandering around the desert, then surely we would have seen at least one or two. We haven't, so maybe they are all somewhere stalking the Valythians." I stared at the map, trying to see what we might have missed. Although the dragons could crisscross the land, some areas seemed inaccessible to people. I pointed to three of the closer regions.

"Four moons have passed. How far could they have gone in that time?" said Iryndal.

I frowned. "If they were being hounded by the fyrsha, then probably not too far. More likely they stayed close and built some sort of secure place to protect themselves. The threat would be massive, worse when they travelled."

"And they'd be at risk of starving if they stopped. Garanniis told me they travelled constantly because they had to. Food was always the issue."

"The river is their most productive land, so they'd not want to go far from it. They'd be able to get a good harvest in these trees, enough to keep them going for much of the winter. But they may have gone out into the desert a little to be in more familiar surroundings. Somewhere easy to defend." I put my finger on an area to the northwest.

Iryndal glanced at the map. "Garanniis is adamant they'd not be there. He said the area was home to ghosts."

"Given a choice between fyrsha and ghosts, the ghosts have a decided advantage," I said.

The icy late autumn night, a hint of the winter to come, gave way to a cool morning, but the clear sky suggested we'd have a beautiful day.

The area Ubree took me to, was strange. All we could see of these caves was the tunnel entrances leading into a low stony hill.

Ubree hovered high overhead for a short time. *Stay on my back. Don't move and don't make a sound. Watch the area in front of the caves.*

He settled on a steep dune about a hundred steps above the tunnels.

I wondered why Ubree chose to stand here to view the area. We were too far away to see if there were prints around the entrance. Not all of the cave entrances were visible, and I didn't think we could would see anyone leaving some of the tunnels.

The ground in front of the caves was strange. Different. There were lots of small humps here. It took me a while to figure out what was wrong. Then it dawned on me, these mounds were laying in different directions. They were all very small. That was an anomaly I had never seen before, dunes, even small ones were shaped by the wind. In any area the wind was uniform. I wondered if my view was distorted by the long early morning shadows.

For a while nothing happened. Then small subtle movement, and finally something I recognised. Large insects scurried across the sand. Most were chorkans going by the tell-tail curved sting hanging over their heads.

Watch them, came Ubree's instructions.

Larger creatures I had never seen before darted over the small dunes, chasing the insects.

They were slightly darker than the sand, but if they stayed still or in the shadows, they were virtually invisible. Eventually I realised they were rodents of some kind. Having caught the insect they wanted, they then sat on their haunches to eat them. They looked quite amusing. Their oversized ears flicked as they licked around their mouths to get all of the juices.

Suddenly the ground in front of the caves erupted. It seemed almost instantly the area was full of large black cats chasing the rodents, hissing and snarling at each other.

Fyrsha! They fought viciously over the few rodents caught and any fallen remains. Once all of the scraps had gone, the fyrsha spread out across the sand and with some wriggling and flicking. Covered themselves with sand. It was a perfect camouflage. The unusual humps were now explained.

I was amazed that black creatures could be so well hidden in the golden sand, but now I knew what to look for. Many of the darker streaks I had assumed were shadows were the hint of what was hidden beneath the sand.

With a downward sweep of his wings, Ubree was in the air. His shadow swooped across the cats and again the sand erupted. This time, we were their focus, and I was amazed at how high they jumped in an attempt to catch us. Some came very close, and I could see their faces, the long piercing fangs and their horns, about a hand-span in length. They had small crests running from their noses, up between their horns and ears and down towards their backs.

Then Ubree shot up, and the air cooled. The cats were a blur on the ground and as we got higher, they disappeared, although their roars of frustration followed us.

"Sand lice settle in the top layer of sand there," Ubree said. "The heat given off by the fyrsha draws them here, although they do live right across the sands. They're too small to attract the fyrsha, but chorcan eat the lice, and gilibars eat the chorkan."

"Where do the gilibar live?" I asked.

"They dig small burrows in the sand. They're fast, have great hearing and sight. Generally most of them escape."

"The fyrsha don't dig into their burrows?"

He chuckled. "Gilibar dig very quickly, change direction frequently and collapse their tunnel behind them. It would be unusual if a fyrsha managed to dig one up. They're the reason the nursery is there. The sand is their camouflage, but the chorcan, their main food source, live in the stony area."

"Do the adults hide in the sand like that?"

"On occasion. They are far more subtle, and they have many other ways of hiding."

Our next stop was a wide plain of gently undulating dunes. Here, Ubree allowed me to climb down and stretch my legs.

I stared around in awe. The air felt so clear, the sky seemed to be closer. The sand glowed golden in the distance. I loved the contrast of it against the deep constant blue of the sky at the far curved horizon. The ripples at my feet reminded me of the patterns left by the waves on the beach.

Initially I marvelled at the silence, but then I became aware of a persistent noise that grew until I felt it would overwhelm me. I concentrated and realised it was simply the constant movement of the sand as it drifted down the steep sides of the dunes or was blown across the surface by even the lightest breath of wind. Once I understood the noise, it again diminished.

Small animals and insects scurried across the dunes. The sounds of them and the moving sand reminded me of a crowd of people whispering in the distance.

"It's stark but beautiful. I can see why Garanniis loves it, but it's hard to think that a place that seems so peaceful could harbour so much violence and death." I stared at the horizon. "As gorgeous as it is, I'd quickly miss the trees. I feel quite lost already."

Ubree nodded. "It's easy to become disoriented here. Generally there's nothing to focus on except the line of the dunes. That changes over the seasons. If you're away for a while, you become instantly lost."

A thin raucous cry came from high above us. A lone vulture circled, soaring closer with seemingly no movement.

"So that's how the fyrsha find people."

"People and everything else moving in the dunes. I imagine any who see or hear the bird will be watching to see if others join it. One or two birds may not get a lot of attention, but more than that and the fyrsha would start their journey here."

"Is there any way to avoid the birds?"

"They don't fly until the land heats, so travelling as the

sun rises or at night is the best way."

"Wouldn't they see you even if you just stayed still?"

"Tents and clothes used here are made from grasses and fibres found in the desert. The colours blend. Garanniis mentioned that his people layered sand over their tents, and stayed under cover during the day. However the birds can catch minor movements or anything not quite right. Their calls travel a long way. It could take the fyrsha a day or two to get to where the birds are unless one happens to be close by for some reason. We'd hear them if they were close. They're not quiet, although they can be if they're stalking something."

"You knew there could be no people at the tunnels, so why did we go there?"

Ubree nodded. "I wanted to show you what we faced. Fyrsha hide well, and they're quick. As they get older, they leave fewer signs of their presence in the sand. If there was an adult hiding, I doubt you'd see it until it moved, and if you were the prey, it'd be too late."

"These were quite young weren't they?"

"That was a nursery. There are quite a few scattered across the desert."

"The other dragons. Are they in danger?"

He shook his head. "They're aware of what they face. We spent a lot of time talking last night."

The bird had now been joined by another, and a number of distant specks indicated more approaching.

"Let's go, Kirym. There must be a kill of some sort nearby. Where one type of scavenger gathers, others are normally close by."

Before he had finished speaking, I was on his back and we were in the air.

As we approached the designated meeting place, Iryndal and Borasyn swooped overhead preparing to land.

We braced ourselves for Borasyn's crash-landing, but Iryndal grabbed his tail and pulled back slightly. Together they slowed as they approached. At the last moment, the older dragon let go.

Borasyn's landing was perfect.

"Didja see, Kirym? Didja see? I did it. Flawless. Another great landing. Didja?"

"Yes, Barasyn. It was perfect."

"See Ub. Kirym said it was perfect, and she knows landings."

"Humph! Did you see any sign of people?" interrupted Ubree.

"Naha. Just sand. Yellow sand, red sand, brown sand, more sand. And stones. Yellow stones, red—"

"No, we saw nothing at all," interrupted Iryndal.

"No fyrsha?"

"I've never seen one, except those you showed me."

"We did," I said. "A juvenile nursery, and that implies the adults are interested in something else, which could be good news and bad."

"Good news?" asked Teema, as he and Egrym swooped in to land beside us.

"The fyrsha are together. The bad news is they're stalking something."

Teema nodded. "If it's the desert people, they're in grave danger. Still that would mean they've thwarted the fyrsha until now. Where is the most likely place they could be holding out, Ubree?"

He frowned. "Garanniis wants us to look at part of the rock plain, but I firmly believe the fyrsha would find it far too easy to stalk them there, especially with the numbers of fyrsha I suspect are hunting them. So," he paused as Arymda and Othyn landed beside us. "There's a large area of bushes north of here. They're tall, thick and covered with thorns. The fyrsha don't like them. The problem is they cover a massive area. There could be any number of creatures in there and in any part of it, or not there at all."

"So we're wasting our time here. Let's go," said Morkeen.

10

Kirym Speaks

We circled over a sea of massive thorny growth. These grey-green thorn bushes had attained the height of trees. They towered over the desert floor. The one difference—trees had a tall trunk allowing access to the ground below them. These plants continued to grow out from the base even at ground level. In the few places where there was a bare trunk, seedlings had sprouted and filled those spaces. It seemed impossible that anything lived in there.

"Maybe I'm wrong," I said.

"No fyrsha at all," said Morkeen. "We waste time."

"Before we leave, I'd like to fly over and listen to the life here," said Iryndal.

"There won't be life in there. Nothing could get in," snapped Morkeen.

Garanniis laid a restraining hand on her arm. "Let them look. While it'd be difficult to enter, it wouldn't be impossible."

We met back where we started, and hovered together to discuss our finds.

"Nothing!" snapped Morkeen.

"Many living things?" responded Iryndal.

"Of course there'd be insects, rodents, birds and…"

"Large living things," interrupted Othyn. "Very large."

"Big enough to be our people?" asked Garanniis softly.

Iryndal nodded. "Possibly, but bigger too, which may…"

"Up!" I screamed.

It was just a blur in the corner of my eye. Big, black and very fast.

The dragons' reaction was instant. Even so, the beast grabbed Ubree's foot with one clawed paw, and was slowly pulling him down when I sliced across its nose with the tip of my sword. It roared with pain and frustration, but let go and fell to the ground. When we again hovered, much higher now, blood dripped from Ubree's foot.

A huge horned creature had raced from nowhere. Had Ubree not been rising, it may have, in view of its size, dragged him down. Ubree and I would not have escaped.

"What is that?" Garanniis gasped.

"A fyrsha. Full grown," snapped Ubree. "The dominant male of the pack."

Iryndal urged Ubree higher, and hovered close to allow me to climb onto her back so I could check Ubree's foot while we remained in the air. Now the fyrsha was aware of us, we couldn't land on this side of the river.

The claws had been long, the length of my hand at least. The wound was deep and nasty. It bled profusely.

I washed it and then sterilised it with some skafarhn, a strong fermented drink Findlow made.

Ubree bellowed and pulled his foot away as it stung. He

winged away from me, glaring over his shoulder.

"Let her do it," said Borasyn quietly. "Otherwise it'll fester like your shoulder did."

Ubree transferred his glare to Borasyn, who returned the look. However, Ubree hovered and allowed me to continue caring for him.

I spread a salve over the wound and bound it up, proper bandages this time, from the large remedy pack given me by Mama before we left.

I glanced below once I'd finished. The fyrsha paced the ground beneath us, tossing his head, snarling, and roaring. He was huge.

The implication of the beast wasn't lost on any of us.

"Straight up," snapped Ubree. "Out of his sight. He may leave."

"I've never seen one so big. No one could survive living near something that vicious," said Garanniis.

"But something is living in the thorns," Teema said. "It may not be people, but we need to find out. How can we search with that thing following our every move?"

"If I can neutralise him, Othyn can check if there are people in there. Let me begin," said Iryndal.

"It won't work," said Ubree.

Iryndal frowned, and closed her eyes, concentrating on the ground. We waited for her to tell us the fyrsha was subdued. Time passed.

"It won't work," reiterated Ubree somewhat louder this time.

Iryndal's eyes opened. "It is difficult."

"There are only two ways to deal with him."

"And they are?" Iryndal inquired.

"Lead him away," said Ubree, "or kill him. I'll try to get him into the desert, but he's experienced, and may not follow. If he doesn't follow, he'll have to be killed. Anyway there'll be more of them here somewhere. First we need to draw them out to see what we're facing."

Egrym snorted. "How do you propose finding out? Do you call them?"

"More or less," said Ubree staring at him coldly. "Iryndal, watch the ground, but don't let anyone go nearer than this until I find out how many we're dealing with down there."

We were so high above the ground, we could no longer see the fyrsha, and although we must have been mere specks or invisible to him, he was obviously aware we hovered high overhead. We could hear him bellowing even at the height we were. Iryndal transferred her keener sight to us and we could see him pacing to and fro below us.

Suddenly Ubree folded his wings and dropped, much as he had when we were above the stone bridge. This time though, he was above the massive fyrsha. Then his head dropped, and his speed increased so he hurtled arrow-like towards the fyrsha.

I watched, my heart in my mouth, and wished him to pull out of the dive. Long moments passed and just when it seemed he must crash into the beast below us, his wings opened and he circled, deftly avoiding the massive fyrsha.

It raced after him. It was fast, but the ground the fyrsha crossed erupted in a lake of black and finally Ubree began to rise.

Even though I had seen the juveniles in hiding, the adult's ability to disappear left me speechless. I'd seen absolutely nothing.

"There must be hundreds of them," gasped Garanniis.

"And how do you suggest we handle all of those now you've woken them all?" demanded Egrym as Ubree joined us.

"If you think they were asleep, then you're a fool. They knew we were here. They were quiet because the big one would've killed them if they'd moved. He disturbed them, too many for him to cope with." The noise below us rose to a crescendo. "And I'd say he's taking his anger out on a few of them now," said Ubree. "We can't handle the problem if we don't know the extent of it. Now we do, and it is possible. I can draw them away long enough for you to bring out any people in there, and protect them until they can be transported to the far side of the river."

Iryndal looked down at the fyrsha below us. "You'll need help."

Ubree frowned. "All right, Egrym can help, but," he rounded on his brother, "you'll stay well out of their reach, unless I call you. No matter what you think is happening you will do as I say."

"Oh all right," snapped Egrym. He frowned and his skin darkened slightly. "Honestly!"

"If they get hold of you, I won't be able to help, so you'll do as I say or you'll die!" Ubree paused. "Just look at what we're going to cope with."

I was shocked. In the short time we had hovered and discussed the problem, more fyrsha had appeared. Many of them were huge, although none as big as the one that attacked Ubree. It was hard to calculate numbers, but I estimated at least three hundred and probably more.

I watched from my vantage point on Iryndal's back. Ubree and Egrym circled away, nearer the ground now.

I wondered if Ubree had made the right choice here. Egrym had a rebellious streak and didn't like being subservient to his older brother. Despite Ubree's instructions, Egrym was arguing with him.

Suddenly Ubree darted away from Egrym. Egrym chased him, pounced on him, and they rolled over and over, roaring and snarling at each other.

Below them, the fyrsha followed their every move.

Ubree broke away and tried to fly off, but Egrym grabbed his tail and wrenched backwards. Ubree's forward momentum was halted and he swung towards the ground. At the last moment, Egrym let go, but Ubree didn't manage to recover. He fell to the desert floor with a sickening thud.

Ubree struggled to his feet, and limped away into the dunes. His wing, broken in the fall, sat at a strange angle. Almost instantly, the fyrsha were on his trail.

I watched, my heart in my mouth. They were fast. Just when it seemed they would grab Ubree, he took a mighty leap into the air and tried to fly away. One wing flapped, the other hung uselessly. He landed ahead of the howling mob, and hobbled on. Again the fyrsha closed in, and once more he worked his good wing, rising briefly into the air.

Another crash landing!

He sat there for a brief moment and struggled to his feet. He slipped and fell. The fyrsha were again too close. He limped on, now on three legs.

The fyrsha were snapping at his tail, and he managed to again get airborne, only to flap helplessly downward.

The fyrsha ran and pounced.

Ubree crawled and leapt. With his broken wing, there seemed no way he could escape.

Egrym hovered helplessly above him.

I could feel his despair.

11

Kirym Speaks

Four dragons landed and we slipped to the ground.

"Over here! Quickly!" called Othyn, pointing to the remains of a tree, now dried and broken. "Light a fire."

"Why?" asked Garanniis.

"Protection," she said.

"What from?" muttered Morkeen. "Fire doesn't scare ghosts, and that's all you'll find here."

I suddenly felt heavy, as if I could lie down and sleep forever. Garanniis and Morkeen looked drained and both sank to the ground. Teema leaned against the tree, his eyes closed. Othyn had placed us in a protective circle, much as Iryndal had placed over the camp when she had taken me to see Mama.

I stared at the edge of the thorn patch, and wondered how we could see if there were people in there, not only because there seemed to be no way in, but also because we couldn't move from our circle. Can the circle be moved with us in it? I wondered.

A patch of bushes grew out to my left, different from the thorn patch, not as prickly although still thick. Perhaps we can begin there. Chop our way into the thorns. But how long would it take? Could Ubree keep the fysha away long enough? And could we cover the whole of the thorn area before they did return?

I stared at the bushes, trying to figure the best way in. Something moved deep in the shadows, but hidden so I couldn't identify it. I moved towards the edge of the circle, wondering.

Light a fire! Othyn's thought roused me.

It was hard to respond, I felt I was wading through honey. Now I understood Teema's description of being unsure if he had been dreaming or not.

The fyrsha's roar raised the hair on my arms.

I swung around. He was so close.

I couldn't help myself, I flinched and involuntarily stepped back, although I knew Othyn's circle would hold.

Behind him, the bushes still shook from his sudden exit.

Oh my stars! He was there. In the bushes I'd been planning to use.

He sprang towards me, his paws outstretched, long claws unsheathed. He roared with anger when he hit the side of the circle. The blacks of his eyes narrow and empty in the yellow. He pushed his shoulder into the invisible wall, snarling when it held him, batted it with a large black paw and roared with frustration. All the time he watched, aware of every movement I made.

I glanced behind me. Morkeen and Garanniis seemed almost asleep, certainly not aware of the fyrsha. The protection Othyn gave them would keep them out of trouble, but I knew I had to move—do something or the sacrifice Ubree was making was wasted.

The fyrsha snarled again. He reared up, testing the extent of the protective cover over us. The tips of his claws seemed to rake through thin air actually piercing the invisible force as he tried to find a way in. He swung his head around, struggling to stab his way in with his horns.

He was so close, I could smell his foul breath, feel it hot on my cheek. My heart beat loudly as I reached out and touched his paw. I had a moment to register the rough pad, some long course hairs and a soft downy undercoat before Othyn's instruction registered properly.

Light a fire! Quickly!

I took off my pack, my cloak, baldric, sword, and shield, knives, my bow and the bolts, everything that weighed me down. Then I collected small dry twigs that had fallen from the tree above us and grabbed my flint.

The fire caught, and I carefully added sticks and then a short thick limb and two longer branches.

Teema brought more wood over as he saw what I was doing. "I feel so tired," he mumbled.

I set up the skin pot, pouring water in and adding a strong stimulating herb to give us a hot drink.

Drink it. It'll help you to concentrate, came Borasyn's prompt.

The huge fyrsha lay at the edge of the circle watching my every move. With his chest and belly on the ground, he still towered over me. The small crest I had seen on the juveniles in the nursery was impressive on this beast, long on his head and neck and growing down his back to his tail.

The branches were burning well. I grabbed the longest of them and swung it at him. He didn't even flinch. I pushed it through the circle, but he stepped away from it, and then casually swiped at it. The branch spun away, twisting from my hand before I registered his paw movement. The force of his manoeuvre shocked me.

I felt frustrated. The fire didn't scare him, it wasn't going to make him leave. If he didn't, Iryndal couldn't find Garanniis' people, and we would never manage to get back onto the dragons. This fyrsha would wait us out, and if any Valythians were here, we could do nothing for them. I felt helpless.

The crown I wore on my wrist until needed, was loose. It kept getting in the way, annoying me as I tended the fire. I remembered Ashistar's words when he handed me the baldric. 'Wear it when you face your enemies or when you want to understand something important.' I slipped it off and placed it on my head.

Ubree's words came back to me. 'There are only two ways to deal with him. Lead him away, or kill him.'

This one wasn't going to be led away. He wasn't taken in by Ubree's ploy. I wondered why not. Fire wouldn't drive him away. How could I kill him without leaving the protection of the circle, and yet if I did, I was sure I'd be dead before I could aim an arrow. His whiskers flicked. He still watched every move I made. It was disconcerting.

I walked to the centre of the circle, and slipped behind the tree trunk and out of his sight. I thought that maybe I could get through the circle on the far side without him being aware.

His speed was phenomenal. I'd only taken two steps towards the far edge when he was in front of me, snarling and spitting.

Teema grabbed my arm. "Don't play with him. This isn't going to work. What was Ubree thinking?"

Back at the fire, I scooped the hot liquid into two flasks, handed one to Teema and sipped the other. A feeling of warmth moved down my body.

"Wow that does make a difference. What now? There's no way to check the thorns and now we're stuck here. Too far away to help," said Teema.

"We have to find a way to kill that thing."

Teema's mouth opened and he turned to stare at the beast. "How?"

"There has to be a way. We work with what weapons we have."

Teema slipped his knife from its sheath. He checked his distance from the fyrsha and threw it. It bounced back towards us. He gasped in horror.

"Something must work," he said as he grabbed his bow, fitted an arrow and fired. His second arrow was following it before the first hit the circle and fell to the ground. He had the third nocked and aimed before it registered. That wasn't going to work either.

"We have nothing else to try," he said.

The fire spluttered, sparked and settled, collapsing as the lower branches became ash. Teema grabbed two big branches and dropped them on the burning wood, pushing aside my weapons as the fire spread.

I picked up my bow and two of the bolts I'd found as we were searching the tunnels of The Rock. They had been used as part of a trap set to kill the last of Churnyg's supporters who were imprisoned in there. The points of these bolts were made of stone, and having sat close to the fire, were rather hot.

The burning branch went through the wall, I thought. *Perhaps that's significant.*

Time seemed to stand still as I nocked the first bolt to my bow. It pierced the surrounding circle and struck the beast in the chest, moments later a second joined it. The fyrsha roared. Both bolts fell to the ground, a tuft of fur with them

As I walked to the edge of the circle, I sucked my finger where the point had burned it. The bolt lay on the ground beside the circle.

"It didn't pierced his skin, but he felt it," I said.

"Try again," said Teema. "Can you hit the same spot?" He handed me two more bolts.

The barrier, where the bolts pierced it, briefly glowed red, but it made no difference. The beast seemed impervious to the bolts.

"It's not working!" Teema sounded shocked—disbelieving—desperate. "But they got through the barrier. Should we heat them more? What else can we do?"

"The last two got through the barrier. They weren't hot, so I don't think that's the answer."

Teema shot two normal arrows, but they were no more successful than the first he shot over.

I pushed a log over as it threatened to fall towards Morkeen. It dislodged the stone shard which rolled towards my feet.

I grabbed it, turned and threw as hard as I could.

The beast reared up—screamed—clawed the barrier trying to get through. Then it fell. Its feet thrashed. Blood gushed from its mouth and it lay still.

12

Teema Speaks

A large area of the barrier blazed white. It slowly faded to red and then disappeared.

The weight pressing down on me seemed to dissolve with it.

"What's happening?" asked Garanniis. He rubbed his eyes, as if just waking from a long sleep. "Where did—" he paused, looking around. "I thought, um, where—" He gasped when he saw the fyrsha, and shook his head. "What happened?"

"Talk later," said Kirym. "How can we search all of that undergrowth?"

"Can you call them?" I shrugged. "It may help."

Iryndal nodded. "I'll know if they respond. Then I'll be able to bring them to you."

"Any call I make will attract any fyrsha who hear it," said Garanniis.

"Leave that to us," said Iryndal. "Just call them."

"Kchheeeehuh! Kcheee, kcheee, kchaar, Kchhaaaahuh."

We waited. I expected to hear the roar of a returning fyrsha, but there was nothing.

"Kchheeeehuh! Kcheee, kcheee."

One of the thorn bushes to our right quivered, and then a solid cylinder of woven thorn branches began to move out from the bushes. It was almost the length of a man when it finally ended and two dark, almond shaped eyes in a white face stared at us.

"Paluniis?"

"Garanniis? Is that you?"

The thorn plug was pushed aside and Paluniis crawled out, jumped quickly to his feet, and looked around cautiously. He was taller than Garanniis, but much younger, perhaps a little older than me.

"Paluniis. I never thought I'd see you again." Garanniis grasped his left hand, the right held a long flimsy looking spear. His look of joy was wonderful.

"I thought you were dead, Garanniis. Come, we've stayed out here too long, the fyrsha don't ..."

"They've gone for now," interrupted Garanniis. "But we need to move fast to get you to safety. I don't think we have much time."

Paluniis leaned down to the tunnel in the undergrowth. "Kcheee, kcheehe."

Two more young men crawled out, followed by an older man and a girl. They all held long spears, flimsy looking compared to the massive legs, long claws and horns of the fyrsha.

"Wharliim." Garanniis smiled broadly and hugged the older man.

"I didn't think to see you ever again." Wharliim had tears in his eyes, and suddenly everyone was talking.

Paluniis bent and called something into the tunnel. It

began to spew people.

Kirym ushered them all over to the fire. "We'll have you safe as soon as you're all here."

Wharliim looked over the people gathered around. "This is us," he said. "The rest are dead."

Morkeen squinted at the people standing around us. She grabbed the shoulder of a girl beside her. "Where's Zyanda?"

The girl shook her head.

Morkeen stiffened. She turned away, picked up a pack, emptied it and slowly, carefully, refolded everything and repacked it.

"Her sister," said the girl to Kirym's quiet question. "She disappeared into the sands a little while back." She glanced over at Morkeen, folding and refolding a cloak. "Morkeen and Zyanda were the only ones left of Garanniis' immediate family. Zyanda was special. The nice one." She glanced at Kirym, her face suddenly red. "Well, Morkeen is abrasive. She irritates everyone, but she was looking forward to being an aunt. It might have made her sweeter. We searched for Zyanda, but there was no trace. There rarely is." She smiled shyly. "Not a nice story to meet you with. I'm Tiannii."

Kirym smiled and offered her water.

I tried to do a head count, but kept losing count.

"Fifty three adults, five children, three toddlers and a baby," said Kirym. "A massive city brought down to this. They've lost so much."

I joined the men and inspected the fyrsha's body. The stone shard lodged deep in his chest. "I'm amazed he managed to roar after that pierced his heart."

Paluniis grabbed the fibre covered hilt and yanked it hard. Bright red blood gushed over his hand as it came free. He shook the shard to get rid of the excess.

Morkeen stamped over, grabbed it and emptied a flask of

water over it, rubbing the stains to remove them. "I want its pelt and its heart."

There was a shocked silence at the waste of water, and the Valythians stared at her and the puddle of water soaking into the sand.

Morkeen tried to push the fyrsha's front legs apart and stab the shard again into his chest.

Paluniis took the knife off her. "We must get to a safe place quickly. The fyrsha will return soon. A heart and pelt are not worth more lives." He handed me the shard. "We wouldn't have survived much longer with this monster around. He learned too fast. We're in your debt—"

"It's not mine," I interrupted. "The knife. It belongs to Kirym. She killed it."

Paluniis looked stunned. "Wha..." He recovered quickly, swung around and took her hand. "I haven't enough words to thank you." He handed her the shard.

She smiled. "No thanks are needed, but we should leave now."

"Leave? Where to?" asked Paluniis. "I don't know how you got here safely, but there's now no way out of the land. We've searched. This refuge is the safest we've found since we last saw Garanniis."

"You'll leave the same way we got here. The dragons will take us."?

"Dragons?" He looked around, and I saw the realisation hit him. "Dragons!"

"They brought us here. They're the only way across the river." I glanced up at Iryndal. "Can you cope with this many people?"

"Of course we can," said Iryndal. "Morkeen, if you wish me to, I will take the beast's body. I'll drop it off at the camp before I go to help Ubree."

"Shouldn't Ubree come first?" asked Kirym.

I could see the Egrym's view of Ubree, struggling again to get into the air. Now he left a trail of blood, his wing dragged in the sand behind him, and his attempts to get airborne were even less successful than before. He held his tail high, the fyrsha now snapping at his heels.

"He was very specific in his instructions," said Iryndal. "We are to get you all to safety before attempting to help him. As soon as we get him away, the fyrsha will return here, and whatever is left here will be torn to pieces. Their frustrations will make them reckless. They may go further to get their prey than they have before, so even being in the thorn patch may be of little protection. We must move fast, sooner or later, they will manage to get Ubree, or tire of the chase and return."

Already I was showing Paluniis how to use the harnesses.

"We have to ride them?" Wharliim was pale.

"Crawl back into the thistles then," snapped Morkeen. "Do it quickly, because we're leaving."

Paluniis rolled his eyes. "Come on Wharliim. We can do this. It's the only choice we have. Now up you go." He physically lifted Wharliim up to get his foot onto Othyn's knee.

Iryndal picked up the carcass and was quickly airborne.

"She's nearer the ground than is safe, Othyn. She'll be vulnerable if she meets a lone fyrsha on the journey. The sun is low, and fyrsha blend well into the shadows. Can one of you go with her as protection?"

She'll be all right, Kirym. She knows what she's doing.

Kirym nodded.

I was thankful Othyn had included me in her answer.

Now almost everyone was safely tied into the harnesses, and Morkeen packed the last of our gear. Othyn, with Garanniis and twenty three other people, was already in the air. Arymda carried nineteen and the baby. She was waiting for me to tighten my harness.

The rest of them waited on Borasyn as Morkeen climbed up behind Paluniis. Once she knew Morkeen was safe, Kirym took her place in front of them. Then we were all in the air.

From above, the baying of the cats was shockingly loud. Some had given up on the chase and returned to their haunt. We only just made it, and despite the long chase they'd had, they still found the energy to leap after us, coming scarily close to Borasyn's feet as he took off.

The dragons banked around the area, giving us the chance to watch the fyrsha discover the bloody spot where their leader had died. The cacophony rose, as the smell of death triggered a frenzy of anticipation. With no prey, a fight erupted and the noise rose.

The sound was relayed to Egrym who amplified it to those below him. A portion of the pack wheeled around and sped back to claim their share. However, there were still too many following Ubree.

"Let's get to safety so you can all go and help him," I said to Arymda.

Despite the heavy loads, Othyn, Arymda and Borasyn made good time. They aimed, not for the camp, which would have taken longer, but straight across the river. Before we reached the bank, Othyn swung around mid-flight and stopped. Borasyn and Arymda paused beside her, motionless in the air.

"Stay in the air, both of you, but get higher." commanded Othyn. Then she showed us the view Egrym was sending to her.

Ubree had struggled to the top of a sand dune. He took a leap into the air, and again drifted back to the sand, but this time, he slipped, and rolled over and over. Suddenly he ran out of dune. Instead of angling gently down as those around it did, this one fell sharply. Ubree teetered on the edge of a cliff.

Unable to halt his forward momentum, he fell in a flurry of sand, wings and limbs. He managed to stop rolling, now sliding along on his stomach. He pushed himself forward, getting faster and faster. He lifted his tail in the air and thumped it down on the sand, propelling himself into the air. Suddenly he was flying.

With one wing close to his body, Ubree wheeled in a circle and swooped back up the hill, skimming over the fyrsha.

Aware of his change in direction, many tried follow, but the sand was loose and they lost all control of their descent.

They tumbled towards the bottom of the dune, their roars, snarls and screams all that followed Ubree into the sky. When the ground flatened, they crashed into each other, and the sounds of the subsequent fight lessened as Egrym and Ubree began their long flight back.

Our view of Ubree and Egrym disappeared, and as one, Othyn, Arymda and Borasyn wheeled south and aimed for the camp.

13

Teema Speaks

Iryndal was waiting at the camp. She and Othyn helped Borasyn to land safely, and we dismounted. Othyn immediately took to the air again and flew north.

The camp had been extended, the fire stoked, and a meal was cooking. The fyrsha pelt sat on the ground, neatly folded, with the head next to it.

Morkeen had her harness off and was on the ground before we had properly landed. She ran up to Iryndal, her eye's blazing. "Why did you skin it? You had no right. I wanted to do it."

Iryndal looked down at her. "You aren't the only one with a claim to this beast, Morkeen. You are angry with it, but why condemn a creature for doing what is in its nature. You wanted to own its death, but many others have as much right. Ubree has dealt with it on a number of occasions, and he risked his life to save you and your people. Is his entitlement any less than yours? Kirym killed it. She too has a claim. You can help with doing what is needed to preserve the skin, and I'm sure you will assist with the decision about later ownership if it is properly cared for now."

Morkeen glowered at her, and stamped away into the growing darkness.

"Make sure everyone has water to drink and wash in," Kirym said.

I nodded. "Garanniis is sharing it out. They treat water with the same reverence Morkeen shows. They're still trying to get over her wasting it on the shard. What was that all about?"

She smiled. "A salute to Zyanda, to victory, I think."

Food would take a while, and although everyone looked as if they could do with a good meal, no one was in dire need. Kirym hauled out Loul's large remedy pack.

I was surprised to see it, I had never known Loul to let it go from her care in the past. She had assembled it for when she travelled to be ready for any emergency. Kirym must have expressed grave concern to have convinced her to send it with us.

The Valythians were still stunned at everything that had happened, but slowly they began to talk and look around.

Kirym quietly approached everyone, offering salves and tinctures as needed. Most had cuts from the thorns, some of the vicious points were still embedded deep in their skin. Two of the men had scratches from fyrsha claws and horns. Those were infected already, in one case quite badly, but she began treatment for them all. In a quiet moment, I offered her a drink.

"Thank you, Teema. Make sure everyone has plenty of food. They've eaten too little for far too long, mainly rodents and roots from what I hear."

The meal was almost ready when Othyn and Egrym arrived back, supporting Ubree between them. Ubree landed with his right fore-foot off the ground. He looked tired.

"The bandage came off, Kirym. It was ripped to pieces before I could retrieve it."

"They'd have been attracted by the blood on it. It doesn't matter, I have plenty more."

Kirym had Ubree soak his foot in an attempt to remove as much of the sand from the wound as possible. She handled the deep slash in his tail the same way, finishing with a wash of skafarhn to sterilise it, and then a coating of salve and bandages.

"Ubree, in the desert, you appeared to have a broken wing," I said. "How did that happen?"

"Oh it's simple. I can do it whenever I want," he said, shaking away his tears. "Watch." He shrugged his shoulder, and suddenly his wing settled on the ground, looking again as if he had broken it.

Now we saw why he had needed help in his return. The wing membrane had a large rip in it, two pieces held together only by the bone structure.

Kirym inspected his wing. "Did that happen as you were flying?"

"A fyrsha came at me from an angle I wasn't expecting. I didn't see him until it was too late. The flight made it a little worse, but Egrym helped me get across the river, and then Othyn helped from there."

"How long will it take to heal?" she asked.

"It won't. I'm stuck with it."

Only rebirth has healed membrane cuts in the past. Ubree can no longer fly. This is the worst I've seen, so bad he couldn't fly even if he wanted to.

I stared at Kirym in horror as I realised what Iryndal meant.

"How will he get back home?" I asked quietly.

To get to your home area, we will have to carry him. It isn't ideal, and it will alter the timing of the meeting at the amphitheatre. An extra two days at least, but we have no choice.

I acknowledged the reproof, and realised that Kirym had delved into the large pack, inspecting containers, returning most to their places in the remedy pack, but putting a few items into a flat basket. An arrow repair kit, gorthan, a powder she used to help plant cuttings to grow roots, and a handful of packets I didn't recognise.

First she washed the rip, removing accumulated sand. Then she ensured the two sides of the wound were sitting flat and together. She sprinkled gorthan over the wound.

I watched in amazement as the membrane rippled and the powder rolled off. "How did that happen?"

"Strange, because the sand adhered to the membrane." Kirym handed me a fireproof container and the gum she used to glue feathers onto arrows. "Can you heat it until it is softened enough to use, but not so hot as to burn the membrane."

When I returned it to her, she had a small pile of rose thorns and a hank of fine thread out. She placed gum on the base of a thorn, attached it to the membrane, and soon had a line of them down each side of the rip and one at the top.

She tied a loop in the thread, and hooked it over the top thorn, and began to zigzag it down the wound to hold it together. Before she had finished, the membrane again began its rippling, and the thorns slid off. She picked up a thorn and looked at it. The membrane had rejected the glue completely.

"Any more ideas?" I asked.

Kirym frowned. Sitting cross-legged on the ground, she pulled the large remedy basket to her and began to sift through the bottom layers. These were powders and plants that were either very strong, ancient or dangerous. Some of them hadn't been used in living memory.

Over at the fire I brushed aside the embers, and began to dish up the meal Irundal had prepared. Garanniis came and helped. Others joined us, and before long, everyone was eating except Morkeen, who was still sitting in the shadows staring in the direction of the desert, and Kirym who was still sorting through the remedy basket.

As I ate I watched her reject container after container. She'd pick one up, stare at it for a few moments and return it to its pocket. Pick up the next, deliberate, place it back. Finally she started on the bottom layer. Some of these had small parchment notes attached.

I wandered over to get a closer look at them. Generally the first notation warned of the danger of using whatever was in the container. One simply said: Poisonous! Danger! Avoid!

"But what is it," I asked.

"The seeds Salcan took."

"Should we get rid of them? You did with Salcan's."

"That's up to Mama and the other healers. Now I can tell her what happens when they're ingested, and others may be able to add information about them."

"Why didn't you give Salcan's seeds to Loul?"

"I knew she already had some, and I had no desire to carry them." She turned away and concentrated on a small flask.

One little container had nothing attached, no indication of its use or danger from what I could see, and Kirym scarcely looked at it before replacing it in its pocket. She went on to the next and the next, before suddenly returning to it. The container was a silver hexagonal pyramid, sitting on a similar shaped base, and with a small dent at the tip. Tassels hung from the six sides. It seemed to be solid, there was no lid and seemingly no way of opening it. It was unlike anything I had ever seen before.

Kirym inspected the container from every side. "Mama's great great-grandmama made a comprehensive list of all of the items here. She said this contained ground bat's wings." She held out the container. The bottom carried a worn picture of a wing.

I nodded. "I'd take that inference from the picture alone, but why would anyone grind bat's wings?"

"A few recipes need it. Most of them are really weird though. Anyway, they've never been used, but what if they're not?"

"Not what?"

"Bat wings. Couldn't that picture equally be a dragon wing?"

"You think someone ground dragon's wings up?"

She laughed. "No, Teema. When I was young I had the thought this contained butterfly wings, but I don't know where that idea came from. But whatever is in here, perhaps it will help. Heavens knows, we have no other options."

It wasn't that simple. The container seemed solid. With no obvious opening, Kirym tried to cut the top off, but the knife made no mark on it. She sat with her eyes closed, trying to feel any differences in the sides and top. There seemed to be none.

Ubree lay beside her, his head on his front feet, watching her. His shredded wing still lay open beside her. Behind us, the meal finished, and Garanniis and some of the women cleaned up and then sorted out cloaks and robes for everyone. On the far side of the river, the roar of a lone fyrsha drifted over. The children, who had begun to settle were suddenly awake and fearful.

Iryndal sat up. We should leave here. We can return for Ubree later.

"If fyrsha get over here, he would be helpless," said Kirym.

"They won't," said Ubree. "They fear the water, and the few who've attempted to, have sunk and drowned. The rivers on both sides of the desert are what keeps them contained. They're not keen on snow and ice either. We're all safe here."

"Kirym. The contents of the container may be simply be what Loul's great great-grandmama thought it was. Her knowledge must have come from somewhere," I said.

"If it opens and looks like bat wings, I'd accept that. But the container is so different, and the material is unlike anything I've ever seen. The knowledge of it has gone, and so I wonder if it's something to do with the dragons."

She stared at it momentarily, and looked up at Ubree.

He still sat there, his head on his front feet, but his eyes were open and he was alert. The fire reflected red in his eyes.

"Oh for goodness sake. How stupid am I." Kirym sounded exasperated. She picked the container up and clicked her blue token to the small dent. There was an audible snap and the sides flicked out like wings. She placed a thumb and two fingers of each hand onto the areas left by the sides opening. Another click, and the pyramid top slowly opened. There was an audible gasp from behind me. Everyone could see the shimmer of colours, reminiscent of the bright colours of butterflies, reflecting out of the container.

"How did you know about the colour? It must have been opened before," I said. "The colours are perfect for butterflies."

Kirym frowned. "Remember spring day? My fifth—when the oak tree fell."

"What, the tree with red leaves?"

She nodded. "I have this strange memory from then, that I saw this. Mama always said I must have dreamed it."

"So how did you know what was in there?"

She shrugged. "I don't know. Anyway, let's see what it does."

I moved closer and stared into the container. Although the container was motionless, the tiny particles moved constantly creating a wonderful assortment of patterns.

Kirym took a tiny pinch of powder and sprinkled it on Ubree's wing. Immediately the membrane seemed to come alive. It rippled and vibrated, although this was different from before. Now it wasn't rejecting the particles, it absorbed them, and moved them down the rip. Thousands of small bright-coloured fibres grew out from the cut edge. Each searched for connections. When two touched, they seemed to study each other. Sometimes they moved away and continued their search, but other times they linked and appeared to absorb each other, almost eating the extra length, until they sat flat on the wing. When all had found a companion fibre and lay flat, longer fibres grew from above the top of the wound, and wove their way to the bottom of the wing.

There was one brief flash of the colours Kirym had sprinkled, and a corresponding glow from the container. As the colours died, the container snapped shut, once again solid.

"Wow!"

Kirym looked up at the boy who had made the comment. "No one else alive has seen that. You'll be able to tell the story for the rest of your life."

He looked delighted.

"Do you think you can travel, Ubree?" asked Kirym

Ubree stood, opened his wings and flapped them strongly,

raising dust all around him. When he stopped, Kirym inspected his wing. "It looks as good as new, but how does it feel?"

He nodded. "It doesn't hurt, but it didn't before so it feels as a wing feels."

"Could you travel back to the meeting area?" asked Iryndal.

Ubree nodded. "I'll keep up."

"We'll travel in convoy. Then if the membrane splits again, I could possibly heal it."

"What do you mean, possibly?" asked Garanniis.

"It may not work a second time," said Kirym. "I just hope we won't need to find out."

With the dragons ready to leave, Kirym walked over to Morkeen and spoke to her briefly. She took Morkeen's hand and together they returned to the fire. Kirym sat her in the shadows while she collected two platters of food. Morkeen's face was red and swollen, tears still ran down her face.

They ate while we loaded the packs and checked the harnesses.

More fyrsha joined the first, the cacophony echoing discordantly across the gorge.

"Iryndal, is Kirym the only one to fly with me?" asked Ubree.

"I'm reluctant to even allow her, although I imagine she will do what she likes. I'm concerned something will go wrong?"

"Your other choice is using Borasyn."

Iryndal shook her head. "Having him carry anything worries me. Sooner or later something will be broken. I would prefer it not to be a person."

"He'll be fine. He is learning. If something happens to my wing, I'll land and we'll deal with it. But probably nothing will happen. If you want to carry everyone, that's fine by me," Ubree huffed.

"I'll go with Kirym," said Morkeen. "He'll care for Kirym, and that will keep me safe."

Iryndal stared at her intently for what seemed like a long time. "Very well. I hope your faith in him is justified."

Ubree almost smiled.

"We'll help," said Othyn. "Take off is the hardest. Beyond that, we float and soar."

Kirym packed the last few items in her pack, and handed a warm robe to Morkeen, helped her onto Ubree's back, and climbed up to sit in front of her.

The fire died with a suddenness that surprised me, and then we were all in the air, and it was too dark to see anything.

The baying of fyrsha followed us up, and then that too faded into the distance.

14

Kirym Speaks

On the way home, I was aware of Iryndal coming close to Ubree to check his wing membrane. He, Iryndal and Othyn landed three times so I could also check it. There appeared to be no residual damage, if I hadn't known there had been a rip, I could not have even imagined it. The edges were solid and the wing seemed to be as good as new. While Ubree was assisted on the first take off, he could have managed by himself and had no problems after that.

I was aware of much more through this flight, than during our trip towards the desert. Dragon speed amazed me. The mountains swooped past so fast, visible only because the snow on them glowed in the moonlight.

As the sky lightened at dawn, I felt Morkeen stir and waken. "How long before we get there?" she asked.

"Not long. Are you rested?"

She ignored the question.

Ubree flew lower now. In the grey dawn light, I realised we

were flying over water, and only recognised where we were when I saw the great arch at the entrance of the bay leading to The Green Valley.

Morkeen gasped as Ubree swooped down to fly through, looped back and went through again. Once into the inlet, he turned east. The sun reflected pale pink on the water as we flew over it. With the cliffs at the southern end of the inlet in sight, Ubree gained height and turned again, this time to the north east. Soon we saw the waters of a small lake reflecting gold from the now rising sun and he banked around and came into the amphitheatre from the south.

Papa's fires to the north no longer glowed, although thinning smoke hung in the air and mingled with the diminishing fog. To the east, Gynbere's fires blazed, bright even in the early morning.

"Most of them are still asleep," said Ubree to my unspoken question.

A small group of people below us were traveling north. I briefly saw the blur of white faces staring up at us, before Ubree began his spiralling decent. The amphitheatre loomed quickly.

The sun shone on the pool by the southern entrance. Borasyn's pictures stood out in sharp relief on the northern bank, already he was hard at work readying another section of clay. He turned eagerly to see us land, and then he was hidden on the far side of the fallen tree trunk.

The other dragons had obviously been there for some time. A fire glowed, and my mouth watered at the fragrant smells coming from a great pot sitting over it. I wondered how the dragons did this. Whenever we needed food, it was waiting for us.

Paluniis had used his time here to open the pelt and scrape it clean. He and a number of the other men were tying a frame together to stretch it out on.

We met near the pool. Teema hugged me. "I was getting worried. Iryndal said there was nothing wrong with Ubree's wing. What took so long?"

"Well perhaps he just enjoyed the trip and didn't want it to end."

15

Kirym Speaks

"Churnyg won't enter the amphitheatre," said Mekroe. "Starshine and Bryn can't convince him it's safe, and he won't listen to anything I say." Mek was exasperated; I suspected this rose from his desire to sample the source of the delicious smells from the cooking fire instead of guarding Churnyg's people. "They're a few hundred steps south o' here. I doubt they'll be there long, Kirym. Churnyg wasn't eager to wait to talk to anyone, not even you."

Churnyg had his pack on his shoulder and was already walking away when I caught up with the group. His people stood near him, all showing signs of being really troubled by something.

"We're not coming in," Churnyg said, as soon as I was within hearing distance.

"All right."

"Nothing you can say will convince—" He stared at the ground when he realised I wasn't arguing with him.

"Why?"

"Ummm," He kicked at a clump of dandelions, his face bright red. "I saw—I—um." He looked up at me. "Kirym, we're not dragon riders. I saw one, a dragon, and I knew. Straight away I—I—it wasn't true. We only saw them from a distance, and ..." He shook his head again. "Not good," he mumbled. "Not good." He glanced up at me, and stepped away, looking scared.

I realised I was frowning, and shook it away. "It's all right, Churnyg. It doesn't matter. It was a story passed down to you. Some stories have no truth."

He wrung his hands. "We have a collective memory. What we know is passed to our children. This morning I knew we were dragon riders, and then suddenly I knew we weren't. I don't know what's changed. They're huge. They're frightening. They always stayed a long way away, and they were so big. Anyway—well—that's it."

"So what now?"

"We'll go and find some trees. Trees are good." He turned away.

"So you'll let Gynbere win."

"What d'ya mean?"

"If you are not with us in the amphitheatre, the rest of your people will have no reason to leave Gynbere for freedom. They need proof the other choices are real. They need a leader. You're it. They won't follow anyone else. So they'll remain Gynbere's slaves. He'll just build a different prison for them. Anyway he knows you're alive, so he'll hunt you down and kill you. You and all of those with you. If you wait and meet Papa, he can protect your people."

Varitza slipped through the crowd around us, and looked up at Churnyg with something akin to reverence on her face. She had been eating sukerberries. The juice had dried on her cheek, and her hair was stuck to it.

"Kirym's right," said Rosisha. "I've grown up believing you'd save us. That you'd bring all of my family together and teach us to be free. I don't want my children to live with the fear I've had. If it means facing a dragon, well, let's do it. If it decides to eat us, I think that has to be better than whatever Gynbere had planned for us."

"But, but," he stammered. "They're so big and fierce—"

"And sweet and kind and helpful and funny," I interrupted. "And they have different personalities. The purple dragon draws wonderful pictures. His name is Borasyn and if you ask him he will draw a picture of the trees you lived in and tell you about your lives in them."

Churnyg looked at his feet, kicking at the dandelion clumps again. The root finally gave up and the leafy top rolled across the grass, the seeds with their feathery wings flying off to drift in the light wind.

"Oh all right. But if one of them licks its lips, I'm off. I'll hide in the biggest tree I can find."

As Starshine and Bryn took charge of the group, Jeresaya handed Amethyst to me. As I kissed her, I marvelled again at how she had grown. She was smiling properly, cooing and gurgling and grasping things. She had a lot of toys, it seemed everyone had made something for her.

"I've found her family, Jeresaya. Her mama's dead, but her aunt and great-grandpapa are lovely. They'll value her."

Jeresaya looked sad. "It's been nice having her with us. I'll miss her dreadfully. I really did think she was yours. When she's with you she's brighter."

"There is a lot of healing to be done and I think she will be a big part of that. I only cared for her until she was ready to return to them."

Garanniis had chosen a spot against the bank west of the southern pool for his people. They were intrigued, almost reverential, with the ready access to water. They would frequently wander over to it to touch the surface.

Together Jeresaya and I walked over and were met by Garanniis, Morkeen and Paluniis. I introduced everyone and told the story of my finding Amethyst.

"She was newly born, and I found no footprints on the ground around her. She must have belonged to Zyanda, and that makes you her nearest kin," I said, handing her to Morkeen.

Morkeen stared at the small bundle, and stroked her cheek. "Zyanda," she whispered.

"What's her name, Kirym?" said Garanniis.

"Amethyst," I said quietly.

"No, Zyanda!" Morkeen stared at him fiercely.

"Amethyst wears a token, Morkeen," said Garanniis.

"She doesn't need to." Morkeen was close to tears. "It doesn't matter. She's mine. She's obviously—"

"Morkeen!" Garanniis looked horrified.

She stared him down and began to remove the token holder.

Paluniis grabbed her wrist. "She keeps it!" He paused. "And her name." He forced her hand away from the token.

"You're hurting me."

"It belongs with her. She will keep it," he reiterated.

She pulled her arm away, shook her robe over the bruise, and turned away towards the shelter erected for them.

"We'll bring her food over and show you how to prepare it," I said to Garanniis.

He nodded, but looked very troubled.

"I'll do it," said Jeresaya, as I turned away

I felt quite empty. I hadn't thought it would affect me quite as much as it did. Jeresaya slipped her arm around my shoulder. "I'm sure it's just shock, realising that Zyanda's daughter didn't die. I'll tell them how to prepare her meals, and make sure they have plenty of harkii. You need to get busy with other things."

I took a deep breath. "Yes, you're right. Ummm, I need to talk to Bryn."

16

Kirym Speaks

Bryn was helping to erect a shelter near the south entrance. We walked away from the noise.

"I need to go and check it," he said, when I told him about the fire damage I'd seen at his lodge when flying past with Iryndal. "See if there's anything to salvage."

"I'll see if one of the dragons will take us," I said.

"Ubree will," said Iryndal. "He needs to strengthen his wings, so he doesn't lag behind on future flights."

Ubree snorted. "I'll do it because I want to."

He extended his leg for me to climb onto his back.

Bryn looked pale. "You come too, Jeresaya. Help sort out everything."

"You don't need me, Bryn, and anyway, I need to take Amethyst's food to Morkeen, and teach her how to prepare it."

"Can I come, Pa?" asked Qwinita. "I can do what's needed."

I leaned down to give her a hand up behind me. Bryn joined us, his body language and face showing his reluctance. "I could've walked. It wouldn't be any problem."

"Except you'd be gone for days, Pa. You are head of the family. Who would you leave the responsibility to? Dashlan?"

He laughed shortly, and then realised we were above the amphitheatre and it was gone.

Qwinita initially held me tightly around the waist, but quickly relaxed. "Oh, this is fun," she laughed.

Once over the clearing, Ubree circled briefly before landing.

Bryn stared around him. "How did it happen? There can't have been a forest fire. None of the trees around the lodge have been burned."

"Lightning strike?" suggested Qwinita.

"No," said Ubree. "There hasn't been that sort of storm in this part of the land this season. Heavy rain—yes, but lightning—no, definitely not."

"But—what about when you were off finding the desert people?" Bryn said.

"It happened before we left," I said. "It must have happened within a day of us leaving here, because a lot of the ash had blown away even then."

"How? We're always so careful about dousing the fire."

"It wasn't anything you did or didn't do," I said. "The ashes were cold when we left. I felt them, sifted through them, and even then, Jeresaya spread them and dug them into the ground."

He nodded. "So what caused the fire?"

"Talk about that later. Is there anything we can salvage?"

He wandered through the remains of the lodge, kicking the occasional pile of charcoal. Then he shook his head. "Nothing left. Well nothing worth taking with us."

"I'll get the speaking stick, Pa"

Bryn shook his head. "I left the basket there." He pointed to a spot that would have been against the lodge wall. "It's gone."

"There's no outline showing that whatever sat there was burned," I said. "The ash is consistent right along the wall. Could someone have moved it?"

"Rargo," Qwinita said quietly.

"He wasn't here."

"Yes he was, Pa. He was out there, and when we all left, it would've been easy for him to come in here and do what he liked. His favourite like was to make trouble."

Bryn looked at me. "Do you think he could have started the fire, Kirym?"

"Probably."

"Oh definitely," said Qwinita. "Just the sort of thing he'd do. And he's done it before."

Bryn gave her a blank look.

"When we found him, Pa, that place had also been burned down. We assumed the people there had been attacked. That whoever did it didn't realise Rargo was still alive. We'd heard all those stories about towns being burned to the ground, and we assumed that's what happened there too. But I always wondered if Rargo started the fire. His clothes hadn't even been singed. Now looking at this, I'm sure he did."

"He'd been badly beaten, Qwinita. He didn't do that to himself, so you could be wrong."

"Maybe he was beaten because he started the fire. Or perhaps it was punishment for something he'd previously done and the fire was revenge. I'm not saying it was right, but I'm sure that you've had the desire to wallop him lately. Maybe someone else had had enough of him too. Pa, he tried to kill Larqeba. He tied him to a tree, and wouldn't tell us where he was. If Larqeba hadn't managed to worry the rope apart, he would've died. We had no idea where to look for him. It's the same pattern. I think Rargo killed those people too."

Bryn sighed. "Those poor people. We could be wrong though. He was so young. Still, I guess it doesn't matter one way or the other. We can't prove it, and the speaking stick has gone. There's nothing we can do to bring it back and there's work to do back at the amphitheatre."

"Let's not rush." Qwinita smiled smugly. She kicked at the dust for a moment before continuing. "It might still be here. The speaking stick, I mean. The basket was where you left it, but I moved the stick before we left."

"What?"

"Not all of it, Pa. The head came off the stick. Ma and I had a hiding place and I put it there."

Bryn looked as mystified as I felt.

"Remember we planned to explore the land soon after we built the lodge? Then I was sick and Ma kept me here while the rest of you went. When I felt better, Ma had the idea to create a secret spot for special things. We dug a cavity under your sleeping platform. Before we left here to look for Churnyg, I put the head of the stick in there. So it may …"

"What made you and Jeresaya do that?" interrupted Bryn.

She shrugged. "Ma said there'd be times we'd be away from here, so why not?"

"Let's see then." He picked up a partly burned platter, and began to scoop the accumulated ash and charcoal away from where the platform had been.

Ubree cleared his throat, and again when Bryn ignored him. "The men of your people seem to be less inclined to ask for help than the women, Kirym."

Bryn looked up. "What?"

"What will take you until sunset, would take me moments. My family does have more talent than just flying people around you know." He gently pushed Bryn back to where Qwinita and I waited. Then he took a deep breath and began to blow. The debris floated away, first the dust and ash, and then the charcoal and eventually all that was left were three of the solid branches that had held up this part of the lodge.

Ubree pushed them aside as if they were twigs, although he grimaced as he did so.

"Are you all right?" I quietly asked, as Qwinita helped Bryn to lift a number of branches that had been tied together to create the base of the platform, to expose an underground cavity.

"I'll get you to check my foot when we return to the clearing. It's fine though. I suspect it's simply that it hasn't fully healed. It doesn't feel the same as my shoulder did, so it's nothing to worry about."

Bryn leaned into the deep hole below what used to be the sleeping platform and brought out a large lidded basket. "The top is burned, Qwinita. The contents may be also."

However the burn was simply across the surface and the contents were intact.

"Ma's treasures," said Qwinita happily. "They smell a bit, but when we've washed and aired them they'll be fine." She held up a tiny jacket. "This was Larqeba's baby jacket. We all wore it. Ma saved it to pass on to one of us when we found someone and lived with them.

Bryn glanced back into the cavity. "That's it. Nothing else here. If it was Rargo, he might have known about the hole, and whether he started the fire or not, well it makes no difference. The head is gone."

"Pa, if Rargo had known, he wouldn't have put anything back. He'd find some way of ruining it, and letting us know it was deliberate. Hold on." Qwinita leaned into the hole and scrabbled around at the bottom. Bryn grabbed her legs when it looked like she would overbalance and fall headfirst. "Pull me out, Pa." She emerged, her face smudged with dirt, brandishing a skin wrapped package.

"Where was that?" asked Bryn.

"We made cavities off the main chamber as well." She opened the wrappings, displaying a strange object.

I moved in closer to try and understand what it was.

Seeing my shadow Qwinita looked up and, smiling broadly, handed it to me. "I don't know why the shaft came off, Pa, but it wouldn't have fit into the chamber with it on. That was why I left the handle in the case. I'm sorry."

"It doesn't matter. The handle can be replaced. It wasn't original anyway. It was just a convenient way to hold it. I vaguely think my great great-grandpa had the idea for it, although it could have been his pa. I wonder why it came off. I've never known that to happen before. It was firmly on when I last looked at it."

I studied it, and now I had so many questions, I didn't know where to start.

It was quite big, I needed both hands to hold it. The top two thirds was shaped like a large closed pinecone. It was clear enough to see through, although there appeared to be a shadow inside it. There was a ridge where the cone-like area finished. The bottom third was divided into three wavy arms. I assumed they held it onto the wooden shaft.

"We didn't use it often," said Bryn, "but if something important needed to be said, the holder could speak without interruption. The last time it was used was when Larqeba told me he'd seen you. If he hadn't been holding the stick, I doubt I'd have listened to him."

"I'm glad he thought to hold it then," I said.

I held it up and stared into the centre. The shadow didn't

seem to be anything, although I wanted to study it further when I had time.

As I lowered it, I noticed a tiny mark on one of the arms, three small wavy peaks.

I checked the other arms. The second had two circles, the first was plain, and the second had seven lines radiating out from it. I turned it to look at the third arm. The mark here showed wavy lines, but these were horizontal.

"Were these made during its creation or do they have some other meaning? I asked as I handed it back to Bryn.

"In all the time this has been in my family, no one has mentioned the marks or the shadow inside it. I wonder if the handle hid them. I would've sworn they weren't there prior to this." He wrapped it and placed it in his pack with the other things found in the hole.

"It's a speaking stick, and I imagine that when you use it, you look out at the people you're talking to, or inward at your own thoughts," I said. "It would've been easy to overlook them. They're very small."

"When I was little, I used to look at it when no one was around," said Qwinita. "I never saw them either. I never picked it up, but I was intrigued with the surface."

"It is time we returned to the others," interrupted Ubree. "Many things are happening and we need to be there."

17

Kirym Speaks

The area outside the north-western entrance of the amphitheatre was full of people, carts and animals. There was a holdup at the entrance as one cart tried to leave the amphitheatre, meeting two others attempting to enter.

Borasyn was again over by the northern wall surrounded by people, more of whom ranged along the wall studying his pictures. Nearby, Egrym, also with an audience, lounged on his back blowing smoke rings into the air.

Othyn and Arymda were at the big tree stump, *surrounded*, I thought, *by girls*.

A number of dwellings were in the process of being erected around the walls.

Iryndal was just west of the centre with a group of people around a table.

"I imagine that's where Papa will be," I said pointing towards it. "You all need to be introduced, to him, Wind Runner and the other leaders."

Many faces looked up as we circled, converging on the open area as we landed.

The low chatter we had heard from the air increased, the occasional comment loud above the others.

"Ohhh, another dragon!"

"It's green."

"Oh look. It's got a sore foot too. Poor thing."

"Isn't it pretty."

"It? Pretty?" grumbled Ubree. "What do they think I am?"

I patted his neck as I climbed down. "I'm sure they will soon realise you are grumpy and unapproachable. But in the meantime you'll have to try to fool them."

"Kirym!"

I spun around.

"It's so good to see you." Oak grabbed me, lifted me off the ground and kissed me.

Teema entered through the southern entrance, saw us, stiffened and frowned.

Oak turned as he put me down and saw Teema. He waved in his direction. "Teema," he called. "Good to see you. Now you can show me hunting in your style, as you promised."

I glanced at Teema as I regained my feet. He was smiling. Oak thrust out his hand to Teema, who shook it, then hugged me.

The noise around us lowered, and I looked up. Papa, and the guild leaders approached, along with most of those who'd been at the western end of the area.

"Papa, this is Bryn and Qwinita of the Southern Escarpment, and Ubree ..."

There were shouts from the back of the crowd. People stumbled aside or were pushed, staggering into others. Something black raced towards us, its head down, making short work of anything or anyone in its way. It skidded to a stop in front of me. Its head came up, giving it height not apparent while it barged its way through the crowd.

I looked into the eyes of a black squilute. It nuzzled against me and gently licked my nose with the tip of its tongue. I could hear its chest vibrating.

"Midnight? My goodness, you've grown."

"What's that?" asked Quinita.

"It's a squilute," I said, smiling. "Her name's Midnight. The people of Faltryn herd them. Isn't she lovely?"

"She's gorgeous. What a glorious fleece. How do you know it's a she?" said Quinita. "I've never seen anything like her before."

"Me neither," said Bryn. "In some ways she looks wrong. Her neck is too long and her legs are too short."

I laughed. "I only know because Oak told me, but the solid coloured ones are female, the mottled, male. Only a few are white, or black like Midnight. Most are brown." I pointed out a few that grazed in the middle of the amphitheatre.

"When they've grown, the Faltryners use them to pull their carts. But the fleece is lovely, and they are fun to have."

Bryn hunkered down and inspected Midnight's legs while Quinita gushed over her fleece, eyes and eyelashes.

"They're lovely and gentle, but they're mischievous. Bryn, you'll need to warn Dashlan and Larqeba that they don't like to be teased."

"I wonder if I could barter for enough fleece sometime so Ma could make me a cloak?" said Quinita.

"I'm sure you could. I'll introduce you to Starshine soon. I know she'll help you." I said. Midnight was again licking my cheek to get my attention."

"Don't let it lick you, Kirym. They're foul. Remember what happened at Faltryn," said Teema, trying to push Midnight away.

"They only retaliate if you annoy them, Teema. Midnight

would never do that to Kirym," said Wind Runner. "They have to be really bothered to do it at the best of times. It's a defence mechanism against annoying little boys."

A number of people laughed.

Wind Runner continued. "Midnight and Kirym belong to each other. This is how squilute greet those the love." She stepped out of the formal group and rubbed Midnight's forehead. "Veld, I imagine our formal welcome has been put in its place. Teema, how lovely to see you again." She stood on tiptoe, and pursed her lips. He bent and kissed her. Then she turned to Ubree. "I'm pleased to meet you, Ubree. My great great-grandmama told of our ancestors meeting dragons, and them helping one of our people who was in dire need. Many times there has been scepticism over the tale, but I'm delighted it's proven true in the time I lead my people."

Ubree stared at her, and hesitated for a moment. He nodded an acknowledgement, brought his head down to very gently rest his chin on her shoulder, and whispered something to her.

She smiled and nodded. "Thank you, Ubree, and yes, Moon was bossy and opinionated. I feel you may find out that I'm like her."

Ubree almost smiled. "I'm pleased to meet Moon's ancestor. She was but a child when I saw her, but even then, formidable."

Wind Runner turned to greet Bryn, who was surprisingly bashful.

Everyone crowded in and the noise rose as hugs and kisses were exchanged. Papa enveloped me in a big hug. "I've missed you, my little one. We all have. I've heard some of your adventures, but you'll have to tell me the rest later."

I hugged him back. "I will. I've missed you too. I've missed everyone."

"Iryndal explained how you thought we should set up here. I've changed a few minor details, but I don't think you've missed anything out. You've done well to get us all here. Loul is in the healing area waiting for you. I imagine she wishes to check you've been eating enough."

He introduced himself to Ubree and then to Bryn and Qwinita.

Although most of the organisation in setting up was done, the area looked chaotic. However Papa was brilliant at getting everyone to do what was needed without obstructing others.

As everyone dispersed, Wind Runner drew me to one side. "On advice from Iryndal, Veld suggested I not approach the Desert people until you had spoken to them. As yet, I haven't met them. I would love to welcome them to my family. Can you find time to talk to them? Sooner or later someone will tell them we are here. They may read much into it, if they think we've been avoiding them."

Paluniis had erected a large frame against the southern wall and laced the fyrsha skin to it. It was massive, and still very scary. A group of boys and young men stood around it. I imagined they were talking about their own hunting feats. Nearby, the huge head with the horns still attached sat on the ground. I wondered what they had planned to do with it. Iryndal had removed the flesh, and it really just needed a few moons in the open air to dry.

Garanniis and his people had started to erect a shelter nearby, helped by Armos and his sons Peet and Young Harby.

All greeted me as I approached, and I accepted Garanniis' invitation to join them as they rested from the heavy work.

Morkeen took Amethyst away from the fire when she saw me approach. She kept her back to us, although she stayed close enough to hear our conversation.

I was a little sad when she gave me no chance to greet either of them. Although I knew I had no claim on Amethyst, I had cared for her since soon after her birth. It was hard to suddenly have no contact at all. *Perhaps Morkeen will relax once she settles down*, I thought.

I came straight to the point once everyone was seated. "One of the families you've not yet met here, comes from the Fortress of Faltryn."

All of the men, including Garanniis, and many of the women jumped to their feet and grabbed knives, bows and other weapons.

"What the ..." Armos stood up, shocked and wary.

I tried to remain calm. While I expected a reaction, this was more extreme than anything I had ever dreamed of.

"Where are they?" demanded Paluniis. "We finally get a chance to claim retribution for the death of our families."

18

Kirym Speaks

I grabbed Garanniis' arm and held tight, hoping no one would leave without him.

I was surprised when he became still in my grip. "Garanniis, before another war begins, I have a question."

He nodded.

"When you became leader, how many people did you care for?"

"About a thousand, although—"

"And were you to blame when those people died?" I interrupted.

"How dare you!" Morkeen spun around, darted between us and pushed me roughly away. "They made the decision to leave us, and he wasn't there when most of the rest were killed. You've no right ..."

"And yet you wish to kill Wind Runner and her people. She wasn't born when your families clashed. None of those alive today were. Were any of you?"

I stood quietly waiting.

"It doesn't matter," said Morkeen. "They sent hunters in to kill our babies."

"And no one in your family has ever done something wrong, something that affected other people? Foheem died, and that was tragic. But you now want to kill all of *their* babies?"

Garanniis sighed and dropped his knife on the ground. "You make a good point, Kirym. It's a stupid feud that's gone on far too long. I never thought about it before. I've always imagined the same person ruling their land now as then. In my mind I created an immortal, multi-headed monster."

I took his hand. "You told me the older woman who led her people over the river to offer you food and shelter was distraught when she found Foheem. According to the journal she wrote, she was very upset about the death, and she worried about Foheem's people for the rest of her life."

"Distressed?" spat Morkeen. "After killing her, those seasons were spent claiming our land. They flooded the landscape with their imitation fortresses."

"She did have them built, cairns not towers, but did anyone ever open one of them?"

"Of course not. We wanted no part of their evil." Morkeen eyed me suspiciously.

"We didn't go near them, Kirym," said Tianni. "We suspected they were some sort of trap."

Garanniis frowned. "Initially they were avoided, and stories about them proliferated. We've long been trained to avoid them and the areas around them. We'd heard the stories of their attacks from birth, grew up instilled in the venom of those actions. I watched from a distance as they checked the towers, the cairns, and built more. I always thought I knew why they were built."

"Had you dismantled one, you'd have found food, clothing,

and an invitation to claim sanctuary in the fortress. Moon, who organised the original cairns, and later Wind Runner, her granddaughter, understood how hard it was living in your land." I took a deep breath. "When you all appeared on the riverbank, did they grab weapons and drive you away? Moon immediately offered food and clothing. There were no ties attached to that." Again I paused, allowing them an interval to think.

"It's easy for them to claim that now," said Wharliim. "There's no way of proving it one way or the other."

"If you really want proof, there is a way. I'll ask Iryndal or one of the other dragons to take you back to dismantle one or more of the cairns. In the meantime, why don't you meet Wind Runner? If you listen to the story from her, you may find you look at it differently."

"Why should we?" snapped Morkeen. "They've had a long time to make their story sound good. They can deny Foheem's death all they want. It won't bring her or any of the others back to life."

"They don't deny her death. They never have, and Moon took responsibility for it, although she personally had nothing to do with it. That was why she tried to find you, to explain what happened. It increased her desire to offer help. Remember though, it happened a long time ago. All of those people are dead. Another thing to think about, Garanniis. You told me that some of your people went to live in the fortress. Given a chance to return, they chose not to. If you meet Wind Runner you can find out what happened to them, meet their descendants."

After a long silence, Garanniis stood. "We'll meet Wind Runner and offer a truce. I'll guarantee her safety."

Morkeen scowled. "I won't."

"Yes you will, Morkeen," said Garanniis quietly. "This gathering is on land we don't own. We will all be peaceful.

I lead this family."

"Then lead it without me," she shouted. "I'll join Paluniis' family."

Paluniis put his arm around her shoulder. "Garanniis leads all of us. I asked him to. I will not go back on my word as soon as his first decision is made. Morkeen," he pulled her around to face him. "It's a good decision. There's been too much death. All Valythians are one family, but we need friends. A lot of sand has drifted away, even in our life time." He paused, and lifted her chin, looking into her eyes. "We all do things we shouldn't. We make amends where we can."

Tears ran down her face. She scowled, wrenched away from his grip, and stamped away.

"I'll talk to her," said Tiannii quietly.

"Well there's no time like the present," said Garanniis. "Would Wind Runner come here? Should we go to her or perhaps she'd like to meet at someone else's camp?"

"She would leave that up to you, Garanniis. Where ever you would feel most comfortable. You can also invite anyone else you wish," I said.

"And I'll get them," said Armos. "Would you like Veld perhaps?"

"If you would stay, Armos, I'd be honoured. Perhaps your sons also. Kirym, you too, if you'd like," said Garanniis.

Morkeen glanced over her shoulder and glared at me.

"I have other obligations, Garanniis, but thank you for the invitation. I'm sure Armos can introduce Wind Runner."

I glanced across the amphitheatre. "She's already on her way over. Unaccompanied. She's happy to trust you."

I took my leave.

19

Kirym Speaks

As I walked in the direction Papa had taken earlier, I got a good look at the layout of the dwellings. I noted where different people and groups were and checked to see what else I thought might be needed.

Everything looked chaotic, worse than it really was, because of the partly unpacked carts and thirty or so squilute wandering the area. One dwelling was finished, the healing area I assumed, because that was always given priority.

Papa and the other leaders clustered around a large table where a map of the amphitheatre was laid out. That was my destination.

He smiled as I approached.

"I see you have Wind Runner and Garanniis talking. I'm pleased. Had they remained antagonistic, it would've created problems."

I looked back to where they stood. Garanniis turned and gestured towards the fire. Wind Runner sat and accepted a tumbler from Tiannii.

"They're very much alike, aren't they," said Papa.

"They probably have ancestors in common. I believe there were border skirmishes a long time ago. Some of the prisoners refused to return to the desert when given the chance. They intermarried and every now and again, it's obvious."

"That may help. It'll be good if they can get over the hostilities of the past. They'll have to live close together if they stay here. If they fight, I can put them on opposite sides of the land, but really, it would mean they'd be a few days apart at best. I don't want any battles."

"Both leaders are sensible."

"But what about their people? I met Morkeen."

"She respects Garanniis. There should be no problems." I paused. "Papa, we should have guards up on the wall, and someone needs to round up the squilute."

He nodded. "I have some men fencing an area outside the wall for the animals, but yes, I will organise some boys to round up those in here. The hunters are checking the whole area, but do you think more are needed? Iryndal tells me they can take care of security."

"There's an army approaching," I said.

"Is Gynbere a threat?"

"There may be no problems, but what if there is? If there's any emergency at the moment, we're in no fit state to react properly. As generous as Iryndal's offer is, the dragons are special guests here. They have less chance to get to know us if they're busy looking after us."

He nodded, turned and issued a series of orders to Tarl and two others standing with him. Then back at the map, he pointed to the outer rim. "Here, here, here and here, I think." He indicated to the eastern and southern entrances, and the walls above them.

"Here too, Papa." I added areas on the western wall. "We

should have the whole of the rim guarded, and we need to check on the army to the east. At this stage do you know where they are?"

"Not exactly. Storm and Peet saw some of them just before the fog descended. Gynbere was travelling very slowly. Since then, Peet found them and estimated they would arrive today, if they manage to find us. He described a large group with well-armed guards."

"If they sped up, they could arrive here before the sun moves a hand width toward the horizon. As Peet and Sundas will affirm, Gynbere knows exactly where the amphitheatre is. He told his soldiers to come here, and he described it well. His guards will have spied out the land and know we're here. Talk to Churnyg, Ashistar and Baketer. They'll have some idea of how he thinks. However, have you thought of inviting Gynbere to join us?"

"Why?"

"They're coming anyway, and it may encourage them to feel a little less defensive."

He smiled. "Do you think they would harm any messenger?"

"I'm not sure, but there we could possibly request Iryndal's help."

"Well Kirym, you're thinking ahead, but in this case, I've beaten you to it. Storm and Sundas took the invitation to them before we even arrived here. I suspect the dragons helped us there, although I'm not sure how. The invitation was very carefully worded, and the peaceful nature of attendance was highlighted. Gynbere wouldn't see them, and the person they did see wasn't very receptive. I'm not sure they'll come."

"They will. Gynbere would still be inside The Rock if he didn't want something, or he would be moving in the opposite direction."

Papa nodded. "I'll talk to Churnyg and Baketer, but Ashistar is missing. I've not met him yet. There are murmurs about him, you know. Are you really sure of him?"

"Yes, I am. He's a loner, used to making his own decisions. It's not easy to change the habits of a lifetime. He'll turn up when he's ready." I paused. "Oh, one more thing. Mix up the family dwellings. They won't get to know each other if they each stay isolated."

He nodded and I turned to leave.

"Kirym." I turned back. Papa pointed to my hip. "May I see?"

Momentarily mystified, I suddenly realised he had seen the rock shard I had removed from Borasyn's foot. I handed it to him.

He inspected it from tip to hilt. "Mekroe described it very well. It looks vicious. I hope you never have to use it as a weapon."

Obviously no one had mentioned how the fyrsha died. Probably good.

"Papa, I haven't seen Mekrar or Arbreu. Where are they?"

"Ahhh, let me see. Mekrar will be helping Loul in the healing area. Wind Runner asked for Arbreu and Mek to help with the squilute." He frowned. "She said Mekroe was experienced in dealing with them. A number of people laughed, but no one will enlighten me. I'm sure if Mekroe is involved in something, there must be some mischief in there as well. It'll be a good story, will you tell me when everything is settled?"

I smiled. "Yes, I'll tell you when we get home."

Few people were in the healing area, one girl in tears with a broken wrist, two boys—one with a deep cut to his leg, the other there as support. One of the cooks had burned his arm badly and a young woman was in the later stages of labour. Mama was there with four healers.

"How lovely to have you back again," she said, hugging me. "I've missed you. You were away far too long. Your stories will fill many evenings around the hearth in winter."

"It's nice to be with family again, Mama."

She told me the news of the family and a little of meeting Wind Runner. "Teema told me some of your journey when he returned the extra remedies. I gather some were needed."

I nodded. "When we get home, we can add the notes to the memory box."

"I think we will have a lot to add, more than we ever have at one time."

"Mama, where's Mekrar?" I asked, as she helped me refill my remedy pack from the supplies the family carried on journeys. "Papa said she was helping you here."

"She is—was," she said. "She wanted to see you, but she's been rushing around managing people all over the place. You know what she's like."

I was disappointed. "I'd hoped to hear all of her news."

Mama seemed distracted.

"Oh well, I'm sure I'll find her soon. First I need something pretty to wrap around Borasyn's foot."

"The purple dragon? I offered to change his bandage, but he refused to let me touch it. He allowed Mekrar to retie the bandage, but only after she promised not to take it off, nor look at his wound."

I smiled. "He's very like Mekroe was when he hurt his wrist, Mama. He will let me change it, but I'll have to do it privately."

"Ohhhh, I see. Well, there is this," she said, holding up a long strip of green, sprigged with small yellow flowers.

"He's purple, Mama. Green will clash."

Mama couldn't decide whether to be annoyed or amused, but then she smiled. "Well what about this," she handed me two long pale pink strips. "I'd like you to change out of that dress as soon as you've sorted his wound. You've ripped so much from the hem of it, it's beyond use as anything other than bandages and patches. I brought two of your old work dresses with me, although I suspect they too may be getting a little short. Go and choose one of them when you're finished with the dragons. The green dragon is also wounded. Do you need special colours for him?"

I smiled. "Ubree will be happy with the plain bandages. He is older. More practical." I took the rolled linen, picked up my remedy kit and turned to leave.

"Oh, Kirym." Mama came close and stared at my tokens, frowning slightly. She ran her finger over the small white one and shook her head. "I don't understand this," she whispered. "Everything I thought I knew about tokens has changed." She shook her head and stepped back. "Oh well. I expect you'll figure it out and tell me at some stage. Later when everything is settled."

I hugged her and turned away.

"If it ever settles," she said quietly.

20

Kirym Speaks

Ubree had moved to the north-eastern part of the open area where there were fewer people. I worried he was isolating himself. As I skirted the stump on my way to talk to him and re-bandage his foot, I bumped into a distracted looking, fully armed Twig.

"Twig. How lovely to see you. Have you been out on patrol?"

He nodded. "Yes, Mam, and it's good to see you too. I was worried about you until Mekrar and Arbreu arrived a few days back with news, well we all were." He paused. "Mam. Oh dear, um, something's not quite right. Yes, patrol, and we found the other camp."

"Gynbere's?"

He nodded. "He has an army and they're setting up for the night. But they're only a few thousand steps east of here."

"Could they have mistaken the distance from there to here?" I asked.

"Oh I doubt it. Their guards have been within sight of the walls. They've seen our people coming and going, that's how I found them. I followed them. The guards don't watch their backs, and they don't actually guard their people, only a few who looked wealthy. Anyway when they got there, the guards talked to some man sitting on a seat up on a box thing. Now he was very well guarded. He was pleased with what they told him, said something to an officer and someone in a black robe and the soldiers cheered and then they set up a fancy shelter."

"Did you tell Papa?"

He nodded. "He thought they may want to make an entry early in the morning. The other leaders agreed with him."

"But you're still worried."

"Yes, Mam. The encampment is strange. It's like they are two different camps. The soldiers and their families are celebrating, but the others, men and women aren't. Actually, they're quite separate. They just sit there. They have no fire, no food, nothing."

"Are they guarded?"

"Not really. There's something else, Mam. Something I thought unusual, under the circumstances. They stayed. Ignored, and with no care, but ..."

"Were the soldiers eating?" I asked.

"Yes, Mam. But the big thing, there were no children. Well a few, but they were in the wealthy group and some with the soldiers. Thing is, I'd have expected a lot more. Dashlan said everyone left the rock thing they lived in, and there were a lot of children then. Out there I saw men, woman and old folks. Almost no children."

"If Gynbere has taken their children, that would keep them there, wouldn't it."

"He'd do that? To his own people?"

I nodded, trying to think of what I could do. I concentrated on Larqeba, trying to think of where he might be.

The children are to the east. There are six guards. There is no food, water, shelter or fire for the children. Few of them have cloaks, and many are very small.

I nodded acknowledgement to Iryndal while trying to decide what to do that could be done quickly. "Right, Twig. I want you to get together ten men like you."

"Like me, Mam?"

"Yes, your height, dark hair. No, wait. Eight like you, plus Bryn and Dashlan. They're blond, but with cloaks and hoods, you'll all look identical. And Ashistar if you can find him. Do you know who he is?"

He nodded.

"Good. Churnyg too. Ask Bryn to get my camouflage robe, he'll know what you mean, and dark cloaks for you and the men, green, black or blue. Um, also get some of the elf bolts and bows, a set for each of you. Bryn and Dashlan will know where they are too. Meet me just outside the west gate."

It didn't take me long to find Starshine. I told her what I needed, and before long I was opening a guild basket, and pulling out the costume I had last seen in our rooms in the Fortress of Faltryn. Starshine helped me put it on. This was different to the clothes those from Faltryn normally used. The cut was plain, but it was highly decorated. It flowed from my neck to my feet, with long sleeves. It was joined in the front with one hundred and seventy tiny jewels. I was pleased that not all of them had to be unfastened and refastened, and that Starshine was there to help me. Had I been left to my own devices, I would still have been struggling with them at midnight.

"It comes with a hat and a pocket," said Starshine, handing them to me.

Thanking her, I packed the items I wished to take with me, including the tokens, in the pocket and stuffed the hat in on top.

I wished I had asked Twig to bring my robe here. I had no great desire to walk across the compound dressed like this.

Just then from outside the dwelling, someone coughed loudly.

"Ahem, Mam. I know you asked me to meet you at the entrance, but somehow, ummm, well I forgot."

I silently thanked Iryndal for the forethought. Then after thanking Starshine for her help, I slipped into the robe and joined Twig.

"I couldn't find Ashistar," he said as we crossed to the entrance.

"Never mind, we'll have to do without him."

Twig had chosen a good assortment of men. Teema, Walf, Peet and Blacknight were there, along with others I recognised from Faltryn.

Teema was handing out identical dark green cloaks to everyone.

"Where did you get these?" I asked.

"Storm handed them to me." Bryn frowned. "He said you wanted them. Is that not right?"

"They're perfect," I said, again sending my thanks to Iryndal.

I glanced around at the men I had, and noticed Ashistar slip quietly into the group.

I smiled my welcome.

"Iryndal sent me," said Arymda, appearing so suddenly, most of the men jumped.

"Oh good," I said. "You'll get us there much faster."

"We have to ride that!" said Dashlan.

"Your sister did it easily," said Bryn. "Would you prefer to change places with her instead? I believe she's washing swaddling clothes."

Mumbling under his breath, Dashlan joined Teema and

me, and the others were easier to convince once he and Bryn were astride.

Not Churnyg though. "I'm not getting on that thing. Nothing will ever convince me to. We are not dragon riders, never were, never will be. My feet are firmly placed on the ground and that's where they will stay."

"Except when you swing from the trees," said Dashlan. "Come on, Churnyg, if I can do it, so can you."

"No!" Churnyg folded his arms across his chest.

Arymda rolled her eyes, leaned over and before he was aware of what was happening, grabbed him by his tunic and sat him spluttering and protesting just behind me.

Before he could move she was in the air. She snaked through the trees, landing in an overgrown dark clearing just south of a small rise.

As I dismounted, Arymda set Churnyg gently on the ground. He was incandescent with rage.

I brought my finger to my lips. Even here, I could hear the cry of small children, and the guttural snarl of the guards.

Arymda showed us the scene, although the view lacked the clarity given me when Iryndal passed on a scene. Arymda's was a good overview, but it gave no close details.

"Can Arymda make the guards forget what they're supposed to do, or stop them from seeing the children leave?" asked Teema.

"Dragons do that? Wow, handy," said Blacknight.

"No!" said Arymda emphatically. "I don't have that ability. Not all of us do when we're young."

I frowned. "We're quite capable of sorting this one out ourselves, Teema. Arymda is here to support us. Anyway, I want to have a closer look. Teema, Twig, Blacknight and Ashistar, you come with me. The rest of you, keep alert, out of sight, and wait until we return."

We got to the top of the small rise and peeped over.

The children were huddled together in a rough circle in the centre of an open area surrounded by thick undergrowth. There were a few women near the northwest corner close to where five guards lounged. One guard walked the perimeter.

"Might've known it," murmured Ashistar. "Grave-diggers."

"They're gonna kill them?" gasped Twig.

"Oh, no, no, no," said Ashistar hastily. "No, I was talking about the type of guard. Brainless! They're only good for digging holes. Ask them to dig a hole to plant a tree, and they dig as ordered, but they haven't the sense to stop when it becomes too deep. They'll keep going down until the sides cave in on top of them."

"Well that's a relief!" said Twig. "Can Arymda tell them to dig holes?"

"Nothing can be that simple. Which one's the leader, Ashistar?" I asked.

"The big one with the cloak. I know him vaguely. Falben. That's his name. Slaslow likes him. Belligerent and a stickler for doing what he's told, well if he remembers that is. Can't think for himself though."

"Would he accept an order from you to let us take the children?"

"Not without the right uniform, and those I have access to, won't pass. I'm sorry."

"Ach, it's the way of bureaucracy," said Twig, patting him on the shoulder.

"Twig, do you see the bush just down there?" I said, pointing to the southern-most path. "The one near to the children."

"Aye."

"Go down and talk to the boy beside it. It's Larqeba, Bryn's youngest. Tell him to stay put, and wait. Otherwise he may jeopardise the rescue. Then join us back at the clearing."

"It can't be Larqeba. He's too dark," said Teema. "Larqeba is as fair as Arbreu."

"I'm fairly sure. Last time I saw Larqeba, he had darkened his hair with mud to camouflage it. I suspect he has continued to do that. Anyway, he seems to have a group of children around him who are far more active than the others, but restrained. Even the younger children. The rest are very subdued. That points to it being Larqeba."

Twig disappeared into the undergrowth, and we walked down the hill.

"I could have gone," said Teema, as we wandered back to the waiting men. "He knows me."

"Yes, but with someone he doesn't know, he will be wary and listen, rather than react. That could save lives."

"Kirym," Teema grabbed my arm and slowed his walking, allowing Blacknight and Ashistar to move ahead. "Why isn't Iryndal here helping us? Or she could have sent Othyn or Ubree. Arymda is no use at all."

"Arymda got us here very quickly, and gave us a general idea of the area. Why would we want more?"

He seemed unconvinced.

"Teema, this is what I meant about relying on them too much. As eager as they are to help us, it's all too easy to expect them to do it all. If we intend to rely on others, why not send Garanniis to do this? Depending on the dragons is no different. If we didn't know Iryndal's talent, we would be in awe of what Arymda has done here."

While waiting for Twig to return, I drew a rough map on the ground to show the men the area.

"The women worry me," said Blacknight. "Are they with

the guards or are they prisoners?"

"They all have newlings, cubs," said Arymda, suddenly appearing behind us.

Dashlan jumped. "Cubs?"

"Babies? New-borns?" I asked.

Arymda nodded. "The newlings are all together on the ground between the women and the guards. The only time the women are allowed access to them is when they cry."

"The women won't escape unless they can rescue their babies first," said Bryn.

"Classic ploy," said Churnyg. "The threat is real. Falben is stupid enough to follow through."

A short time later, Twig returned. "Canny kid, you've got Bryn." He chuckled. "Mam, he said to tell you he'd almost given up on you coming to rescue him. Thought he'd have to do it all himself. Asked if you'd like to wander by and hear his plan." Hey," he said, holding up his hands as Teema bristled. "I'm just the messenger."

"He'll be ready for whatever happens, then. All right, let's get this done," I said.

"So what's your plan, Kirym?" asked Blacknight.

"Each of you take a bow and quiver of bolts. Bryn and Dashlan, I want you hidden in the trees near me, but on the ground about there." I pointed to a spot on the map. "If the need arises, step in behind me. Keep your hoods up. The rest of you, get yourselves a good position along the western and southern sides of the clearing. Half in trees to get good oversight, and the rest on the ground. Remain hidden. Be sure you can shoot accurately, but without being seen. I don't want anyone dead unless there's no other choice. Remember these bows are light and springy. The bolts are heavy tipped, but over a short distance, that should make no difference at all. Shoot only if it seems necessary, and initially put your bolts between the feet of whoever is threatening."

"That'll be Foben," said Ashistar.

I nodded.

"Why do it this way, Kirym? Wouldn't it have been easier to bring more men and overwhelm them?" asked Bryn.

"What would be the fun in that? Anyway, it would scare the children. They've seen enough of large men with weapons. If this ploy fails, we can always fall back on that, but I would prefer to have everyone come along with us more or less of their own free will, even the guards."

"But we're hooded," said Dashlan. "How is that not intimidating?"

"I'm working on their own deeply ingrained beliefs. Baketer believed this land belonged to elves. He thought I was one simply because I carried the bolts you now carry. He believed he couldn't kill an elf. So I'm hoping that'll give us an advantage."

Ashistar nodded. "Yes, the story was originally given to guards who were picked on. It stopped them from walking away when guarding the tree. Elves were said to live extremely long lives, and will come back for revenge if crossed. Stepping on their land was considered crossing them. We were shown pictures of their bolts, and a copy of it engraved into a door would keep the hardiest of guards from crossing the threshold."

"So why don't you believe in that?" asked Teema.

"I'm part Oak. We never believed it."

"And yet you're a guard."

"I have Ash heritage as well. I always saw things differently, the mixture of roots does give you a different point of view, I imagine. Anyway, I thought I could help, and I had to survive."

"Do you think the ploy will work?" asked Twig.

Ashistar nodded. "It may be the only thing that does, short of bringing in an army. Kirym, once you have the children, what then? What will happen to the guards?"

"We take them with us if possible. If not, we'll tie them up, and return for them with more men. If everyone keeps their hood up, we have every chance of keeping the subterfuge until it is too late for them to object."

"Even with a hood and cloak, they'll never accept me as an elf," said Ashistar.

"True, you'll need to stay out of sight. You can't be recognised at this point. I want you and Churnyg to watch from the trees, and if we get the children, follow us back to the amphitheatre. If something goes wrong, you'll need to go and warn Papa. However before then, Ashistar, can you walk with Bryn in case I need advice?"

He nodded.

21

Kirym Speaks

"That dress will stand out as soon as you appear, Kirym. Won't the leader send someone to check on where you've come from?" asked Twig.

I picked up the camouflage robe. "Not if I appear out of nowhere. I shall be as invisible as possible until the last moment."

"Don't forget those," said Arymda, pointing to the shinning items sitting on the ground.

I picked up the pocket containing the tokens, tied it into place, and shook out the hat. Not a hat as I had envisaged it. This was more a mask, made to show off my tokens. It was decidedly weird having something across the top half of my face. The crown sat just above it, seemingly made to match.

"Wow! Elven queen. That changes you," said Dashlan. He smiled. "Looks good. Must make me one."

Teema nodded. "It's regal. Impressive." He handed me my

bow and a quiver of bolts.

I hooked the quiver to my hip, but Dashlan and Bryn both shook their heads.

"It ruins the effect, Kirym," Bryn said. "I suspect you will need to leave them."

Dashlan took them. "You hold the bow and one bolt, I'll carry the quiver. If you need them, I'll be right there."

I thought for a brief moment. They were correct. It didn't feel right wearing them. "Very well. Now is everyone ready?"

There were various grunts and nods of agreement.

We skirted the hillock and I waited with Bryn, Dashlan and Ashistar, hidden in the trees until the men had time to get into their positions. All disappeared nicely, even I saw no sign of them.

I walked through the trees parallel to the path. A guard was again walking the perimeter. He looked tired.

"Is that the same guard as before?" I asked, once he was past us.

"Aye. The lowest of the low," murmured Ashistar. "I'd say he's probably done all of the perimeter checks since they arrived."

"That's not fair," said Dashlan. "Why don't they spread it around?"

"It's all a power play. The others have seniority or family influence. There isn't any real power here, so they create their own."

I waited until the guard was walking north along the eastern path.

"They're sloppy," said Bryn. "They're watching him walk instead of checking the rest of the perimeter. Still, makes it easier for us."

A thick tree hid me from the guards as I removed the robe and handed it to Ashistar, who tucked it into his belt.

He, Bryn and Dashlan lifted their bows.

I took another quick look around and stepped onto the path.

22

Teema Speaks

I sat high in a tree above the path. Just below me and to my right, one of the jewels on Kirym's robe sparkled as she removed her cloak. From the corner of my eye, I saw a pale hand, thumb up. So yes, probably Larqeba. He'd seen her too.

"I've come to claim the children for the Elven nation." Kirym's voice rang out clearly. She was already on the path.

The guards were totally confused. They had no idea what they'd heard, nor where it came from.

The perimeter guard saw her first. He shouted and pointed. There were a few moments of turmoil as the leader looked around, and then struggled to his feet.

"Below me, Ashistar shook his head. "Appallingly trained," he murmured. "They're looking at the guard. Not for what caused him to shout."

The leader, Foben, finally spotted Kirym, and strode towards her. The others, were still watching the perimeter guard as he jogged towards them. Once he had passed, they scrambled belatedly to their feet.

"Who are you?"

"I'll take the children with me now," Kirym said.

Foben whipped out his knife and threw it at her.

The ping, as a bolt hit the blade, echoed around the clearing. The blade flicked away and dug into the ground beside a young girl.

Moments later, eight more bolts, one being mine, seemed to erupt from the ground around the guard's feet.

I looked for the knife. It had disappeared.

Foben hesitated, then whipped out his sword.

He faltered as Bryn and Dashlan stepped from the trees, their bolts pointed at his chest.

The perimeter guard grabbed a bolt from the ground.

"Don't, Foben. They're elves. Look elf bolts. She's an elf queen or something."

"Ya fool. There ain't no such thing. Them's all made up stories ta scare the dwarflings."

"Slaslow said they were real. He said this was their land. That's why we were to keep everyone quiet, but now they're here. What do we do?"

They both retreated a little, conferring in loud whispers as the other guards joined them.

Kirym seemed to glow in the dim forest light. A miniscule gem amongst the massive trees.

"I claim the children. You're using my land and that is my price." said Kirym.

Foben's voice cut through my thoughts. "It's a trick, Jargeel. There's nowhere for elfs ta live here. There's nothing but trees and stuff. It's not real."

"The bolt's real," said Jargeel. "Anyway they live in the trees. Right inside them. "They'll imprison us all there if we don't do as they say."

A flurry among the women caught my eye. They were frantically collecting their babies and a few of the smaller children.

"Come along children," said Kirym. "It's time to go."

Movement began over near the bush where Larqeba was. A few dwarflings stood, and picked up some of the younger children. They encouraged others to their feet and suddenly everyone was standing. They surged forward and surrounded Kirym and the guards.

A child's voice was heard above the general noise. "Come on! We're gonna be elfs."

"Oi!" bellowed Foben. He grabbed a girl from the crowd of children, held her to his chest, his sword across her throat.

"PUT! HER! DOWN!" Kirym stepped towards him. Her tokens flashed. The white token appeared to grow. Its light settled over her and she suddenly appeared tall and imposing.

"You will not threaten my children. They are mine to take whether you wish it or not. You are a guest in my land, and you will behave as one, Foben."

Foben faltered.

"See, she knows who you are," hissed Jargeel. "Elves can own you if they know your name. They can make the tree's grow up around you. The branches'll grow through you. Is that what you want? It's a painful way to die." He grabbed Foben's sword hand and pulled it away from the girl.

Foben paused and the girl squirmed until she wriggled out of his grasp. She was pulled into the crowd of children.

"Gynbere will be here soon," he said.

Kirym, no longer tall and imposing, still looked mysterious and regal. She turned to stare directly at Foben. "Really? Do you think so? Why would Gynbere do that? Then he would have to feed and shelter the children. And he'll have lost his hold over their parents. You're stuck with them, I'm afraid.

If you keep the children here, you'll need to provide food and shelter, and quickly. The night will be cold. Or you could allow us to take them and we will care for them. You can come too of course."

The children swarmed around Kirym, and she turned to lead them away. The guards were drawn along with the crowd.

Foben grabbed another guard by the arm, and tried to slip to the back.

Blacknight and Crag were beside them so suddenly, Foben jumped. They were ushered forward, their weapons taken from them.

"Just for now," said Blacknight. "We wouldn't want you to have an accident with them."

As I swung down from the tree, I glanced over to where the bolts had stuck in the ground. They had disappeared. I wondered who had taken them.

Twig was waiting for me at the bottom of the tree, and we dodged through the trees to close in on the group.

"Whose bolt hit the knife?" I asked.

"It had to be Ashistar's. The angle was wrong for everyone else."

I was surprised. "Could it have been Bryn or Dashlan?"

"They were both on the ground."

"So was Ashistar."

"When the guard, Foben, reached for his knife, Ashistar moved fast. He ran up the trunk of the tree next to you. I only saw it because I happened to look at him when he moved. He stopped about half way up the trunk, and out on one of the branches. Had the bolt come from any other angle, the knife would have flicked into one of the children. It was a clever shot. Even standing there, I couldn't have done it. It was amazing. Then he disappeared." He glanced over at me. "You don't like him, do you?"

"I don't trust him. Someone's passing information on to Gynbere and it can only be him. Where was he when you were asking us to help? How come he joined us when he did?"

Twig looked troubled. "Well I'll watch him too, but I've not seen him step out of line. Kirym believes he's loyal."

"Kirym sees the best in everyone, but I think she's wrong this time. He seems to have been one of the most influential guards under Gynbere. I think he may very well be as powerful as Slaslow. He got to go anywhere he liked in The Rock. I caught him listening when Veld was discussing our plans with the other leaders. Who knows what information he's handed over?"

"Well when we did the perimeter check, he was in my sight all of the time. He did nothing out of the ordinary," said Twig.

"Maybe he knew you were watching, but there are a lot of ways you can pass things on. Especially if it's been arranged in advance. A hand signal, even a nod."

"Only if it's seen, Teema."

"I'll prove it eventually," I said.

"Well I'll watch too. If he is passing on information, he'll give himself away sooner or later. Did you see what happened to the knife?"

"No, but I suspect one of the children has it. I'll ask Larqeba to find it when I figure out which one he is. What about the other bolts? Did you see who got them?"

Twig smiled at me. "Yes. I retrieved four, one was given to Bryn, and a young lad handed the other three to Blacknight."

Our men now ranged along the sides of the group, ensuring everyone kept up. They were helped a little by the women, although they looked as scared of us as they did of the guards.

On Kirym's advice, we kept our hoods well forward and didn't explain who we were, nor where we were going.

"Best get everyone to safety," she said, "and show them we mean no harm. The stories that have gone around are better dispelled that way. They might not believe the telling, and it's easier not to have them slipping away because they fear false knowledge."

I picked up a small boy who was beginning to lag behind the others, and cut across a curve in the track to the centre of the group gathered around Kirym.

A little boy near me stumbled and I grabbed his shoulder to steady him, wishing I had enough arms to carry the lot.

"Will the pretty queen really give us food?" he asked.

Kirym turned, smiled at him and took his hand. "Of course I will. There's a wonderful meal waiting for you already. Venison was already being slowly turned and basted over the fire-pit when I left. Root vegetables were prepared ready to bake in the meat juices until they are soft inside, but crisp and crunchy on the outside.

"I tasted venison once," said one girl, brightly. "It was delicious."

"No you didn't. You're just saying that." The voice came from the far side of Kirym.

"Yes I did," the girl responded. "Just 'cause you haven't."

"Well soon you both will have," said Kirym. "The bakers were making bread too. Flat bread cooked on a heated stone, or soft bread baked in the oven. It'll be so light you'd think it'd fly away. Some will have spices and honey in it, or fruit and nuts. Other loaves will have boiled curd chopped into small pieces, and because it's warm, the curd will have melted and it'll dribble down your chin."

All around me there were ooh's and ah's of appreciation.

"They've made stews and soups too," continued Kirym. "Vegetable cooked with grains, and shanym with crispy greens around it. Shanym will be also be baked with trandor berries in the gravy. Lots of green leaves have been picked and steamed with onion and garlic."

"I'm looking forward to the kellich pie," said Dashlan. "They'll serve it with soft dumplings cooked in the gravy."

"And after that," continued Kirym, "there'll be fresh fruit heated with honey and cooked in pies, or covered with sweet sauce. Nuts and dried fruit will be roasted with spices, and they'll serve lots of dandelion cordial, fruit juice and fresh spring water."

The children had all listened quietly as she described the meal waiting for them. Even the guards drew closer.

"Huh," snorted Foben. "You'll never get enough of any of that to give even half of them a taste. Most of those things are made up. Just fables."

"Will you believe in them when you eat them?" Dashlan asked. "I can smell the kellich pie already."

"What's kelitpi, Keebe?" asked the boy I carried.

"Bobble tails," said an older lad who walked nearby. "I'll take him, sir," he said, holding out his arms.

I hesitated ever so slightly as I stared at him. He looked much the same as the other dwarflings, swarthy skin and brown hair. But I knew the piercing green eyes that looked out of the dark face. I had seen them almost every day since just before leaving The Land Between the Gorges. This had to be Larqeba, Arbreu's brother, but he looked so different.

He brought his finger to his lips, took the lad I held and disappeared into the crowd.

"It was, wasn't it," said Dashlan in my ear. "Larqeba? Where'd he go? Oh Pa will thrash him for running off again."

"Leave him." I grabbed Dashlan's arm and pulled him out of the crowd. "He may have a good reason to keep his identity a secret for now. He's helped to save a lot of lives today. He has a connection to Kirym, and he has knowledge we don't. I'm sure the time will come when he's ready to return. Just wait."

He nodded thoughtfully. "Should I tell Ma I've seen him?"

"Do that, and tell her he's safe."

23

Teema Speaks

The trees on either side of the path were now swathed with mist, unusual at this time of the day. I wondered if a storm was brewing. I tried to gauge the distance we had to go to the amphitheatre, but as we had travelled to the children at dragon speed, it was difficult to tell. I didn't recognise the land around me.

The children would have been miserable out overnight in rain and wind, although I doubted if there would be enough shelters at the amphitheatre to cope with the numbers now descending on it.

I wondered if we'd get the children back to the amphitheatre before they ran out of energy. They hadn't been fed today at least, and I wondered how much they'd been given over the last few days. I could see how clever Kirym was to talk about the coming feast. It kept the children up close to her and thinking of what was coming, rather than how far they would have to walk to get it.

In the trees to my left, I caught a glimpse of something moving in the shadows. Then it was gone.

I quickly looked over the crowd, accounted for the guards and the women. It had to be one of the children.

Ahead, I could see the top of a steep bank, and wondered if it was the amphitheatre. If it was, the children had been kept surprisingly close. I wondered why Gynbere would do that, unless he wanted them to be found and cared for so he wouldn't need to, while still having control of their parents. However I really didn't think he was that caring about his people.

I wandered towards the trees, checking through the undergrowth. The noise of the children disappeared in the mist, and the trees suddenly seemed closer and bigger. I felt momentarily disoriented, and reached out to steady myself against a nearby tree.

Many strange things had happened over the seasons, but this was the most unexplainable.

"What happened?" Not really a question, there was no one to answer, but spoken because I needed to hear my own voice. Despite my nervous quiver, I was convinced this was not a dream I'd soon waken from.

I knew I was awake and suddenly I was very scared of whatever had brought me here. A moment of dizziness might have taken me a step or two further into the trees than I thought. But to realise that the step I took placed me at the top of a tree was frightening.

The trees were close and a thick mist twined around them. It cocooned me, cutting off all vision other than the nearest trunks. The sky was invisible, as was the ground. I had no idea of direction.

I grabbed the branch above my head, and stared out into the mist, trying to get a glimpse of the wall of the amphitheatre. The mist was too thick for me to see much, although as the breeze wafted the tendrils around, I caught a glimpse of what might have been the edge of the trees or perhaps a clearing. I'd flown over this area twice recently, and I couldn't remember forest this thick anywhere near the amphitheatre.

I dropped to a lower branch, again and again, until there was only grass below me. The trunk was thick, and the branch I sat on was higher from the ground than I'd prefer. I wished I had Churnyg's climbing ability. I dropped my bow, quiver and knife onto the ground near the base of the tree, then grabbed the branch and lowered myself to arms-length. My feet were still a long way from the ground, but I had no choice. I let go, dropped and rolled.

Quickly back on my feet, I grabbed my knife and backed up to the tree, feeling more secure there than in the open. If there was anything close, I would have either attracted it, or scared it away. I flexed the shoulder I had rolled onto, it hurt, but not enough to stop me from using it if need be. It might be different in the morning once any bruising had time to settle.

Slowly the noises of the forest resumed, comforting sounds I recognized. Birds called, small creatures nosed through the undergrowth disturbing the leaf cover. An early owl, glided by and I wondered how I knew the bird was early. Solely because of the position of the sun when last I saw it, and I doubted even that now.

I took a handful of bolts, hooked the quiver onto my hip, picked up my bow, nocked a bolt into it and held it ready to tension if needed. My knife was back in its sheath, but available at a moment's notice.

Something big rushed past me in the mist, simply a dark shadow, although close enough for me to see the swirl of mist, and feel the movement of the air. I shrank back against the tree, hoping whatever it was had no interest in me.

However, it disappeared into the mist, intent on what it was doing.

Another noise caught my attention, *an animal in pain*, I thought. It reminded me of something I'd heard before, but didn't associate with trees. It didn't come readily to mind though, so I put the thought aside until later. Sound seemed to echo around me, I couldn't work out where any noises came from.

The trees here all looked similar, but as I moved, I noted differences in trunk size. A small amount of moss at the base of a number of trees indicated south, not a lot of help in telling me where I was, but all information was useful.

As I moved, the small sounds of nature disappeared. I stood still and took stock, waiting for them to begin again. It was difficult to move anywhere outside with the wildlife unaware of you. I knew of only two people who could do it. Kirym and Findlow, and Findlow was only partially successful.

The trees here were a little further apart, but the mist was still thick, and I could see little. The noise came again, and I, for a second time, sought the protection of a large tree trunk. I paused listening carefully. The sound came from my right, but even so, I didn't rush. Feeling I was already in deep trouble, I saw no reason to hurry into more. This place, this mist and the unknown were just too strange.

I jumped when a seed pod hit the ground beside me and exploded into pieces. My heart raced. I made myself stop and take deep calming breaths, before moving on.

Closer, the sounds were sharper. Something was whimpering in pain. More care needed, injured animals could be dangerous.

Suddenly the trees opened up. Whatever was making the sound was now very close.

I edged around a large tree. The noise I heard came from

something young. Young didn't mean harmless. It might possibly have an over-protective parent, I hoped I wasn't being similarly stalked by a larger version of what I was looking for. While the danger was real, I couldn't leave an animal in pain without checking on it.

I was about to glance around the tree when the bushes on the far side of the clearing rustled.

I tensioned my bow, aimed and waited.

24

Teema Speaks

The bushes parted and a dwarfling carrying an armful of twigs and dragging a large branch pushed his way through.

"See we'll soon get—" he stopped and stared open-mouthed at me.

I moved into the clearing, glancing behind me to see what was beside the tree.

A tiny girl sat hunched under a bush. Her clothing, more a shift than a dress with a thin strip of material tying it at her waist, was tatty. Her ankle and leg were blue and swollen.

"Leave us alone!" the boy yelled.

The sound of the smaller branches hitting the ground brought my attention back to him. He had a solid branch hefted over his shoulder, ready to use as a club.

"I can't help your sister if you hit me with that."

He faltered a little, but then grasped it tighter. "I'll help her. We don't need you."

"Unless you know how to set a broken leg, you'll leave her

crippled for life, or possibly you'll kill her." I gave him time to think about that. "I'll need to have a good look at it to see how bad it is."

"All right. You can look, but if it's not broken we're going, and you can't stop us."

I placed my bow and bolts on the ground beside me, taking the time to look carefully at the swollen ankle.

This little girl was tiny, about the same size as Triji, Siba's youngest, who had seen six seasons, but I felt that this girl was older. She had finer features than any other dwarfling I'd seen. She looked unkempt. Her hair was dirty and hadn't seen a teasel in a long time. Her face was grimy and streaked with drying tears, which didn't help her appearance. Bruises, old and new covered every part of her body I could see, including her face.

I bent over her leg. The skin was hot to touch, not that that told me much, but swelling wasn't a good sign. The black bruising hid much, and a bulge in the skin pointed to a break worse than any I'd ever seen. I knew instantly I was out of my depth. Her leg was so badly broken, it was beyond my ability to fix. I desperately wanted to get her back to the amphitheatre so Lantiah or Loul could tend it. "What's your name?"

"Don't tell him."

"What happened?"

"I was running. There was a hole in the ground. I didn't see it."

Her speech didn't sound childish. There was something in her eyes that spoke of knowledge.

Something heavy hit me between the shoulders. I heard something crack, the girl screamed and everything went black.

25

Kirym Speaks

Mama was waiting at the southern entrance of the amphitheatre, accompanied by a number of other women, all carrying platters of bread and fruit.

The children hesitated briefly and then surged forward to take a share. They were ushered over towards the cooking area where food was already being dished up for them.

"I didn't quite know what to expect," said Mama, "but definitely not this. Iryndal told us to dish a meal and expect many visitors. Mekroe thought it might be the army to the east."

She ushered the final few children towards the cooking area. Leaving only Wind Runner, who linked her arm through mine and guided me towards a dwelling.

We paused as two women walked slowly past us. I stopped when I recognised Jinda.

"Oh my, she looks—" I hesitated, searching for the right word.

"Absent?" suggested Wind Runner.

I nodded. "That's it precisely."

"She's been like it for a while now. Hopefully she'll find herself and return to us, but Danth took her with him, as much as we tried to stop him." She sighed. "She seems to have no awareness of anyone, not even herself. She's docile enough, but someone must be with her day and night. She doesn't sleep much, won't feed herself, or do anything else really. If left alone, she wanders away."

"That's horrid. How did she react when she met the family?"

"Nothing. Loul tried, but Jinda seemed to have gone far away. She wasn't even aware of young Tarjin, who's not as upset as I thought he'd be. Loul took him under her wing. She keeps his spirit up. Jinda is no bother, well she's nothing really. Certainly not here." She frowned.

"I haven't had a moment to ask about your trip here," I said. "Talk to me while I get changed. How was it? Were there any problems?"

She chuckled quietly. "It was a little rockier than I imagined."

I remembered how easily she climbed the steps and paths of Faltryn's Fortress and paused, remembering her age.

"Oh no," she laughed. "Nothing really bad. Sundas wanted to carry me or haul me on a frame as if I was ancient. When I refused to allow him, he hovered over me every time I moved, arms out as if I was an infant just learning to walk."

I laughed with her. "Oh dear. Poor Sundas."

"I must be getting old, though. It took me half a day to convince him I was quite capable. He finally conceded with a few conditions."

"You agreed to his demands?"

"Oh no, but I made sure I never slipped, never looked tired, and gave no sign of hesitation when the terrain got difficult. Actually I think it did me good. I feel better now than I have for many seasons"

"So all in all, the trip was smooth?"

She nodded. "Bokum, Sundas and Findlow did well. We didn't travel as fast as when you did it, of course. Still, even the time we took was so much less than the stories indicated. I'm still amazed at the different landscapes we travelled through. I was able to spend quite a long time at the stone circles, Bokum took me through the stream with the first group, after he and a few others had gone through to enlarge the rest areas."

"How did you manage the deepest water?" I asked.

"Ah well, I did that in a boat, and most of us did. It took a bit longer, but the alternative was being carried."

"Sundas?" I said, laughing.

"Hmmmm! You'd described the stones well, but I hadn't dreamed of the size of them. How could it possibly have been built by one man? I could have stayed for twice the time I did, and I'd still find new things. Mind you, we all wanted to get here. Bokum in particular was eager to get to his family. He had good reason. His family is beautiful."

"His throat?"

"Improved. I think the shouting he did trying to organise us was good for him. He took us through some amazing land. That forest was formidable. We'd never have made it through without your guidance. It was daunting, although not as frightening as seeing the crowd of people waiting for us as we walked out of the trees. I felt sure Veld would tell us you'd misunderstood him, and he didn't want us here. I quailed at having to tell him his daughter wasn't with us, but he didn't seem at all surprised. The tokens I imagine. I must admit, I didn't expect a new adventure before we got to your settlement. And there's so much more coming. The wide plain made by the leader of The Green Valley really exists. After we all meet here, we get to see your settlement. I'm looking forward to exploring this canyon too. Starshine told me you'd taken her to see it. Do you think you'll enter it again?"

"Of course. Our cave is there," I said. "There may be changes in it when we do, but not many. I imagine it's flooded many times over the seasons, although perhaps not often to the extent it did this time."

"You said the tribes would gather, and I have no idea how you knew that. I never imagined so many people in one place."

I smiled at the surprise in her voice. "How did you get on with Garanniis?"

"I must thank you for that," she said. "It's not perfect, but there's a chance we can be good friends as time passes. I'm horrified at how our intentions appeared to them over the seasons. They accepted our explanations, although I think that may have been because of your prior input. I hope with a bit of time, the rest of the differences can be put aside. Some of them are still a little hostile."

"Mmmm, Morkeen. She can be sharp. I hope her stance will soften soon."

Wind Runner stared at me, her eyebrows drawn together. "I'm sure we have ancestors in common. Any of their people we found, we welcomed and cared for. They were given the choice to return to the desert, and almost all refused."

"Can you identify them? Proving kinship could help."

"Our history is written so I'll have to check. Theirs is spoken and Garanniis remembers his family back for many generations. When we're settled, we'll get together and compare them. However, as we discussed what I did remember, Garanniis mentioned one of the people they lost, a young man, who they believed to have been captured. I believe he was talking of Moon's great great-grandpapa, a young man who'd been injured. If it's the same person, then Morkeen is related to me on her mama's side."

"How did she take that?"

"Not well, I'm afraid. I hoped it would bring us together, but ..." Her voice drifted off.

"Give it time," I said, taking her hand. "They value family ties, and they have respect instilled in them. With that, she must accept you, and really, everyone from the fortress."

"With Morkeen, well I'm not so sure. In the time I was there, she spent most of it snarling at everyone, except the baby. She only stopped when Paluniis pointed out how upset Amethyst was getting every time she yelled. She has so much anger. What, in Faltryn's name, made you hand Amethyst over to her?"

"Morkeen's her closest relative," I said. "Amethyst needs to be part of them. They all love her, Morkeen particularly. This gives Amethyst everything she needs."

"Except her mama."

"Who is dead!" I said.

"No she isn't!"

I looked up from the jewelled buttons I was struggling to undo.

"You!" said Wind Runner. She held up her hand to stop me interrupting, and began to assist me with the buttons

"Without you, Amethyst would be dead. Even had they found her, she would probably have died. Garanniis told me they had no one who could have given her the care needed for her early birth and aftercare. More though."

Again she stopped me from interrupting.

"Their law is similar to ours, from what I can gather. They probably came from the same base. If it's as I think it is, you have a better claim to Amethyst, and if nothing else, she needs you. Morkeen only sees the sister she lost. I gather from comments made by Jeresaya and Garanniis, Amethyst hasn't settled well since you handed her over. Garanniis is worried about her, and he may make a decision despite, or perhaps because of Morkeen. That lass is the only one against them joining us. She threatened to walk away from everyone if we even talk again. She holds them all to ransom. The only reason she hasn't left is because Paluniis said he wouldn't allow her to take Amethyst, and Garanniis backed him up."

I closed my eyes, trying to make sense of it. Finally I took a deep breath.

"A resolution?"

I nodded. "It takes time, and they have been together less than a day. They need to get to know each other. It'd be unfair to reverse my decision so quickly. Morkeen also needs to come to terms with her sister's death. If Garanniis decides to intervene, then I will think of another way of dealing with it. If I wade in now, we may lose Morkeen and that wouldn't be good."

"I'm not sure I agree. However it's your decision. So I'll leave it for now, but I'll watch carefully. If need be, I'll intervene." She paused. "Kirym, listen to me. Both Paluniis and Garanniis think Amethyst should be with you. There is something else going on there, and I don't know what. But I will not allow damage to you or Amethyst. What will you do now?"

I stared at her, thrown by what she was implying. "Oh, umm, I have dragons to deal with. Borasyn and Ubree both need my attention, and then I'm sure there are other things I need to do."

"Don't leave it too long, or the damage done may not be reversible."

I stared at her.

"To you and Morkeen, my dear. It's not good for you to lose your child this way. Whatever you think, there is more going on than meets the eye."

26

Teema Speaks

I struggled to my knees holding onto the nearest tree trunk, trying to clear my head. I gingerly felt the lump on the back of my head. There was blood on my fingers. Next I felt my shoulder. The pain at my touch was so bad, I almost passed out again. My stomach rebelled and I vomited. I slowly sat up and waited for my vision to clear. I washed my mouth out with water from my flask, spitting out the first mouthful and then swallowing the second. I felt better—a little better. My head still hurt. The branch lay on the ground beside me.

I twisted around and sat against the tree, taking care not to lean back to firmly. I closed my eyes and breathed deeply willing the pain in my head and shoulder away. Every movement, even breathing hurt it to the point I almost passed out again. My shoulder ached, and it was surprisingly hard to think straight.

The dwarflings were gone, my knife with them, although they had left my bow and quiver. I'd fallen on my pack, so it remained as well.

The bushes on the eastern side of the clearing showed signs of their passage. I had only blacked out for a few moments. I could hear the girl whimpering. They weren't far away.

I stooped, picked up the bow, tightened the quiver on my belt and followed them.

The ground was rough, although the trees were further apart here. They went slowly, I suspected the boy found his burden heavy. He blundered through undergrowth and over rough ground, even when there was a smoother route. I doubted he had ever been in this sort of forest before. Well of course not, he had never left The Rock before, so would have no knowledge of this type of terrain.

I caught up quickly, cornering them between a small rocky cliff and a deep stream.

"You'll not get across," I said as I came up behind them. "The flow's too strong, and it's far too deep unless you're really good at swimming."

"Leave us alone!" the boy yelled. "If you don't, I'll throw her in!" He belied the threat by clutching her closer.

"That'd be silly. Far better to let me share my meal with you, and then I can do something for her leg."

He glanced around. "You can get us some food?"

I sat down, opened my pack and took out a small woven basket full of dried fruit, nuts and oats. To that I added my flask.

"Push it over here."

"No. I'm sharing my meal. You'll show some manners and sit down with me. You can't eat while you're holding her. You'll keep hurting her."

He sat the girl carefully on the ground and took a handful of food, tipping some into her hand. He bit into a piece of dried apple. Her food had disappeared, and although she chewed, I didn't think there was much in her mouth.

"My camp is nearby. I've fresh bread there. Fruit too and meat. Lots of it. Why don't you come and ..."

"We're not going back."

"Fine, but you won't be going anywhere until I get her leg supported." I walked to the nearest tree and swung on a branch to break it. "I need to trim this. Can I have my knife back, please?"

He scowled, but handed it over. I stripped the smaller twigs off the branch and cut it in half. With little else to bind the support to her leg, I took a leaf from Kirym's repertoire and grabbed the bottom of my tunic, ready to cut some strips off it.

"Don't ruin good material." He grabbed the rag from her waist and handed it to me. "Use that."

The material was as worn as her dress, and had covered a long frayed rip.

I inspected her leg again, still unsure if it was a two breaks or three. "What's your name?"

"Don't tell him," he said as she took a breath to reply.

I carefully tied the splint on. "You said you don't want to go back. Back where?"

Silence.

"You escaped from somewhere or someone. Were you with the other children?"

"For a little while. Then I got taken away," said the girl.

"He'll take you back to them," the boy said, his mouth still full of food.

"They took the two of you?"

She shook her head. "Only me."

"Stop talking, Teliq. You'll ruin everything."

"Is that your name? Teliq?"

She stared at me solemnly.

The boy nodded and smirked. I wondered why.

"It's nice of you to look after your sister."

"She's not my sister." He grabbed her arm and hauled her roughly to her feet. "Come on. We're going."

"Stop! You're hurting her!"

In fairness, he looked mortified, and put his arm around her shoulder. Her grimace of pain softened as tears coursed silently down her cheeks.

"You may as well tell me what happened. I can't help you unless you do. Even if I let you leave here, where would you run to?"

"Away. We'll manage."

"It'll be dark soon, and it's gonna be a cold night. Winter will be here before you know it. You've no shelter, no food, no weapons, and even if you had them, there's little enough out there to keep you warm and fed. You won't survive without my help." I waited patiently, watching his indecision.

"Shormel," Teliq said. "His name's Shormel." She leaned back against the cliff, suddenly very pale.

Shormel. There was something to the ring of the name, but I couldn't put my finger on it.

"I want to help, Shormel. But I can't if you don't trust me. I could've walked away and left you. I didn't have to share my food. I could have let you throw Teliq into the stream. It'll be night soon, and you'll freeze out here. I'm concerned about Teliq. She needs more care than even I can give her. I'll keep you both safe, but you need to trust me."

He eyed me, obviously torn. "No. We're going." He pulled Teliq to her feet.

She gasped in pain, and tears streamed down her face.

Shormel looked resigned. "Oh all right. But-you-got-to-protect-her." He spoke with a rush, turned away and rubbed his eyes with a grimy fist. "You got to 'cause otherwise—" He sniffed and wiped his nose on his sleeve.

"Shormel! Shormel Willow?"

He looked alarmed.

"You're Larqeba's friend."

"So?"

"Larqeba's brother Arbreu is my token brother." I pointed to the token I wore.

He looked at me blankly. Obviously Larqeba hadn't explained the significance of the tokens.

I remembered a name I had heard earlier. "Keebe. That had to be Larqeba, and he would have talked of Kirym, if not of the rest of his family."

Shormel's eyes gave him away, although neither of them said anything.

"We'll keep you safe, but your families will be worried about you."

"She doesn't have a family, an' Slaslow will kill 'er if we go back."

"I said I'll protect you both, and I will. Slaslow won't get Teliq, I promise."

She eyed me silently.

Shormel sighed. "You'd better not call her that. It means stupid."

I was appalled. "What! Oh, I'm so sorry, little one. What is your name?"

"Doesn't have one. Never did." He was quite matter-of-fact about it. "Everyone in The Rock called her that." He paused. "Well almost everyone."

"Do you remember …?" She was already shaking her head. "Then we will find you one. Something really pretty, just like you."

She stared at me gravely.

Shormel snorted. "More like ugly," he said under his breath.

I thought back to when Kirym chose Amethyst's name and glanced around.

Nearby was a mishillian bush, the green berries just

beginning to form. The berries were pretty, although they didn't smell nice, but the flowers were wonderful and the choice for summer joinings.

"What about Mishillian?" I asked. "Would you like that? It's pretty."

She shook her head, and I resolved to wait and ask Kirym or Loul. It was something they did easier than I did.

With my quiver over my sore shoulder, I picked her up, and settled her on my hip. I was shocked at how tiny she was and frail. I could feel her bones beneath the thin ragged shift. It was far too big for her and she wore nothing beneath it, no petticoat. She had no shawl, no cloak and no boots.

I thought about the other people from The Rock. Only those around Gynbere had worn bright colours, but everyone had been warmly dressed and their clothes fitted well, although most of it had been dull browns and greys. There was a marked difference between them and this little one, and I was troubled by it. Still, I decided to let Kirym or Loul deal with her.

I wasn't sure where the amphitheatre was, but I knew if I could find fush grass, I could at least keep them warm overnight, and even without a flint, I would start a fire somehow.

I knew too, that I'd be missed and hopefully Kirym could somehow come and find me. Maybe one of the dragons would help.

"Let's get going. There's a lovely lady there who will make everything fine. Let's see if we can get to safety before night falls." I decided to walk east until the land became more open. If I could get a glimpse of The Rock, I'd know what direction to go in.

Shormel looked tired. I took his hand and thought about how Kirym had kept the children intrigued while she travelled with them. I decided to copy her.

"You know, when we get back, there will be a wonderful feast waiting for us. There will be venison on—"

"Don't promise her things that may not happen," interjected Shormel.

This was harder than I thought. How did Kirym do it so effortlessly? She made it sound enticing, an adventure, and she took the children along with her. I obviously didn't have the special something she had.

With no idea of where the sun was, I based my direction on where the moss grew on the trees. Despite that, I felt as if a particular tree trunk came into view far too often for my liking. I had not been this disoriented since I was a small boy out with Veld on my first hunting trips.

A small cliff barred our way. I lifted the girl as high as my shoulder would allow. She grabbed a small bush growing near the top, planted her good foot securely on my head, managed to climb over the edge. Using the same bush I hauled myself up, somewhat ungainly because of the damage done to my shoulder. I leaned down to help Shormel. He too grabbed the bush, but its roots had loosened, and as the ground around it began to come away, I made a frantic grab at his arm, and by sheer willpower, dragged him the final distance.

As I twisted to allow him room to roll onto the grass, I heard a resounding crack in the centre of my back, and at the same time, pain shot down my leg. I rolled into a ball, as the pain threatened to overtake me. Darkness at the edge of my vision told me how close I was to blacking out. I couldn't, I didn't want to chance the children running off again.

Something cool was pressed against my forehead. Panting, I tried to relax and contain the pain. More cool, now on my temple and down around my neck. Water dripped into my eyes, and when my senses returned, Shormel handed me my flask. I cautiously sat up, wary of any movement that may further damage my back.

"Sorry, I think I hit you too hard before."

"Not just that. It was an accumulation of things that happened today," I said. "Give me a few moments and we can get moving again."

I sat up, wary of any sudden movement. It took me far too long to get to my feet. Every movement sent pains shooting up my back and across my shoulder.

Turning to pick the girl up again, I felt nauseous. I hadn't eaten a proper meal since early morning.

Shormel leaned forward, clutching his stomach also. He too was feeling the lack of food. I figured his family had probably had fewer meals of late.

I hunkered down beside him. "Are you all right?"

"Just a bit sick. Maybe it was thinking about the food you talked about."

I put my arm around his shoulders. "Been a hard day, hasn't it."

He nodded, tears welling in his eyes.

I opened my flask and handed it to him.

When he had finished, I too drank. The girl had fallen asleep.

"Let's keep going. Climb on my back and I'll carry you."

He looked at me and shook his head. "I think I'd hurt your shoulder more. I'll walk."

He was right, I would never have managed it, my shoulder and neck hurt badly. It was hard enough picking up the little girl. I wasn't looking forward to sleeping on the hard ground tonight.

Shormel took my hand and we set off again.

A few steps on, we came to a stream, and followed it downstream. Although I would have normally gone upstream, the bank was overgrown and would be difficult to manage while carrying the girl. A short distance further the stream dwindled to nothing and the trees thinned. I glanced around, shocked but delighted to see the ridge that surrounded the amphitheatre. I knew I had travelled south and east, so being here made no sense. As I tried to think of the distance I'd walked and the time it had taken, I glanced back through the trees. The mist had lifted and I could see clearly to an open meadow about three hundred steps away.

We all have gifts, came Irundal's voice. *That's Arymda's. She can contrive to have you not see her, not be aware of her, even when she carries you.*

I was suitably chastened. "I'll personally thank her." I said.

"Thank who?" asked Shormel.

"A friend who suggested I look for you."

He stiffened. "Who? No one knew we had escaped except the guards." He struggled to take the girl off me, and waking her as he did so.

"Not them," I said, holding tight. "My friend, Arymda must have seen your tracks. The guards couldn't have done that, they don't know how to. Anyway, she was helping to get the other children away from the guards."

He nodded, frowning. "We're not staying though. Just get her leg seen to and ..."

"Perhaps a meal too," I suggested. "And a good night's sleep. Then think about what to do."

We approached the north-western entrance and I was relieved to see Loul standing there.

"Arymda said you needed me."

Everything inside the amphitheatre looked surprisingly calm when you added the addition of the extra children.

"The children are eating. They'll be sorted and cared for until dark. Then they should sleep."

"How did you know what I was thinking?" I asked.

She shrugged. "It's what I'd have asked, and I assumed you'd want to know. Bring these two straight to the healing area. There's food waiting for them there. We'll be able to look at that leg, the scratches and find this little one some clothes. Then they too can sleep. Tomorrow we can sort out everything else."

"We're not staying," said Shormel. "Fix her leg and we'll leave."

"Very well. We'll get both of you fit and healthy and sort out some supplies," said Loul calmly. "Let's work on those things first."

I was no longer worried. Loul was used to dealing with recalcitrant children. I didn't think Shormel had a chance.

I handed the girl to Loul to be cared for. I could tell by the look on her face when she inspected the leg that she was most concerned.

"Can you fix it?" I asked quietly, as she got padding out to ensure the splint didn't rub and do more damage.

"I can do nothing more than splint it for strength and pad it carefully until the swelling has reduced somewhat. She may yet lose her leg. I'll talk to the other healers. They will have their own ideas. She'll need a bath and some clean clothes first. Then a meal. Poor little thing, she's had little enough over the seasons, I suspect."

Loul handed the girl a platter of food. "You get off, Teema. Come back after you've had a meal."

Shormel had also been bathed and fed. Once he had eaten, his eyes shut, and Loul sent me off with instructions to rest and return later to check on the two children.

I grabbed a platter of food and wandered the length of the

clearing to find Kirym.

People, or more probably the dragons had been hard at work while I was away. The tree trunk had been moved over to lie parallel and close to the northern wall. That had opened up the centre of the area.

I was near the tree stump when I spotted Kirym talking to Ubree and looking at his wounds.

She had changed her dress, now wearing one of her old favourites, which although well-made, was rather shorter on her than when she had worn it last. She was a lot taller than when we left the settlement in the early spring to travel to Faltryn.

I felt a little annoyed that everyone demanded so much her. We'd scarcely been able to do more than say hello since we arrived back from finding the Valythians, and while searching for them, we had spent very little time together.

Suddenly I wanted some time by myself. Time to think. I quietly slipped out through the south entrance, ignoring a shout that may or may not have been my name.

27

Kirym Speaks

Ubree sat alone in the clear area between the stump and the eastern entrance. When I approached, he straightened his leg so I could tend to the wound. It hadn't healed as well as I had hoped, but it had progressed. I wished I had replaced the dressings much earlier today.

Ubree took the application of more skafarhn stoically, although he did flinch. His tail was easier to deal with, the wound there was healing nicely, and the other scratches were almost healed. I replaced the bandage, checked his wing, which showed no sign at all of the massive wound he had sustained so recently. With everything cared for, I sat beside him.

"Everyone wants to get to know you, Ubree, but they respect your desire for privacy when you give them the impression that's what you want. I really think you've had enough loneliness over the seasons."

"They won't like me."

"Why do you say that? I like you. Why shouldn't they?"

"Borasyn does his pictures, and Egrym blows wonderful smoke rings and anyway, they're just children. Arymda and Othyn are pretty, and Iryndal is so wise. I'm not. There's always one they don't like."

"Who said? The others are being themselves, getting stuck in to help with setting up and caring for the children while dwellings are prepared. Your brothers and sisters have their worries and fears too. They're special and different, but you are too. You're so brave. You've risked your life for many of these people and for the other dragons. They haven't done that."

"They would've if they'd thought of it."

"But they didn't. You did. Tonight we'll gather around a big fire, and everyone will eat and talk. Come along, listen and join in. But before then, see what you can do to assist." I paused. "Actually there is something you can do to help me with now. I want to change Borasyn's bandage. Can you distract the children so they don't see his foot?"

"He doesn't need a bandage. His foot is fine," Ubree said quietly.

"I know that. It's not a physical injury, but he thinks he needs it now, just to be accepted."

Ubree frowned. "He's a wonderful artist, and he knows things. His knowledge isn't normal, but he helps everyone see their memories. What difference does a stupid bandage make?"

"None. But he's scared that he isn't enough. It's a little bit of reassurance. We can do that for him, can't we?"

Ubree almost smiled as he stood. "Let's go and indulge the child then." He folded his wings across his chest again.

"Why do you hide the scar?"

"What if they ask about it?"

"Tell them."

"That I foolishly underestimated the fyrsha and almost died. They'll think I'm an idiot."

"That you were injured while learning how to defeat the fyrsha who were terrorising the people in the desert. Or you can just say it's private. Mind you, then they'll imagine momentous battles in which you came out victorious and they'll hail you as a hero."

Ubree looked mortified. "But I'm not. I was stupid."

"Then tell them the truth, and tell them about the brave man who helped heal you."

He nodded. "I liked Salcan. He was scared of me, but he stayed. He told me," he paused. "Well he told me things. I think we were friends. It was good."

Borasyn's foot was fully healed, but he winced when I touched it, and that worried me. I wondered if there was perhaps a fragment of the shard still deep inside, although his skin wasn't hot to my touch.

There isn't, came the thought from Iryndal. *You were right about his need for the bandage. If you can find a different way of allowing him to be rid of it, that would be better for everyone.*

"I'd like to leave the bandage off for a while, Borasyn" I said.

"Noooooo! It'll huuurt."

"It needs some fresh air. But," I said quickly as he was about to object, "you could carry the bandages, in case I need to put them on in a hurry. I was thinking I could tie them to your horns. They'd look like streamers."

"What are they?" he asked dubiously.

"Like long flags. You'd have a choice, this material or I could use a piece off my old dress." I pulled the blue remnants from my pocket.

He looked the two choices over. "The blue is nicer. Can I have the pretty pieces with the sparkly lines?"

I tied them to his outer horns.

He shook his head, whipped them to and fro, and smiled as they cracked in the wind.

Borasyn bounced back to where Ubree waited with the children.

I had to supress a smile.

As Borasyn had limped away from the wall for me to look at his foot, Ubree had moved in between us and the children, successfully containing them in a small area next to the wall. He sat in front of them, growling very quietly, his wings extended to limit their view.

The children sat, eyes wide, intimidated into silence.

Borasyn jumped over Ubree's tail. The children looked relieved, but remained quiet, eyeing Ubree tentatively.

Borasyn beamed. "This is my big brother, Ubree. He's very brave. Look, Ub, Kirym gave me some florgs."

As if released from a spell, the children crowded around him, laughing and chattering.

"Does your foot still hurt?" asked Varitza.

"Naha. Well, it does a bit, but I'm very brave too. If it hurts more, Kirym will bandage it up again. That's what the florgs are for."

Ubree joined me as I walked away. "Ub? Florgs?"

"Well at least they're on his horns and he's no longer limping," I said. "Let's go and see what the leaders are planning for tonight."

He stopped. "I'm not the oldest. I can't push Iryndal aside, that's her job."

"We're not doing that. I'm not the oldest either, but I'm interested in what they decide. It's good to know how they make the decisions. You will be leader after Iryndal."

"That's a long way away. Faltryn is still the oldest. We each have our position."

I stopped and looked at him. "Ubree, a position can be created, often by the person who wants it. I'm not saying you should oust Iryndal, but if you are interested, be there and learn. Your age or position doesn't matter. Othyn and Arymda are vastly different in age and size, but they are doing things together with some of the girls, and the girls range in age from just toddling to those with their own children. Borasyn and Egrym both got stuck in to amuse others. They weren't asked to do it, but it really helps the families who are trying to get so much done, especially with all the extra children here. If you give the impression you want to be alone, people will accept and respect that. Join in and they'll welcome you. Now come on, let's see what's happening up there."

Mekrar and Arbreu came out from behind a large cart that was travelling slowly across to the south entrance. I called out to them.

They were holding hands, but as soon as they heard my voice, they jumped apart.

Mekrar was bright red. She looked as if I'd caught her doing something wrong.

Arbreu looked embarrassed.

When they were about ten paces from me, both of their tokens suddenly connected to my green token.

I registered the shock on their faces, mirrored I was sure, on mine. Everything went grey. I heard someone scream. From a distance, someone called Teema's name. Then everything went black.

28

Teema Speaks

I followed the outer wall of the amphitheatre east and then north. There was little close growth south, but trees a near the eastern wall would have given a hunter good cover to wait for prey. However there seemed little prey about. Probably too much recent coming and going in the area had scared them away.

I was impressed with the silence. The ridge that loomed to my left cut out all noise from the amphitheatre. If I didn't know about it, I could easily walk past without being aware it was full of people.

I came to a place where the trees grew closer to the ridge. Broken branches were scattered across the ground, partially covered with dried leaves. Although it was now late autumn, this tree still held its leaves and they were still green. That so many had fallen was an anomaly. Something big and violent had happened here recently. I waited for a short time to see if there was any hint of what had caused this, or a suggestion that one or more of the perpetrators were still there. It all seemed peaceful though, and when something glinted in a shaft of sunshine and I went to investigate.

A small shield shaped disc, partially hidden by dried leaves, gleamed in the sunlight.

It was firm, flexible and warm to my touch. It glowed, the colour ranging from soft apricot in the centre to deep bronze at the curved edges. The top straight edge was different, creamier in colour and slightly jagged. It didn't have the same sheen as the rest of it.

I was surprised at the size of it, almost the length of my thumb, and slightly less for width. It was thick, supple and yet my thumbnail made no mark on it.

I spied another and another and soon had fifteen of them. They were strange and didn't fit into the scene. They hadn't fallen off any tree, and seemed too widely spread to be the shedding of a bird or animal. Anyway this wasn't off any animal I knew, but thought Kirym might like them. I slipped them into the bottom of my pocket, and continued to quarter the area, looking for anything else out of place.

I kicked at a mound of leaves near a pile of broken branches and something else caught my eye. A larger disc with a similar glow, but this was a different colour, green, and now I remembered two dragons, Ubree and Egrym, showing off for us until Othyn barrelled into them and knocked them over the edge of the ridge. These were their scales. I continued to search, but there seemed to be no more.

I was calmer when I continued on my way. I could just imagine Kirym telling me off and giving me something steeped in hot water to lighten my spirit.

TEEMA!

I looked around, but I knew no one was there, and that probably no one else heard the call. Then I was running—as fast as I could.

Kirym's token changed. Suddenly! So did Arbreu's. It was weird. They both faded, and seemed to almost disappear. This was totally unlike what happened to Kirym's token when she was taken by Salcan. This time they had both changed, but there were other things there—something huge. It was intruding on me—I felt it was trying to take me as well. It was massive, overwhelming—multi-headed, a shape-changer.

Panic rose, my chest already ached from running, and my legs felt heavy. Everything seemed to be moving past me in slow motion. I hit the ground, jarring my sore shoulder and back as I landed. Then I was on my feet again and pushing myself to cover the distance to the north east entrance.

Already my heart was pounding. I cursed myself for leaving the amphitheatre, for going so far from the entrances, so far from Kirym. The ridge that encircled the amphitheatre was too steep for me to climb—a perfect defence, but I wished it wasn't.

The scale I held was warm, getting hotter. I clung to it for some reason, as if holding on to hope. Finally the entrance was in sight. I powered on and raced through it.

Everyone was converging on a group near the centre of the open area. Ubree was there, his head low over something on the ground.

I drew a sharp breath.

Ubree was mauling Kirym. Her body looked like a ragdoll, as he pushed it round. He was over her face, and I had memories of a vulture eating a dying animal without waiting for it to breathe its last. It had started with the eyes.

I felt physically sick at the thought.

Few people were close to them, but those there were doing nothing, just standing and letting it happen.

I was enraged. I pushed myself harder to get to Kirym, wondering how I could get Ubree off her. I knew I would have no impact if I hit him somewhere solid, so I aimed for his snout, barrelling into it with my shoulder.

His head flicked away, and I braced myself, expecting him to return to attack me also.

To my relief, he moved off and all I saw was Kirym.

She lay crumpled on the ground, her face white, dark circles around her eyes. Her face showed a darkening bruise and although her token's still glowed, they were different.

I didn't have time to think about it. I leaned over her and clicked my token to hers.

I expected the familiar drain of energy, but this was bigger than anything I had ever felt before. Everything began to go black and I struggled to push the void away. I clicked her token again, and then I knew nothing.

A cold damp cloth was draped across my forehead—more than damp. Water pooled in my eye sockets and dribbled down the side of my face and past my ears. Someone mopped it up.

"He's coming round."

That's Findlow, I thought. *Why isn't he helping Kirym?* Everything went black again.

"Come on, Teema. Wake up." Someone was patting my cheek.

I opened my eyes.

Veld hovered over me, looking concerned.

Findlow helped me to sit, and the cloth fell from my forehead onto my lap. It was still too wet, and soaked into the leg of my trousers from my knee to my groin.

"Drink this." Loul knelt in front of me, holding a water flask.

"How's ..." I was too scared to finish the sentence. I

couldn't feel her tokens.

"She's fine. Drink," said Loul.

I took a mouthful, coughed and spluttered, spraying my trouser leg with fluid. Who carried skarfarhn in a water flask?

My head ached and everything seemed blurry. Then reality hit me like a boulder. "What happened? What did Ubree do to Kirym?"

"More!" Loul insisted, and this time, the smaller mouthful went down, followed by another. I felt very tired.

"What did he do?" I asked. My voice sounded harsh, angry.

"Kirym says he saved her life until you could get here," said Loul gently.

"You'd gone, Teema," said Arbreu, "and no one knew where you were. I don't know what Ubree did, but without him, I think she'd be dead."

I stared at him. He was deathly pale, but what was most arresting was his token. It had changed. Ordinarily it was green with a small white inclusion, his connection to Amethyst. Now though, it also had a gold spot beside the white.

I wondered what it meant. Could his connection to Kirym be growing?

Mekrar appeared beside him. Her gold token now had a green inclusion.

I grabbed Arbeu's face and forced him to look at me. "Did you two try to sort this because I wasn't here?"

"No! What gives you that idea? Anyway I didn't get the chance. Ubree was there, and he handled it."

"Handled what? He was mauling her!"

"No! That's not what she says." Arbreu explained how Kirym's token had connected to his and Mekrar's.

I felt as if someone had punched me in the belly. It didn't

make sense to me. My tokens felt different. I recognised the difference in the green token now, a small bit of someone else, and that had to be Mekrar. I just didn't know why she was there. And I knew there was something else in my blue token. I couldn't explain it.

Then Kirym was on her knees in front of me. Her face had a massive bruise down one side, both eyes were black and she was very pale, but she was otherwise fine. Her green token also had a gold inclusion, but her blue token was different.

Deep in the centre was something else. It was formless, not really obvious, but when I stared at it, it seemed to grow, and although it never took over, it seemed to be everywhere I looked. It changed the colour, but whenever I tried to focus on it, it seemed to be as it always was, except it wasn't. It didn't make sense. It seemed to be more green than blue, vast and to my mind, threatening. I didn't know what to think.

"Thank you," she said quietly. "Are you all right?" She helped me to my feet, swayed and grabbed my shoulder for support.

Pain shot through my back, and I gasped.

"What's wrong?"

"Nothing. I'm fine. I just feel a bit light-headed."

"All right, it's all over" called Veld. "Back to what you were doing." His voice lowered as people turned away. "Teema, I want to talk to you, Mekrar, and Arbreu. You too, Kirym, at our dwelling. Now!"

"Where's Ubree?" asked Kirym.

I looked around. It took me a while to find him. He had crept into the branches of the fallen oak. Despite the tree now having no leaves, he blended in, well hidden. Kirym's squilute, Moonlight was with him, standing guard by his stance.

"Leave him until later, Kirym. I need to know what happened," said Veld. "Then we can make decisions about the dragons and our safety."

"Ubree has just saved my life and I will thank him, even if no one else will. It's nothing to do with safety. He protected me." Kirym didn't actually lose her temper, her words were forceful and to the point.

"You need to rest," insisted Veld.

Kirym stood in front of him, a look on her face I had only seen a few times before. "A few moments will make no difference at all, Papa."

Veld took a deep breath, he was angry. "I ..."

"Stop!"

Everyone did, and I realised who Kirym inherited her assertiveness from.

"Veld, you will thank Ubree for Kirym, and invite him to our porch to see her. Teema, if you feel up to it, could you ask the other dragons to join us also. Arbreu, we will need to see Bryn and Jeresaya sometime very soon. Kirym, you will come with me to change that appallingly short dress and allow me to see to your bruises." She took Kirym's arm, and marched her away, leaving the rest of us standing with our mouths open.

"So that's where Kirym gets it," said Arbreu.

Veld nodded. "You don't see it often. I see it so rarely, I forget. I'd prefer to face one of those fyrsha, than Loul when she's annoyed."

"She has the ability to make you feel like a naughty child," laughed Findlow. "Come on Teema. Let's go and talk to Iryndal. Veld, you have a job to do too."

I glanced after Kirym as we walked away. Sundas was with her.

Findlow grinned. "I imagine Sundas thinks he has someone new to fuss over and nurse. He won't get her as easy as he got his other victims." Seeing my mystified look, he continued. "He cared for every waif and stray with a bruise or bump on the way from the fortress. As you can imagine with that number of people, there were no shortage of patrons. Willing or otherwise. He tried to carry Wind Runner when she almost slipped on some loose stones. They had a right argument." He laughed quietly. "It held us up for half a day. He is formidable though, and he has a special spot for Kirym, so I see another battle coming."

"He might win, you know. Could Kirym stand up to a united front of Loul and Sundas?"

Findlow chuckled. "She's about the only person I know who could. It won't be easy though. We live in interesting times."

Despite Loul's instruction, I found myself with a large crowd of other people assembled near the stump in the centre of the amphitheatre. Those who weren't there already, were on their way. Only the guards on the surrounding ridge were absent, and most of those were watching what was happening.

"Why are we here and not at Veld's hearth?" Findlow asked.

I nodded over at the large blue dragon. "I imagine this is Iryndal's doing."

"But we were supposed to tell it to go to Veld's."

"Her! Not it, Findlow, and she obviously had different ideas."

The various family heads and the guild leaders congregated around Veld, who looked a little harassed. He tried a number of times to send everyone away, but no one actually left.

When Loul and Kirym finally appeared, I was shocked.

Kirym was still pale, but the bruise on her face was darker and more obvious than it had appeared to be earlier. The dress she wore was an old one of Mekrar's, too big for her. She looked fragile and lost. However Sundas wasn't in attendance, and I wondered what had happened inside the dwelling.

I felt a weight against my leg and glanced down. The girl I had rescued not so long ago looked up at me, her eyes big and a little scared. I felt guilty. I had not even thought of her or Shormel since leaving them with Loul.

I made myself smile, and hunkered down to look at the changes in her.

"Don't you look pretty," I said. She was clean and smelled sweet, her hair, no longer tangled in knots, was a lot longer than I had realised. She wore a fresh dress, long sleeved and warm, with a small shawl around her shoulders. The dress was one Sarel had worn many seasons ago, although I had the feeling this girl was older than her. The shawl had belonged to Kirym.

She smiled, the first real smile I'd seen from her. "Look," she said, holding out a small pocket, another of Kirym's. "It's got some nuts in it and Loul gave me some fruit. I had a big wash with warm water and it smelled pretty. Loul got me a sleeping robe and a cloak for later when it's cold. She said I could have a meal soon too."

She looked so excited I had a pang of embarrassment that I had been so put out because I didn't have Kirym's full attention all of the time. This little one was excited because she had been given a bath, some old clothes and a few nibbles.

"Tell you what," I said. "We'll eat that meal together. Then you can tell me about the things you like."

She put her arms around my neck and hugged me. I carefully picked her up. She also wore a warm petticoat under the dress and I was sure she had a shift under that. Her leg was thickly bandaged, and I wondered how she had managed to walk here from Loul's dwelling. It was a long way. Why didn't Loul given her a crutch, I wondered. I'd seen other children using them.

I looked up and saw Shormel watching. He smiled, nodded and disappeared into a group of dwarflings standing nearby.

29

Teema Speaks

Loul approached with Kirym and saw the line of people waiting for news. She did not look pleased. "Meeting here may be easier for everyone else, but Kirym can't rest here."

Findlow stood in front of her and held her shoulders. "They need to know, Loul. They love Kirym too, and this affects everyone, it seems."

"Everyone should be here, Mama," said Kirym. "They either saw what happened or will have heard about it. The story will grow out of all recognition unless it's all explained."

The dragons stood around the stump, Ubree almost hiding behind Iryndal.

Kirym walked up to him, laid her face against his, and closed her eyes. I had no doubt they were talking.

I watched, as did everyone there. Slowly, Kirym's bruise faded. It appeared briefly on Ubree's face and neck, and then disappeared.

Kirym smiled, kissed his nose and together they turned

and walked slowly around the large stump.

Oak joined me as the last few stragglers arrived. "It's amazing how she deals with those dragons. She's so small and fragile, and they're so big."

"Given a battle of wills between Kirym and any one of the dragons, I'd back Kirym every time. She does have a way with them. Any animal really. Where were you when all of this happened?" I asked.

"I was putting the last of the squilute into the pen when Midnight bolted. I chased her. I came around the tree trunk in time to see you charge into the dragon. I had my sword out then. I thought he'd turn and attack you, but he just slunk away. I've never seen a creature look so devastated. I was stunned."

"I didn't see his face. All I saw was Kirym. I thought Ubree was mauling her. She said he wasn't. Veld wants to find out what to do for the best."

Oak looked around. "How did everyone know to gather here?"

I laughed shortly. "Dragon organisation? They think it, and it happens."

He stared at me incredulously.

"Remember the fog a few days back?"

He nodded.

"Kirym tells me Iryndal made it, and organised it to stay while we were away. It kept everyone hunkered down until we were ready to bring you all here."

"Why the hold up? Where did you go?"

"To find the Desert people."

Oak nodded. "So that's how it happened. I was with Wind Runner when she was told they were here. She wanted to go over straight away. Iryndal and Veld said not to, that Kirym had to arrange it. Storm just told me that Kirym organised it as soon as she returned. It all went off fine. Wind Runner has invited the Desert people to join our family if they wish to. Even if they don't, she has guaranteed them our protection forever. They'll sit with us tonight when we eat."

"Wow, having listened to some of them, I never thought I'd see that happen. Mind you, both Kirym and Wind Runner are formidable when they set their minds to getting something done. With two of them working together, Garanniis wouldn't have had a chance."

Sundas jogged past us and caught up with Kirym. He handed her a flask and a small platter.

She accepted the flask, but refused the harkii. "Perhaps Teema could use it," she said.

Sundas' eyes lit up.

I accepted the platter from him—it took a brave man to refuse Sundas anything much— and I always wondered how Kirym managed it so often.

The noise around me rose. Everyone chatted excitedly, describing what they had seen, or asking for details of what they missed. There seemed to be a lot of underlying hostility against Ubree.

I knew Ubree could hear the murmurs.

He looked unhappy. The other dragons closed in around him. Despite that Ubree still appeared to be isolated.

"You know, that dragon is an enigma," I said. "I don't know what to make of him. I've talked to all of the others, they're fine. I can't even approach him. I doubt anyone has, other than Kirym."

"She likes him."

"I think she sometimes overestimates her ability to read people properly."

The chatter diminished quickly when Veld stood up. "I need to know what happened. Ubree, what did you do to Kirym?"

If a dragon could shrug, Ubree shrugged. He shuffled

backwards, shook his head, but didn't answer.

"That, Papa, is not the question to start with," said Kirym. Her voice was clipped and icy.

I wondered if Veld would realise how angry she was.

"Then where would you start?" he asked, in equally icy tones.

"I'd like to know why Mekrar and Arbreu are not allowed to be joined."

Everyone looked surprised, Mekrar and Arbreu looked shocked.

"That's family business and will be sorted in private," said Veld. "I'm disappointed in Mekrar. She promised me she wouldn't tell you."

"She didn't. You just confirmed what I thought. It's relevant to what happened, and I'd like the answer."

It was the first time I had ever seen Veld look uncomfortable. "It's simple. They're too young."

"Mekrar is less than a season younger than Mama was when you joined with her, and Arbreu is three seasons older than you were."

"Loul needed my support when she was chosen to be headwoman."

"Arbreu is an eldest son, Papa, or do you think someone else is destined to be headman of his family."

"We don't have the token cave."

"I don't think we need it. Look at their tokens. That is what we were being told."

Veld looked embarrassed and angry.

"You said once that the tokens never hurt you, Kirym," interrupted Wind Runner. "It seems this time they did."

"They didn't, Wind Runner. This request should've been shared with the family and the large tokens, as it normally is. It was put off. I think it would have been easier had it been discussed, and the tokens and dragons involved in the decision. For some reason, their decision to join is important. Anyway, she is days away from not needing permission. Arbreu has been making his own decisions for many seasons."

"Age is not the only decider, and I'd like more time to think about it, Kirym. The biggest problem I have at the moment is that you were hurt by Ubree. Your face is—um was badly bruised. I thought you were dead and I'm not happy with you continuing to have such close contact with him," said Veld.

"Um, Veld," I interrupted. "I really think the bruising might've been my fault." My face felt hot, I was sure it was bright red. "When I got to Kirym, I wasn't sure what was happening. I pushed Ubree's head away. He wasn't expecting it and I think his jaw banged Kirym's face. That's probably when the worst of the bruise happened."

"I'm not sure how the bruise happened, Veld," said Ubree. "It may have been then, or earlier. I don't know what I did. Her life force was going. I tried to hold her, bring her back."

"Nevertheless, there are things happening here that I don't understand. We need to be very careful, Kirym. There are dangers here, and until I understand it, I don't want any token connection—"

His eyes widened! "Don't."

Kirym turned to Mekrar and touched tokens.

Veld's shout of warning came too late. However there was no adverse reaction, and nor was there one when her token connected with Arbreu's.

"There is no danger for her, Veld," said Iryndal.

"There is something else you should know, Veld," I said. "Kirym's tokens have changed, well the green and blue. The green is obviously influenced by Arbreu and Mekrar, but I don't know what has affected the blue. My connection to

Kirym is now different. It's as if someone or something else is there. Something big."

"Something has aligned with us, Papa, and I suspect it's the dragons. The connection isn't malevolent."

Loul was beside Kirym in three quick strides. She stared at the tokens, touched them carefully, and then clicked hers to them. Her connection with Kirym was no different.

She stared at mine and shook her head. "I just don't know," she murmured.

"Mama, I'm fine. Right now there are three dragons who also need to be linked to the tokens."

Veld stared up at Egrym, Othyn and Ubree. "No! I forbid it. This could hurt you. This thing that's now aligned to you, we don't know what it will do."

"Papa, it can't hurt me any more than you can. Three dragons are already connected to us. Othyn, Ubree and Egrym are entitled to also."

Veld frowned, shook his head, and looked to Loul. "This is moving too fast, Kirym. Can it not wait?"

"Look what happened when we demanded Mekrar and Arbreu wait," said Loul. "Perhaps we're being overly cautious."

Veld sighed and shook his head.

"It's possibly not a decision you can make, Veld," Oak said.

"Papa, I wasn't hurt when the tokens connected to Borasyn, Arymda and Iryndal. It's not about my connection with them. We all connect with them, including the other dragons."

Veld shook his head. "Can we wait until we get back to the cave?"

"Kirym pointed out that we've never waited before," said Loul. "If our excuse was the inaccessibility to the cave, well we've just been shown it isn't necessary."

"The time seems right, Papa. If we wait, it might not be."

Veld was pale, but he nodded. "You know more about the tokens than we do, Kirym, but it seems there is even more about them that's unknown, than known."

Loul frowned as she considered the implications of all she had learned. "Are you sure?" she asked, and when Kirym nodded, "All right. What do you need us to do?"

"Each person does what they feel is right. They can leave or stay, join in or be a spectator."

"And you're sure we don't need the cave?" asked Loul.

Kirym smiled. "If the cave is needed, the tokens will tell us."

I approached Kirym to offer support, beaten by Qwinita who murmured a quiet warning. "Two tokens are missing. The green and yellow."

Kirym smiled and nodded reassuringly. Quinita wandered away.

"What will you do?" I asked. "Othyn and Ubree won't have a connection."

"Teema, if the tokens have to all be here, then nothing will happen and we'll wait until we have them. But something tells me we need to do this now, and whatever the end result is, at least we did it."

I knew better than to argue with her, but as I wondered what it all meant, Shormel walked up to Kirym and held out the green token.

I'd forgotten he had it.

She accepted with a smile, talked to him quietly for a few moments. Then he disappeared back into a group of dwarflings.

The children crowded around Kirym, as she pulled the rest of the wrapped tokens from her pocket, oohing and ahhing as each new stone appeared. The little girl I held was one of the few children not there. Probably the only way she could have seen what was happening was in someone's arms. She was so small, and I guessed she was not one to push her way to the front.

Kirym placed the tokens on the top of the stump. This time she made a pattern different to any other I had seen her use. She placed the tokens in a straight line about an arm's length away from the edge of the stump, first the orange, then the red, purple, blue and the green.

The rainbow token sat at the edge of the stump in front of them. The pattern looked unbalanced because it was opposite the space between the purple and blue.

Slowly, the children returned to places further from the stump, with only a few remaining close to Kirym. Most just chatted and asked questions, and one girl, a dwarfling, helped fold the cloths the tokens had been wrapped in.

When Kirym had finished setting the tokens up, the children wandered away to stand in front of the crowd. At the last moment, a boy darted out and handed something to Kirym. At first I thought it was the yellow token, but almost instantly I realised that the shape and colour were wrong.

Nevertheless she accepted it with a smile, talked to him for a few moments and then added the stone to the end of the line. Now it looked balanced.

The boy turned away, but instead of joining us, he stared at me for a few moments, winked and then disappeared into the crowd of children.

"Larqeba?" I asked as Kirym joined us. "Is that the stone Churnyg gave him?"

Kirym nodded.

"Will it work?" I was worried, scared Kirym had made the wrong decision. "What if nothing happens?"

"Something always happens, even if it's not what we expect or hope for."

30

Teema Speaks

The dragons stood opposite us, the tokens on the stump between us. I stood behind and to one side of Kirym, and moved the wee girl to my right hip. I would have preferred her on my left, but the ache in my shoulder was becoming intense. I'd never realised that carrying a child could be such a strain. I was amazed that parents did it all the time. Kirym had carried Amethyst every day as we travelled here from Faltryn. Although a little bigger than Amethyst, this wee girl was not much heavier. I never realised what Kirym had gone through.

Arbreu stood next to me, Mekrar on his far side. Oak moved around to Kirym's other side. It was strange having him there, because he wasn't part of our group, but when Sundas stood behind us, I was surprised to realise that even with the strangers beside us, the group actually felt whole.

I was just about to ask Kirym if the substitute yellow stone would work, when an intense argument started between

Morkeen and Paluniis. It ended when Paluniis took Amethyst off her and brought her over to Kirym.

"She should be with you for this," he said, and walked back to a glowering Morkeen.

I was shocked at the venom in the look Morkeen gave both Kirym and Paluniis.

The evening sun now sat below the western edge of the amphitheatre wall behind us. The last vestiges lit the tokens. The light inside the rainbow stone reached out to touch each of the other tokens and the yellow stone. It then soared from them over to Kirym's tokens, and then on to Iryndal, Arymda and Borasyn. The light then washed across Othyn's, Ubree's and Egrym's foreheads. From them, it returned to the rainbow token. There was a long moment when all the lights flowed into the token, which appeared to swell and cover the whole stump. The other tokens glowed out of it. Again the light erupted out and zigzagged between the six dragons and the smaller jewels of the token wearers.

The lights returned to the tokens and disappeared into them.

My eyes adjusted to the darkness of the clearing. The sun had now set and the cooking fires had been covered. The other fires hadn't yet been lit.

Suddenly lights, coloured this time, streamed out of the tokens. They spiralled into the sky, back again into the rainbow token and white lights exploded out of its base in hundreds of smaller rays that raced crazily around the open area.

From awed silence at the beginning, now there was a lot of delighted laughter. The lights were friendly and the children jumped up to try to catch them as they raced past, or around them.

The girl giggled as one light whizzed between us, circled her head and then raced away. Another zeroed in on Kirym, hit her tokens, ricocheted onto the girl's forehead and exploded into a hundred smaller lights. These too raced around, colliding with whatever was in their line of fire. Slowly the lights broke up, getting smaller and smaller, until it seemed the whole area was glowing moving light.

Small groups of lights charged together, but now when they hit, they changed colour, and soon it seemed we were standing in a gently moving rainbow.

The lights slowly gathered in a massive multi-coloured ball above the amphitheatre, and one by one fell into the large tokens. There was a final eruption of light when everyone was bathed in colour. It faded, and looking almost as ghosts of their former glory, they gathered together above the dragons, connected to them, brightened and dropped into the rainbow token. It slowly shrank back to its normal size getting paler as it did

Suddenly everything was dark and quiet, the only light being the glowing tokens.

I had been lost in the glory of the display, and when everything stopped, I was amazed to see the moon was a hands-width above the embankment rim.

Everyone was awed by what they had seen and been part of. There was a short time with no sound, and then one of the cooking pits sparked as the embers collapsed and fell. Flames shot up to the food above, and the cooks ran over to control them.

After a moment of quiet awe, everyone began to talk excitedly about what they had seen.

I stared up at the dragons. They all had token marks on their foreheads.

Kirym clicked Amethyst's token, kissed her cheek and started towards Morkeen, who almost ran across to grab her. I wasn't close enough to hear what Kirym said to her, but Morkeen's scowl softened as she turned away.

Kirym then went to the stump and began to wrap the tokens. I was concerned to see a tear slide down her cheek.

The girl wriggled out of my arms and limped over to Kirym, and hugged her.

I watched, and made a note to ask Loul how bad the damage to the girl's leg was. The bandages were heavy and when she took a step, she avoided using her damaged limb, hopping instead on her sound leg. Even then, she grimaced with each movement.

I felt she needed more support for the leg, and I made a mental note to talk to Loul about a crutch of some sort.

Kirym wiped her face on her sleeve, and together they packed the tokens away. Then Kirym picked the girl up and took her over to talk to the dragons. The rest of us joined her.

The lump on each of the dragon's foreheads was more prominent now than before. They pulsed, the glow getting more intense until it was almost as if they would explode. Light shot out, one or the other connecting with each of us who had stood together, although all touched Kirym.

The pale red light touched mine, and I felt at peace, the best I had felt all day.

When I began to think again, I wondered why the girl and Oak were also chosen by the dragons. Neither wore a token, and even now, their foreheads were blank. I wondered what it meant.

I held my arms out for the girl.

"She's a sweet wee flower," Kirym said. "She's taken a liking to you, hasn't she?"

I thought about what Kirym had said.

"Hey, little one," I said. "A name. What about Flower? Would you like that?"

She was already shaking her head. "It's pretty, but it's not mine."

"Well you'll figure it out eventually."

She nodded seriously. Her shawl slipped to the ground, and I carefully put her down to pick it up.

Kirym frowned. "What was that about?"

I briefly explained.

Kirym picked the girl up and sat her on her lap. She pointed to the stars. "They're shining brightly tonight. Perhaps they wanted to see what the tokens have for the dragons." She indicated one star all by itself near the horizon. "When I was very little, an old wise-woman who visited us one winter told me a story about that star. 'A small flower roamed the world looking for someone to belong to, someone who would give her a name. No one knew who she was and no one would accept her into their family. 'You have no fur,' said the wolf. 'You can't belong to us,' said the swan, 'you've no feathers.' 'You don't swim, do you,' said the fish. 'You have no roots,' said the tree. 'You have feet,' said the snake. The little flower was very sad, but she continued through the land, across the water, up tall hills and down into deep valleys. Still she found no one who would take her in and give her a name. One night after she had trudged all day across a wide desert, she sat at the top of a big sand hill and stared up at the stars.

'Perhaps if I was as beautiful as they are, someone would want me and give me a name' she cried.

At that moment, the moon rose above the horizon and heard her. 'But you are beautiful,' she said. 'Some are blind to beauty, others only want to see themselves. You do have a home, you can come and live with us. A name is waiting here for you.'

The little flower was overwhelmed. She felt so happy when the moon lifted her high into the sky.

'Your place is here with us,' the moon said, 'where everyone in the world can see you. When they do, someone special will share their name with you. Only that person will know it. You can have her name if you like.'

The flower sat in her place in the night sky, and all of the plants and animals looked up and were in awe of her beauty." Kirym paused and looked at the wee girl. "Everyone really knows her name, because the moon whispers it to them when they're born. What did she whisper to you?" Kirym asked.

The child stared at the star. "Trethia," she said. "Her name's Trethia."

Kirym smiled and nodded.

"How did you know that?" I asked the girl.

She shrugged.

"Because that star has the same name this little one was given," said Kirym.

"Is it?" I asked. I lifted her out of Kirym's arms and sat her on my hip.

Trethia smiled and nodded. "It's pretty."

Kirym leaned over. "I think so too. It means beautiful one, and it suits you."

Trethia shrugged, then whispered back to Kirym, and they both giggled.

I suddenly felt left out

31

Kirym Speaks

Lantiah woke me while it was still dark. "There's someone to see you," she whispered. "One of Wind Runner's people."

I carefully lifted Trethia's arm off my waist, pleased when she turned over and snuggled into Mekrar, who we shared the set with.

Throwing my cloak around my shoulders, I slipped out through the heavy door covering.

Oak waited nearby, holding a hooded lamp. "I think Teema needs some help. He hasn't slept, his shoulder is troubling him. He wouldn't go to see the healers, and forbade me to go for him."

I glanced at the sky. No moon, it had set, and although it was still dark, the sky was beginning to lighten. Dawn wasn't far off.

"Give me a moment to get dressed," I said.

Inside the dwelling, Lantiah had a bowl of warm water waiting. "Will you eat now?"

"There'll be food over with Papa. Save what is here for the others. Trethia will be hungry when she wakens. She ate so little last night, it'll be good if she doesn't have to wait. Ask Mekrar to ensure she eats and has another meal midmorning if I'm not back to take her." I quickly washed and put on my petticoat, an overdress and my boots. Grabbing my cloak, I again slipped through the door.

"Where is he?"

Oak guided me over to a dark area against the northern wall. Teema was curled in a ball on his knees. He was deathly pale and sweating. His skin was clammy.

He was pleased to see me, but scowled when he saw Oak.

"Can you take your tunic off, or should I cut it?" I asked.

He tried to pull it over his head, but the pain was too much.

I slit the side seam and along the arm, and began to ease it away from the wound. "The tunic can be repaired. Take it to Seba once it's been washed. Oak, I'll need two bowls of warm water. The material will come off easier if I wet it, and I'll need to wash the wound to see the extent of the damage."

Teema straightened up and before I could stop him, he wrenched the material away from the wound.

"Teema!"

"Quicker than all o' that nonsense," he said, gasping with pain.

I was exasperated. "Quicker maybe, but now the wound has to begin healing again."

"There was no guarantee water would've worked. You know that as well as I do."

"It would have been nice to try," I said, appalled at the damage I could now see.

Both shoulder blades were bleeding, the scab had stuck to the material when he pulled it away. I suspected there was more than one break. His head had also bled, his hair there was plastered to his head.

"What happened?"

"I landed awkwardly when I jumped from a tree. Then Shormel hit me with a branch. Neither would be a problem by themselves, but together ..." He winced as he touched his head.

"Why'd he hit you?" asked Oak.

"He was scared, didn't know who I was. Mind you, I barrelled into Ubree soon after that. Altogether I was a bit careless yesterday."

"Teema, you've broken a number of bones, and they won't be an easy fix. Your left shoulder is too bruised for me to deal with. Mama will have to look at it. She will bind it up, and she'll want to put leeches on it to help with the bruising, although that may be a bit late by now. The bruise is well set."

"I can't have it bandaged up," said Teema. "I can't use my bow if I'm wrapped up like a baby. We need be ready for anything with Gynbere so close."

I knew Teema's arguments of old, and resolved to end them quickly. "If you can draw your bow fully, I'll agree to argue against the bandages. Oak, can you get a bow please."

Teema tried to flex his shoulders while waiting, but stopped abruptly when the pain became too much. He was on his feet, pale and breathing deeply in an attempt to ease the agony when he took the bow. He checked the string was properly attached, grasped it and slowly tried to straighten his arm. He quickly faltered, shuddered with the pain.

"That's definite. You will go see Mama. Leaving it this long hasn't helped it at all."

"I can't stay in the healing area. Veld needs all the help he can get."

"You're no use to him like this, Teema. Even had you gone

to see Mama as soon as you did the damage, you'd still have all of these problems. She would have been able to reduce the bruising and swelling. As it is, if you don't do something about it now you'll have problems for a long time."

Teema, come here.

I looked up to see Ubree watching us. Oak had obviously heard him too.

"What does he want?" asked Teema.

"Possibly to help you," I said.

"Why would he?" asked Teema. "I doubted his motives and actions, and I did it in front of everyone. He has good reason to hate me."

"Ubree could have shown his annoyance at any time. He didn't. Trust him."

Teema looked sceptical.

"Trust me," I said softly.

He walked over to stand in front of the dragon. Every step showed fear, but it was a journey he had to make by himself.

Ubree lowered his head until his forehead rested on Teema's. The wound closed over, the bruises faded, the swelling disappeared, and the bones moved visibly under his skin.

The injuries appeared on Ubree's shoulder, oozed blood, scabbed over and healed. The bruises faded.

Teema's stance slowly changed. He stood taller, flexed his shoulder. The stiffness in it disappeared. "Thank you. Thank you so much." He frowned. "Why did you help me? I've not been nice to you."

Ubree shrugged. "You didn't know what was happening and you had doubts. You're entitled to. It's a protective reaction. You care for Kirym. So do I."

"That's your gift, isn't it? You heal things."

Ubree nodded.

"I feel stupid. You saved Kirym's life. She didn't need me at all."

"She definitely needed you. Without you, she would be alive, but still asleep. A wholeness is needed and that can't happen unless we work together."

"Can you heal Trethia's leg?" Teema asked. He went red. "Sorry, I'm being presumptuous."

"Asking for others is never wrong. Bring her to me."

Trethia's reaction on being woken was of terror until she recognized me.

I reassured her first, then: "Ubree has asked to see you, all right?"

She nodded tentatively.

I wrapped a cloak over her sleeping robe. She clung to me as we left the dwelling.

"I'll keep you safe." I wasn't at all sure she believed me.

The sky was now grey, and everything was visible although still indistinct. Ubree sat in a darker area, a black shape against the hill.

Trethia was scared. It showed in her face, but she bravely hobbled up to Ubree.

He brought his head down to her level. His head was bigger than her whole body. He carefully touched his nose to her leg.

Ubree's leg suddenly distorted, no longer bearing his weight.

Trethia patted his cheek, and leaned her forehead against his and the leg slowly straightened and returned to normal.

"I wonder who is healing who," murmured Oak.

Then the moment ended.

They stayed together for a short time longer, until Ubree's

wounds seemed fully healed.

When Trethia walked over to me she no longer limped.

"Ubree said my leg is fixed and I can have the bandage off now."

Oak knelt to help her.

I walked over and sat in front of the dragon. "Thank you for doing that. Can you tell me anything about her?"

"Why?"

"Because she's an enigma. She lived in The Rock, but wasn't part of them. She would play happily with the children from there, but even the kindest avoid her. Some of them are downright nasty to her. Few adults even intervene. She accepts that without complaint and walks away. She won't go with the other children at meal times and seems to expect nothing."

"She doesn't eat?" he asked.

"She does, but she never expects to be fed. She'll pick up food that's been dropped or thrown away, and stores food away when she finds it."

Ubree frowned, but said nothing. He seemed to be looking inward.

"Mama initially gave her a crutch to help her walk. The first time she used it, one of the boys kicked it from under her. She just walked away. She left the crutch, like it wasn't worth fighting for. Someone returned it to Mama later in the evening. Her leg was broken, wasn't it?"

He nodded. "Yes, in two places, and there was a vertical split in her lower leg bone. You've seen most of what there was to see, and you've seen more than anyone else. You have to discover the link to the enigma, the mystery. She is a key. Protect her. Keep her close. You are her future, and I think she's important to yours. You will keep each other alive." He closed his eyes. I had more questions, but I knew I'd have to wait for the answers. They would come eventually.

Trethia's leg looked good. No bruising, and the swelling had gone.

"I'll take these back to Loul," she said picking the splints and bandages up.

"Good, and then we can get dressed and get something to eat," I said.

As we approached the healing area, I held Oak and Teema back and watched what Trethia did.

She cautiously peeped through the corner of the skin that covered the entrance. Then she quietly pushed the bandages and splints onto the worktop that was just inside. She did it so unobtrusively, I doubted anyone in there would have been aware unless they had actually been watching the door.

"Oh my," said Oak. "Why would she do that?"

"I imagine Mama isn't in there. Possibly she's unsure of who is, or more probably she knows the people who are."

"That isn't good, is it? What has she been through?" asked Oak.

"I intend to find out," I said.

Trethia skipped back to me and we went to our dwelling to choose a dress and shawl for her. Then we joined the men to go to the food area.

Although everyone was encouraged to eat at set times through the day, food was always available, especially for those going on and off guard duty. Those in the healing area ate when they needed it, as they were not always able to keep regular meal times, and some of those being healed needed to eat more frequently.

Trethia skipped ahead of us and picked up four platters, bringing one each back for Teema, Oak and me. Then she bounced back to the service area, and held her platter out.

There were two servers there this morning, Seba, Zelriff's granddaughter who was dealing with two hunters, and Shiarta, a woman from The Rock.

Shiarta ignored Trethia, and smiled at Oak and Teema as they approached.

I was mystified over her behaviour. She had seemed to be a kind compassionate woman.

"She was in line first," I said, pointing to Trethia.

"Children wait until the hunters and guards are served." She turned away from Trethia and me and waited as Teema and Oak carried on their discussion.

"Teema and Oak are neither at the moment. She was in line first."

Trethia put her platter down and walked away.

I followed her and took her hand. "Come on, we'll do this together."

"I'm not hungry."

I hunkered down beside her. "Yes you are. No one should treat you like that. We don't allow it here."

She shrugged. "It doesn't matter. It's always been like that."

I now understood why she was so small and thin. In a community where food was sometimes scarce for some people, she was on the bottom of the heap. I just couldn't understand why. They loved their children from all I had seen. A dwarfling who was orphaned was always taken in by another family.

"Why?"

She shrugged.

"Do you remember your Maman?"

She looked at her feet. "People like me don't have them."

The sun was up now, and people were beginning to leave the shelters, calling greetings to each other across the open area.

"Will you join us for a meal, Kirym," called Lyndym, as she, Mekrar and Bildon passed.

"Soon," I called. When I turned back to Trethia, she was

gone. I stood and scanned the growing crowd. A small movement of the door covering to the dwelling I'd slept in, caught my eye. I walked over, standing aside as the last few people left.

Lantiah was the last person out. "Did you need something, Kirym?"

"No, I just wanted to change my cloak for a shawl."

She ran to catch up with the others.

Inside, I was surprised to find the room in chaos. Generally sets were tidied, rugs and clothes folded, or taken to the cleaning area before people left in the morning, unless there was an emergency of some sort.

There was no sign of Trethia.

I picked up a rug from the set I'd slept in, folded it and placed it on the bench ready for the night. A second, third and fourth cleared the set and I straightened the covers. I opened the big trunk that held Mekrar's, Lyndym's and my clothes. Mama had put clothes for Trethia in there too. I pulled out a shawl and the prettiest dress Mama had given her.

"Trethia, come out and get dressed. Then we can go and see the squilute."

While waiting, I removed my overdress, one of Mekroe's older ones and put on another Mama had found for me. It wasn't as new, but I chose it because it was the same colour as the one I'd chosen for Trethia. Then I sat on the floor and lifted the set cover that was hanging to just above the ground. I peeped under.

Trethia stared back at me.

"Come on out. Let's do things together from now on. Stay close to me, and I'll keep you safe."

She reached out and touched the material of my dress. "Pretty."

"Just like the one I've chosen for you." I held it up. "Come out and get changed." I helped her with the ties on her dress, and wrapped the shawl around her shoulders. I had no boots for her, and made a note to ask Mama to find some. However, I wasn't wearing mine, so it was easier to ignore the omission at this stage.

In the corner of the clothes chest was a small woven basket that held the pretty decorations Halse, Mekrar and I wore or had worn when we were younger. I rummaged through it and chose a little necklace and matching wrist band I'd grown out of. I had intended to give it to Tarl's daughter, but she was still too little. Now I was glad I hadn't. I showed Trethia how to tie them on.

She looked at them for a few moments, and then slowly untied the wrist band. "Keep them here safe. I'll probably lose them."

"I want you to wear them, Trethia. These are my gift to you. If you do lose them, they'll be found and returned to you."

"Are you there, Kirym?" called Teema. "I thought we were eating together."

"Come in, Teema." I called. "We're almost ready."

32

Kirym Speaks

We ate just outside the dwelling and then introduced Trethia to Midnight. Squilute are very good with children, and soon the two of them were running around together playing. Delightfully, Trethia was laughing, something I'd never seen before.

I told Teema and Oak what had happened to Trethia at the food area. Neither had been aware of it, too busy talking about hunting, but they were appalled and promised to watch for anything else.

The sun had moved a hands-width before, Oak put Midnight back in the pen and we returned to the amphitheatre.

Twig walked over to meet us. "I thought you'd like to know, Mam. Gynbere's crowd is preparing to move."

"Does Papa know?"

"Yes, and the dragons. Veld's discussing it with the other leaders now."

"I'd have thought Gynbere would be here by now," said

Oak. "They were ready to move last night."

Twig shrugged. "His camp has been in an uproar since before the moon set."

"Is his pavilion down yet?" I asked.

Twig shook his head.

"You don't think his arrival is imminent, do you Kirym," said Teema.

"No. Papa sent a delegation to him last night and invited him to be our guest."

"So this is his answer? That's just bad manners."

"It's to do with power, control and manipulation, Twig. He chooses when and how he arrives. He enjoys having people wait for him, and he isn't an early riser by all accounts. Let's go and see what Papa has learned."

The leaders had gathered with Papa at the table, and listened carefully to comments made by the hunters and guards, as they came in with reports. Papa occasionally made notes about things said or needing to be checked up on.

I handed Trethia to Teema and slipped in close to see what he felt was important. Most of the notes were about where to place the men so as to appear friendly, but be prepared to defend ourselves if need be.

"Papa, why are we only fortifying the one entrance?" I asked when there was a lull in the conversation.

"It's the only one Gynbere's guards knows of, Kirym," said Peet.

"Why are you assuming that?" I said. "Even if the guards don't know about the others, Gynbere does."

"He can't," said Peet. "Mrilan said he's only recently found out leaving The Rock isn't a death sentence. Anyway if he knew about them, he'd have his men check them out, and they haven't."

"That you know of." I turned to Papa. "Gynbere told his people that leaving The Rock was death, but he followed

Churnyg to kill him. Why do that, if he believed Churnyg would die anyway. He was planning to bring everyone out of The Rock before the wall came down. I've seen a copy of the order he gave his guards. Having left, he came straight here. I asked Iryndal, and she confirmed it. Just because he took a long time, doesn't mean he was lost. Gynbere would like us to underestimate him, to catch us unprepared. We can allow him to retain his illusion, but make sure he's wrong."

"And how would you do that?" Papa asked.

"Have two carts block the north-eastern entrance, so they can't enter or exit there even if they want to. Get enough men on the walls to protect us properly, but without appearing to be an armed camp. Keep weapons handy, but not visible, and be prepared to assume the best. Offer generous hospitality and see what happens."

Papa nodded.

"What about the southern entrance," said Peet.

"We don't want to look as if we were scared of him," Tarl said. "But Kirym's right. We mustn't underestimate him, nor allow him to think we're scared. If he aims for the south entrance, we'll have plenty of warning."

"Perhaps we'll place carts near the south ready to cover it if necessary," said Papa. "Both of you are right, Tarl and Peet."

"What if he attacks?" asked Wind Runner.

"Harumph," snorted Storm. "We fight."

"Let's hope Gynbere doesn't. Do you think he will, Kirym?" asked Papa.

I shook my head. "Not initially. Gynbere wants something, but if he doesn't get it, he may decide he has an excuse. Expect a show of power though."

"So we need to be ready to fight."

"Let's not over-react, Peet," said Papa. "It would be silly to pre-empt something. That may be just what he wants.

Armos, can you warn all the guards, please. If there are any you're unsure of, find other duties for them."

"I'll do it now," said Armos, and walked away, signalling the head guards to meet him.

One of the cooks brought over a large platter of baked bread, cocooning meat and vegetables. Everyone took a share, and for a while, the only sounds were groans of pleasure and appreciation.

I looked for Trethia. Tarl had hunkered down and was sharing his platter of food, enticing her with extra tender titbits. He used to do that for me when I was little and more recently did the same thing for his own two children when they were with him.

He saw me watching and smiled. "She's a sweetie. Would you like to share with us?" I joined them with thanks.

A large basket of flasks arrived, and I took mine over to the centre of the amphitheatre to get a general idea of what had been done.

On the whole, Papa had covered everything I would have, and a few things I hadn't thought of. The biggest change I could see was mixing the family dwellings up so no area belonged specifically to anyone. It would make targeting a particular group very hard. Two carts were being pulled in and placed strategically to cover the north-eastern entrance, but left movable in case the exit was needed.

Papa joined me, looking around as I had. "Have I missed anything?"

"Possibly, but you can't think of everything. What will happen when the children we rescued yesterday see their parents?"

"Loul talked to them and asked them to stay hidden until it was time to send them back, or until their parents came to collect them. They understood, the older ones in particular. They have no intention of becoming Gynbere's pawns again.

I'm not sure if it will work in practice though."

"It may depend on whether Gynbere knows we have them," I said.

"Could he?"

I shrugged. "I doubt he would send anyone to check on them, but even if he did, he'd have no way of knowing where they had gone. We would be the obvious ones to accuse though. What about the guards?"

"Ah, they've been well fed and seem to be very happy. We offered them a change of clothes, and most accepted. Two held out though. They're all under guard—out near the squilute. Findlow had a chat last night and asked them how Slaslow generally reacted to his men failing in their duty. It gave them something to think about, although the big one, Foben was heard later concocting a story of being overwhelmed by an army. If he manages to escape, he could be a problem."

"He enjoyed the food we've offered?" I asked, as we wandered back towards the table.

Papa nodded.

Teema joined us. "Some of them eat like filun."

"Dose a platter of stew with batheran," I said. "You'll only need a pinch, it has no flavour and it should make them sleep until late afternoon. By then we should know what's happening. You can always repeat it if you need more time."

Papa smiled. "Oh very clever, Kirym. Teema, can you organise that now? Ask Loul or Lantiah for some."

"It may still be difficult to contain the situation. Once Gynbere sees the children, he can accuse us of kidnapping them," I said.

"Their parents may not back him. However if he wants to attack us, he won't need an excuse."

"Talk to Iryndal, Papa. She may be able to help."

Papa raised an eyebrow at me.

"The dragons don't want a war either. Even if we lined the children up ready to hand them over, Gynbere could still take offence if that was his desire. No matter what we do it could be the wrong thing. The women said the children were only taken from those who had no value or refused to fight for or serve Gynbere and Slaslow. Why would anyone take a baby or child from its mama, even if they don't support you?"

Papa nodded. "Play it by ear, I guess."

Despite the early movement from Gynbere's camp, the sun passed the meridian without his entry into the amphitheatre, although our trackers reported his camp packed and waiting.

"His people are treated so badly," reported Twig, after another excursion out to check on them. "Some of them were made to stand with packs on their shoulders before dawn. After the sun rose they all sat down. Splinter said there was a lot of screaming from someone who I assume was Slaslow, but they stayed sitting. It was ridiculous to make them stand and wait. Gynbere's pavilion is still up and the rest of them are all seated, eating and drinking. I don't think I've ever heard of anyone treating friends that way."

"He doesn't have friends, Twig. Just people who'll pay homage to him," said Teema.

It was almost mid-afternoon when the hunters reported that Gynbere had appeared and his pavilion was being taken down. He ate, and climbed onto his ibith. It was shouldered and they began to move.

His entry into the amphitheatre was staged to be spectacular. A small group of fully armed soldiers entered through the north-eastern entrance, and secured it, arms at the ready.

"That's a bit over the top, isn't it?" said Armos. "It's not as if there has been any threat made to them. They were invited here."

It's all show," said Papa. "Leave it for now."

Next a large group of people were ushered in, and pushed over to the south east corner. They were well guarded.

They were followed by an even larger company of soldiers, many of whom were carrying flags on poles. They fanned out across the width of the open area, cutting over a third of it off.

A third group entered. I suspected these were families who were sympathetic to Gynbere, they were not guarded and there were a large number of children with them.

The next group to enter were quite different, brightly clothed and rather loud. They were guided to an area where seats, food and drink was provided.

"That's disgusting," said Arbreu. "They ate while they waited for Gynbere. The group in the corner have gone hungry right through. It really shows who's favoured and who isn't, doesn't it."

More soldiers entered and joined the line, extending it further into the centre of the open area.

Then there was a long pause when nothing happened. I initially thought Gynbere was trying to create suspense, however it went on for far too long. The wait was explained by Dashlan who had been on the wall. "The brackets holding the carrying rails on Gynbere's ibith have failed and he's just outside waiting as his men fix it."

Eventually there was a resounding cheer from Gynbere's favourites, echoed with less enthusiasm by the group who were guarded. I suspected there was a bit of bullying encouragement from the guards, who moved in among them and forced them to their feet.

Gynbere's ibith was carried on the shoulders of eighteen men. He was surrounded by armed guards. The ibith was now very ornate. Almost every part of it was studded with lines of bright orange stones. The finials at the top of the chair were hung with yellow tassels and the arms were fringed with purple. The chair back and legs were swathed in rich red material fringed with grey, although the base was largely uncovered. Rather than looking rich and impressive, it jarred horribly.

All of Gynbere's people bowed low as he was paraded along the east wall past them.

"Now that's new," said Ashistar, suddenly appearing at my shoulder. "Only those currying favour have done that in the past. I wonder why they agreed to do it."

"He has their children. He's showing off his power to them as well as us," I said.

Gybere's ibith was carried to the centre of the amphitheatre just behind the line of soldiers, but also surrounded by his personal armed guards. He stared around the open area, not at anyone, more a sneering perusal.

I looked for Papa, wondering how he would cope with this.

He was already on the move, striding down the length of the amphitheatre, his cloak flying out behind him.

"Gynbere!"

I was surprised at how his voice carried. Everyone within the amphitheatre heard, stopped what they were doing and watched.

"You were invited here as a guest. It was stipulated that this is a peaceful gathering. Sheath your weapons right now!"

Before Gynbere could respond, most of the soldiers obeyed. Gynbere could not argue without appearing silly.

"Oh," he laughed lightly. "A misunderstanding, I assure you. My people are so very protective of me. There have been threats, you understand."

"The only threats I've heard, were made by him," muttered Shuryn.

Papa glanced along the lines of soldiers. "This area is open to everyone, Gynbere. We would like you to stay, but everyone here must have free access to move around the amphitheatre. Your people are welcome to join us and share a meal. It's about to be dished up."

"On their behalf," said Gynbere, "I thank you. However, my people have already eaten, and many of them are very shy. They prefer to keep to themselves."

"Oh dear, he doesn't give them food, and won't allow us to. What can Veld do?" said Shurlyn.

"Perhaps you can convince them otherwise," said Veld. "We are neighbours, and our homes will be close. Settlements need to help each other. Have you not the power to convince them of the need to get to know us? Or perhaps you should just order them to."

Gynbere took a deep breath and made himself smile. "I will tell them, although some may still be reluctant. However, let us know when you are ready for us."

"He's calling guards to him," said Dashlan. "I wonder what he'll tell them."

Ashistar growled in the back of his throat. "He means to keep the non-supporters in their place. See a number of the guards are wandering over there now."

"It'll be obvious though, won't it? I mean when none of that group come over?"

"No, Dashlan. Gynbere, Slaslow and the Urfits are very good at managing people. Gynbere may have lost the war of words with Veld, but he won't on this," said Mrilan. "People will come from there, but they will be managed, and I imagine it'll be mainly guards, their families, and a few of the not quite so influential, dressed in their oldest shabbiest clothes."

"What can we do?"

He shook his head. "Probably nothing, Kirym. I think

Gynbere will have his way with this one."

"Not if I can help it," I said.

I wandered casually over to Papa, and explained what was probably happening. "Any ideas?"

"It's a difficult one. How can we let them know their children are safe, if we can't get close to them?"

"I have an idea. It might work, but ..." I paused. "Well it should. Why don't we take something over to them? To everyone, even Gynbere. Umm, a drink, no better, a piece of friendship loaf or something like that. He could scarcely refuse it. And for those who are repressed, get a few of the older children to do most of it with a few adults to assist. Larqeba could help. He'll probably be recognised by Shormel's maman, and he'll be able to pass on a message."

"Would the guards recognise him?"

"Probably not. If he changes his clothes, why would they. Just warn him not to be smart to them."

"Very well, I'll talk to Loul, you find Larqeba."

33

Kirym Speaks

Mama was very good when faced with an emergency. She quickly organised the cooks to change their meal plan. Friendship bread was already cooked. It was a regular part if our meals when we were away from home or had visitors.

While waiting for the loaves to be cut and placed on platters Mama grabbed a number of the older children and told them what she needed them to do.

Three basins of water and a flask of concentrated soap nut mixture removed the mud from Larqeba's hair, although Lantiah managed only to lighten his skin.

"How did you do it?" Oak asked.

"Nut oil. After I went with Shormel I applied it every day except for the last two days."

"It'll take time to fade," said Lantiah. "Rubbing your skin with dronger fruit has done a little to lighten it, although it may over time." She handed him a brightly coloured tunic and jerkin, and with his hair back to its usual golden bouncy curls, he looked quite different. I thought he would probably get away with it unless someone knew him well.

The first of our people to go over approached Gynbere personally. Mama chose Harnita to speak to him and she was joined by a group of our prettiest girls and handsomest young men. They wore their festival clothes and all of the jewellery we could find.

Gynbere was quite gushing in his acceptance, pinching Harnita on the cheek as she explained our tradition. He immediately invited Papa over to share a drink in friendship.

As the loaf was dished up to his close supporters, a large group of us who had been waiting at a discrete distance descended on the other groups. Gynbere could scarcely object, when he had already accepted the gift in principle. Harnita had explained it was an old custom of ours and had been very specific in using words that included all of the people from The Rock.

I joined the group who approached those under guard. Each guard was offered bread, and a conversation was started, to keep them occupied. The rest of us worked quickly, handing out food and offering encouragement for them to join us soon for the meal. I also watched Larqeba who had been instructed to try to point out Shormel's maman to me.

The proportions of the gift were larger here. We knew these people hadn't eaten in a number of days. They were very thankful. Many tried to offer us a gift in return. One woman handed me a small carved button. Her generosity made me want to cry.

"All we require is your friendship," I said.

"I want you to have it," she said.

A sudden movement to one side caught my attention. One woman had slipped the food under her shawl. I offered her more, she shook her head.

"No, no. I've had mine. It's so kind of you. Thank you very much."

I glanced around to see if anyone was watching. Larqeba saw me, nodded and smiled.

By that, I assumed this was Shormel's maman. I hunkered down beside her. "Eat the food before the guards are told to remove it. Your children are safe, and being well fed and cared for. Shormel is with them," I murmured. Shielding my body from the guards, I carefully pointed to the right. "Larqeba."

She glanced casually in the direction I indicated. She recognised him, I was sure, but gave no indication. She took my hand. "Thank you. Keep the children with you. Don't let them come back."

I squeezed her hand. Again I felt like crying. I handed her a large portion of bread. "Eat it, we'll get more food to you later."

I carried on distributing all the food I carried. When I came away, I held a handful of small keepsakes, five carved buttons, a small bunch of flowers, two embroidered kerchiefs, four pretty stones, a scarf, a small embroidered pocket and a tiny box.

Mekrar had tears in her eyes. She put her arm around my shoulder. "They were so generous. With almost nothing, they gave us gifts. Did you manage to tell anyone about the children?"

"I talked to Shormel's maman and a few others. I guess they'll pass the information around to those who need it. We just need to watch that there are no repercussions."

"Papa has a couple of guards watching them specifically. Any problems and he will wade in to sort it out, although hopefully they'll be safe enough while here in the amphitheatre."

"Jetara likes you," said Larqeba, slipping his arm around

my waist.

"Was that Shormel's mama?" I asked.

He nodded.

"Did you talk to her?"

"She kissed my hands. Then she said I needed a bath." He sounded outraged. "She wants you to keep Shormel."

I nodded. "She told me. We will manage to get them all back together though, I promise you. Papa will get them over here."

"I was given the same message," said Mekrar. "They said it again and again."

Now the cooks had the meal prepared and set out in the centre of the open area on big wooden slabs—the sides off two of Wind Runners carts.

Armos took the message over to Veld, who was still sharing a drink with Gynbere.

They and Gynbere's favourites were escorted over by his guard.

A quarter of the way across the open area with Gynbere, Papa paused and turned back. He looked at the people still seated. "All of you," he called. "Come and eat now while it's fresh and hot."

I willed them all to stand together and begin to come over.

The guards are threatening them. Iryndal sounded disgusted.

"Not if I have anything to do with it," said Wind Runner. She strode over to the group and started chivvying them to their feet, remonstrating with the guards as she did so.

Storm and Sundas each took a step to follow her, but were halted by quiet words from Mama. "Wait. A show of force could cause more trouble than it's worth."

They weren't needed.

Everyone ate, but those less well dressed were ushered back to the eastern wall very quickly.

"At least we got some food to them, although they didn't get much chance to mingle with us. We can keep working out ways to visit them," said Lantiah.

After the meal, preparation began for the next meal. More game, fish, fruit, vegetables and wild grains were collected.

Gynbere's people kept to themselves. Gynbere claimed they were tired after their long trek from The Rock. He obviously didn't expect to be challenged.

I spent the late afternoon grinding wheat for bread, sorting and chopping fruit for the cooks.

More dwellings had been erected, but Gynbere refused shelter for his people. After a brief evening meal, they all left and spent the night just outside the wall.

His pavilion had been erected for him, although only two smaller tents for his chosen ones. Most of his people would be in the open overnight.

34

Kirym Speaks

The moon was about two hand-spans from the dawn horizon when I joined the guards patrolling the top of the bank. I was placed on the north-western side, just above Gynbere's camp.

Patrolling along the top gave us a good view of both sides of the bank, except to the north where there was a thick copse of trees. Papa had guards watching there also.

After an uneventful shift, I was relieved by Teema just on dawn.

"Quiet?" he asked.

I nodded. "Wet though, but it'll be a warm day and everything will dry off by midmorning."

"Not so good for them." He gestured down to those of Gynbere's people who had remained in the open overnight. "Without any cover at all, they must've had a miserable time.

"Worse than in here actually," I said. "The wind affected

them far more than us."

As we watched, a group of guards and soldiers picked up some large packages that sat beside the grassy bank and carried them into the amphitheatre. They opened them and began to sort out the contents.

"A spare pavilion," said Teema. "Why didn't they erect it overnight to shelter some of those out in the rain? The other tents must've been really crowded."

I shook my head. "One tent housed the ibith. Six people slept in the other. Many of Gynbere's favourites sat out over-night."

He shook his head. "Why didn't Iryndal divert the rain? She could have."

"Why should she? She doesn't create weather, except for fog. To stop it raining here, she must send it elsewhere. That has huge implications here and there. It changes the balance of nature. What if it caused a flood or some other disaster?"

"Couldn't she send our rain to the desert? No one lives there. And the sand would just absorb it."

"The desert is full of life, insects, rodents, and even the fyrsha. They too deserve to live as they have. Grasses and trees here need the rain. Nature is finely balanced, and we interfere at our peril. But look at it this way. Being made to sit out overnight in the rain lets them know how little Gynbere cares for them. They all knew there were enough shelters in here. They'll draw their own conclusions. Mind you, some may look on it as an honour to do that for their esteemed leader," I said.

We watched the pavilion being erected.

"Oh, that's interesting," I said. "This pavilion isn't as fancy as the one he used overnight."

"He'd want to sleep in the best though, wouldn't he?" said Teema.

"And yet I think he's a great one for impressions on strangers. From what I've seen of him, I'd have thought the fanciest would be in here. So today we may see his plan put into action."

"What plan?"

I shrugged. "I'm sure we'll find out."

Gynbere's guards were quick and efficient, but there was a lot of coming and going. Quite a few guards stood and watched the work. They wandered in and out of the pavilion, seemingly for no obvious reason. When they left six men remained, one at each corner of the pavilion, and one on either side of the entrance. The rest returned to Gynbere's camp.

"I wonder why he had it erected." I asked.

"Maybe he wanted two available. Less fuss when coming into the amphitheatre," said Twig, coming up behind us.

"Maybe he doesn't trust us," said Teema.

"He can't be too wary of us. He allowed our guards to protect his camp. I saw no more than four of his men awake and on guard, and they all stayed under that awning against the embankment."

The other guards here made the same observation, Kirym," said Twig as he joined us. He frowned. "Not the actions of someone who is scared or showing distrust."

With my time on guard at an end, I knew I would soon get in the way. "Twig, will you let me know when anything happens down there?"

"Yes, Mam. Anything in particular?"

"Anything you perceive as unusual."

35

Kirym Speaks

Papa was already sitting at the big table he'd set up for the leaders to gather around later in the morning.

He was reading the stack of overnight reports, copies of what went to Mama, but smiled when I sat beside him. He pushed a platter of chopped fruit and nuts towards me. "Loul will ask if you've eaten. It's always nicer if I can reassure her."

"Mama obviously needs more things to care for, Papa. I seem to eat all the time."

I told him what had happened during my shift, and about the men who had entered the arena to erect the pavilion.

"I watched them. You'd have seen more details from the top of the rise," he said.

I nodded. "And fewer men left than entered."

Papa pulled a couple of leaves of parchment towards him. "Yes, six. They're on guard now."

"Eight!"

Papa immediately sent a runner for the senior guard on the eastern bank. We waited.

Raff approached at a fast jog. "Veld. I'm not sure young Limian got the message right. There are six guards at the pavilion, one at each corner and two at the entrance. You can see five of them from here."

"Yes, Limian repeated my request precisely, Raff," said Papa. "Did you notice anyone entering the pavilion and not coming out?"

Raff went very still, as he understood the implications of Papa's question. "I asked the other guards what they'd seen. No one counted how many men came in. One of the bigger baskets was dropped and somehow everything was spilt. Mainly furnishings from what I could see. All in all it was a bit of a mess. Gynbere's fancy tent was erected. They brought in a number of ground rugs, some were taken out again. The chests went in and out of the pavilion six or seven times. Five large trunks were carried into the tent, two remained outside. The contents from them were carried in piece by piece. Cushions, stools, tables, lidded baskets, trays holding goblets and platters. It'll be comfortable inside. Quite a few of those items were brought out, we assumed they were surplus to requirements."

"What do you think, Kirym?" asked Papa.

"Such a big carry-on for a pavilion he will spend very little time in. When his pavilion was erected last night, fewer items went in. It would have been very comfortable, luxurious even, but this doesn't make sense. Why take five chests in, but leave two outside? There was plenty of room inside. Perhaps they wanted us to see what was in those two chests so we'd assume the others contained the same things.

I would swear the boxes that remained outside were almost as full when they left as when they entered."

"What do you think was taken into the tent?" asked Raff.

"The chests were big, bigger than is practical. Two were a lot lighter when they left the amphitheatre. Six men carried them in, only two were needed to remove them. Four were needed to carry the others. It's only a guess, and I could be wrong, but those two were each big enough to hold a man."

"What?" Raff looked shocked.

"We don't know," cautioned Papa, "but we do need to find out. If we asked Gynbere outright he could perceive it as an insult, and that could damage our plans here."

"Right," I said. "We need to find out who hasn't been seen."

"Who would know?" asked Raff.

"Churnyg, Baketer or Ashistar."

Papa shook his head. "They've kept hidden up until now. I didn't want anything to interfere with saving Churnyg's people. They haven't been in a position to see anything. We'll just have to wait and see what happens."

I nodded and left them pouring over the rest of the reports.

Oak joined me as I walked away. "You're worried about that aren't you? Why?"

"You heard? I didn't notice you."

He laughed. "No, I was too far away. But I was on guard with Raff. He asked what I'd seen, and when he reported to you and Veld, I knew I'd missed something. What are you thinking?"

"That anything Gynbere is doing in secret can't be good for us."

"Well we'll know when it happens, and Raff will make sure everyone is on high alert. Come and eat with me."

"I need to talk to Churnyg, Baketer and Ashistar first. They may have remained in hiding, but I don't believe they haven't been watching."

Churnyg's people had been dispersed among the dwellings, and many of them spent their time helping with the children we rescued.

Churnyg, Ashistar, Baketer, and Mrilan had the use of one of Wind Runner's wagons. This one had remained covered, the sides intact. Storm had backed it into a space between two of the shelters, and with the rear covering pulled down it was impossible to see into, but easy to see out of.

Oak and I were invited in, and offered food and drink. "Loul and Shurlyn make sure we're well cared for, Elf," said Baketer.

"Elf?" Oak looked mystified.

I smiled. "Baketer thought I was an elf when he first met me," I explained.

"I still do," he said. "Seen nothing to change my mind."

I accepted a flask of cool water and explained why I was there.

"Ahh," said Ashistar. "While I've been looking to see who the present favourites are, I never thought to check that."

"Do the favoured ones change?" asked Oak.

"Sometimes daily. There are alliances and factions. Gynbere will choose one over another as he fancies. Occasionally a number of families will join forces to oust someone they think is acquiring too much power, or gaining too much support from Gynbere. Effectively it keeps them all on a similar footing, and Gynbere enjoys watching the in-fighting. He figures if they're plotting against each other, there'll be less intrigue against him."

"So as to those not there," said Churnyg, "Old Burath. Bit of an idiot though, so it's probably not significant."

Ashistar frowned. "His son was there. On the outskirts of the inner group, so I wonder if the old man is dead. His health wasn't good. The boy will be feeling his way if he's trying to take over the family tree. He's not the oldest, but he is the brightest, although that's not saying much when talking about Burath's sons."

"Is he dangerous?" I asked.

"Nah," said Ashistar. "Hasn't the strength of the old man. Gurath was so scared of being knifed in his sleep, he didn't allow his boys any training. A nonentity. Put him aside. He's there, the old man isn't, so Burath is either dying or dead. However, I don't remember seeing the remaining two Urfit triplets at all yesterday or today."

Churnyg went pale.

"Quite a few men stayed just outside the entrance yesterday," said Baketer. "They wore cloaks," he said defensively, when Mrilan snorted. "and there was a lot of coming and going for food and stuff. I got good eyes. Gotta have if you're on the wall. Gotta see things a long way away."

"What did these men look like?" I asked quickly as Mrilan took a breath to reply.

Baketer shook his head. "Funny thing, elf. They had hoods and cloaks on, and they kept the hoods up. That's unusual. And it wasn't that cold."

"He's right," said Oak. "One of the guards mentioned it to Raff."

"How many?" I asked.

"Not really sure," Baketer said. "Ten, twelve maybe. Two were a lot taller than the others."

"But men did come from there," said Mrilan. "I know, 'cause I saw them. They took it in turns, but I'm sure they all came in."

"I'm sure four or five of the men in black stayed out there, and I think one or two of them wore grey robes under their black cloaks."

"Huh, can't even decide on a colour to lie about." said Mrilan.

Baketer frowned. "They milled around a lot. And groups of them did come over. But I don't think the numbers add up."

"If you're just trying to make yourself look important ..."

"No no, Mrilan," Ashistar interrupted. "Baketer's loyal to Kirym, as we all are. He knows that if Slaslow gets hold of him, he's dead, so his information is sound."

"Unless Slaslow planted him here," Mrilan snarled.

"He could've planted you here too, old man," said Baketer.

"I trust all of you," I said. "Baketer's information is sound as much for what doesn't make sense, as what does."

"What do you mean?" asked Churnyg.

"Grey robes belonged to the Urfit triplets. No one else wore them, did they?"

Ashistar shook his head.

"So one or two of them were Urfits. And the taller black-cloaked men. Who could they be?"

"Well that proves it's a lie. Gynbere is taller than most of us. Only by one or two finger widths, and that's because he has specially made boots." Mrilan glared at Baketer. "Slaslow and the Urfits are as big because they get the best of food."

"So the taller people must be a recent addition. I can only think of Rargo."

Oak looked mystified.

"Hmmm. I hadn't thought of him," said Churnyg. "Why wouldn't he walk around openly though? We know he's there. Of course it may not be him. Gynbere may very well have lost patience with him." He laughed dryly. "Gynbere may have left him tied up in the forest. By all accounts Rargo's a bragger, so the story of what he did to Larqeba will be well known by now. Many will be disgusted to hear o' that done to a dwarfling. Gynbere doesn't have the same feelings of compassion, but copying Rargo's action with him as the target would amuse him."

"If Gynbere did it, and we can't assume that, Churnyg. Rargo's very good at keeping himself alive," I said.

"Baketer saw two tall men though. If one is Rargo, who's the other?" asked Oak.

Ashistar frowned. "I don't know. But if Baketer is right, then we may have a problem. Wearing hoods and cloaks in Gynbere's presence is not normal. I've known men to be flogged for less."

"And if they didn't join us for a meal yesterday, they're hiding from us," said Oak.

The sun had not yet risen when the first of Gynbere's people were pushed into their corner by the eastern wall. With wet clothing, they looked cold and miserable.

"Well at least we will get a chance to feed them before Gynbere gets in and stops it. The cooks are already getting it ready to take over," said Oak.

I glanced over. "Oh no!" I gasped. "They mustn't. We'll never get a better opportunity. Oak, tell the cooks to stop dishing now. Papa will send instructions." I was already running over to him.

Oak raced past me just as I arrived at the table. Papa looked up to see what the fuss was.

"Rather than take food over to them, let's invite them here," I gasped. "There's only three guards there, and they look as wet and cold as their prisoners. One was guarding out there for most of last night. He must be the lowest of the low. Persuade the guards to come over. They can't stop the people if they're here."

Papa glanced across the open area. "Yes, it's a good idea, but if Gynbere is told and objects, well, I don't want a war, Kirym."

"Send a formal delegation to Gynbere now, inviting him to eat with us now, followed by the first formal meeting of the guests of The Green Valley. Any guards at the entrance will escort the delegation to their leader. Gynbere may assume the invite is for him alone, and technically accept for both. If he has consented, he can't complain that his people arrived first. If he declines the meal he will still come to the meeting, and he will look petty if he complains because his people have eaten."

"What of the guards at the pavilion? Won't they object?"

"When those guards are given a direct order, they follow it to the exclusion of everything else. I suspect their orders are to guard the pavilion and not let any unauthorised person in or out. They won't question anything else."

Papa nodded slowly. "Who would you send in this delegation?"

"Make sure it's formal. Gynbere is impressed by novelty, so have Storm or Findlow lead it. Add a large guard of honour and some attractive attendants. He was taken with Harnita, so send her too. Give her take a platter of pamchii nuts. It's early for them, but I'm sure I saw a basket of them somewhere. Just make sure they're perfect. Nestle them in a basket with leaves and autumn fruits."

"Won't he refuse to eat a gift of unknown food?"

"Harnita could eat one or two. She will have no problem with that, they taste like nectar. However it's the gift that's important, even if he doesn't eat."

Papa sent a runner over to get Storm, Harnita and a few

others, and explained what he wanted them to do.

Everyone had anticipated the coming formal gathering, and were already dressed in their festival clothes. Harnita had been threading autumn leaves and flowers together to make headdresses for the children, and these were handed out to the delegation to add to the celebratory appearance. A basket of posies were given to be handed out as well, and they were ready.

The delegation left the amphitheatre, and as anticipated, the entrance guards escorted them to Gynbere's pavilion.

Cindra and Lantiah came with me to encourage those already here to come and eat.

The guards were easy to convince, but everyone else remained sitting.

Once the guards were out of hearing, I spoke to Jetara. "Now is your best chance to get to your children. Once you are down there, and mingling with us, there is little Gynbere can do. He no longer has power over you, except what you give to him."

The young woman sitting next to her groaned and grabbed Jetara's hand, her face distorted with pain. She looked exhausted. I felt her forehead, she was warmer than she should have been, but very pale.

"Clatheta's pregnant," said Jetara. "She has been too long in labour."

I signalled a message to Bryn who was on the wall above me. Send someone to carry a very pregnant woman to the healers.

"We have experienced midwives. Let's get her to them. Better her baby be born in privacy and comfort," I said.

"And freedom," muttered Clatheta.

Between contractions, we helped her to stand, but she immediately doubled over in pain. "Can someone come with her?" I asked.

All of the women stood.

The men glanced at them, and they too stood. Lantiah helped Jetara to support her. Moments later, Sundas jogged over, swooped Clatheta up into his arms and started back, followed by Jetara, five other women and two men. Cindra, and I ushered everyone else towards the food area.

The guards were busy eating and made no comment. One had removed his body armour, the others their helmets.

Those with the wettest clothing were taken to one of the carts to borrow whatever robes we had until theirs were clean and dry. Within a short time, almost every item of spare clothing was in use, and the drying lines were loaded.

The children were reunited with their parents, and the noise and smells brought everyone else out to mingle, although it was too early for many of them to eat.

The men joined Papa and the other leaders, some eager to know the schedule for the day and the others wanting to know about protecting themselves and their families.

After meeting the newcomers, many people congregated in the open area of the amphitheatre to talk with friends or join in some of the casually organised games.

When Papa had a moment of respite, I approached him again to ask one vital question. "What will you do with the men who were guarding the children?"

"We can give them a choice of where they want to go," he said.

"Ashistar thinks Gynbere will say either the guards are idiots who acted outside their instructions, or that they were a rogue element trying to make trouble for him. Either way, he'll distance himself from the kidnapping."

Papa nodded. "They may be glad to join us, simply to protect themselves."

I glanced along the top of the rise where Teema was signalling. "I think we're about to find out."

"Gynbere was quicker than I anticipated," said Papa.

"It is early for him. Perhaps he has finalised his plan," I said.

The first of Gynbere's guards entered and formed up in two lines to create a wide diagonal avenue from the entrance to where the table had been set up.

They were followed by Gynbere's favourites. The guards pushed them into the line to bulk it out.

Gynbere's ibith was even more decorated now. While the chair decorations remained, the material that had covered the legs of the chair had been replaced with grey. While it looked thick, it was dull. However it also covered the box base and part of the now enlarged platform. The whole thing was carried by twenty porters, all needed by the strain they showed. The back of his chair now had twenty prime tail feathers from the giija bird attached to the top. They were interspersed with secondary plumes.

A boy stood behind the chair fanning Gynbere with more of the feathers.

"That's so sad," I said to Oak. "Gijja don't moult until after they've mated. That won't happen for a while yet. Even if the guards didn't kill them, they don't mate without their feathers."

"That's a shame. Findlow told me about them when we found a feather on our trip here. He drew in the sand to show us what it looked like. He said they weren't good to eat, so it wasn't worth killing them." Oak stared at the feathers. "Twenty birds, I'd say."

"All male for the big feathers, so ten and a similar number of female. Those are the dark blue feathers being used in the fan. That's between thirty and forty eggs destroyed.

Probably a whole community."

He stared at me. "You think they took mating pairs?"

I nodded sadly. "When we began to teach Shurlyn and her group to forage, they understood the necessity of never taking all that nature offers in one place. The lesson must be well known. This destruction was for vanity alone."

"We should introduce Gynbere to Morkeen," Oak said with a laugh. "He'd think twice about taking anything after receiving the sharp edge of her tongue."

Gynbere waved and smiled to everyone as if they were there just to see him. The people lining the avenue cheered as he passed. When he was almost at the table, the ibith was placed on the ground, to the obvious relief of the porters.

Gynbere stood and waved to his people, especially his nobles as they bowed to him. He stared over at the other leaders, who congregated around Papa.

When it was obvious they were not going to bow to him, he allowed Slaslow to help him off the ibith and conduct him towards the table.

Papa met him half way and together they walked back to where many of the other leaders and family heads were gathered.

Gynbere eyed the chairs with distaste. All were identical. Gynbere would have sat in the chair in the centre, but Storm pulled it aside and offered it to Papa.

Gybere had no choice but to sit on his right. Before he sat, he glanced casually around the amphitheatre. His face hardened when he saw the empty corner to the southeast.

36

Kirym Speaks

"I must get Trethia up and dressed," I said.

Oak and I walked over to the dwelling I slept in. This was put aside for single women, and while I would normally have stayed with Mama and Papa, their dwelling was overflowing with other leaders and it had been easier for me to settle here.

I stood aside at the entrance as a group left, still adjusting their festival dresses.

We always had one 'awake' person in charge of each dwelling at night. They made sure problems were sorted quietly, and people were called to attend whatever job they had. Through the early morning, Bildon had the job, and she was still there, tidying up the last few things before taking a break.

"Is Trethia still asleep?" I asked.

"She must be," said Bildon. "I haven't seen her this morning." She pulled a pile of bedding aside. There was no one there. Bildon went pale. "She can't have left without me seeing. Where could she be?"

A quick check of the dwelling, including under the set where Trethia had hidden before showed nothing. Her dresses were still there, although her sleeping robe and over robe had disappeared with her.

"Don't worry, Bildon. She'll be close. You're not expected to keep an eye on everyone coming and going," I said, although I felt nothing like as calm as I sounded.

"Perhaps she went to play with the other children?" suggested Bildon.

I smiled my thanks, and nodded in agreement as I picked up the clean robe I had set out for Trethia and slipped outside.

Oak was reassuring when I told him, and made the same suggestion Bildon had.

"She won't be with the children. Shormel and Larqeba are fine with her, but those from The Rock follow their parent's guide. At best they ignore her, and she avoids them. The children from Faltryn and The Green Valley are wary of her because of the dwarflings." While I was explaining this, I scanned the vast area, hoping to see her.

She's safe, Kirym, Iryndal reassured me. *She's with Ubree.*

Oak followed me over to where the dragons were. Trethia was curled up asleep with her head on Ubree's left front leg.

"She arrived soon after you went onto the wall," said Iryndal softly. "She crawled in next to him and fell asleep immediately. Leave her until she is ready to waken. It won't be long."

"Kirym, I wanted a few moments with you. I have a small gift for you. No, no, nothing big or of value," Oak said, as I began to object. "Just something I picked up as you disappeared down the gorge." He pulled a wrapped package out of his hip pack and pressed it into my hands.

I opened the folds of material to find a shiny black stone. It was a similar size to the tokens, and seemed to pull me into it. When the sun hit it, there seemed to be a fire in the centre of it. It was one of the most beautiful things I had ever seen. I didn't know what to say.

"I found it lying on the ground after everyone had left. It was different to the other rocks there. It seemed like it didn't belong and I thought you may like it."

"Oh, it's lovely, Oak. Such a thoughtful gift. Thank you so much."

I thanked him profusely, rewrapped the stone and slipped it into my pocket as Trethia yawned and stretched. Oak and I moved closer to be with her when she woke.

I was surprised at how warm the area around Ubree was. He had kept Trethia comfortable and safe. "Thank you," I said, rubbing his shoulder.

"I like having her with me," he said.

Trethia's eyes opened, and she smiled up at us.

Oak went over to let Bildon know we had found Trethia, and to pick up her cloak and some soft boots Mama had found for her.

Trethia snuggled into me as the last vestiges of sleep left her. I was removing her night robe when Oak returned. Together we got her dressed. When she was ready, she hugged Ubree and thanked him for looking after her through the night.

"She's a treasure," said Oak.

"I can't understand why some dwarven family hasn't taken her in," I said. "She's so appealing."

"Well, come on, let's get some food before it's all gone and we have to beg it from the cooks." Oak picked Trethia up and swung her onto his back. She giggled with delight.

Platters of food had been placed along the long sides of two carts, and pushed into an area in front of the table. Papa and Gynbere were serving themselves. Many others ranged along the tables piling their platters high.

Papa guided a very sour looking Gynbere back to the table to eat.

"I wonder what's got up Gynbere's nose," said Oak as we wandered towards the carts.

"I think it's easy to make Gynbere unhappy," I said.

We joined the throng, and were waiting for it to move ahead, when Jetara quietly took my arm. "Can I talk to you?"

Shormel wandered up, and took Trethia from Oak's shoulder. "I'll look after her until you've chosen your food," he said.

Oak smiled. "I'll bring plenty over, Kirym. You keep out of the crush."

I allowed Jetara to guide me away.

Shormel produced two fibre balls. He sat on the ground with Trethia and threw one ball to her. She caught it and as she threw it back, he threw the second. Jetara watched to see that they were settled.

"I don't quite know how to put this," she said. "Kirym, you need to take care. The child is strange, and many people are unsettled by her."

"She's just a child, Jetara."

"Oh no. Not just anything. I've known her a long time. She never changes."

I waited as she struggled to choose her words.

"When I had seen the same seasons she had, she looked as she does now. She hasn't changed since then. She comes and she goes, but she always looks like that, although here she is obviously more cared for. She's strange, and unexplainable."

"Is it possible the child you knew," I said, "grew up as you did, and had a child?"

"I thought about that. But when Shormel was born she was there then, and every season since then. I could understand if it were many seasons between seeing her, but twelve winters have come and gone and nothing about her has changed." She paused. "The thing is, other people notice too. Many from The Rock are suspicious of her. Some are now saying she was planted there by you people."

"What? Why?" I paused. "How? We've only recently returned to The Green Valley."

"Kirym, I know that, but others are suspicious. They have been for many many seasons. My maman talked about her, and she says her maman did too. There's been trouble lately whenever she turns up. Anyone who helped her was threatened. A few people disappeared when they ignored the threats. I did what I could for her, but I had Shormel. I'd leave her food occasionally. Once I gave her a dress." Jetara smiled wistfully as she remembered. "She was so pleased. She was wearing it later that day, and so proud. Then a couple of guards, young lads really, came along and started in on her. It was the only time I ever heard her speak. She looked at me and shouted, 'Go away'. Then she turned and walked away. She didn't run, didn't acknowledge the guards, nothing. Later that day, one of the guards grabbed my arm, as I walked past, and handed me the dress. It was ripped to shreds and filthy. All he said was, 'Don't deal wi' scum. We know you.' It was a real threat, and I was frightened, for her as much as me and mine. When I saw her again, she just scuttled past." She shrugged.

"Were the guards always involved?"

Jetara nodded, frowning. "It seemed to get worse for her

when this Gynbere took the throne. There was a whisper that he'd ordered the guards to search for her hollow and destroy it, her too, if they could find her. I gather they filled her hollow in, although it was little more than a hole in a wall, but since then she's been sleeping in odd corners, under eaves, wherever she could find, and she never stayed in the same place for more than a night or two. She was kicked awake if she was found and ordered to move on." She had tears in her eyes. "I'm just saying be careful. She could ruin any chance there is of having peace. That's the general whisper."

I glanced at Trethia and realised that Shormel had arranged her so she was facing away from the crowd. I turned back as Oak placed two loaded platters in front of us. The children were called over, and again Trethia was sat so she wouldn't be obvious.

I squeezed Jetara's hand. "I'll sort it out." Oak looked at me inquiringly. I shook my head.

"Evidently Gynbere isn't happy he had to get his own food." Oak grimaced. "That others were able to eat at the same time he was, is apparently a bone of contention too."

Teema hunkered down between Oak and me. "The pavilion out there has been taken down. The workmen took it west. I sent Mekroe to follow them. He's just returned. He said they followed the trail they came in on and left it with a pile of other packs on the side of the path. It's not hidden, but then again ..." He shrugged.

"Why would Gynbere order that?" asked Oak.

"Because he doesn't intend staying," I said. "I imagine if he doesn't get what he wants, he'll leave quickly and plan some other way to get it. Teema, tell Papa quietly, or if he's not available, tell Armos."

"Why don't you tell him?"

I smiled. "I need to talk to Iryndal. Anyway, you saw it,

and as guard, you need to pass it on. It may not have been noticed by anyone else."

The dragons were all together as I approached. I knew that at least Iryndal had heard the conversation and I suspected they all had. It made it easy. No explanations were needed, no long-winded questions, and I could get right to the point. "Where did she come from?" I asked.

Iryndal, who normally answered my questions quickly, this time paused as if searching for words. Finally, with a look of resignation: "We don't know."

I waited, the uncomfortable silence lengthening.

Arymda sighed. "Borasyn spoke a while back of his mind skittering when he tried to think of something. This is happening to us all when we put our minds to her history. We know there was a time she wasn't here, but we can't pinpoint it in your history."

"When I think of her," said Iryndal, "I see her in The Rock. My knowledge of what happened inside that ghastly mausoleum is limited. Even Borasyn has nothing that makes sense."

"But he did have something?" I said.

"It was this, Kirym," said Ubree. "A double yolk emerged from that blighted nest. One went to light the morning sun, the other brought darkness to the western lands. Both became what they weren't. The gatekeeper lost control of the gate."

"Which means?"

No one answered.

"I can say that all Jetara told you is true," said Ubree, "and that the child is an important part of our past and future."

"When you say our future, do you mean that of the

dragons, the whole of the land, or you and me?"

Ubree had no answer for me.

We were distracted by a rise in the noise from over near the food table. Gynbere pushed through the crowd to his ibith. He climbed on and was carried down to his pavilion.

"What happened there, Iryndal?" I asked.

"He said the crowding around the table was overly excessive. He will return when the meeting begins."

It was mid-morning before everyone was ready and settled down in front of the big map table. Although there were a huge number of people there, the area wasn't crowded.

The dragons gathered in a circle near the stump, I sat chatting with a group just to the south of them. Trethia, Shormel and Larqeba sat nearby rolling balls to each other.

Runners had informed the various leaders that the meeting was about to start, and all had arrived except Gynbere, although he was on his way.

Because everyone was already seated, he was unable to bring his ibith close, and it sat at the edge of the crowd while he decided how to proceed.

37

Kirym Speaks

Thunder rolled across the sky.

Everyone jumped.

I looked up, but could see no reason why it would happen. The sky was blue, clear of clouds, and there was no wind. Thunder was the last thing I would have expected. A second peal of thunder sounded, and at the same time, my tokens thumped firmly on my forehead. Most unusual.

Again the tokens pulsed, and this time a large shadow flickered across the clearing.

I scanned the sky.

It could have been a large and distant bird, but I knew instantly. "Faltryn," I murmured.

"Is that what we saw at the inlet?" Teema asked quietly.

"Taking into account the heavy fog there at the time, I rather suspect it was," I said, standing to get a good look.

"It can't be Faltryn. Borasyn said he was white."

"He did," I said. "But that was when he was born and on

their planet. Time changes many things, and I am absolutely sure that *is* Faltryn."

The dragon hovered high above us for a moment. Then he folded his left wing in close to his body with a snap we could hear from the ground. With his right wing extended, he spiralled downwards like a sycamore seed, landing across the southern entrance to the amphitheatre. He blocked the entrance, his head and front legs west of it, and his tail snaking down to the east.

He was pitch black and huge, much bigger than Iryndal. He turned his head to look at the group I was with. His eyes opened, one deep red, the other blank.

Starshine gasped. "So he was in the cave. Oh, Kirym ..."

"No he wasn't," I said. "It's a trick."

He laughed and his eyes changed, now both dark grey. "Hmmm! A gathering I have not called."

"The Green Valley has never needed your permission to gather in their own land," said Iryndal.

Faltryn hissed.

"And," she continued, "we have an obligation to be here to help as and where we can."

"Really?"

"Yes, we do," interrupted Borasyn. "That is part of our obligations to the guardians of the land. Those promises were made when we first came here."

"And how would you know that?" asked Faltryn. "The eldest is the keeper of the early memories. You, need I point out, are not the eldest."

Borasyn rose to his feet, his scales erect. "The eldest is supposed to sing his memories so life can continue. You broke the cycle!"

"The youngest always retains some memories," said Iryndal gently. "They fade as the songs are sung, and the knowledge passed on. With no songs Borasyn's memories are growing.

He has shared them with us and we too remember. There's a reversal here, and there's only one way to stop it, Faltryn."

"You're the oldest and you're supposed to care for us and protect us. For many seasons, you have cared only for yourself," said Ubree. "That is against nature, and now nature is turning."

Faltryn took a deep breath, stood and drew himself up to his full height.

More than a few of those watching drew away from him, and a few slipped out of sight, into or behind dwellings. The rest sat big eyed and silent.

"These meddling interfering eavesdropping pests have poisoned your minds," he roared. "I am the oldest, and I forbid it."

"Forbid all you like," I said, shocking myself. "You cannot change it. It's not your place. You're here to assist those of the land."

He turned and hissed at me.

Something black shot across the open ground and skidded to a stop in front of me. Midnight stamped her foot. Her chest rumbled, sounding very like a growl. She stamped again, her head aggressively forward.

"Hinka, hinka, hinka." Faltryn sank down on his belly. "Your friends are loyal, Kirym. Perhaps I'll concede this round to you." He settled again, closed his eyes and ignored everyone.

Across the clearing, conversations started up again, initially subdued, but then becoming more normal as everyone realised there was no threat against them. We were all aware of the resting dragon, though.

Midnight trotted over to me. I put my arm around her and scratched her chest. She snuggled against me for a few moments, and then began nibbling at the grass.

"Gynbere looked positively sick when Faltryn arrived,"

said Oak. "I wonder why. I thought he'd collapse when he first saw him."

Kirym! Iryndal hadn't spoken, but it felt like she had screamed at me. I spun around, alarmed.

Borasyn lay with his head on the tree stump.

I ran over to him, arriving at the same time as a distressed Arymda.

His breath was shallow, he looked pale. "It's time," he said. "The best time in my life, was meeting ..." His eyes closed. He was dead.

"It will soon take us all," said Iryndal. "This may be the last death we have. We lack the knowledge to take life forward. Only Faltryn can change it."

As she spoke, Arymda and Egrym slumped beside Borasyn and closed their eyes.

"Somewhere there is knowledge," said Othyn. "Find it, and use it for your people, Kirym." Then she too was gone.

Moments later, Ubree and Iryndal joined them. All six dragons were dead.

Faltryn lay, as still as his siblings, but his chest rose and fell as he breathed.

"Are you all right, Kirym?" Mama's arm was around my shoulder. She hugged me to her.

I nodded numbly.

"What can we do?" she asked.

I felt stunned, empty. I wished I could join the dragons, lie down and sleep, put off the decisions and the responsibilities.

I felt everyone was watching me, waiting to see what I decided. I glanced around. Even Faltryn was watching from across the amphitheatre, and I had the distinct impression he was holding his breath.

"We carry on as planned," I said in a loud clear voice.

Faltryn breathed out and closed his eyes again.

38

Arbreu

The leaders all gathered at the table. Veld formally called everyone to meet the leaders of the families of the land.

"I would introduce you to Bryn from the Southern Escarpment, Churnyg of the Oak Branch of the Tree People, Findlow of the Lakes, Garanniis of Valythia, Gynbere of the Yew branch, Imolay of the Ash Branch, Lorythma of the Willow Branch, Loul of The Green Valley, Raff of the Hills, Sirasha of the Beech Branch, Tartharn of the Chestnut Branch, Wind Runner of the Northern Caves named Faltryn, Storm of Faltryn, and I am Veld, Voice of The Green Valley."

As he called their names, each leader stood, acknowledged Veld and the crowd, and sat again, except Gynbere who merely lifted his hand in response. There was a pause as everyone settled.

"Why are Storm and Loul up there?" asked Larqeba.

"Storm is there as Wind Runner's adviser," said Kirym.

"He sat beside her in that capacity at Faltryn. Mama is our headwoman. She's not just Papa's wife, she's headwoman by birth."

"So if Loul and Veld disagreed," persisted Larqeba, "who would decide?"

Kirym smiled. "I've never known them not to agree. They talk things through, however, Mama makes the final decision."

"Why are the guild leaders not there?" asked Shormel.

"Because they're guides," said Oak, "not leaders."

"And why is Gynbere looking so sour?" asked Lyndym.

"He wanted Papa to introduce him as supreme leader of the amalgamated tribes of the land between the seas," said Mekrar. "The other leaders objected before Papa could say anything. The Beech leader said he had no right to claim that title, especially as it covered The Green Valley, Faltryn's Fortress and Valythia."

Arbreu glanced around the open area.

Those loyal to Gynbere and his guards remained together in the eastern part of the clearing, but everyone else mingled. The dragons, except Faltryn, lay dead near the tree stump, ignored by almost everyone there. Kirym sat near the dragons, surrounded by a large group of friends. Faltryn lay where he landed and seemed to be as dead as his siblings, although occasionally his eyelids flickered.

Veld called for silence, but before he could say anything else, Gynbere stood and cleared his throat loudly.

"I would speak to the people, Veld."

Veld looked questioningly at the other leaders, and getting no objection from them, nodded.

"You've set yourself up as arbiter of the land and the people," Gynbere said. "I don't agree you should hold this position. However, before we debate that—"

"There is nothing to debate," interjected Garanniis. "Veld

is Voice of The Green Valley and this is The Green Valley. We are here as his guests, and we should be thankful he has extended friendship to so many people in such a short time."

"Gynbere has changed his way of speaking," Arbreu murmured. "None of the waffle he used when he condemned Churnyg."

Kirym smiled stiffly. "He's not a fool. He realises he wouldn't get away with that here. I wonder what his people think about it."

"He's ignoring Mama," said Mekrar. "He obviously doesn't think she's important."

Arbreu's attention returned to Gynbere, who again cleared his throat loudly.

"Ahem! This land has been empty of all except we who lived in The Rock. I own it by right of long possession and use. Veld's people deserted this land. I should be standing where he is."

Kirym stood, waiting to be recognised. Gynbere ignored her. It was a deliberate snub, and flouted the accepted protocol which had been explained to everyone.

There was a murmur of annoyance from many in the crowd.

"I see you, Kirym," said Veld, cutting Gynbere off as he cleared his throat again.

"Only recently, Gynbere, you said The Rock was impenetrable, and we of The Green Valley could stand outside and do our worst. By implication, you separated yourself from the rest of the land."

Shurlyn raised her hand and was acknowledged. "Gynbere always told us we were unable to live in the land. It was off limits to the Tree People. He claimed we should be separate from The Green Valley because the people of this land would enslave us or kill us. He accepted that we were part of The

Green Valley but by staying separate, he could decide our fate."

Amid a lot of head-nodding, Gynbere turned his back on Kirym, and glanced at the heads of the families. "It's irrelevant how I sought to protect my people from the lies our enemies told us in the past. The fact is I've spent time in the land for many seasons, and it has been empty."

Kirym stood again and was acknowledged. "A wanderer has no right to claim to a whole land just because the part he saw was empty for a time. You were still in The Rock and claiming separation when you learned we had returned. You avoided us. Was that because when you did visit over the seasons, you simply stole what we stored behind bolted doors? Having taken all you wished, you hoped we wouldn't find out about you. When Salcan visited and you realised he may have figured out the truth, you tried to kill him."

"This whole land thing is really unimportant," snapped Gynbere, "and perhaps left to a later debate. There is something of more significance to discuss and it may resolve this whole issue. I accept Veld as headman of his people, but there is a higher title everyone needs to acknowledge and that is my position."

"And what position is that?" Wind Runner asked caustically.

Gynbere drew himself to his maximum height. "The title of Great Leader of all Lands. That title is mine by right of birth."

"This was not an office held by your sire or grandsire," said Lorymtha of the Willow branch. "You can scarcely claim it as an inheritance."

"My sire gave me nothing," snarled Gynbere. "I have long held the knife, shield and sword of power. Ownership of them gives me all I claim."

"These items of power. Where are they? You don't seem

to be carrying them," interjected Wind Runner, eyebrows raised.

"They've been mine for hundreds of seasons, but recently I was robbed. I demand the return of my property," Gynbere screamed, "I demand satisfaction."

"But where are they?" asked Loul calmly.

Gynbere pointed at Kirym. "She stole them."

"That's a serious accusation, Gynbere," said Storm. "I hope you are sure of your facts."

Gynbere's eyes bulged, his face red. "She's wearing them! They're mine!" he snarled. "They were in my possession until just a few short days ago. My family have held these," he paused and looked around, "these precious items," he took a deep breath, "safely for many generations. I am required, indeed it is part of the obligations to my ancestors, to retain these treasures for my grandchildren, their grandchildren and theirs beyond that. This girl, this thief, crept into my private rooms and stole the box that held them."

"How big was the box?" called Findlow.

Gynbere paused, thrown by the question, but one of his guards stepped forward. "As wide as that man is tall, and twice that for length," he said pointing to Storm.

Findlow laughed. "Oh I can just see Kirym throwing that over her shoulder and walking off with it."

Gynbere paused, suddenly pale. He growled under his breath. "How she did it matters not," he said, "She has them! They're mine! I WANT THEM BACK!"

"What other information is there about these items?" asked Veld.

"You shouldn't need more information. My word should be enough. When the moon was last dark, she did not have them. I did!"

"No, you didn't." A labyrinth guard stood and silently acknowledged Veld.

"How can a labyrinth guard live outside the labyrinth?" murmured Shurlyn.

"Who dares oppose me?" Gynbere thundered.

"Thirteen winters past," continued the guard, "you sought to destroy the items in the box. Using all of the wood you could scrounge, you built a huge fire and threw the box containing them on. The weapons have not been seen since. You wanted to have no part of them then, because you were unable to remove them from the box. Fearing to touch even the ashes, you had them thrown to the winds."

"Is this true?" asked Veld.

"It has no relevance. They belong to me," snapped Gynbere.

"When something is thrown to the winds, the winds take them and do as they will," said Wind Runner.

"I threw the ashes, not the weapons. They were placed on the fire to fulfil an old prophecy."

"And when the fire was done, what did you do with the weapons?" asked Garanniis.

Gynbere took a deep breath.

"Oh, they weren't in the ashes." the guard interjected quickly.

"Lies!" screamed Gynbere. "Kill him!"

Four guards unsheathed their swords and advanced towards the labyrinth guard.

"Stop!" shouted Veld, leaping onto the table. "Anyone who causes a death here, will pay a similar price, as will the person who ordered it." He looked around the amphitheatre, his face like thunder. "Put away your swords. If you raise your weapon to another, even on the order of a leader, you will pay heavily. You are all warned."

"And how would a labyrinth guard know what happened in Gynbere's private rooms?" muttered Shurlyn. "They live in the labyrinth, and as I understood it, they die if they leave."

"And yet he is here," murmured Kirym, "as I think are many others from the labyrinth. Another lie perpetrated by Gynbere, perhaps."

"None of this is relevant," snarled Gynbere. "Whatever has happened to the contents of the box while in my possession, they are still mine and have been in my family for all remembered time."

"No, they haven't. The knife Kirym carries was never in your possession and indeed, it only recently came to this land." Zelriff stepped out of the crowd. "May I speak, Veld?"

He nodded. "I see you, Zelriff."

"The knife lived in the land between the gorges for as many seasons as our families lived there. It is written about on the first page of our memory book and there was a fine drawing of it alongside. Kirym claimed it from when she first saw it. Therefore Gynbere cannot have held it, and if that is a lie, what else is? Kirym claimed it early in her life." Zelriff looked up at those sitting at the table. "When was that, Loul?"

"Kirym took possession of the knife at the beginning of spring," Loul paused, "thirteen season cycles ago."

Gynbere was white with anger. "It matters not that they were separated over the seasons. They go together and they are rightfully mine."

"I'm sure they do go together," said Zelriff. "But perhaps the rightful owner is Kirym. She carries them, it seems you never did."

"It matters not where they have been, they were given to my family, for me. It was foretold there would be a prophesy telling what the future held. That prophesy was revealed at my birth. It said then that I would hold them for eternity. It is written down in the scrolls that tell our history. Check those if you doubt me."

"These scrolls should be studied," said Loul, "and discussed. Who holds them?"

Sirasha, the oldest dwarf at the table stood and shuffled forward. "The Beech family are holders of the history, and certainly it goes back past Gynbere's birth. A prophesy was given at that birth, but we have no knowledge of it being foretold. Nor was it ever made public as to when or how the sword arrived in the care of the Yew family. Sadly, that part of our history was destroyed in a fire."

While Sirasha was talking, four younger men brought a large woven basket forward, placed it at his feet and removed the lid. It was full of scrolls.

"The men are his grandsons," explained Shurlyn. "They protect those scrolls, with their lives if necessary."

"So how did a fire destroy some of them?" asked Kirym.

"Many people would like to know that."

Sirasha studied the collection of scrolls in the basket and pointed to a section. His eldest grandson chose a scroll and held it up to him. Sirasha studied notations engraved on the edge of the roller and handed it back. A second, third, fourth and fifth were returned before he nodded and approached the centre of the table.

Veld cleared a stack of parchment off the table in front of him, and Sirasha rolled the scroll out. He bent over it, studying the long lines of writing, back and forth, up and down along the columns. As he rejected each portion, he rolled it up. Eventually he straightened up and pointed to a section.

"This is it." He cleared his throat and held the scroll up. "It says: The news went out that the dwarfling's arrival was imminent. Those needed were called together, and with them came Finnama, ancient sage of the Willow family. She watched the birth, and when he breathed his first breath, she took him and wrapped him in a cloak made of fine willow fibre. She closed her eyes and began to speak. Her words were thus: 'In the days of this child, a great leader will rise and bring peace to the land. This leader will liberate the tribes from their fetters and, as in the days of times gone by, they will roam free in the lands and they will again explore to the edge of the universe. They will not live enslaved one to another. They will again be friends and help each other. This Great Leader will take Melith, Oakenrock, Tamweir and Zandahem and will unite the tribes into one family.'"

Gynbere looked triumphant. "Now give me the power!" he demanded.

"There is more," said Sirasha querulously. "I will read to the end." He studied the writing to find his place. "Ahem. 'The claimant of the sword must be worthy of it. Such power will turn on the pretender who is undeserving. The price will be monumental.'" He looked up and began to reroll the scroll. "That is all that was written, but I can assure everyone here. It is scribed exactly as it was said on the day of the birth. Whether it means what you think, well that is for the wisest of the wise to decide."

Handing the scroll to his grandson, he bowed towards Veld and returned to his seat.

Kirym walked into the centre of the amphitheatre and drove the sword into the ground. It quivered with the force of the thrust.

Faltryn opened his eyes, rose to his feet and stared down at Gynbere. "Take it if you have the courage, little man, but think carefully about that prophesy. Did you free your people? Had you done that, you may have had a legitimate claim to the weapons. Have you not done the opposite and further enslaved them? Did you fostered what they held dear? What happened to those who stood up to you? It is said that those with knowledge have a greater responsibility to guide those without. What knowledge did you have, Gynbere?"

In the silence that followed, Gynbere frowned. "The knowledge you gave me, lizard," he spat.

"Hincka, hincka, hincka. Perhaps you didn't really listen to the conversation. Maybe you heard the words but totally missed the meaning. It is within the realm of possibility that you heard what you wanted to hear."

"Which items are you claiming, Gynbere?" asked Loul.

"The sword, the knife and the shield."

Loul nodded. "And yet four items were mentioned in the scroll."

"Melith, Oakenrock, Tamweir, Zandahem," intoned Faltryn.

"The sword and knife connect." Gynbere spoke slowly. "I believe the connection was important enough to be named."

"Hincka, hincka, hincka." Faltryn sank onto his belly, his head on his front feet. His body vibrated with laughter. "Self-given belief is a dangerous game. Would the four belong to someone who has no knowledge? The girl has far more understanding. Hincka, hincka, hincka."

"What would a mere child know?" demanded Gynbere. He advanced towards Kirym. "What knowledge do you have?" he screamed.

"Keep your secrets, child." Sirasha's querulous interjection cut through Gynbere's screams of rage. "The wise know of riddles and mysteries and secrets. Only a fool would share with those who are undeserving. When time lightens, you can use your knowledge, for then it will not be able to be taken by those who'd steal what they neither own nor deserve."

Gynbere swung around with a curse. "The loyalty of the Beech was promised to me under oath, Sirasha. You shame your family with such treachery."

Sirasha slowly stood. "I have shown no disloyalty. I tell

the truth, as my family are required by birth, by occupation and by old law to do. I was most careful in the words I used in that oath. Would you like me to read out what I was required to say, and what indeed I did say?"

Gynbere stared at him, frowning.

"While we have remained silent in times past," continued Sirasha, "we did so because we had no other choice. Now we do. Good or bad, right or wrong. Everyone now makes a decision. Failure to do the right thing could cause calamity. We are at a dawn of a new time. Decide whether your actions will stand the full light of day."

"We people of The Rock must stand together to overthrow those who threaten us," screamed Gynbere.

Tartharn Chestnut stood and advanced towards Gynbere. "These people are not our enemy. They do not threaten us. They have shown us nothing but kindness. They have not killed my family, threatened them with extermination. They have not starved them, subjugated them. It is NOT a case of them against us."

Gynbere heaved the map table over, stamped across it, pushed his way through the crowds sitting on the ground around the table and threw himself into his chair. "Slaslow," he barked.

With the porters scattered around the amphitheatre, only twelve of the twenty were close enough to get to the ibith quickly enough. The order to pick it up came too early, they were unable to cope with the load. The platform teetered alarmingly. With too much strain on the chair, and one of the brackets holding it to the platform broke.

Gynbere screamed with fright.

Five soldiers grabbed the platform to support it. Being taller than the porters, it seesawed wildly. Gynbere's progress to his pavilion was fraught. The chair rocked from side to side with each step. Unable to remain on it, he finished the journey on his hands and knees.

An undignified exit.

On arriving at his pavilion, Gynbere stalked over to the doorway, and yelled for a chair.

About ten of his followers finally caught up with him, and joined Slaslow around Gynbere's seat. Voices occasionally rose and the group scattered occasionally as he lashed out at them with his whip.

The throaty echo of Faltryn's laughter vibrated in the background.

In the lull the table was righted, the maps and platters picked up, and the mess of ruined food was cleared away. Loul checked that no one was hurt and then spoke to the cooks and servers.

A basket of flasks was offered to those sitting at the table. Others were circulated through the crowd sitting around them. It seemed the right time for a break, everyone wanted to talk about what had happened.

Arbreu turned to Mekrar. "Does he have any claim to Kirym's knife?"

"Of course he doesn't. It hasn't been in this land for hundreds of seasons. He has never held it, and I don't see how any of his ancestors can ever have held it. I suspect he didn't know about it until recently. If he knew the four names, he might have leapt to claim the knife to make his claim seem more plausible."

"But how could he know about it at all?" asked Arbreu

"Kirym brandished it when he tried to kill Churnyg," said Mekrar.

"There was a picture in The Rock," said Churnyg. "It was said to be drawn by one of Gynbere's ancestors. It showed a young woman holding the sword and shield. I never realised what it meant, but thinking about it now, I'd say she was the previous holder. The knife was attached to the woman's thigh. She wasn't a tree dwarf. I wonder if she was headwoman of The Green Valley. The picture disappeared soon after this Gynbere took over. I heard a whisper that it was in his rooms. Rargo may have seen it and made the connection." Churnyg laughed. "Gynbere must be cursing that he tried to claim it. It really put a doubt on his whole assertion."

"It doesn't matter what he says. It was Kirym's from the first time she saw it. Papa let Kirym hold it long before I was allowed to carry a knife," said Mekroe.

Teema laughed. "Really? Not quite, Mek. You were given the use of a knife a season or so earlier. As I remember you indiscriminately stabbed a stag carcass, ruined the pelt, cut most of Mekrar's hair off, sliced her ear, chopped the toe off one of Veld's festival boots, decimated five fruit trees and wandered around slashing at anything and everything in sight. We were scared for our lives."

Amid the laughter, Starshine took Mek's hand. "Come on, let's get some food before it's all gone. Show them you've learned the proper use of a knife."

"Kirym, why do so few people see the dragons?" asked Teema. "The dead one's I mean."

"Well I think it's partly to protect them while they're dead."

"But we see them."

"Because we know them, their personalities. We've spent time with them," she said.

"I don't see them all the same. I mean, to me, Arymda is much clearer than the others."

"I think you've had a good experience with Arymda. You know a little more about her than some of the others. It takes time to become friends."

Around them, everyone mingled and talked over the morning's surprises as they shared their food.

Kirym wandered over to check on the dead dragons. "Things are happening over there," she said as she returned.

Arbreu stood and studied the scene. A group of men were entering the amphitheatre. They were all wearing armour and carrying weapons. "Where did they come from?"

Teema glanced to the eastern guards. "The signal from the wall says they came through the trees from the south."

There was a small commotion at the pavilion door and then Gynbere, two men in grey robes and one in a full length black cloak paraded south along the eastern wall. All except Gynbere had their hoods pulled forward. It was impossible to see their faces. Gynbere carried a thick pole.

"Oh my goodness," said Kirym, when she saw it. "Where's Bryn."

"On his way over here," said Mekrar. "Papa's coming too."

"You see what he's holding?" demanded Bryn, as he approached.

Kirym nodded. "It proves what we really knew."

Bryn half smiled. "And yet I was angry. I guess because I hoped Rargo hadn't started the fire, and this really proves he did."

"What's going on?" asked Teema.

Kirym explained what happened to Bryn's dwelling and possessions.

"Why is Gynbere carrying the pole?" asked Bryn. "Does he think I'll force Veld to attack to get it back? It isn't important."

"Did you ever explain that to Rargo?" Kirym asked. "Because if you didn't, then he may assume he has something of huge value. It was only held when you talked of important things. And it was the only item remaining in the case when you left the lodge. Perhaps neither of them realise the pole was only a piece of wood."

Bryn started to laugh. "You have to see the funny side."

"So what do you want me to do?" asked Veld.

"Ignore it," said Kirym. "That may make Gynbere angrier. He's looking to get a response of some sort, and he's more likely to react when he doesn't get it. Be prepared, Papa. Then wait and see what he does next."

It wasn't long in coming. One of the men removed his cloak.

Rargo.

Arbreu glanced around the amphitheatre. No one was taking any notice.

After parading up and down for a while longer, an obviously irate Gynbere led the way back to the pavilion.

39

Teema Speaks

"What happens now, Kirym?" I asked.

"The talks will carry on as planned. Mama and Papa will listen to everyone's needs. They plan to give each family a few options. Some family groups will want to be near each other, others will want strong support nearby."

"I guess some families will make obvious choices. There's a chestnut grove northwest of here. I imagine it will become the preserve of that family"

"Not necessarily, Teema. They may want to live near the Beech family. I gather they're close, and as both groups are comparatively small, they may opt to live together. There's a copse of beech trees near the settlement. But both families have a choice. Originally all of the dwarves lived in one community, so that may eventually be the ultimate aim."

"How do you know these things, Kirym?" Oak asked.

She laughed. "I studied Borasyn's pictures. From listening to the dragons, I gather the pictures are fairly accurate."

Enliah knelt in front of me, smiled and handed me a large platter of bread and fruit. "Can I get you anything else, Teema?"

"Oh good, I'm really hungry." Arbreu grabbed the platter, took a large piece of bread and handed it to Larqeba. "Mmmm." He bit into a roll of bread. "We could do with a platter of meat, Enliah."

"It's generous of you to share your meal with us, Enliah," said Kirym. "But join us, perhaps someone else can get the meat, if we really need it."

Enliah squashed herself between Kirym and me. It was a squeeze, but Kirym moved over to give her more room.

Kirym took the platter off Larqeba and offered it to Enliah. When the basket of flasks arrived, she offered them to Enliah first.

Moments later, Dashlan joined us. "Who was the labyrinth guard who challenged Gynbere? It can't have been Ashistar. His uniform's still with our stuff."

"I tried to have a look at it," said Larqeba through a mouth full of food, "but Pa wouldn't let me."

"You weren't looking, weed," Dashlan laughed. "You were trying it on. That's what Pa objected to."

"Such a nosy little beast," Enliah sneered. "Poor Ashistar will end up with all your nasty little guublies."

Fists clenched, Larqeba launched himself at her. "I don't have guublies!! You have!"

Sundas leaned forward and hauled him back by his tunic. "Men don't hit girls, Larqeba."

"She's not a girl, she's my sister and anyway she started it."

Enliah smirked.

"Well, be man enough to rise above her petty childish comments, lad," said Sundas.

Enliah gasped, burst into tears and flounced off.

Kirym spun around, her eye's blazing. "Go and apologise—"

"But—" interrupted Larqeba, indignantly.

"Sundas," she continued, as if Larqeba hadn't spoken. "If you intend to tell her off, do so. But don't make mean backhanded remarks. She doesn't deserve that."

Sundas took a deep breath. "Aye well, she started it."

"Then be man enough to rise above it."

Sundas chuckled. "Ahhck! She's right, lad. Come on, let's go and do it together."

Hand in hand Sundas and Larqeba wandered after Enliah.

"She is strange," said Arbreu. "She's so sulky. Cries whenever anyone even looks at her."

"She's sensitive and overwhelmed," said Kirym. "She's trying to fit in and finding it hard. It doesn't help that everything she was sure of has changed. All of her hopes and dreams have been dashed."

"She's hard work," grumbled Arbreu.

Kirym shook her head. "When I was upset and scared about my life changing, you were there for me. Her needs are no different. Because she's your sister, you should be more aware and caring, not less."

"She only wants to fit in with Teema, and anyway I don't know her like I know you."

"You didn't know me at the start either. She's lonely. If you include her, you will get to know her."

"Qwinita fits in. Why can't Enliah be like her?" I asked.

"She's not Qwinita, Teema, and didn't she just try to fit in? You two were no help at all."

The noise in Gynbere's camp rose. Many of his armed guards seemed to be milling around aimlessly. There was a bit of pushing and jostling.

I watched them, wondering what was going on.

A small group of guards removed their helmets and walked away, aiming for the area where the fyrsha skin was leaning against the wall. For the first time I got a good look at them. Their tree affiliations were obvious now I knew what to look for.

"Ah, there you are, Kirym. A message for you." Twig hunkered down and handed her a small package. "One of Gynbere's guards asked me to give it to you. He said to tell you armed guards were to come through the south gate. They couldn't because there was a dragon in the way. He sounded quite amused. Do you know what it means?"

She opened the package. Laying in the centre of the leather was a single cream dragon scale.

"That's one of the things Ashistar st..." I paused, "well it was taken from your pocket, Kirym, and whoever took it betrayed us. It had to be Ashistar."

"If Ashistar took it, why would he now return it and warn us? This came from Borboncha. He's told us that Gynbere planned an attack, but was thwarted by Faltryn. Where is the guard, Twig?"

"He disappeared into the crowd."

"We've got to tell Papa." She slipped the scale into her pocket and stood.

I glanced across at Gynbere's camp.

Another group of guards appeared to be following the first. These were in formation and they carried their weapons at their sides. A small armour-clad figure ran out from beside Gynbere, and joined them.

"It's just an argument between the different groups of guards," said Shurlyn. "Happens a lot. Gynbere plays them off against each other."

"Something's wrong," murmured Kirym. "Teema, run! Warn Papa! Quickly." She pushed me firmly. "Go!"

The small figure in black had surged ahead of the others.

Then he turned sharply off his path, raced towards the sword Kirym had stabbed into the ground. He grabbed it, swung it around his head and let go.

The sword flew straight, and pierced Faltryn's chest. He roared with pain.

The armed soldiers faltered in their walk away from Gynbere's pavilion. Then they sped up. Their battle cry echoed across the amphitheatre and, weapons now pointed, they and aimed towards the table where many of the leaders still sat talking after their shared meal.

"They're attacking!" screamed Kirym.

"To arms!" yelled Arbreu, and knife in hand, ran to intercept them. Men from all over the camp grabbed their weapons and raced forward. The men on the ramparts picked up the bows and arrows we had stored up there. I was pleased Kirym had suggested every guard up there have them to hand.

I was dimly aware that the soldier who had grabbed the sword had dropped to the ground.

Kirym moved fast. With her knife in hand, she turned in her run towards the top table and raced towards Faltryn, screaming.

In the moments it took for me to register that Kirym was not sprinting into battle, I realised what she had shouted.

"SING! SING OR HE'S WON!"

With only my hunting knife at hand, I sprinted after Kirym, cursing at having left my bow rolled up beside my sleeping gear. A guard raced towards her from my left. I sped up and punched out. My fist glanced off his cheek and jammed into his helmet. He raised his sword, but faltered and fell. An arrow protruded from his neck. Then Oak was at my shoulder, and we swung around to protect Kirym.

She had her arms around Faltryn's neck, comforting him. Three guards charged towards us, their swords raised.

The middle one faltered an arrow in his armpit. He fell, but the other two came on, and we were fighting.

One raised his sword defending, as most fighters do, against my right.

My left-handed thrust took him by surprise, and as he shifted his stance to cope, my knife slipped under his guard and slashed his left leg deeply. He paused and I stabbed again, this time I aimed for his hand. He fell to his knees. I grabbed his sword and kneed him in the jaw. He toppled to the ground.

"Teema!" Mekroe threw me a bow, I grabbed a handful of arrows from a fallen guard.

Five soldiers raced up the length of Faltryn's body towards Kirym and as I aimed for the front runner, Faltryn swung his tail across the ground, sending them rolling head over heels. The dwarf I aimed for summersaulted and my arrow pierced his behind.

With my back to Kirym, Oak at my left and Wind Runner's men on the bank above us, I shot arrow after arrow at Gynbere's soldiers.

"Aim for their neck or armpit," panted Oak. "They're less protected there."

Mekrar joined us carrying three full quivers. "Only the helmeted ones," she gasped. "The others have joined us."

Gynbere's soldiers were now retreating. Bunched together, their armour now proved effective against our weapons.

"They have hostages," yelled Sundas. He picked up a club from the ground and threw it. Deadly accurate, and thrown with force, one guard fell.

The rest stepped away from him, closed ranks and continued their withdrawal.

Sundas darted in, grabbed the club and threw it again. Another guard down. He followed them down the amphitheatre, stunning guard after guard.

The hostages had been hooded, completely covered and had their arms tied to their sides. Each captive had a guard on each side, and one back and front. They were all surrounded by more guards.

I wondered who had been taken.

As they passed to the east of us, Faltryn again flicked his tail. A group of eight, one of them a hostage, went flying. Arrows flew into the group, not doing a lot of damage, but giving Churnyg, Arbreu and Armos time to race in, grab the hostage and haul him to safety.

Then the soldiers were at Gynbere's camp, and beating a controlled retreat to the north-eastern entrance.

Tarl had men lined up to impede the retreat and Oak and I raced to join them.

"We need to capture Gynbere," gasped Tarl.

It was impossible. Quite a few people had been herded along with the attacking army, having raced to the southern area of the amphitheatre to escape the initial fighting. They were pushed along by armed guards. The odd body lying in their wake showed the futility of resisting. Already healers were bending over them to sort the dead from the living.

Our attack was hampered, we were reluctant to attack any who weren't soldiers.

"He's too well guarded," said Armos, "Try to free the hostages. I wonder why Gynbere's taking his seat thing. It's unwieldy. It'll slow him down."

"The porters are well trained," said Arbreu, slipping in beside me. "He's protected by the back of the chair."

Arbreu was right, the thick wooden back bristled with an assortment of arrows and spears.

The porters reached the entrance to the amphitheatre. At the same time, Grenin led a group of men along the top of the bank above it to fire arrows and clubs directly onto them. Gynbere, in full armour was safe, but a number of the guards fell.

Following Sundas' example, clubs and spear shafts were used against the porters, rather than arrows, for they were not in armour and had never used a weapon against us. Those left standing couldn't carry the bulky base and chair.

As they fell, the ibith swayed and tipped. Gynbere felt it going. He leapt onto the back of one of his bigger guards, was surrounded by others, and they ran.

Those left carrying the falling ibith found themselves overrun and surrounded. Two of the front porters abandoned their load and tried to push their way to freedom. One managed to break through, but as he entered the trees to follow Gynbere, he slowed, turned around and gave himself up.

"Here I may have a chance of living," he said as he returned.

40

Teema Speaks

"I wonder where they're going. The Rock isn't as easy to defend as it was." Armos grunted with satisfaction as his arrow pierced the armour of one of the rear guards.

Churnyg laughed dryly. "Parts of it will be. If he gets men on the walls, they can shoot at any who approach."

"They won't," I said. "They can't," and I told them about seeing the complete collapse of the walls while flying with Borasyn.

Mekroe laughed. "So that was the rumble we heard. Churnyg's people packed up and walked on before we'd even eaten. They thought it was one of Gynbere's dastardly plans. We travelled a long way that day."

Armos organised for the captured and wounded to be collected, taken to a healing area or guarded as necessary. A new larger healing area was set up east of the stump.

I headed a group of men to follow the captives.

Gynbere's guards were well trained. They moved fast, much faster than when they travelled before, but not so fast as to allow those at the back to fall behind and become vulnerable.

Initially they seemed to want only to get away, but just before midday we found ourselves at the top of a small tree-lined incline facing the charge of a solid wedge of soldiers. Although we had the higher ground, they had the advantage of surprise and numbers. Our lack of armour was a disadvantage, although we could move faster. In the race from the amphitheatre, many of us had picked up swords and shields, and most of us held bows. In this type of fight, arrows were of no use and our opponents were more experienced with swords than we were.

Because they came at us from close quarters, in the ensuing battle we sustained more wounded than previously. A trumpet called their retreat before they could push their advantage. They left eight on the ground. Five were wounded and three dead. Four of our men were wounded beyond their ability to fight.

We tied the prisoners up, made the wounded comfortable and took a short breather.

"Our arrows aren't doing too well against them," said Oak.

"Ashistar said the armour is made of multiple thicknesses of leather," said Granite.

One of the prisoners laughed. "Oh they're much better than that. The armour is made of metal disks stitched onto padded linen and covered with layers of leather. Even a direct hit will deflect your arrows. Our men are invincible. Your weapons and protection are sadly lacking."

"We trusted that no one would attack after promises of peace while at a family gathering," I snapped.

"Only a fool depends on others thinking as they do," he said, smirking.

Oak grasped my arm and shook his head.

We re-formed into a fighting group to follow the hostages.

"The prisoner gave us vital information about the armour," I said. "Why?"

"I suspect it's a loose boast, and they're more vulnerable than they care to admit?" Oak frowned. "We've held our own for the most part. Despite his boast, their hands, neck, lower leg, and face are generally unprotected. Under their arms too. That's where we aim."

"So when they raise their swords to charge," I said, "we shoot."

The land here was covered with trees. Most had seen twelve to fourteen springs, interspersed with massive older growth. Little of the undergrowth had been deprived of sun for long enough to have died out. Aware of the ease of concealment, we were forced to keep our speed down.

We caught occasional glimpses of our opponents as they ran ahead of us, never close enough to shoot, but sufficient to encourage us to follow.

Secondary growth ahead was thicker though, and I scanned the area to see if there was a less dense path. There was a flash of sunlight between the trees to my far right. That seemed to me to be the obvious path. Why bring us so far over this way? I wondered. They appear to want us to follow them.

"Ambush," I screamed, grabbing Storm's arm and halting his momentum.

He hesitated and looked back at me

They attacked!

They had lain in wait in the thick undergrowth. My scream had pushed them to break cover earlier than they planned. Their swords were heavy and unwieldy, and in the close fighting we were able to rely on our knives. We manoeuvred better in the dense growth without armour than they could with it. Because they had further to come to get to us, it gave us a slight advantage.

They fought fiercely. Just as I thought they were gaining the upper hand, they were again called to retreat. Oak, standing at my right shoulder mirrored my deep sigh of relief.

As they backed away, a small group of them broke cover from the bush to our right, pushed past Mekroe and Arbreu and surrounded Storm. Taken by surprise, he was quickly disarmed. In one swift movement he was captured, knocked out, and they retreated.

With a scream of rage, Mekroe threw himself at them, grabbed Storm and hauled him back. They all fell in a jumbled heap, and guards from the main group stepped in with clubs and swords.

We raced to protect Mekroe and Storm, but six guards shouldered Storm's body and ran. We were faced with a wall of soldiers, who backed off slowly, giving the bearers time to get away. They left three of their own unconscious.

Mekroe too, lay senseless on the ground. Two more of our men were injured, one groaning, the other, silent, but breathing.

"Come on," I shouted, grabbing Oak's arm. Arbreu mirrored my steps, his bow primed. Twig and Blacknight fell in behind us.

We cut across the grove to where the trees were clear of undergrowth.

The soldiers had a good advance on us, but I aimed and fired. One fell, the arrow deep in his back. They closed ranks and left him. Another stumbled, an arrow in his shoulder, one more limped, a shaft protruding from his leg. They were not as protected as the guard had boasted.

"Run," I gasped, as the trees thinned. "We need to get closer."

We covered about thirty steps when a line of arrows thudded into the ground in front of us. I jumped over them, but saw the second volley arch up, followed by a third. I slid to a stop and jumped back. Too late, an arrow pierced my upper arm, one hit the ground between my feet, the others around me. I dropped my bow and clutched at the shaft, grimacing with pain.

Line by line the arrows thudded into the ground in front of me. I grabbed my bow and stepped back. More arrows, closer and closer to my feet encouraged retreat.

"I wonder who ordered we not be killed." I asked. "Not Gynbere or Slaslow, I'll warrant."

Oak hunkered down, gasping for breath. "Why did they want Storm? That ambush was well set. If they'd wanted to, they could've killed us."

"Why not take Mekroe as well?" said Arbreu. "Surely he has as much value as Storm or Veld."

"Perhaps they didn't know who Mek was," I said. "Storm sat at the table with the other leaders. If Gynbere finds out, someone will pay a dear price.

"I suppose we were lucky. They could've killed us all. I reckon someone has a plan," said Twig. "What do we do now?"

Then Mekrar was at my side.

"Stop," she said. "Leave off the chase."

"Why?" asked Blacknight.

"We need a proper plan. They've managed to get extra hostages, and we don't want them getting more."

"If Gynbere gets to The Rock, we may never get them

back," said Twig.

"He's not going there. Kirym said he has a different plan," said Mekrar.

"But he's retracing his steps."

"There are a lot of other places out there. Anyway what would be the point of taking hostages if there is no intent to exact a price for their return?"

We regrouped, picked Mekroe up and, assisting the wounded men, retraced our steps to collect the dead, wounded and prisoners.

Mekrar broke off the fletched end of the arrow in my arm, pushed the head through and bound it tight.

"That hurts more than the initial wound," I said gasping with pain. "I hope the arrows weren't poisoned."

Mekrar shook her head. "Your flesh looks healthy. I was talking to one of the Willow healers. She's dealt with poisoned wounds. Her description of the flesh was ..." She shook her head. "Be assured, you're not in the running. They shoot accurately. We're going to have to learn how to cope with their fighting abilities. Our knives are too short unless we're very close. Arrow for arrow, we're better shots, but their armour puts us at a disadvantage. They're more experienced at sword-play."

Mekroe groaned as he gingerly pressed a cloth to a long cut that ran from near his ear across his cheek, stopping just short of his nose. "He'll have a scar from this."

"Finally," laughed Twig. "Arbreu will finally be able to tell you two apart."

Snorts and guffaws echoed around the small clearing.

Mekrar went pink, and hid her smile as she tended her brother.

"You can carry him back, Twig," she ordered. "And I guarantee he'll waken just after we get there."

More laughter.

"I want to get the soldier we shot," I said. "If he's dead, he deserves a decent burial, and if not, well he'll not survive the night by himself."

Laden with dead and injured, it was a slow trip back. We were tired, hungry and thirsty, and few of the walking wounded could hurry. Those who could carried heavy loads. After one particularly gruelling trudge through thick undergrowth, as we discussed leaving the dead for later recovery, Paluniis, Morkeen and Lyndym and eight guards arrived, laden with drink flasks, food pouches and stretchers.

I checked the sky, surprised to find it was only just mid afternoon.

We hunkered down in the shade of a tree and thankfully grabbed the flasks.

I had trouble removing the stopper with my wounded arm.

Morkeen took it and opened it for me.

"Don't waste it," she snapped. "Others back there need it too."

"Then why did you bring so much," demanded Paluniis, his eyes bright with laughter.

She glanced over the wounded. "A little fight and half of you are too tired to walk back," she said. "Fortunately more men are coming to carry you all."

Arbreu nudged me. "Teema, I can't find Kirym. I mean she's there, but, well I think she is, but I don't know what ..." His voice faded. "I don't know."

I closed my eyes and concentrated on her. Arbreu was right, something was weird. I could see different scenes, but none of them made any sense at all.

"What does it mean," Arbreu asked.

I frowned, trying to come up with an answer. "Maybe the dragons are talking."

"But they were killed. They're dead."

"Well perhaps they've been reborn."

"WHAT!"

Everyone looked at me, their faces reflecting Twig's exclamation.

I grimaced and clutched my shoulder which ached with every movement.

"It was something Borasyn said. They die but they don't." I shook my head. "I don't know. It's complicated. I'll explain later, but maybe everything's all right." I turned away, more worried than I wanted to appear. Oh please let those dragons be reborn.

"Teema!" interrupted Oak. "Why did Gynbere bring his people in this direction?"

"Ask Kirym," snapped Morkeen. "Men are so stupid." She slipped the flasks over her shoulder, grabbed one end of a stretcher and waited impatiently until the other was picked up.

41

Kirym Speaks

"Sing," I sobbed. "Please tell them the things I don't know."

Faltryn's head lowered, he rested his chin on my lap. I could feel his breath through the fabric of my dress. "I'm tired," he said. "It's been such a long time."

"You can sleep soon," I murmured. "But they deserve the chance to live. I'll try to let them know what I can, but you have to help me."

I clicked my token to his forehead. His sad laugh was throaty. The large tokens vibrated at the sound.

"It's a long time since I was offered the acknowledgement of a token. It feels different."

The sounds of battle had faded. I hoped everyone was safe. I reached into my pocket and brought out the first token my hand came in contact with. The large blue token trilled as it touched his forehead.

"So you tie me to yourself and your family," said Faltryn. "So clever."

"You've always been part of us. You all are. I want that to continue."

"Remember this, Kirym. You have a strong link to the dragon family. Stronger than any I've known before. The bond never dies. When you need it, it's waiting. There's one secret you've not yet found, but it's in your grasp. Soon someone will ask for it. Don't let it go until you've discovered what it holds. It's yours by right."

There was a long silence.

"The song may work for them," he said, "but they will never forgive me for what I've done."

"Together we're whole. If others can forgive, they must too."

"You are noble. More than anyone I've ever met." He paused. "I imagine there is hope for the future, but I'll not be holding my breath for mine. Vengeance is a strange thing, and many will want to extract it." As he spoke, blood dribbled from his mouth into my lap.

Although Faltryn made no sound, I was under no illusion when he began to sing. I felt his passion well up, at first excitement, delight, the soaring flights, the new lands, enquiry. Then resentment, anger, resolution. Shock, more anger and frustration, sorrow and finally fear. So much fear.

I was sure everyone here felt the same emotions.

If the other dragons heard or felt the message Faltryn sent, they gave no sign, but I hoped it registered in some way, as it had in the past.

Faltryn's song brought pictures to mind, the land from above, massive snow covered ledges along the cliffs beside the river, small dwellings clustered together on them. The settlement looking different—fewer trees, smaller houses and formal tended gardens. Six massive oak trees bigger than any I'd ever seen, their branches intertwined and festooned with walkways and dwellings.

Faltryn was weakening. He moaned with pain as he tried to move.

"Stay still," I murmured. I brushed his forehead. He was very hot.

I was aware of people hovering nearby, time passing.

"Should we remove the sword?" Starshine asked quietly.

"No, he would bleed heavily," I answered. "Can I have some cool water for him, please?"

Mama placed a bowl of water and a soft absorbent skin beside me. "Will a drink help?"

"No." I squeezed the skin and wiped his forehead and down his nose. His eyes closed.

I saw a huge square block with a tented roof in the middle of the dessert, the image slightly different to Borasyn's engraving on the bank, in that the walls were not as straight and forbidding, but were terraced down to the sands, with smaller buildings clustered around it. Only the massive doors were identical. A massive creature emerged from the desert, its walk lizard-like, its head dark, but indistinct. The huge city crumbled, and became a desolate waste.

I saw my birth place, The Land Between the Gorges, as it was when I was young. Prominent in the picture was a huge red leafed oak tree. As I watched, the tree slowly fell over.

I remembered it happening. We were in the midst of our spring celebration, my fifth. Papa had just agreed I could own the knife and carry it with me.

Faltryn had been there.

In the back of the crowd, Churnyg began to sing with help from Larqeba. A harp joined in, a pipe—not Mekroe's—and a number of drums softly picked up the rhythm.

Faltryn's chest rasped as he breathed in. It sounded painful. He coughed convulsively, spraying me with fine drops of blood.

"You know the secrets of the weapons. Keep them close until

you're sure there is no other danger. But follow your heart. It won't let you down." He was silent for a long moment. "I should never have done it," he whispered. "Curiosity! It was my downfall. That and pride. So futile!"

He breathed out and in again.

I waited.

He breathed out.

In.

Blood dribbled from his mouth. I wiped it up. He breathed out. His head was suddenly heavy. Blood gushed across my lap and down my legs.

The singing and music stopped.

Time passed. Everything was quiet for such a long time.

Teema and Oak were there, helping to raise Faltryn's head off my lap and lifting me to my feet.

I felt lightheaded, and my legs gave way momentarily. Many hands supported me.

I grasped the sword, and gave it a sharp yank. Initially it resisted, but then Faltryn's body gave it up. More blood gushed onto the grass, splattered the hillside, my feet and legs.

Faltryn's forehead where I touched it with the token was white, but in the centre was a raised blue bump.

Then Mama was there, with a soft damp cloth for my face. I smiled through my tears and took a deep breath.

"Who is injured, Mama? How many are dead and who was kidnapped? We need to get a meal for everyone and reorganise the guards."

"Others can worry about that for a few moments," she said briskly. "You need to change your clothes."

I glanced at the sky. The sun was halfway to the horizon.

I took a deep breath. "Mama, the wounded may not be able to wait," I said. "Where are they?"

Teema took my arm, and glanced at Mama.

She clicked her tongue, but nodded. I knew they would humour me for the time being.

I didn't care, as long as I got to check the things I needed to.

As Teema guided me to the area where the wounded were, I had a good look around. Someone had organised the guards, double the number stood on the top of the bank, and many guarded each entrance, above and at ground level.

Gynbere's ibith sat in the middle of the south-eastern entrance. Wind Runner's wagons now all stood inside the walls. On the eastern side of the ground was a clear area with more sentries lined up, ready to take over from some of those on watch. I was shocked at how many wore bandages.

"Arbreu, get some men to bring the ibith and base into the compound. Guard it. I want no chance of it being further damaged until I can look at it." I paused. "Oak, spread the wagons out. Utilise them to help healers with the wounded. The cooks could use them also, shelter if we run out—anywhere they're needed. Although I doubt Gynbere will attack again, have two across each entrance with a third ready to add extra security in case I'm wrong."

He nodded and hurried away.

A healing area had been created east of the stump where the dragons lay. There was a water nearby and two fires had been lit. Concoctions were already being prepared over some of them.

Healers bustled around plying their trade. The members of the Willow family were prominent here.

Lorythma bustled up and bowed.

I inclined my head. "If you need anything, please ask. Mama has access to most remedies, and what she doesn't have, she may know where to find."

"Lady Loul has already offered, and ensured we have all we need. She and the cave healers have interesting ideas. This will be an exciting day for us. So much to learn. Is there anything we can do for the dragons?"

"No," I said. "They're dead, and their future is already decided. Give them space and peace."

He turned away to attend a soldier who had regained his senses, and was in a great deal of pain.

I walked down the space between the lines of wounded. One body was covered, ready to be taken to be placed with the dead. I talked to each of those injured as I passed. One man, a tree dwarf but unknown to me, sat against a pack. His leg was heavily bandaged, but the blood showed through the linens. I offered him the flask of water someone had pushed into my hands.

He drank. "We did our best, Mam. I'll be ready to fight again soon." His eyes closed.

"He'll survive, Kirym," said Lantiah softly. "He's weak, but time will sort his wound." She lowered her voice. "He'll lose the use of the leg. I fear his ability in the trees will be very limited."

"Where one leg won't suffice, perhaps three or five will. Otherwise we'll have to find another solution. I'm in awe of these men," I said. "This was a fight they didn't expect, but they rose to the occasion against seasoned warriors. These men showed true bravery."

The hot metallic smell of fresh blood came to meet me as we approached the next man. Healers surrounded him, working frantically to stem blood-flow.

I felt bile rise in my throat, and swallowed convulsively. Unable to do anything to help, I moved on down the row, assessing needs and offering what little help I could in the way of comfort and assistance.

The last man in line had been placed apart from the others. His uniform, at a quick glance, gave him the look of a guard, but it was ill-fitting, obviously not his. It was too big in the body and far too long to be practical. His eyes were shut, his breathing irregular. No one tended him, he looked as if he had just been thrown down.

"Find someone to care for him, Teema."

"It won't do any good," said Lantiah putting her arm around my shoulder and trying to turn me away. "Initially we thought he was dead, but Lorythma says there is no saving him. He threw the sword that killed Faltryn."

I was outraged. "All the more reason to try," I snapped, although it was not her fault.

I knelt and felt his neck. His pulse was weak and fluttery, but still there. Teema helped me ease his helmet off.

He was past middle age, but while his hair was silver, he didn't look old. I took him to be from the Yew family.

"Lorythma," I called.

He came, along with his son and two women who were helping him with the injured.

"This man is alive, but he won't be if he's not cared for."

Lorythma frowned. "Lady Kirym, we try to save those who have hope, and we make death for those who will definitely die as easy as possible."

"Neither is being done for this man."

"In that I am remiss, but others had more need and our history tells us he will die, because he betrayed his people. Gynbere said anyone who touches the sword without having the authority would die."

"But he isn't dead, and no one has deemed to make him comfortable," I snapped. "If death was the price paid for betrayal, Gynberre would have died long ago." I took a deep breath. "I understand the principles of a battle hospital, but this man he has information I need."

"He's never ever been part of us," said one of the Willow healers. "No one knows him. He held the sword. He wasn't chosen to, so according to all that is known, his death is a matter of time. He made a choice and helped Gynbere."

"Legend rarely tell the whole story, and there is more to his tale than you know. Help him to live, so we can find out what happened and why."

Lorythma stared at me for a few moments, then nodded and waved one of the women beside him to help.

"We are always learning," he said frowning. "Perhaps I've let our folk tales influence me wrongly. Allow me please to make amends. Gynletha is one of our most talented healers."

"Thank you," I said. I watched for a few moments. She was skilled and very gentle with him.

"I'll help her," reassured Lantiah. I nodded and turned away.

42

Kirym Speaks

The dead lay near the north-eastern entrance. Sadly three porters and a boy had joined eighteen of Gynbere's guards. Four of the dead were ours. Armos' son Peet had been placed next to Pinecone, one of Twig's cousins. Two I didn't know were from The Rock, one a member of the Ash family, the other a Willow.

"What are their names?" I asked.

"Oshunta is Imolay's great-grandson, and Sharchenta is Gynletha's nephew." said Churnyg. "They fought well. Our bards will sing of their bravery."

"Does Armos know about Peet?"

"Yes," said Findlow. "He carried him here himself."

"Get the names of these men." I pointed to the other dead. "I'll talk to the families later." I stared at the boy. He appeared to be too young to have been a soldier. "How did he die?"

Findlow shook his head. "He was found behind the

pavilion. Our men above thought he belonged to one of the men Gynbere had on guard there. We initially thought he was asleep. When we checked, well he had no wounds, so perhaps he'd been sick."

I stared at the boy, he didn't look like any dwarf I had seen before. His tousled hair was a different silver to the Yew family. His skin was fair when most of the dwarves were swarthy. What hit me most was that although his skin was pale to the point of blue, I felt he looked a little—well not pink—but not quite right for someone who had been dead since early morning.

"What are his family connections?"

"I've searched for anyone who will claim him. None will," said Findlow. "I thought he was Yew. We have a few of them here, but they say, no. What do we do with the dead?"

"We'll bury them tomorrow." I pointed to the northern edge of the grounds. "With everyone's agreement they can be laid on the far side of the bank in the grove of trees there. Ask Lantiah or someone equally experienced to double check they're all dead."

Findlow frowned, and drew me away from the others. "What are we looking for? Dead is dead. Even I can recognise a corpse. There's a feel about them, and these men all have it."

"The boy looks different. His skin is pale and blue, but after death the skin changes. His hasn't."

"Dwarves look," he paused, "well, different, but he's young and perhaps in death that's, well that's how they are."

"You look as doubtful as you sound, Findlow. I know no one claims him, but does anyone know him?"

"Oh. Yes I see what you mean. Yes there is a difference. I'll find out."

The prisoners were gathered in front of the map table, well-guarded and muttering together.

"Get these men food and water," I said, "and find them robes to change into."

"Take our uniforms if you will," snapped one, "but Gynbere will not be fooled by their use. You are all too tall, and some are positively gormless." He looked pointedly at Sundas.

"What's your name?"

He hesitated.

"It's easier to speak if we know each other. I'm Kirym."

"I know who you are. I'm Thyshult."

"I thought you'd be more comfortable in robes, Thyshult. I know you wear uniforms only when on guard."

"We prefer the discomfort of our uniforms to keep our honour," he said stiffly.

I nodded. "Very well. However, the robes will be there for you anyway. Food and drink will be brought here. Rugs also as the night draws in."

"Don't bother; we won't be staying that long."

"Gynbere won't return for you," I said.

"He has hostages. He'll set up an exchange."

"Why would Gynbere do that? He could have left here at any time, and taken all of you with him. He was very specific in whom he took. I'm afraid you're surplus to his requirements."

He looked unhappy, but from the murmurs around him, the news wasn't as unpalatable to others as it was to him.

"If you swear you'll not return to Gynbere until we have peace, nor fight against us again, you can have your freedom and join your families here," I said.

Another of the prisoners cursed. "I'd rather die," he snarled. "You won't hold us."

I shrugged. "Darknight," I called. "Build a cage. Give them plenty of room, but make it solid. Ask Churnyg to arrange for the wood you'll need."

Darknight nodded and turned away, calling for men as he went.

"Sundas! Guard them well in the meantime. Ensure there are plenty of men to help you."

I walked over to Teema who was deep in conversation with Findlow and Mrilan. "Who was taken prisoner?" I asked.

Teema looked uncomfortable. "Soon, no one," he said. "We have his men. We'll exchange them." He pressed his bandaged arm and winced.

"Don't annoy me with banal comments that bear little resemblance to reality. Gynbere doesn't value his men. I know he has Papa, so who else?" I took his hand away from the wound, feeling heat around the dressing. "Go to the healers and get that seen to before it turns bad on you."

He hesitated.

"Go now," I ordered. "Findlow, take him please. Make him cooperate."

Sirasha walked slowly from his seat on the dais.

"Old age can be a bonus, Lady Kirym, but I fear they left you a burden. I cannot move fast, and Gynbere saw that when he took most of the other leaders. There was no attempt to take Lorythma nor me with them."

"Gynbere is a fool, Sirasha. Your limbs may be slow, but your mind isn't. His lack of foresight is our gain, if you're willing to help us. You, Churnyg, Lorythma and Findlow have skills I need. I'm grateful you're here."

"Garanniis of Valythia was left with us too. He was wounded, although not badly. He refused to take the healers away from their patients, but Lady Loul sent him to rest. Bryn of the Southern Escarpment evaded capture also," said Sirasha. "He'll join us presently. He's handling a family matter."

"They got Enliah too," interrupted Larqeba, his eyes big. "She was down near Gynbere's pavilion. Me an' Sundas was going after her when the attack happened. We saw her leave. Pa's telling Ma not to cry."

I tousled his hair. "Tell Jeresaya we'll get her back. Papa will look after her."

He ran off.

"If she lets him," murmured Harnita.

I looked up enquiringly.

"By all accounts, they shrouded every one of them except her."

I frowned at the implication. "It may not be as it looks. Where was Rargo when she was taken?"

"He was near her." Shurlyn frowned. "You're right, she may not have gone willingly. I think Rargo had hold of her arm. Zeffun Urfit was on her other side. Well I think it was Zeffun. It's hard to tell."

"Did Gynbere take anyone else other than the leaders?"

"Zelriff," said Harnita. "I imagine the guards were unsure which old lady was Wind Runner. Old Harby went into battle for them and young Harby also. Both were taken."

"They got Storm, as well," said Oak. "While we were out chasing them. It was planned, Gynbere must have ordered it. He had Findlow, but Faltryn was rather accurate with his tail."

"I'm pleased," I said. "We need his talents. Anyone else?"

"Ashistar is missing," said Mrilan. "I never trusted him. He's not been here much and he disappeared soon after you left us this morning. No one has seen him since."

"I have," I said.

There were looks of surprise and, from Teema, disbelief.

I ignored them and mentally went over the resources we had in the men left to us. "Ensure all of our leaders are guarded. As much as I don't think Gynbere will return, we need to be sure. Mama, where's Tarl? He needs to take his position as warlord until Papa returns."

"He's on the bank organising the sentries," said Twig.

"Get him down, he needs to make decisions for more than just the guards. He needs to prepare everyone for what comes next."

There was a muffled scream. I jumped.

Mama laid a reassuring hand on my arm. "I'd say we're about to have a new little tree dwarf. Clatheta is nearing the end of her labour."

"Who's caring for her?"

"Lantiah was, but Clatheta sent her to help with the wounded. Illukra is with her, and Harnita keeps an eye on them."

I glanced at the sun. "It's been a long labour. Ask the other families for assistance. There's a lot of midwife experience here. Let's use it. If it's beyond their abilities, get Lantiah back. This baby must be born healthy."

Tarl jogged up wearing body armour borrowed from one of the dwarves. "I'm glad you're free now, Kirym. What do you suggest we do?" He slipped the armour off, handing it to one of the Chestnut Dwarves. "Pass this on to someone who needs it."

"You've done most of it, but you need to plan ahead," I said.

He nodded, looking worried. "But what? You should take over, Kirym."

I stared at my boots, realising with shock they were covered with blood. My dress was black with gore. Folds of it had stuck together and stiffened as it dried. I felt very tired.

"I've not been in battle with them. You were, Tarl. Talk to Mama and take advice from your key men. You're doing well."

He grabbed my arm and pulled me away from the others.

"I can't," he whispered loudly. "I can't make the decisions. They go wrong. I just want to be—. I don't think—" He paused. "I don't want to do it." He looked troubled and distracted.

"Think how Papa deals with his men, Tarl. Take advice. You've made good decisions so far. Ask Mama, she is headwoman. Armos too. It'll do him good, and take his mind off other things."

Tarl paused and nodded. "Bad that. I'll miss Peet."

"Yes, we all will. But you now need to keep everyone else alive."

He looked unhappy, but took a deep breath and nodded. "Tell me what you need, Kirym. And any ideas you have. I know you have the dragons to think about, but you know more of Gynbere than most of us. I'll need your help." He walked away, more confident now, calling out names of men he wanted.

"Oak, have you seen Garanniis?"

He shook his head.

"All right, I'll look for him. Can you find Starshine for me?" I rubbed my jaw as he left, surprised to find it too was caked with dried blood. *I need to wash first*, I thought.

I found Garanniis in the dwelling Mama and Papa shared. Mama was just retying a bandage on his arm. He assured me he was fine.

"Did you understand Faltryn's story?" I asked.

Mama stiffened as he nodded.

"Is there anything we can do? Do you need help to explain to your people?"

"No," he said. "To my mind, Faltryn confirmed what happened back then. I've thought about it. It was a long time ago. We were nomads by heritage before the city, and afterwards we again became nomads. We had the desert, and it was a good home for many long seasons. We had freedom.

Our downfall was in assuming hate and anger in those from the fortress. We were offered sanctuary in Faltryn often, and each time, we rejected it. Some of our own people told us, you know, urged us to live there. We decided they were leading us into a trap. Given a choice, they returned to live in Faltryn. But when one who came to us died, we assumed his death was orchestrated by those in the Fortress. In our wooden stupidity, we condemned ourselves to death. We're fortunate that some of us were saved. We will hold no grudge against Faltryn."

"Morkeen?"

"She was away from the amphitheatre attempting to save those who were kidnapped. It was the most normal I've seen her since she learned of Zyanda's death. She'll have to know, but I have hopes she has begun to heal and will accept Faltryn's story as something from the past."

Mama shook her head as he left. "I fear he's being optimistic, but hopefully I'm wrong." She turned her attention to me. "Now let's get you cleaned up." She guided me over to a section of her dwelling where screens provided an area of privacy for washing. She handed me a flask and pointed to a platter of fruit.

I hadn't realised how thirsty I was and drank. I declined the fruit. The thought of food made me feel sick.

She had laid out clean clothes, and Mekrar brought in a bowl of warm water.

The water was changed twice before I was rid of the blood and dirt. My clothes were taken away and I dressed in one of the outfits Wind Runner had given me. "You are so hard on your clothes," Mama murmured, as she helped me tie the sleeves on. "No wonder Wind Runner saw the need to give you so many."

The material was warm and I realised how late in the day it was. I slipped the crown onto my damp hair and strapped the token pocket to my hip. With the baldric across my shoulder, I clipped the knife onto the sword, and picked up the shield.

43

Kirym Speaks

Oak and Starshine almost knocked me over as I stepped from behind the screen.

Starshine hugged me. "How can we help, Kirym?"

"With Wind Runner away, you'll need to make the decisions for your people."

She went pale. "She's dead? I don't become matriarch until then."

"She is alive, but she isn't here and you are. Liaise with Tarl, tell him what you want and need. Oak can help."

"I will too," said Mekroe, appearing at her side. He put his arm protectively around her shoulder. He had an ugly wound across his cheek. It had been skilfully stitched and smeared with a yellow cream to thwart infection. *He would,* I thought, *always have a scar there, although it would fade over the seasons.*

"That's Oak's position, Mek," I said. "You'll need to help Tarl. He needs your support now Papa is gone."

"No! My future lies with Starshine. I asked Storm if we could join."

"He said, yes?" asked Mama.

"He didn't say no," said Starshine. "And nor did Wind Runner when I talked to her. So if we have a ceremony, then Mek can stand alongside me."

"Do we have time, Mama?"

Mama sighed. "It's a complication, Mekroe."

"There'll be more fighting, and we could all die," he said. "We'll all be fighting together, it makes sense for us to be joined. It forms a connection between our families. Anyway, Storm isn't here. Gynbere got him."

"I think they should join," said Oak. "As Starshine's closest family here, I'd be asked. Mek and I get on, and we fight well together, and I can liaise with you Kirym."

"What is needed for the ceremony?" Mama asked. "Who arranges it and who presides?"

"Normally it would be Wind Runner," said Oak, "but she isn't here. Our guild leaders could do it." He paused. "In the end it's Starshine's choice. She doesn't have to ask, because there's no one here to ask."

"I'd like it if you and Kirym gave your agreement too, Loul," said Starshine.

I frowned as I thought over the implications of the suggestion. "Mama, she's right about that. Mekroe doesn't really need permission either, so perhaps the Guild Leaders can arrange it."

"Why don't you organise it, Kirym?" asked Mama.

"I have other things I need to do." I paused. "Where's Trethia? I've not seen her since just before the attack."

"Mama went to her travelling desk and flicked through a stack of parchment, pulling out a number of sheets. She scanned through them. "This is the list of children we have here." She ran her eyes down the lists. "Harnita made it after the armies left, to ensure those without parents weren't overlooked. Trethia is not on the list, and no one has mentioned her. Amethyst's name isn't here either, so they're probably both with Morkeen."

"Evidently Morkeen helped carry some of the wounded back," said Mekroe. "She wouldn't have left Amethyst alone."

"She might be in her dwelling." I stepped through the door and glanced around the open area. The prisoners sat against the bank, armed guards above and around them. Many of them had exchanged their armour for robes, but Thyshult, Rookham and a few others remained defiant. The cage had two walls already erected. A third was being attached, the long branches being jointed onto what had already been built. The frame of the fourth wall and a roof were lying on the ground.

The walk to where Garanniis and his people slept seemed to take three times longer than usual. My call at the entrance of the dwelling was met with silence.

"Morkeen, is Trethia in there with you?"

There was no answer. I thought I heard some movement inside, but knew Trethia would have come at my call.

I walked away, asking people I met if they'd seen her. No one had. Most people were rushing to do various vital things, already Tarl was organising us into an armed encampment.

"Can I help, Kirym?" asked Oak.

"I can't find Trethia. There's no answer from Morkeen—"

"Hold on. I'll check. Maybe she fell asleep in there. Why don't you go and look in the dwelling you use. I'll catch up."

Trethia wasn't in her usual hiding place under the set. I was looking under the others when Oak arrived.

"Morkeen hasn't seen Trethia. She wasn't with Jeresaya when she picked Amethyst up. It may be that Morkeen didn't notice her because she wasn't looking, so," he shrugged. "Anyway Mekrar said Jeresaya was with the healers, and we know Trethia isn't over there, so let's check the healing place Loul took her to when she first arrived. She more comfortable there."

"I doubt she'd go there if Mama wasn't there, but it's closer than Bryn's dwelling."

There was a lot of noise in the healing area. I peeped in. The dwelling was full, unusual under normal circumstances. Then I realised Clatheta's baby had arrived. I turned away.

"Trethia wouldn't be there with so many from The Rock present."

Oak started to look uncomfortable. "So where would she be?"

"See if Jeresaya knows, I'll check the dragons."

"But they're dead."

"She's gone to them for protection before, and I'm running out of places to look."

Now I was near the dragons. I wondered if Faltryn's song had affected them in any way, but Iryndal, the dragon I'd thought would waken first, lay as she had. There was no sign of Trethia with any of them.

I was getting more and more concerned. I had no idea where to look next. "Could she be with Midnight?" I asked Oak, when he returned with no news.

"I'll look. You stay and talk to the dragons. That may help." Oak ran, and I knew he was now as worried as I was.

I told the dragons about Trethia, and got the anticipated response. I felt silly. "What did I expect? They are dead," I said to myself.

While waiting for Oak, I wandered over to the tree trunk, and looked around it, remembering how Ubree had hidden in the branches when he felt ill at ease. Trethia wasn't there. But on the ground was an embroidered band with stones, the arm jewels I'd tied on her that morning. One of the ties had been cut through.

When Oak returned, he had others with him. Some were dismissive when they realised who was missing, but it was easier to ignore the comments than argue. A few of them were really concerned. Many places were suggested.

"Morkeen took Amethyst to Jeresaya to keep her safe. Although Trethia wasn't sent there, perhaps she followed Morkeen and hid in Jeresaya's dwelling."

"I've already been there, asked and searched," said Mekrar breathlessly. "I looked under the sets, and behind things. Is it possible Gynbere took her?"

"No," said Jetara. "She'd be beneath his notice. He'd be more likely to swipe at her with a sword, but that would've been seen. I doubt he'd be able to convince any guards to grab her, anyway, they were all running for their lives."

"Would she be with Shormel?" Mekrar asked.

Jetara shook her head. "He's over with the other dwarflings. He'd never take her there, and she wouldn't have gone anyway. But what about Larqeba? Would she have run to him? That would explain the arm band being here. She'd have had to come past the tree to get to him."

"He wasn't here," said Sundas. "When the attack happened, I grabbed him and threw him up to a guard on the wall. Figured it may keep him out of trouble. He spent the battle dancing around screaming oaths and insults at Gynbere and his men."

"Where is he now? Perhaps once the fight stopped, he came and collected her," said Jetara.

"He did come down, he told me about Enliah," I said. "He has been trying to get up there for ages, but Bryn wouldn't let him. Now he has a precedent, he may have gone back, especially when he realised Bryn was preoccupied over Enliah. Sundas, can you go and ask the guards, please."

Sundas quickly returned. He shook his head. "You're right, Kirym, he is up there. He said he hasn't seen her. None of those I asked have. Well not since before the fight."

"Then perhaps it's time we told Tarl, and had a proper search outside the walls," said Oak.

"He'll be taking the men to rescue the prisoners. We can't interrupt that."

"You're right, Lelth. They're more important than this waste of time."

"If it was your child, you'd want us to search," I snapped.

"But she's ..."

"She's a child of The Green Valley," interrupted Oak. "We are guests of The Green Valley. Remember that!"

And suddenly everyone was arguing.

I turned away, and again scanned the amphitheatre. Where could she be? With absolutely no idea, I started west of the northwest entrance, and began to search methodically behind and under everything along the wall. Dwellings, carts, stacks of equipment, wood piled high for the fires, and among the myriads of items brought from the fortress and stored until we were ready to return home.

I was halfway along the west wall when Mekrar, Arbreu, Oak and Sundas joined me.

They're still arguing," said Mekrar. "We'll move faster without them. Do you want some of us to start searching outside?"

"Could you and Arbreu look outside the entrances? If she went after the armies left, there may be tracks. It's unlikely, but ..." I shrugged.

She nodded. "I'll tell Garanniis as I go past. He may have seen something from the wall, or perhaps one of the other guards has."

"Larqeba was on the wall, but he didn't see her at all," said Sundas. "That may imply she ran along the north wall.

There were fewer guards to the south, because Faltryn had blocked the entrance there."

"If she left the amphitheatre during the fight, no one would have noticed her. Most of the men were trying to retrieve the prisoners," I said.

"She's a strange one, and she was close to the dragons," said Arbreu. "Could she have died with them? Just a thought, but, is it possible?"

I frowned, concentrating on her. "She didn't die with them, and she didn't know Faltryn so it's unlikely she'd die with him. But it doesn't matter, dead or alive, I have to find her. If she's dead, find her body. I'm sure she's alive."

In reality, I wasn't. I didn't have a token connection with her, and I only assumed she hadn't joined the dragons because she wasn't with them.

I had searched as far as the tanning frames when Bryn approached me. "I've just been told about your wee girl. One of my men heard there was a girl near the black dragon just after he died. Maybe it was her."

44

Kirym Speaks

I spun around and raced towards Faltryn's body, wondering if there was some nook or crevice she could have slipped into while everyone concentrated on his dying.

The body had few real hiding places. Nevertheless, I checked under his wings and around his legs.

She wasn't there. I felt sick.

I was looking to see that she hadn't managed to climb in behind his tail when Mekrar, Arbreu and Sundas came towards me from the east.

"Nothing. That springy grass hides footprints too well, and where the grass has been worn away, the ground is too firm to hold them," said Arbreu. "In other places where it's been used a lot, it's been flattened. No help at all."

"Kirym, there's no obvious answer," said Sundas. "But perhaps Tarl should organise search parties now. Go further and in different directions."

Mekrar put her arms around me. "What do you want to

do? We've covered every obvious place."

I looked around the amphitheatre. "I haven't checked everywhere. Trethia is used to hiding. Shormel said she could get into the most unusual places, places no one would ever think to look. I've missed one of them." Again I scanned the amphitheatre from where I knew she was last. "I've not finished searching this wall so that first, and then I'll talk to Tarl and Mama."

Mekrar shook her head, but she stayed with me, and I could hear Abreu, Sundas and Oak behind her as I ran west along Faltryn's long torso.

When we reached the ibith, Mekrar realised what we had missed.

The monstrosity leaned at an angle against the east wall. The chair was held on by only one bracket, and one of the long poles the porters used had split at the end where it hit the ground when they dropped it. The material that covered the box was irregularly put together, and it had been bunched in places to make sure it didn't pile up too much on the platform. In other places, parts of the box were visible.

I hunkered down to peer behind it, wondering if she could have crawled in there. It was hard to see because the material bunched up there too.

"Maybe we need some men to move it," Arbreu said.

"Kirym!" I turned, hearing the insistence in Sundas' voice. "It was moved. Had she been hiding near it, she would have been seen. It's more likely she …" His voice died away.

I paused, thinking about where Trethia was when I saw her last. My eye's travelled from where we ate our last meal, east past the tree where I'd found her arm jewellery, and then down to the exit, where the ibith had been abandoned.

I held out the arm band. "Trethia was alone and unguarded because of the attack. I found this by the tree, so she'd been sensible enough to get away from the fighting. Something happened there. This isn't ripped, it wasn't caught on a branch or anything. It's been cut! Gynbere was leaving. Men were milling around the entrance. More were racing down there. She wouldn't have crossed in front of those running into battle, so she'd have gone east or west. Could she have gone west, Bryn?"

He looked over to the western wall, signalled the guards and watched their response. "You can ask the guard who was there, he's on his way over."

The man who approached at a run came from Faltryn. Oak quickly explained what we needed to know.

"I know the girl, Oak. I saw her as the battle started. She was suddenly standing by herself in the middle there." He indicated where we'd been sitting. "She went towards the north wall, out of the way of the fight. There were a few people there, Walf ran towards the fight, most of those there followed him. After that, well I concentrated on the battle. I never noticed her again."

"Was any of that area vital to the battle?" asked Oak.

He shook his head. "It was pretty much a path to get to the east entrance. Clear o' bodies and an easy way past the centre skirmish. Had I wanted to get to the east entrance fast, it's the path I'd've used. West o' there were a few o' the men. Most o' them raced out into the centre there."

"Once the battle finished, what did you do?"

"I was ordered down to carry the wounded to the new healing area. Didn't see any of the children then. I was worried, my son had been down here, so I asked where they all were. A healer said the Lady Loul had taken them to safety."

"Doesn't help much, Kirym," said Oak, as the guard was dismissed.

"It implies she may well have hidden in the tree through

the battle."

"So why didn't she stay there?" asked Arbreu.

"Possibly something happened that scared her enough to make her run again."

"So we're no further forward than before," said Oak.

"She hid during the battle, and probably came out once the army left. So we need to look at the only place we haven't looked, and then consider that she may have left the amphitheatre. Bryn, can you let Mama and Tarl know that we may need to organise a search outside the walls."

I started to push the material up the sides of the box. It was thick and heavy especially in the areas where it had been bunched up. If she was under it, she wouldn't be immediately obvious.

"Can we pull it out from the wall?" I asked.

Sundas organised the men. The platform the box sat on made it awkward to even move, but soon it was sitting straight.

Arbreu tried to lever the chair off the top, but the spears and arrows made it unwieldy.

Sundas grabbed the nearest leg and yanked hard. The bracket broke with a loud crack, and he hurled it away. The attached back came away and fell to the ground. Three of the seven spears fell out and one broke with a loud crack.

The heavy material hung down over the sides of the box and pooled on the platform. Now I got a good look at it, I realised it was a patchwork of different materials, many of them woven wall or floor coverings, all cobbled together to form one big piece. Originally many colours, they had been boiled with miffut leaves to give it a uniform grey. It was a waste of beautiful rugs.

Together we pushed the material up from the sides. Mekrar and I climbed up using the pole as a step to get on top. Once there, we began to fold the heavy cloth over to expose the box.

Because the material was so bunched in places, on three occasions, movement I hoped might be someone, proved to simply be the weight of the material moving as it slipped and settled.

Mekrar and I were soon straining to move the thick heavy material, far too much for us to cope with. Oak and Arbreu clambered up to help and together we struggled to lift it off the places it was fastened to the box.

Trethia was near the centre. She was curled up in a ball, shaking and looking terrified. She recognised me and came to me with a sob. Her dress was in shreds.

I sat and hugged her as the others jumped off the box.

"We need to get you down from here. I want you to be very brave and jump into Mekrar's arms. She'll catch you and I'll be right behind you."

She glanced down hesitated and then launched herself off the box, and clung to Mekrar, still sobbing.

Sundas helped me down and Trethia came straight back into my arms.

"Why didn't she come out when you called earlier?" asked Sundas.

"She'd never have heard us from under that heavy pile," said Mekrar. "It was a good hiding place really, no one would have found her unless they striped the material off. I'm just amazed she managed to get under there. She must have been truly terrified."

I stood her on the ground and hunkered down to look at her. In places, the shredded dress was covered with drying blood. She had cuts on both arms and one leg, and two across her back, one across her buttocks. Parts of her dress had stiffened with drying blood and it oozed down her leg into her boot.

Her tears were as much of shock and relief, as pain. "I'm s-sorry," she hiccupped. "He c-cut your pretty dress. I couldn't stop him."

"It's only a dress. We'll find you a new one. Did you know the person who did it?"

She slowly shook her head.

"It's all right. When did it happen?"

"You were with Faltryn. I hid in the tree, but when Gynbere left, I came out. I was going to come to you."

"Well, let's get those cuts seen to, and then we'll get you another lovely dress. Can you walk, or do you want me to carry you?"

She glanced around the amphitheatre and looked up at me. She took a deep breath. "I can walk, but you hold my hand."

I smiled. "Good. You're very brave."

I took her hand, and flanked by the others, we walked across the open area towards the healers.

Conversations stopped, and heads turned to watch us as we passed. Trethia walked with her head high. The tatters of the dress blew in the light wind, and showed everyone the full effect of the attack, not only to her dress, petticoats and shift. Some of her wounds were very obvious.

Although the healing centre was busy, no one was in crisis. Lorythma came to meet us as we approached. He was horrified at the attack on Trethia. "I know she's considered a problem, but she's a child. This is untenable." He ordered an assortment of salves and powders to be brought over. "Teema told me how his shoulder was healed, and I wish I had the same healing powers as that dragon. However I will work with what I have." His hand poised over one pot after another, and finally he chose one. "This is very good, special. I'll give Lantiah a copy of the recipe for you. I did promise it to Lady Loul also."

He cleaned the wounds himself, spread salve on, and bandaged two of the deepest cuts. "If she gets a temperature or if the wounds become infected, bring her directly to me. And bring her back this evening for me to check there are no problems. Again in the morning after she's eaten. Ask for me, even if others feel they can deal with her."

It seemed a long walk back to the dwelling, and again, Trethia held her head high. Although she was well supported by us, she wasn't surrounded and hidden. I was determined for everyone to see what had been done to her.

The men waited outside while new clothes were found. Jetara came in as I was tying the shoulder ties to Trethia's dress. "Is she all right?" She fingered the ruined material and shook her head. "Much the same happened to the dress I gave her. Those soldiers have a lot to answer for. Would you like me to get rid of it?"

"No," I said. "It's one thing to take a dress and shred it, quite another thing to do it while she's wearing it. Attacking the child takes it to another level. This has gone far enough, and it has to stop. Everyone will be made to face this."

"It'll make it worse. People will resent it," she said.

"Resent it? I think that's Trethia's right, not theirs. If these attacks aren't stopped, it'll get worse. Actually, it has already escalated. Talk to Shurlyn, Mrilan. Talk to Rosisha. It must not continue."

"But the guards and soldiers have gone. What's the point?"

"It happened after Gynbere's men had left, Jetara. So the person is probably still here. Also, it happened quite openly, and someone must have seen what happened. And yet no one did or said anything. Then or later."

I handed the dress to Mekrar. "Put that away safely. It's

evidence I don't want to lose." I took Trethia's hand. "From now on, one of us will always be with you until we are sure of your safety."

Sundas had scrubbed the blood off Trethia's boots, but they were still damp, and I opted to leave them off until they were fully dry. Then we went to meet Oak, who had gone to the cooking area for food and a drink for Trethia.

"I've been looking for you, Kirym," said Bryn. "Tarl is organising the retrieval group. He plans to leave first thing tomorrow. Do you foresee any problems?"

Tarl was surrounded by the remaining headmen and guard leaders. Most were talking, nothing was being decided. Bryn and I were the last to arrive.

"Quiet," Tarl bellowed. "Now, we need some order. Everyone can make a suggestion, but decisions will be made quickly, and once made, will not be altered unless there is a change in the circumstances."

"Why should you make them?" asked one of the Tree Dwarves.

"Hold on, Girk," said Armos. "This is The Green Valley. Because Veld is away, Loul has decided that Tarl should take over as War Lord. That's her right as Headwoman of The Green Valley. There should be no argument."

"I intend to follow him as much as I'm able," said Mrilan. "We need to stick together. Veld was a good leader, and healthy trees spawn healthy saplings. Tarl has been well trained, and Armos is Veld's right hand man."

"He's young," said Girk. "Too young."

"Is your son less capable for his youth?" asked Mrilan.

Girk growled under his breath.

"We leave in the morning," said Tarl. "That gives us the evening to get organised, rest as necessary and decide who will come and who will stay."

"What organisation?" asked Blikall. "Why would anyone stay? And if we leave now, we get our people back quicker."

"We need stores to sustain us," said Tarl. "The women, children and injured will stay here. They'll need to be protected. The prisoners need to be guarded as well. It's almost evening and we've had a long hard day. We'd not get far tonight, so we eat, and rest. In the morning, we'll be better able to see the trail and spot any traps on it."

45

Teema Speaks

Those not working ate. Workers were relieved of their duties, they ate and slept. Kirym did too much work and not enough eating and sleeping.

She spent time with the injured, the families of the dead, the healers, the guards and the dragons. She spoke to the prisoners, asking if they were comfortable. She arranged for them to have more rugs overnight, and ensured they had enough food and drink.

She sat for a time with the man who had thrown the sword, and many murmured angrily about that. She spoke to the few Yew family members who had stayed back with us, trying to find out something about him.

They continued to deny all knowledge of him or his family.

"All we know," said Darchet, "is that his sire and his sire before him, was closely protected by Gynbere. His family, for generations back, have kept themselves apart from us.

We haven't seen him for many seasons. I didn't even realise he was still alive."

With no one other than a healer with him, she asked Mekrar, Arbreu and me to ensure he was never alone. She joined us when she could, as did Loul and others of our family.

"You'd think his family would be embarrassed into doing it," grumbled Bildon. "I wonder if Kirym thought they'd relent if total strangers started doing their job."

"No, I didn't," said Kirym, coming up behind her. She hunkered down beside us. "They have no obligation to sit with him. They've said they don't know him."

"But we don't either," said Lyndym. "At least they're related, even if it is as distant as they say."

"That's not how they see it, but there are lots of unknown things happening here. Perhaps later they'll look back and see the situation differently."

"What do you know about him, Kirym?" asked Mekrar. "I'd have thought you'd hate him for killing Faltryn and condemning the other dragons. And it's his fault Gynbere managed to attack so easily. We were all watching him and wondering what he was doing."

"As I see it, this man had no reason to kill Faltryn. I don't hate him because I know nothing about him, but if he doesn't fit in anywhere else, he belongs to us. That's why we sit with him."

"But—" Lyndym frowned.

"Even if the worst is true, we don't condemn a man without listening to his explanation. Let's hope he has the chance to tell us why he chose the action he did. He's a mystery, one of a number I need to get to the bottom of."

The moon was well risen before Kirym agreed to rest. Through the afternoon and evening she had kept Trethia beside her, explaining what she was doing, and allowing her to help as she could. When Trethia fell asleep, Kirym carried her. I was pleased Trethia was so small, but either way, it was a burden Kirym shouldn't have had.

There were patches of light and movement around the amphitheatre, intense areas where few slept. The cooks prepared food for the journey. The prisoners were guarded, although the light there was less and those under guard slept. The healer's area continued to be busy.

Soon after sundown, another of Gynbere's guards died and was given to those of his relatives who had stayed with us.

I took over charge of the guards at midnight and increased the number on the perimeter bank and around the prisoners.

I was on my way to get a late meal when Twig raced over to intercept me.

"Teema, I think you should waken Kirym. She needs to see this." He looked as if he had seen a ghost.

Kirym was instantly awake when Mekrar touched her shoulder.

"It's Faltryn, Mam," said Twig, when she joined us outside the dwelling.

Kirym questioned Twig as we walked towards the dragon, but he was unable to explain what it was he had seen.

Faltryn's corpse was in a dark area next to the southern wall of the amphitheatre.

It took me a while to understand what I was seeing, and I appreciated Twig's inability to describe it. Faltryn's body looked slightly shiny, and appeared to be moving, writhing.

Finally Kirym took the lamp Twig was holding and held it close to Faltryn's head. He was covered with long thin silvery worms. "Is this happening to the other dragons?"

Twig raced away to check.

I followed Kirym as she walked along the length of Faltryn's body. Worms were streaming out of the bank above and dropping onto him. They flowed up and down the corpse, twisting over and around each other. We returned to Faltryn's head as Twig arrived back from checking the other dragons.

"They're the same as before. No worms, nothing like this. Shall I brush them off, Mam?" asked Twig.

"No," she said. "It's nature doing what it does. Maybe this is what happens to the eldest, or perhaps it's to do with the way he died."

The higgledy-piggledy mass of worms turned and began to move towards Faltryn's head. For a short time they piled up on each other around his horns and ear frills.

Twig, standing closer to his face than I was, turned away and vomited.

I grabbed the lamp, held it up, and Kirym and I both saw what Twig had seen. The worms were wriggling down Faltryn's face and forcing their way into him, through his eyes, nostrils, mouth and the sword wound. For a while they bunched up, and got tangled around his horns.

It took surprisingly little time for them to disappear into him. After the few that had seemed to be lost finally disappeared, he was again bare, and now the blood that had gushed from his body was also gone. We could see the wave of worms moving slowly down the inside of his body. It was a gruesome sight.

Kirym turned away. "Keep everyone back from him, please. Let him decompose in peace."

Twig, now recovered, but looking pale, nodded shortly. "I'll put two guards on it."

Kirym sat on a rug against a wagon wheel and closed her eyes.

"Why don't you go and get some more sleep?" I asked.

"I need to think for a bit. Then I'll go. If I fall asleep, waken me at first light. Don't leave it any later, I want to get back to Trethia before she realises I've gone. There'll be a lot to do in the morning."

"I'll get you a hot drink."

She smiled and nodded.

When I returned, she was sound asleep and Trethia was snuggled in beside her.

I brought over a warm rug and covered them both, then turned away to check the camp.

Bryn strolled towards me with two platters. "I was just about to have meal break. Thought you'd need one too. Anything in particular you'd like me to do? I've been up at the north-eastern entrance, but there are more than enough men there to keep it safe."

I took the platter thankfully. I had missed my usual food breaks. "Yes, I do have a job for you. Organise a guard over Kirym. Don't let anyone waken her without coming to me first."

He nodded. "Aye, the lass does too much, doesn't she? I think she's aware of everything happening in camp. Earlier she talked to each of the guards to see they had all they needed. She does that almost every shift. I've never known anyone like her."

He turned away, but spun back. "Oh, I meant to tell you. When I began my meal break, I took a garland of flowers over to the black dragon. Miessa and her wee sister asked me to, the guards wouldn't allow them near. Anyway, I leaned the garland against the beastie's head, and they withered instantly. Weird that was. Kirym needs to know, but I guess it'll wait until morning."

I nodded, and walked over to check the dragon. The flowers sat against Faltryn's cheek and true enough, the few petals left appeared to have been burned. The rest had turned to dust or perhaps it was ash.

I picked a handful of grass and sprinkled them across his front leg. As with the flowers, they went black and disappeared with a puff of smoke. There was a strange smell with them. I leaned in for a closer look, taking great care. However, the hem of my cloak touched him, and that too dissolved with a hiss.

I took it off, staring at the damage. Whatever was on it continued to eat its way up the material. I dropped the cloak on the grass, and turned to the nearest guard. "Make sure none come close to the beast. It seems he's as dangerous now as he was alive."

He stared at me as if I was a raving idiot, but nodded.

"Where's Twig?"

"Here, Teema," he said from behind me. "I was chatting to Bryn. Couldn't believe what he said, but," he looked at my cloak which was only obvious as a cloak because of the hood. The rest was just a blackened mess of fibrous ash, "well, it seems he was right. What do we do?"

"Increase the guards here to seven. Move those on top of the bank, away. Ensure the closest guards are experienced men and warn them to take care. At least one young fool tries to run down the bank every few days. Here it could be disastrous. If it does that to leaves, flowers and fibre, who knows what it'll do to skin. Keep everyone away, but don't tell anyone else for now. I'll talk to Kirym about it in the morning."

As much as I wanted to tell her now, Kirym's instructions were specific and telling her would not alter what had happened.

I woke her as requested, bringing a platter of bread filled with meat and vegetables straight from the food pit and a bowl each of hot broth and fruit.

"It's the first meal I've enjoyed since yesterday morning," she said.

I told her what had happened over night, very little really, although one of the boys on his first guard duty had slipped and rolled down the bank of the amphitheatre. "He's broken his wrist and sprained his knee. He's more embarrassed than in pain." Then I told her about Faltryn.

"What effect has it had on Faltryn's skin?"

"None that I can see, although it was night and the light wasn't good. What are you thinking?"

She shrugged. "Is it normal, or the effect of the worms?"

"That's anyone's guess."

She stood, picked up a still sleeping Trethia and drew her cloak around them both. "Well, you've done the right thing with the guards. I'll have a look before we leave to follow the Gynbere."

A low whistle sounded from the guard on the perimeter wall.

We spun around to see what was happening.

46

Arbreu

It was only just light enough to see the guard's hand signals.

An envoy approaches. One man, thirty guards. They carry peace blooms, a chinttal branch and white lyncca flowers.

Arbreu raced over to the table where Tarl had his command centre. He arrived as Tarl gave orders.

"Armos. Take men and go meet them. Don't allow them the upper hand."

"Don't believe the peace symbols either," said Kirym. "If they wanted peace, they wouldn't have attacked us in the first place. Accept nothing on face value. Listen to everything said and think carefully before giving an answer or making a decision."

The guards at the entrance were signalled: Hold them outside the entrance for now.

Arbreu joined Armos, Sundas and forty guards to see what the envoy wanted. It was light enough for him to make out the men being held at the entrance. One, obviously the head of the envoy, was not in uniform. He wore a grey leather cloak over a similar coloured robe. The cloak had a series of thick black chevrons just below one shoulder.

Arbreu remembered seeing a similar emblem on the dead body they'd found inside The Rock, when they were rescuing Churnyg's supporters. *It's one of the Urfit triplets.* He sent the message to Kirym.

Warn Armos. This one is very dangerous. Take great care.

Armos nodded when told. "I expected someone like that. Don't worry, I have it in hand. Just let me do the talking. The rest of you keep quiet. Just march and look grim."

Four shields had been laid together on the ground, with another on top of them.

Urfit stood on the top shield. He was still shorter than Armos, and refused to look up at him. "My Lord Gynbere sent me to collect his ib—"

"You can enter with four of your men," interrupted Armos.

"My guards are with me to protect me," exclaimed Urfit, talking to Armos' belt.

"You can enter with three men," said a stony faced Armos. "Your safety is guaranteed here."

"I protest ..."

"It's down to two."

Urfit took a deep breath, stared at Armos with his mouth open and then turned to his men. "You and you," he said pointing.

"They can leave their weapons here."

Urfit took a breath, thought better of it and nodded briefly.

"And their armour."

Again he nodded compliance, but his eyes narrowed. He was furious.

"Yours too," said Armos, as the guards removed their armour.

Urfit looked sour, but handed the leather cloak to one of the guards, removed his helmet, arm and thigh protectors without complaint.

"Any more weapons? Armos asked. Despite assurances there weren't, he ordered two guards to search them all.

Urfit couldn't object, especially when Twig removed a knife he had in an arm sheath.

Urfit had trouble keeping his temper under control as he and his two men were surrounded and silently marched across the open area to the table where Loul, Tarl and others were working. Those at the entrance were kept there under guard.

When they reached the table, Urfit stared around the amphitheatre, pointedly ignoring everyone there. Eventually still staring around the amphitheatre, he took a deep breath.

"I have a message from My Esteemed Lord Gynbere for ..." he shrugged. "Well, for whoever is trying to be leader here I suppose. I've come for Lord Gynbere's possessions. His ibith, pavilion and the other items he left. I'll also take the guards you've unfairly imprisoned." He sneered. "And of course, our people, of whom you have so maliciously deprived of their freedom."

Tarl lounged casually back in his chair. "Will you return our people?"

"My Esteemed Lord Gynbere has not authorised me to offer ..."

Tarl picked up his quill and pulled a sheet of parchment towards him. "Then you're wasting your time. We may consider an exchange at some stage. The men and women you kidnapped for a few of those we captured when you attacked without provocation." Tarl began to make notes, pointedly ignoring Urfit.

"But, but ... but it—they're his. They belong to him." Urfit took a deep breath. "My Lord Gynbere will meet with you. Leave here in two days and go to The Rock. I will meet you there in ten days and escort you in ..."

"Don't be silly," interrupted Kirym. "Gynbere is scarcely likely to take people back to that mausoleum he previously imprisoned them in. Especially when his latest lie is that we created it. His claim to have freed them would mean very little if he returned. I somehow doubt many would follow him, no matter what threats he makes against their families. Anyway, it collapsed just before the last full moon. Even if you wanted to return there, you couldn't. Gynbere won't have gone there, so Vellysh, why lie and suggest he has?"

Urfit, his lips compressed to a hard white line, stared coldly at Kirym.

"You—you know. How did—?" He went very still, obviously annoyed at his response.

Tarl shook his head. "Do you have a real message for us, or shall I have you escorted out?"

Urfit turned back to Tarl. "My Esteemed Lord—"

"Vellysh Urfit!" said Tarl. "We are quite capable of tracking your army without any of this mucking about."

Urfit blanched when someone wearing a labyrinth-guard uniform sauntered up.

Urfit turned back to Tarl, his face hard and his eyes narrow. "Very well. These are our rules, and you break them at your peril. I'll leave you a map, the path is marked. You will not leave here until after the sun sits on the western horizon in four days' time. If you attempt to follow me sooner, every single prisoner will die. Painfully! When you arrive, we'll— My Lord Gynbere will have an arrangement for you. You'll follow the path we set, towards the rising sun, and then you'll travel with the morning sun on your right shoulder for an equal distance. If you take a shortcut, your people will die." He laughed nastily. "You have no choices here. We'll have men watching you and we will know if you ignore these instructions. The journey takes four days."

Tarl leaned across the table. "Very well, but let me warn you. If one of our people is hurt, you, your brothers, Gynbere and Slaslow will die. I guarantee that." Tarl slowly stood, towering over Urfit. He stared coldly down at him. "We also have rules. You have my word, we will not follow you for four days, but I imagine a man's word counts for little where you're concerned. So leave your guards to watch the trail. However your men will stay out of our sight. If our guards on the wall see any of them, they will shoot. We'll hunt and forage to the east, west and south as usual." He grabbed a clean sheet of parchment from the pile in front of him and drew a circle in the centre, leaving three gaps in the line. "The amphitheatre!" Then he slashed two lines across the page. "This line goes east from the northeast entrance," he pointed to the first line, "and this," he indicated the second, "goes north from the northwest entrance. We will shoot any of your men we find west and south of those lines. You will not spy on us. Make sure your men comply. Now go back to Gynbere and take care no harm comes to those you kidnapped. Your life depends on it."

Urfit grabbed the sheet Tarl pushed in front of him, turned on his heels, but had second thoughts and turned back. "Gynbere would like a few of the things he left here. Perhaps just his ibith. My men will come in and get it, or yours could deliver it to the entrance."

"No!" said Kirym, before Tarl could answer.

"What!" exclaimed Urfit.

"You can't have it."

"But as a sign of your good will..."

"You want good will?" she demanded. Kirym suddenly

looked tall and imposing. Her tokens glowed brightly on her forehead. "We welcomed you here. We extended a hand of friendship, offered you food and shelter. You willingly accepted. You ate our friendship loaf after its significance was explained. You were happy for us to guard your camp at night. That was our goodwill. In response you attacked us without provocation. You killed our dragon and our people. You kidnapped our leaders." Her voice lowered, and Urfit leaned forward to hear her. "You broke old law. That is indefensible. Now you ask for more goodwill? What in Faltryn's name gives you the idea we have any left to give?"

Everyone stared at Kirym, mouths open. This was so unlike her not to try to accommodate everyone if possible.

Urfit's face had grown progressively redder as Kirym spoke.

Escort him out!" she snapped.

"We! Have! Your! People!" he sneered.

She leaned over the table, her face close to his. "Listen to me very carefully. If any of my people is hurt or even appears discomforted, we will hunt you down. As long as one person from these families here is alive, you will need to fear, for you will end up dead, as will your remaining brother."

Urfit's face went from red with anger to white with shock. "Remaining?" He paused, and took a gasping breath. "Where's Thipin?" he whispered.

"Didn't Slaslow tell you? Thipin was sent to herd a group of dwarflings, defenceless men, women and babies into the death tunnels. Slaslow mustn't have trusted you enough to tell you what Thipin was doing"

"How did you ...?" He took a deep breath and turned to Tarl. "Don't believe will-o-the-wisp tales from demented idiots like Churnyg ..." He blanched when Mrilan and Shurlyn stepped up to the table from behind him, where they had been standing listening.

338

"Really? You knew about the traps. You, Thipin and Zeffun created them. You'd sent people in before and knew how deadly they were. This time we escaped," said Shurlyn.

"Where's Thipin?"

"He stayed there!" said Kirym.

Urfit was thoroughly shaken. He turned on Shurlyn. "I'll hunt you down, old woman."

Tarl stood. "Be warned, Urfit. Anything you threaten against my people will be visited on you, and many here are listening." He paused, and shook his head. "Take him away." He picked up a quill, sat and carried on writing.

Urfit turned on his heel, but faced a solid line of men.

"A map," said Kirym. "You have a map for us."

Urfit turned back and stared down at her with distaste. He pulled a large pile of parchment sheets from his robe, and began to sort through them.

Kirym drummed her fingers loudly on the table. "Perhaps you forgot it," she said. She leaned over, grabbed a handful of the sheets and pulled them.

Urfit moved fast. He tried to snatch them back, but they fluttered to the ground. He snarled at her.

His eyes bulged as five knives suddenly hovered just below his nose. "Uh, he guaranteed my safety." He pointed to Armos.

"Then don't threaten our Lady of The Green Valley," said Sundas.

Urfit went red, and glanced sideways at him.

"Just go away," said Kirym. "We'll find you. We don't need a map. We'll ..."

"Keep them," snarled Urfit. He grabbed the more ragged sheets off the ground and stuffed them quickly into his robe. "Study them carefully and make no mistakes. You are warned!"

He pushed past two guards, but was surrounded. Arbreu

and Armos escorted him back to the entrance and arranged for them all to be taken away from the amphitheatre.

"The oak tree beside the small stream is the closest your men will come to the amphitheatre, Vellysh." said Armos. "Explain it carefully to them. Their lives depend on it, and later yours, if we find our rules have been broken."

When Arbreu and Armos returned from seeing Urfit out, the maps had been picked up and piled on the table. Loul, Kirym, Tarl and Sundas were casually talking about their visitor and his message.

"He's messing with us," said Arbreu, looking at one of the parchment sheets now sitting on the table. "This is all meaningless scribble."

"From their point of view, this is the journey they made," said Kirym. "They haven't the experience we have with making maps. In fact if you know the land, it does make sense."

"You've been to where they are?" asked Arbreu.

Kirym shook her head. "No. I saw the land from the top of the ridge when we made our way towards the fountainhead in spring, and then a few days back I caught a closer glimpse when Iryndal took me to find Garanniis and Morkeen. Knowing what I saw, and seeing this, yes it makes sense." She placed the map in front of her, and picked up a quill.

"Think north, south, east and west," she said, noting letters on the four sides of the parchment. "This," she pointed to a small curve in the southwest corner, is the amphitheatre. These three concentric circles in the northeast corner is where Gynbere will wait for us. We're to follow a path that goes east until it meets the path that comes north from The Rock. By their rate of travel, it'll take them four days to get there. They'll expect us to take the same length of time."

"So they want four days to do whatever they're organising. What are these things?" asked Tarl, pointing to an area that looked as if a small bird had stepped in ink and darted across the parchment between the amphitheatre and the circles.

"It's a marsh. I vaguely think there's a path through there, but I doubt they'd know about it anyway. Of course the map is wrong—"

"You mean he's sending us on a wild shanym chase?" interrupted Sundas.

"Oh no, not on purpose, and knowing the map is wrong gives us yet another advantage. Remember I said they have no real knowledge of maps, nor of the land. Gynbere's normal progression from The Rock to these circles was, in what he thought, a straight line north from The Rock. Somehow Gynbere knows about the marsh, but possibly the story was passed down to him."

"Have his men been there?" asked Arbreu.

"I don't think so. By what is drawn here, he thinks it covers the whole area."

"I accept he has left The Rock in the past," said Tarl, "but everyone said he never went very far."

"Rookham was searching for the amphitheatre when we met him. He'd been here before, and he described it to his men. Also the tree here was chopped down relatively recently. Now back to this map. Urfit held quite a few of them, and one was very old. That was probably the original. He panicked when I tried to take it. The others, including this one," she flicked the sheet she held, "are recent copies. Now this line they think goes north actually angles more westward. From what I've seen, I'd put the circles here. Northeast of where we are." She grabbed a bigger map of the area and pointed to a spot.

"That's quite close," said Arbreu. "Whatd'ya reckon? Half a day?"

"Three quarters, a little more maybe."

"Travel for four days? There's no way—"

"That's how long it took Gynbere. He assumes we couldn't possibly move faster than he does, especially if we take a lot of people and supplies with us," said Kirym. "I wonder if he thinks you'll take everyone with you, Tarl. Women, children, the injured and the prisoners. I suspect he would, because some of his people would be happy to walk in the other direction, given half a chance."

"What this means is we could leave now," said Arbreu. "If we can find the path through the marsh, we could be at these circles before Gynbere even gets there. Meet him on the path. We'd possibly get to him before Vellysh reports back. He'd be at a massive disadvantage, because we could choose the meeting place."

"No, for two reasons—"

"Tarl gave his word, Arbreu," interrupted Loul, "and we will stick to that. What else, Kirym?"

Kirym nodded. "They may kill the prisoners if they see us. Gynbere and Slaslow would happily kill others just to prove a point. Have no doubt Arb, life holds no value to either of them. We'll obey the rules to stay here or our people may die."

"So he holds all the power?" asked Arbreu. He sounded dejected.

"Oh no," she said brightly. "We have knowledge and an ability to act outside the way he thinks. And he wants something from us."

"Kirym, you said Gynbere and Slaslow," interrupted Sundas. "But Gynbere makes the decisions."

"Urfit is Slaslow's man, even though he was probably sent by Gynbere. Slaslow wants power. He's been angling for it for a while. Gynbere's personal guards are probably loyal to him, but orders to the rest of the guards have come from

Slaslow lately, not Gynbere."

"You imply that Slaslow wants to take over," said Mrilan. "He could have done it at any time in the past, so why wait until now?"

"Gynbere holds something Slaslow wants or needs, but I'd say Gunbere's merely a figurehead at this stage."

"Does he know?"

"I doubt it. He may suspect something's going on, which could be why Gynbere didn't send Slaslow. Gynbere may be trying to limit Slaslow's power. Together Slaslow and the Urfits were lethal, but now Vellysh'll be rethinking his loyalties. Slaslow didn't tell them where Thipin had gone. He must have suspected Thipin was dead, but he didn't tell anyone. Now Vellysh will distrust Slaslow, and I'm sure he'll pass his suspicions on to his brother."

"Why did Slaslow want us dead?" asked Shurlyn.

"Perhaps Slaslow thinks you know something about him. Whatever he suspects could affect his ability to keep command. He intends to take over from Gynbere, and he's far more brutal. Gynbere thinks he can manipulate us to join the rest of his adoring slaves. He wants to rule us all, and he imagines himself to be benevolent."

"That's benevolence?"

I shrugged. "Slaslow knows we're strong, Tarl. He wants to own all we have, but he isn't fool enough to think we'd meekly hand it over, sink to our knees and submit to slavery. So he has a plan, and it's probably not the same plan Gynbere holds."

Tarl frowned as he thought over what Kirym said. "These three circles where they want us to go. What is it?"

"I'm fairly sure it's a hollow flat top hill—"

"Like the canyon hill?" asked Armos.

"Sort of, but no. It's almost the opposite of the canyon. If the hill stood alone on the land, we'd call it a tor. It has steep sides and a flat summit. However, the top of this one is not much higher than the land around it. It's only a hill because there's a deep gully surrounding it. Think the canyon, with a tor in the middle. Much smaller though, and not nearly as wide. The eastern side of the gully is narrower than the western, I think. The land to the east rises gently to meet it, but the top of the tor is still a bit higher. On the south side, it drops off quite sharply, and there are some boulders there I think."

"How big is the flat area on the hill?"

"It would hold two or three hundred men, maybe more."

Tarl frowned. "How do they get onto it? Can they climb up and down the gully?"

"I just caught a glimpse, but I think the gully is too steep to climb. There was no way onto the tor when I saw it, but it would be easy enough to build a bridge across. The eastern side would be the best place."

"If it's as you describe, Gynbere would be an idiot to make his stand there. It doesn't sound defensible and his people would be free to leave."

"I imagine he'd be on the hill, and he'll put his archers in the gully," she said. "They couldn't see what to shoot at, but with a little practice, they'd be quite accurate. They couldn't aim for one specific person, but they'd have a good chance of getting someone, and any strike would be a bonus."

Arbreu looked perplexed. "It'd be hit and miss, but we could just return fire. We may not hit the person who shot, but ..."

"And if they were surrounded by women and children?" Kirym asked.

Tarl shook his head. "Yes, you're right. It's the obvious answer. Why do they stay with him?"

"Sometimes the black unknown is more frightening than a known horror, particularly when they've lived with it for so long. They've been told that doing anything without Gynbere is a death sentence." Kirym looked bleak.

"What can we do then?"

Tarl shrugged. "We'll have to think of something, Arbreu, but what? Vellysh said they'd watch for us. He'll have a system set up to warn him if we leave here early. He thinks he has the upper hand. The land isn't difficult, but we can't approach without them knowing, if it's as Kirym remembers."

"How deep is the gully?" asked Armos.

Kirym closed her eyes. "I'm not sure, but count on it being very deep."

"Ahh, too deep for them to climb out unaided," said Armos. "We'd better make some ladders to take with us."

"Kirym, you've always accommodated people wherever possible. Why not this time?" asked Tarl.

"What do you mean?"

"Well, Urfit wanted his guards and the pavilion. Why not let him have them? Neither are that important, and one or two more guards would make little difference in the long run. They might appreciate being allowed to return. Refusing Urfit made him really angry."

"Gynbere knew when he put the pavilion up that he'd leave it here. I think it was put up simply to hide his perceived assets. Rargo, and possibly someone else. His guards? Well he sees them as being faceless, arrow fodder. If we returned them, they would all see it as weakness. I think Gynbere really wants his ibith, and that's what I refused him. Did he ask for it at the entrance, Armos?"

"Yes, although I didn't allow him to finish his request."

"So the box was important enough to bring from The Rock, and while Gynbere camouflaged it to keep it with him, the chair is clearly not of the quality he prefers. He could have brought one of his other ibiths. From all accounts he had quite a few."

"Well why couldn't we let them have the stupid monstrosity?" interrupted Arbreu.

"It's not stupid, Arbreu," Kirym said. "His men weren't porters. It would've taken at least half of them to carry the ibith, and it'd slow them down considerably. So of all of the things they could have asked for, why that?"

Arbreu frowned. "It places him above his people, a symbol of his power. It's his throne. Maybe Slaslow was trying to keep him happy. It's just a box and a chair."

"Oh not just a box. Urfit asked for it first, and three times in all. When Gynbere was running for his life, he attempted to take it with him. He thinks it's valuable? We need to find out why."

"How?"

"Search it, Arb. And very carefully."

"Do you think Gynbere or Slaslow will kill Urfit when he turns up without the ibith?" asked Tarl.

She laughed dryly. "No. Neither Gynbere nor Slaslow can afford to kill either of the brothers. Vellysh and Zeffun hold the balance of power now. They have the knowledge to destroy both men. If Vellysh is killed, Zeffun will turn against the killer."

"So who really sent for the ibith? Gynbere or Slaslow?"

"I'm not sure, but I suspect that if we had let it go, Slaslow would have ended up with it."

"It's convoluted, Kirym," said Arbreu. "How do you figure it all out?"

"Old Harby has many fine sayings. One is, know your enemy. I just watch and listen."

"What if Gynbere and Slaslow fall out? Would the Urfits take over?" asked Tarl.

"The Urfit's could kill them both if it suited their purposes, but they aren't well liked. They need a figurehead. Without a leader, I suspect they'd lose most of their power. However

I'd back Slaslow in the end. He's far more ruthless."

Loul nodded. "I think Kirym's right. She generally is when it comes to people."

"By the way," said Arbreu. "Urfit was annoyed when you refused to hand over the ibith. Then you told him about Thipin. He didn't know that, but it made him even angrier. With us! What was the point?"

"Mainly to let him know we weren't intimidated by him— most people are. Also he was so thrown by the news, he made a massive mistake. He gave us information we weren't meant to have."

Those around the table went very quiet, and all eyes turned in Kirym's direction.

"All right. What?" asked Tarl, when the silence had stretched.

She pulled a piece of parchment from the pile and held it up.

"It's the map," said Tarl.

"Yes, he had quite a few of them, and from what I could see most were identical. But two were a bit different. The original map, and I wonder why he had it, but I think this too was one he didn't intend to show us."

She turned the parchment over and they all saw what was written on the back.

IT'S WAR!

The End

If you have enjoyed The Sands of Valythia, please leave a review on the website of the seller you purchased it from. Good reviews are the life blood of independently-published authors, so please take a few moments to let others know what you thought of the book.

Thank you for reading.

Do look for further adventures as
The Token Bearer series continues.

www.wordlypress.com